THE TUNNEL

broadview editions
series editor: L.W. Conolly

THE TUNNEL

Dorothy Richardson

edited by Stephen Ross and Tara Thomson

Introduction by Stephen Ross

broadview editions

Library and Archives Canada Cataloguing in Publication

Richardson, Dorothy M. (Dorothy Miller), 1873-1957, author
    The tunnel / Dorothy Richardson ; edited by Stephen Ross and Tara Thomson ; introduction by Stephen Ross.

(Broadview editions)
The tunnel is the fourth chapter-volume in the thirteen-volume Pilgrimage, Dorothy Richardson's series of novels detailing the inner life of Miriam Henderson.
Includes bibliographical references.
ISBN 978-1-55481-110-6 (pbk.)

    I. Ross, Stephen, 1970-, editor II. Thomson, Tara, editor III. Title.
IV. Series: Broadview editions

PR6035.I34T85 2014   823'.912   C2014-904361-9

Broadview Editions

The Broadview Editions series represents the ever-changing canon of literature in English by bringing together texts long regarded as classics with valuable lesser-known works.

Advisory editor for this volume: Michel Pharand

Broadview Press is an independent, international publishing house, incorporated in 1985.

We welcome comments and suggestions regarding any aspect of our publications—please feel free to contact us at the addresses below or at broadview@broadviewpress.com.

North America
PO Box 1243, Peterborough, Ontario K9J 7H5, Canada
555 Riverwalk Parkway, Tonawanda, NY 14150, USA
Tel: (705) 743-8990; Fax: (705) 743-8353
email: customerservice@broadviewpress.com

UK, Europe, Central Asia, Middle East, Africa, India, and Southeast Asia
Eurospan Group, 3 Henrietta St., London WC2E 8LU, United Kingdom
Tel: 44 (0) 1767 604972; Fax: 44 (0) 1767 601640
email: eurospan@turpin-distribution.com

Australia and New Zealand
NewSouth Books
c/o TL Distribution, 15-23 Helles Ave., Moorebank, NSW 2170, Australia
Tel: (02) 8778 9999; Fax: (02) 8778 9944
email: orders@tldistribution.com.au

www.broadviewpress.com

Broadview Press acknowledges the financial support of the Government of Canada through the Canada Book Fund for our publishing activities.

Typesetting and assembly: True to Type Inc., Claremont, Canada.

PRINTED IN CANADA

Contents

Acknowledgements

Thanks are due first to those scholars who have worked so hard to put Richardson back on the map: Gloria Fromm, Kristin Bluemel, Averill Buchanan, Scott McCracken, Gillian E. Hanscombe, Sydney Janet Kaplan, Thomas Staley, George Thomson, and Joanne Winning. We have benefited enormously from their work, and our literary lives are much richer for having followed their lead. Miriam Brown of Softprobe Computing Services did excellent work to scan in the edition we used, and to make sure we had an error-free text to work with. Thanks to Charlotte Bruton of the Marsh Agency, Ltd., literary executors of Dorothy Richardson's estate, for permission to reprint the Foreword to the 1938 Collected Edition (Appendix C7). Thanks also to Sean Garrett at the University of Georgia Press for permission to reprint letters and notes appearing in Gloria Fromm's *Windows on Modernism* (Appendix B).

Scott McCracken has been unfailingly supportive of this project; his advocacy for Richardson studies is exemplary. Don LePan and Marjorie Mather at Broadview Press have been delightful to work with; Don first by soliciting a proposal, and Marjorie by demonstrating almost eerie patience. The manuscript was late, very late, and still she remained cheerful, professional, and helpful. Finally, we owe Michel Pharand a huge debt of gratitude for his incredibly close and careful reading of the texts, and for his probing queries. His attention has greatly improved the finished product. Of course, it goes without saying that any errors remaining in the texts are our own. Thank you.

Stephen Ross and Tara Thomson

I would never have taken on the task of editing this edition were it not for Tara Thomson's interest in Richardson. I am grateful to her for helping stoke my interest to a sufficient level to tackle editorial work. I would also like to thank Katie Tanigawa whose final read through of the Introductions improved them in quiet but very important ways. Above all, I thank my wife Stephanie, my children Kathleen and Adam, and all my family, for their love and support as I've worked on this project.

Stephen Ross

I would like to thank my colleague and friend David Oswald for his ongoing support through this project. Our many conversations about Richardson and the book have helped immensely to focus my thoughts and keep me excited about the work. I would also like to thank, as always, my family; my mother Deb, in particular, who has taken an active interest in this book, and my partner John, whose love and support are invaluable. And finally, thank you to my co-editor Stephen, for bringing this project my way, and for his ongoing patience and mentoring. I would not have been able to take on the task of editing without the benefit of Stephen's expertise and determination.

Tara Thomson

Introduction

Richardson's Life

Dorothy Miller Richardson was an intensely private artist who preferred to be obscured behind her work, allowing the novels to take the spotlight. Biographers have found it difficult to discern even the basic outlines of her life, at times even turning to her novels to supply or confirm details.[1] For the most part, the information we have about her life comes from letters she wrote and references to her in others' diaries and correspondence, in addition to the self-proclaimed autobiographical works that make up *Pilgrimage*. Here is what we know:

Richardson was born at Abingdon, near Oxford, in 1873 to a relatively well-off family. She was given a typical education and enjoyed a comfortable childhood. When she was seventeen, however, her father suffered some financial reversals. The family were forced to move into more modest circumstances, and Richardson went to Germany to teach at a finishing school in Hanover. After that post ended, Richardson continued to work as a governess for a couple of years, before leaving off to care for her mentally ill mother, who took her own life in 1895. Her father having become bankrupt in 1893, Richardson moved after her mother's death to London to work as a secretary/assistant in a dental office. In 1896 she met H.G. Wells, with whom she would later have an affair, miscarrying a child conceived with him in 1906. Around this same time, Richardson began to write reviews, articles, stories, poems, and translations. Her interest in the Quaker religious movement resulted in her first book, *The Quakers Past and Present*, in 1914. Her first novel, and the first chapter-volume of *Pilgrimage*, *Pointed Roofs*, was published in 1915. In 1917 she met the much-younger bohemian Alan Odle, and was married to him until his death in 1948. In 1918 May Sinclair published the landmark review of *Pointed Roofs* in which she applied the term "stream of consciousness" to a literary work for the first time. *The Tunnel* appeared in 1919, marking something of a new start for Miriam Henderson in *Pilgrimage*, and consolidating Richardson's talent as a leading experimenter with novelistic form. From 1918 until near her death

---

1 See, for example, Gloria Fromm, Gillian Hanscombe, and Joanne Winning. See also the headnote to Appendix C in the Broadview Edition of *Pointed Roofs*, p. 247.

in 1957, Richardson supported herself and Odle with her writing, remaining prolific and committed to the project of *Pilgrimage* even as her reputation gradually waned. In 1954 Richardson entered a nursing home; in 1957 she died. The final work in *Pilgrimage*, *March Moonlight*, was published posthumously a decade later.

Pilgrimage

Pilgrimage begins in 1893, when seventeen-year old Miriam Henderson leaves her family to take up a job teaching English in a boarding school in Hanover, Germany. As she matures, Miriam moves back to England and through a series of the sorts of jobs typically reserved for young women at the time: teacher or governess. As she moves into her early twenties, Miriam takes up a post as a secretary/assistant at a dental office and begins to flourish as an independent woman in the wake of her mother's death. Miriam gradually becomes more involved in London's public intellectual life, and meets writers and intellectuals, becoming romantically involved with Hypo Wilson (modelled on H.G. Wells). Miriam's increasing confidence sees her also begin to write reviews for publication. Eventually, Miriam evolves into a professional writer as she comes fully into her maturity. She has a lesbian affair and explores both her sexuality and her intellect more fully as she approaches middle age. Finally, as she closes in on her fortieth birthday, Miriam determines to write a novel and begins composing what many critics, noting the close parallels between Miriam's life and Richardson's life, take to be the first chapter-volume of *Pilgrimage*: *Pointed Roofs*.

This summary of what happens in *Pilgrimage*, useful as it may be, fails to capture what it is really about, and why it is so important. As the series title indicates, *Pilgrimage* is about a journey, one with a quasi-sacred objective. It's a quest to write what had not yet been written in English literature: a woman's life from a woman's perspective and using what Richardson herself thought of as a feminine style. Fusing stylistic innovation with thematic and substantial daring, Richardson's *Pilgrimage* manages to be *avant-garde* in its technique at the same time as it introduces into English literature a female protagonist whose chief concern is not to get married or to eliminate her competition, but to grow into a fully realized mature woman with intellectual and artistic ambitions equal to those of any man. At the same time, *Pilgrimage* brings to light the trivial, mundane realities of everyday life that, though shared by us all, were commonly thought to be chiefly a concern for women. Along with later novels that would follow a similar path, such as James

Joyce's *Ulysses* (1922) or Virginia Woolf's *Mrs Dalloway* (1925), *Pilgrimage* recognizes the potential for illumination, insight, and even epiphany in the banal events of daily life. Moreover, *Pilgrimage* first initiates and then develops more fully than any other body of work in English the stream of consciousness and free indirect discourse techniques that would come to be hallmarks of modernist prose writing. Ten years before *Ulysses* appears, Richardson introduces stream of consciousness into the world of the English novel, challenging her readers to navigate the shoals and rapids of the protagonist's mind, often without a compass and rarely ever with objective confirmation of its contents. Though it was long neglected, largely because it was written by a woman (the same fate hardly attended Marcel Proust's parallel achievement in French),[1] *Pilgrimage* is at last receiving its due recognition as a mammoth accomplishment. It is one of the earliest and certainly the most sustained works in all of English modernism, perhaps even all of twentieth-century literature. More than any "New Woman" novel,[2] *Pilgrimage* fused form and content into an aesthetic and political tsunami whose rising water raised all boats and pointed the way for both a new feminist aesthetic and a new way of writing.

The Tunnel [3]

The Tunnel is the fourth chapter-volume in the thirteen-volume *Pilgrimage*, Dorothy Richardson's series of novels detailing the inner life of Miriam Henderson. The first three books follow Miriam through a series of fairly conventional posts as a teacher and governess, as she first leaves home and tries to find the financial means to support herself independently. In *The Tunnel* and its successor, *Interim*, Miriam enters urban life, work, and the public

---

1 That is, the seven-volume *A la recherche du temps perdu* (*In Search of Lost Time*), the first volume of which appeared in French in 1913 (the first English translation, published under the title *In Search of Lost Time*, began to appear in 1922).

2 "New Woman" novels dealt with the new social phenomenon of the career-minded, politically aware, and romantically (and sexually) independent "new woman," appearing in the late nineteenth century and finding its apotheosis in the "flapper" of the 1920s.

3 The material from here to the start of the section, "Auto/biography" is unique; the immediately preceding section, and those from "Auto/biography" forward, are nearly identical with the same sections of the Introduction to the Broadview Edition of *Pointed Roofs* (i.e., the examples there are from that novel, while here they are from *The Tunnel*).

sphere. Though there is a logical tendency to approach *Pilgrimage* from the beginning, with *Pointed Roofs*, *The Tunnel* is the ideal gateway into the series. *The Tunnel* is more representative of *Pilgrimage* as a whole, displaying its qualities as a groundbreaking modernist text, and narrating the story of a woman navigating the modern world and challenging traditional roles and discourses. Though it is the fourth in thirteen chapter-volumes, *The Tunnel* also functions as a stand-alone work, as it marks the beginning of an entirely new phase of Miriam's life in a new city, in a new job, and with mostly new secondary characters. Stylistically, it also marks the point at which Richardson consolidates her experiment with a feminine psychological realism and begins to draw the attention of prominent readers such as Virginia Woolf and Katherine Mansfield. *The Tunnel* is also where the thematic experimentation really emerges, as Miriam moves to London, takes on a secretarial job, and immerses herself in independent urban living. Richardson's innovations in *The Tunnel* drew significant critical attention and a wide contemporary readership for the series, as well as setting the gold standard for experimental renderings of consciousness in prose.

Readers of *The Tunnel* encounter a much stronger and more mature technique and voice than in the earlier chapter-volumes, in addition to a more mature protagonist. Having honed her method in the preceding three novels, Richardson *arrives* in a sense with *The Tunnel*, and her restriction to Miriam's consciousness is undertaken with greater confidence. Where earlier chapter-volumes such as *Pointed Roofs* at times falter in their use of stream of consciousness, or supplement Miriam's perspective with a third-person point of view, in *The Tunnel* Richardson moves deftly from scene to scene scarcely ever letting the veil drop. Throughout, we are restricted to what Miriam sees and knows—and does not know—and to her often humorously flawed understanding. At the same time, *The Tunnel* affords a privileged view into the opportunities for social, sexual, and intellectual exploration that were newly available to English women in the wake of World War I. Though the narrative perspective is like a spotlight in what it reveals to us, the scenery it moves across has expanded geometrically. The close focus on the everyday Richardson first undertakes in her experiments with free indirect discourse, stream of consciousness, and unreliable narration in *Pointed Roofs* remains in *The Tunnel*, but the scope of what counts as the everyday has broadened enormously. In this sense, readers of *The Tunnel* encounter the earliest and among the most sophisticated experiments with modernist literary technique in English, and a sustained engagement with the changing dimensions of women's experience in the first half of the twentieth century. In the works that follow *The Tunnel*, Richardson brings Miriam to full maturity and the beginning of her writing career; *The Tunnel* marks a turning point in that progression, as it introduces key characters—most significantly Hypo Wilson and consolidates Miriam as a character worthy of our interest and complex enough to sustain it over the long term.

The Tunnel takes Miriam to London, where she enters the largely male world of professional work, lives independently, and begins to develop a feminist consciousness. Having left the work of teacher and governess behind, Miriam now lives on her own in a rented room, and comes and goes as she pleases. The solitude appeals to one side of her enormously, and she rather jealously guards her privacy from her landlady. This growing sense of independence fuels some of Miriam's most modern activities in *The Tunnel*, including the bold decision to learn to ride and then make trips by bicycle. One such trip takes Miriam to visit her sister Harriet, now married and expecting a child. It was still very much a novelty for women to ride bicycles, and not considered entirely proper behaviour; still less was it proper for a young woman to ride a bicycle alone in the countryside, as Miriam does on at least this occasion. Miriam's growing feminism and sense of independence fuel her determination, though, and she completes the trip.

As this adventure indicates, Miriam is becoming something of a New Woman (about which more below), exploring her independence and pushing against social boundaries. To that end, in *The Tunnel* Miriam cultivates the friendship of two New Women, Mag and Jan, who live together, talk philosophy and art, and even smoke cigarettes. Mag and Jan importantly show Miriam things that will be key to her future development: that women can be friends and not simply rivals, and that women can think and create alongside men. They also encourage her to write, starting Miriam's transformation into a full-time writer. They make her believe that the constraints that would keep her from doing what she desires are merely social, and therefore arbitrary, and they urge her to develop herself as a full person.

That Miriam is able to do all this independent living is itself an indication of the changing time in which *The Tunnel* is set. Miriam is a working woman, with a job as a receptionist, secretary, and assistant in a dental office in Harley Street. There, she rubs shoulders with other professionals who find a sense of worth in their work, converses with cultured people, and develops a sense of her worth outside of the traditional framework of marriage, child-rearing, and domesticity.

In this vein, *The Tunnel* gives Miriam the chance to meet two people who will take her well outside her usual ambit: Hypo Wilson and Miss Dear. Hypo Wilson is the husband of one of Miriam's old school friends, and Miriam gets to know him over the course of a short visit to their house. She is fascinated by his opinions, and luxuriates in the open invitation to talk and dispute about matters intellectual, philosophical, and aesthetic. Miriam's attraction to Hypo is palpable, and the encounter, which takes up a significant portion of the chapter-volume, lays the groundwork for the affair she will have with him in *Dawn's Left Hand* (1931). If Hypo presents Miriam with intellectual potential and the prospects of extra-marital sex, Miss Dear affords her a wholly different perspective on things. When Miriam meets her, Miss Dear is in a hospital being treated for consumption (the archaic name for tuberculosis). She is also in dire straits financially, and scheming to secure a husband as a means to financial security and comfort. Where Hypo introduces the possibility of love without marriage, Miss Dear introduces the possibility of marriage without love. Both are unsuspected alternatives to the Victorian household in which Miriam was raised, and certainly a significant remove from the rather pious household of Fräulein Pfaff in *Pointed Roofs*.

Still tentatively, Miriam begins to challenge and cross some of the many boundaries that otherwise constrain women at the *fin-de-siècle*: gender, class, sexual, social, and professional lines. She finds the various worlds of family, work, friendship, and leisure messily overlapping and converging in ways at once confusing and arousing. On all fronts, Miriam's world is expanding and opening up new vistas for her to explore, and the chapter-volume's ending promises more to come. Miriam learns at the end of *The Tunnel* that the building she lives in will be converted into a boarding house, ensuring a steady rotation of interesting characters for Miriam to meet.

Main Themes

The Tunnel's primary themes concern Miriam's emerging sense of herself as an individual, apart from the various social roles she inhabits. *Pilgrimage* starts with Miriam striking out on her own because her father can no longer support her. Chapter-volumes two and three, *Backwater* (1916) and *Honeycomb* (1917), see her return to England and care for her ailing mother, who dies at the end of *Honeycomb*. *The Tunnel* ratifies the break indicated by this trauma, and sees Miriam move to London to live on her own and support herself. It shows her in the world of work, invading traditionally masculine spheres of activity, and testing the boundaries of her independence. Typically, these investigations leave Miriam confused as often as they elate, frustrate, and sometimes just perplex her. Miriam enjoys her independence and values her capacity to live on her own, learn, study, explore, and befriend whomever she chooses. At the same time, Miriam chafes at the restrictions of working for a living, having to rise every morning to be in the office at the same appointed time, doing repetitive and dull tasks, dealing with unpleasant or awkward people who also work at the office, and navigating misunderstandings about friendship or budding romance in the workplace. She loves having tea and conversation with her employers, but is nearly driven to distraction by some of the tedious demands of her job. In this respect, *The Tunnel* presents a sophisticated perspective on the issues associated with women's broader entry into the workforce in the 1890s. It neither celebrates the development as a utopian liberation of young women from the tyrannies of domestic life, nor condemns it as unnatural or socially divisive. In truth, it adopts both perspectives at times, and presents a complex, human vision of both the positive and negative aspects of women in the workplace.

Much of this complexity is due to Richardson's ongoing focus on the nature of human consciousness and self-narration. Though this aspect of *Pilgrimage* is most often discussed in relation to its method, it also forms a key element of the thematics of *The Tunnel*, since Miriam's interior monologue frequently returns to questions of why she thinks or feels what she does, and how those unlooked-for reactions feed into her sense of herself. The challenge presents itself in starker terms as her New Woman friends, Mag and Jan, begin to encourage her to write. Miriam begins to think of narrative and consciousness more explicitly in *The Tunnel* than she has in the past chapter-volumes, and to consider writing as a concrete engagement with them. When Miriam surprises herself or others, she often reflects on why this is so and considers how such surprises justify an ongoing close attention to her own consciousness and the role it plays in shaping the world through which she moves.

Key to that world are gender roles. *The Tunnel* takes the earlier chapter-volumes' sustained engagement with the differences between men and women to a new context and provides a richer frame for its consideration. Miriam often tries to sift the differences between men and women, though almost always in terms of what they do rather than essential qualities. These reflections are often complicated by two additional factors, though. First, Miriam herself does not often identify with other women. That is, she often exempts herself from the understanding of women she is developing, so that she seems to be at once a woman in biological terms and not a woman in social or behavioural terms. As she puts it at one point, "I am something between a man and a woman; looking both ways" (p. 226). Second, Miriam's ideas about men and women are nearly always focalized through her experience of them. That is, Miriam's encounter with men is never with them just as men, but always with them as men engaging with her as a woman. The same is true of her encounters with women; they are nearly always with women who are relating to her as another woman. Naturally, this complicates matters, as it both troubles and personalizes the consideration of gender difference presented in *The Tunnel*, and captures the inextricable binding of gender to sex and sexuality. In doing so, it lays bare one of the primary *fin-de-siècle* concerns about the increasing number of women in the workplace: it is not their gender that is problematic, so much as the fact that their gender is sexualized in any integrated working environment.

Quite naturally, then, *The Tunnel* circles around questions of sex and sexuality, particularly where men and women interact on a daily basis and in novel situations. Miriam's evaluation of the dentists she works for is at times flavoured with her sense of their personal attractiveness as well as her opinion of them as her employers. In one striking case, she mistakes Dr. Hancock's intentions towards her after he first escorts her to a play and then invites her to a country weekend with a group of others. She believes his interest is personal and even romantic. It is not. The ensuing embarrassment and outrage when he treats her curtly and professionally, and when he writes to make clear that he is not romantically interested, is exquisite and provokes one of the funniest moments in all *Pilgrimage*: Miriam in her heightened state of anxiety and anticipation, not sure whether to expect a confrontation or a declaration of love, enters an examining room to clear up after a patient: "The patient had gone. He would be alone. They would be alone. To be in his presence would be a relief ... this was appalling. This pain could not be endured" (p. 244). Dr. Hancock is there, "standing impermanently with a sham air of engrossment at his writing table" (p. 244). Miriam enters the room rather grandly and crosses to the instruments to begin cleaning up, anticipating either that Dr. Hancock will simply leave or that he will speak to her: "She reached [the table] and got her hands upon the familiar instruments ... no sound; he had not moved" (p. 244). Miriam gives way to her thoughts, a racing tumult of reassurance and doubt, then turns to face Dr. Hancock: "Steadily with her hands full of instruments she turned towards the sterilising tray. The room was empty" (p. 244). While Miriam has been rattling around inside her own head, imagining a scene of high drama, Dr. Hancock has quietly finished writing in his record book and left the room. The stark gap between what she imagines and reality achieves comic dimensions, which Miriam quickly transforms into pathos: "the room was stripped, a west-end surgery, among scores of other west-end surgeries, a prison claiming her by the bonds of the loathsome duties she had learned" (p. 244).

Miriam's forwardness in this episode is crucial for the chapter-volume's depiction of both her own burgeoning sexuality and a more general tendency of women to take control of their romantic as well as their economic lives. *The Tunnel* supplements this progressive vision with some other alternatives now available to women, in Miriam's visit to her sister Harriet (who is married and pregnant), her friend Alma (who is in a more or less open marriage), her friends Mag and Jan (who may be more than friends), and her new friend Miss Dear (who introduces Miriam to a good-naturedly scheming approach to securing marriage as a living in itself).

What much of this amounts to is that Miriam is becoming a woman in the high age of the New Woman, an age in which Woman (in the abstract) was a primary topic of discussion. Miriam's own self-reflective approach to gender and sexuality captures this much broader concern with the status and role of women in debates over The Woman Question and the New Woman (about both of which more below). One of the most telling moments in this regard comes when Miriam sees the new encyclopedia in the tea room of the dental office, and immediately turns to the index to discover how many articles it now has devoted to women: "Her miserable hand reopened the last page of the index. There were five or six more entries under 'Woman'" (p. 255). In her assessment of the index, Miriam reveals that she is already familiar with the number and nature of the entries pertaining to women: there are five or six *more* than before. She has looked into the matter before, and doing so again peculiarly makes her hand "miserable," suggesting a kind of abjection or suffering tied to being made an object of scientific inquiry. The increased number of entries also indicates the rising interest in The Woman Question more broadly, as turn-of-the-century English society came to grips with an irreversible change in gender dynamics. Finally, and perhaps most interestingly, the index category "Woman" testifies to how much women have become an object of scientific inquiry by the end of the nineteenth century. This positioning of women as objects of study both clashes and is consistent with Miriam's own attitudes, as discussed just above: she is at once the object of inquiry and the inquirer. Science, or intellectual inquiry more broadly, takes women as a category about which an increasing number of articles need to be written to fulfill the mandate of providing a "liberal education in twelve volumes" (p. 255). Insofar as she identifies as a woman, and is identified as one by those around her, Miriam is therefore the object of inquiry, a mystery to which the methods and techniques of science must be applied. Insofar as she feels herself almost constantly at a distance from other women, and puzzles over or deplores their behaviours, Miriam is the scientific inquirer, seeking to understand the strange creatures known as "women."

This dual role underwrites the final theme that we will discuss here, that of Miriam's intellectual discovery. From the earliest pages of *Pilgrimage*, Miriam has been revealed as a progressively educated young woman. Her bookshelf at home at the beginning of *Pointed Roofs* has works by Charles Darwin and William Lecky[1] on it, and she is clearly familiar with basic scientific facts and ideas. Her father regularly attends lectures of the Royal Academy, and she is to all appearances a well-educated young woman. Richardson complicates this vision, though. When, in *The Tunnel*, Miriam finds herself invited to attend a Royal Society[2] lecture

---

1 William Edward Hartpole Lecky (1838-1903), Irish historian whose *History of the Rise and Influence of the Spirit of Rationalism in Europe* (1865) argued that Europe's historical progression was due to rationalism rather than faith. Charles Darwin (1809-82), English naturalist who originated the theories of evolution and natural selection.

2 Richardson mistakenly refers in the novel to the Royal Academy. Chartered in the 1660s, the Royal Society's fundamental purpose is "to recognise, promote, and support excellence in science and to encourage

she discovers that the Society welcomes children to some of its events, and realizes that had her father wanted to he could have taken her to some of the lectures. That is, Miriam's education is just as ambivalent as everything else about her: she is considered intelligent and free enough to read Darwin, but not to be taken to hear lectures about his work.

This duality plays out in the tension between her desire to know facts and to learn, and her tendency to let impressions and feelings take priority. Miriam has opportunities to educate herself as richly as she would like, and yet she mostly opts for pastimes that focus on the social or the aesthetic. Miriam is, it seems clear by the end of *The Tunnel* if not sooner, of the artistic and creative cast of mind more than the scientific. She knows much and has opportunity to learn more, but appears to feel that facts provide but an impoverished account of the world. Instead, she bicycles across the countryside, visits the quietly scandalous pair Mag and Jan, or adopts the stranger Miss Dear as a special project. She is infinitely more interested in the social side of life, not in any derogatory sense, but as the sphere in which humanity is played out most fully and where it may with most profit be observed.

Contemporary Concerns

The Tunnel was published in 1919, just after the end of World War I, though it is set in 1896, providing it with two historical contexts to take into consideration. The Great War, as World War I was known, began on 4 August 1914 and lasted until 11 November 1918. Over ten million young men died in the battles, many of them drowning or freezing to death in the mud and filth of "no man's land": the ground between the trenches occupied by the Entente powers on one side, and by the Central powers on the other.[1] Though people initially believed that the war would be over by Christmas of 1914, the advent of trenches dug nearly clean across France from the English Channel to the Mediterranean saw a stalemate settle in that threatened to be interminable. Senior commanders who had learned their battle skills

---

the development and use of science for the benefit of humanity" (<https://royalsociety.org/about-us>). Throughout its history, it has sponsored public lectures by its members as part of that mission.

1   A further six million died of disease, infection, and starvation, making World War I one of the deadliest conflicts in human history. The Entente Powers included Britain, France, Russia, and the Commonwealth; the Central Powers included Germany and Austria-Hungary.

in the wars of the nineteenth century found themselves outpaced by the development of killing technologies such as the machine gun, the tank, and eventually aerial bombing, and continued to order infantry and cavalry charges against fortified positions well into the war. The war quickly became a war of attrition, in which the side that would win was the one that could withstand the most casualties without giving up its positions. That grotesque point was finally achieved in 1919, when the Central powers surrendered and signed the Treaty of Versailles.[1]

Aside from the vastness of its geographical and temporal scope, the Great War was also notable for its proximity to the civilian populations of the countries that fought in it. Londoners were often exposed to wounded soldiers and those spending their leave in the city. Maimed bodies and the shattered minds caused by shell-shock—later called "neurasthenia" and, later still, PTSD—mingled with civilian populations going about their daily business. At times, it was even possible to hear the big guns laying down artillery barrages in northern France all the way over in the seaside resorts on the English south coast. When the war ended, more or less an entire generation of young men had been exterminated, leaving a social and professional vacuum that yielded unprecedented opportunities for young women.

The Tunnel appeared while World War I was still fresh in peoples' minds. Indeed, its title may well have spoken to a collective sense that a dark period had just been overcome and a light was perhaps glimmering at the other end of this dark time. Thomas Staley suggests that *The Tunnel* refers to Dante Alighieri's *Divine Comedy*. Dante's work begins with the narrator lost in a dark forest. He finds a guide in the Latin epic poet Vergil (author of the *Aeneid*) who takes him through Hell (*Inferno*), Purgatory (*Purgatorio*), and Heaven (*Paradiso*), all the while teaching him moral truths and showing him the eternal wisdom and justice of God. "In *The Tunnel*," Staley writes, "there are thirty-three sections just as there are thirty-three cantos in each of the three books of Dante's *Divine Comedy* along with allusions to the 'inner circle,' 'outer circle,' and 'rim of the world'" (62). The religious trappings of Dante's work are absent from *The Tunnel*, but the sense of the chapter-volume as a transitional period, from the old

---

1 The terms of the treaty were notoriously harsh and punitive, virtually ensuring that Germany would re-arm and the hostilities recommence within twenty years.

to the new, persists. Certainly the cast of characters Miriam meets in *The Tunnel* could correspond to the vignettes in Dante's work, and the language of "inner circle" and "outer circle," drawn from the *Purgatorio* indicate both an element of Miriam's distaste for the invidiousness of some of her new acquaintances and the larger historical sense of having just lived through Hell on Earth in the war. Further, the reference to "the rim of the world" suggests a bold new departure, reaffirming the sense that in *The Tunnel* Miriam truly is starting a new chapter in her life, just as England was embracing a new world order in the wake of World War I.

Richardson cements this fusion of the historical and the personal by having *The Tunnel* pick up only months after Miriam's mother has died at the end of the previous volume, *Honeycomb*. Miriam's experience of her mother's death is so traumatic that it very nearly eludes narration altogether. It is only revealed very obliquely in *Honeycomb*, and remains almost entirely buried in Miriam's unconscious throughout *The Tunnel*. We might well speculate that part of the reason for this is the close parallel to Richardson's own life: she, too, returned home to care for her mother, whose mental illness deteriorated until she finally took her own life. Naturally, the event was deeply traumatic for Richardson, and we may well conclude that its repression from the narrative of *Pilgrimage* is itself evidence of Richardson's own inability to process it. As Richardson's life intermingles with Miriam's throughout *Pilgrimage*, and the trauma of the war casts its shadow back over the events of *The Tunnel*, the interfusions of madness, illness, generational upheaval, and suicide coalesce to infuse the intimate world of *The Tunnel* with an additional sense of historical import.

One of the chief consequences of the war's mass depopulation of England's young men was a relaxation of social constraints on women in the workplace: there were simply not enough young men to fill all the vacant positions at the end of the war, so women filled them. In this respect, World War I only accelerated a general change that was already in motion in the 1890s, when Miriam begins work in Dr. Hancock's dental surgery. Delaying marriage or refusing it outright, often for political reasons, young women increasingly sought employment in the cities as clerks, receptionists, assistants, and secretaries in addition to the traditional posts to which they had access: teachers and governesses. Miriam's own career arc describes this transition nicely, as she begins as a teacher/governess and by *The Tunnel* has become a secretary/assistant. As the fortunes of women in general go, it seems, so go Miriam's.

This shift in employment patterns underlaid a much more fundamental public conversation in England at the turn of the century: what is the status and role of women in a modern society? Known as "The Woman Question," this conversation dealt with issues pertaining to women's right to vote, reproductive rights, medical rights, property rights, bodily autonomy, and marriage. Feminists demanded the right to vote; to own property; to decide when, where, and with whom to have sex; to control fertility; and to enjoy a greater equality in marriage. Opponents argued that women were naturally weaker, less logical, and less fit for public roles, such as owning property and voting; that they were meant to be cared for by men and should be protected from the rough demands of the world. Thomas Hardy's *Tess of the D'Urbervilles* (1891) chronicles the devastating impact of one woman's efforts to fight back against these traditional notions, and advances the notion that marriage ought to be dissolvable when it becomes a cruelty to either party. Emotions quite naturally ran high, reaching a peak (or nadir) in 1913, when a Suffragist named Emily Davison stepped in front of King George V's horse (being ridden in a race by jockey Herbert Jones) in protest against denying women the vote. Davison was killed in the collision, and instantly became a martyr to the cause for some, a dangerous anarchist for others.

All this is still to come in the England of *The Tunnel*, but it is in the works, as manifest in Miriam's evolution into just the sort of "New Woman" who embodied these changes. The "New Woman" was an educated, independent career woman who broke many of the stereotypes associated with femininity. A precursor to the "flapper" of the 1920s, the New Woman of the turn of the century might scandalize by cutting her hair short, wearing trousers, smoking cigarettes, or riding a bicycle. She might walk the city streets alone, talk to strange men, or hold a job that might previously have been thought indecent for a woman to hold. She may even (scandal!) indulge in extra-marital sex for pleasure rather than reproduction, drink alcohol to excess, or expose herself to ridicule by writing for newspapers or other publications. Miriam does not do *all* of these things, but one can begin to see in *The Tunnel* how she increasingly fits the bill. Mag and Jan, the friends who encourage Miriam to begin writing, are full-blown New Women, and chart a path of possibility for Miriam to consider as she figures out what sort of woman she wants to be.

Perhaps the single greatest influence on Richardson in this respect was H.G. Wells, who had become a significant figure in the literary and journalistic worlds by the time Richardson met him in 1896 (the same year Miriam meets Hypo Wilson, who is modelled on Wells). Richardson was well aware of him, and admired him greatly. Wells's stock in trade at that time was science fiction, including *The Time Machine* (1895) and *The War of the Worlds* (1898). He was a well-known progressivist and utopian thinker who advocated open marriages (which he claimed to have himself) and supported women's rights. Richardson had a romantic affair with him, concluding when she miscarried a pregnancy in 1907. Aside from appearing for the first time in *The Tunnel* as Hypo G. Wilson, Wells clearly influenced Richardson's burgeoning feminism, and informed her desire to move in intellectual and artistic circles. Drawing on her own experience in this regard, Richardson has Miriam revive her thirst for the intellectual novelty of Royal Academy lectures, and for the freedom of movement promised by new modes of transportation.

Wells is famous for reputedly having said, "Every time I see an adult on a bicycle, I no longer despair for the future of the human race." As the age of horse-drawn transport began its long conclusion and the age of the automobile took hold, the bicycle intervened as an affordable and reliable alternative to both that was also easy to learn. Women embraced the bicycle as affording them enhanced mobility without the need for a groom for the horse, or a mechanic/chauffeur for the automobile. When Miriam rides her bicycle to visit her sister Harriet, she actualizes the potential of the New Woman: free, mobile, independent, and autonomous. She is in total control of her itinerary, route, and schedule, even alarming one of the men she meets on the road in her intrepid willingness to ride through a wooded area that might not have been entirely safe for a lone woman.

Miriam may not be a New Woman in all her glory just yet, but with her artistic friends, her steady income, her lack of other responsibilities, her intellectual curiosity, and her unwillingness to be reined in by social constraints, she is well on her way. *The Tunnel* charts this shift in relation to the 1890s phenomena most obviously pertinent to the action of the novel, and to the 1910s context most directly pertinent to the time of its composition.

Auto/Biography[1]

It is virtually impossible to discuss *Pilgrimage* without reference to the question of autobiography. Beginning with Miriam's setting out at the age of seventeen to teach at a finishing school in Germany in *Pointed Roofs*, just as Richardson herself did, virtually every significant event and relationship in *Pilgrimage* derives from Richardson's own life. At the same time, Richardson was intensely private about her personal life in all other respects, putting very few details into her letters or articles, so that the primary source for much of what we know about her is often *Pilgrimage* itself. Joanne Winning provides an excellent account of the difficulties this circularity presents to critics and especially biographers: "How is one to write the life of someone who spent forty years writing it herself? ... Since fictionalizing her life was *the* aim, the revelation of facts about her real identity, such as birthdate or birthplace, could potentially reinscribe the text, in the public eye, as autobiography" (18). Complicating matters further, May Sinclair, writing in 1918, turns the tables, repeatedly insisting that Richardson "has taken Miriam's nature upon her" (p. 238). For Sinclair, *Pilgrimage* does not fictionalize Richardson's life so much as it records Richardson's occupation of Miriam's life. We must, therefore, be cautious about the natural impulse to read *Pilgrimage* as the record of Richardson's life. Despite the temptation to use Richardson's life to lend structure to Miriam Henderson's life, and *Pilgrimage* to fill in the gaps in Richardson's life story, we must resist the impulse to equate the two.

Perhaps, then, it is best to think of *The Tunnel* as autobiograph*ical* rather than autobiography per se. Just as James Joyce's *Portrait of the Artist as a Young Man* and Marcel Proust's *A la recherche du temps perdu* are autobiographical, so *The Tunnel* draws upon Richardson's own formative experiences for its material, but then reshapes and remakes them to take on larger significance. And just as we do not read *Portrait* or *A la recherche* to learn about Joyce or Proust primarily, but for the pleasure and joy of how they explore concepts of memory, youth, identity formation, experience, consciousness, history, the self and the other, so should we read *The Tunnel* not to learn about Richardson but to

---

1   The material from this point to the end of the Introduction is nearly identical, aside from examples, with that in the same sections of the Broadview Edition of *Pointed Roofs*.

experience how she explores the nature of perception and subjectivity itself. Of key pertinence here is the question of gender that concerns so much of *Pilgrimage*. The ease with which critics have accepted this point in relation to Joyce or Proust and yet not with regard to Richardson has led Bonnie Kime Scott to suggest that there is a "tendency to sensationalize the biography of women writers rather than to explore their works with care" (11). That is, to read *Pilgrimage* only as auto/biography is to read in a gendered fashion, to cut against the very grain of what Richardson (and Miriam) sought to achieve in generalizing from the intensely personal to the wider experience of modernity. Rather, *Pilgrimage* ought to be read as an early entry into the modernist fascination with the fragmented self that achieves coherence and unity only in retrospective narration. It presents not Richardson's life, nor a thinly-veiled retelling of her life, but a long-term engagement with the very problematics of subjectivity itself as a function of language and narrative. Contrary to what Hugh Walpole wrote in *Vanity Fair* in 1923, Dedalus is not Joyce, Marcel is not Proust, Clarissa Dalloway is not Woolf, and Miriam is not Richardson (see Walpole, *Pointed Roofs*, p. 233). Rather, all are efforts to understand what it means to have an identity in light of rapidly changing and unsettling ideas about consciousness such as those of Sigmund Freud, William James, and Henri Bergson (about which more, below; for James and Bergson, see *Pointed Roofs*, p. 219, notes 1 and 2).

Feminism

Western modernism, and thus Richardson, emerged at a critical moment in the history of feminism and women's rights. As a consequence, much modernist experimentation is layered with a concern for rendering hitherto subordinated aspects of human experience, including women's experience. As Liesl Olsen, Lorraine Sim, Shari Benstock, Bonnie Kime Scott, Kristin Bluemel, Susan Stanford Friedman, and many others have shown, modernist formal experimentation itself derives from impatience with the conventions of the realist novel—including its standard gender roles—particularly as it developed in England in the nineteenth century. This tradition relied upon a transparency of language, verisimilitude between the world in the novel and that of the reader, moral clarity, clear narrative arcs with well-defined beginnings middles and endings, chronological narration, and reliable narrators who could be trusted to provide all the relevant information necessary to make sense of the narrative. Richardson understood this tradition as fundamentally masculine, and sought to counter it with a feminine equivalent: "Since all these novelists happened to be men, the present writer, proposing at this moment to write a novel and looking round for a contemporary pattern, was faced with the choice between following one of her regiments and attempting to produce a feminine equivalent of the current masculine realism" (Foreword, p. 375). Doing so meant that Richardson focused not just on consciousness, but on a woman's consciousness, and sought the proper language, form, style, and techniques for rendering feminine consciousness.

Before we move on to discuss the stylistic innovations and hallmarks of *The Tunnel*, it is necessary to say something about the concept of a specifically feminine consciousness just invoked.

The history of Western feminism has in general moved through three waves. First-wave feminism (from the late eighteenth through the nineteenth centuries) sought equal status as humans and legal persons for women; it sought a very basic level of human rights that had historically not been accorded. Second-wave feminism continued this struggle through much of the twentieth century, achieving victories such as the universal franchise for women, but also shifted focus towards celebrating what had historically been deemed shameful about being a woman. Thus, in addition to asserting that women were every bit as capable intellectually, morally, emotionally, politically, and physically as men, second-wave feminism also sought to redeem those qualities coded as feminine that had been used to shame or belittle women: emotionality, talkativeness, sociality, the body, and so forth. Third-wave feminism moved beyond both first- and second-wave feminisms by attacking the very notion that there are any essential qualities of masculinity or femininity at all, instead arguing that men and women are not born but made by cultural norms and unconscious biases. Third-wave feminism attempted to do away with the notion that there could be anything like a "feminine consciousness" that was in any respect different from a male consciousness, except perhaps by dint of the ways in which it is shaped by the experience of being raised a woman. That is, third-wave feminism holds that there is no innate difference between how women and men think, or between how women think and their biology: if there is a difference at all, it is a cultural product.

As even a passing familiarity with contemporary gender issues makes clear, the waves of feminism are not consecutive, but syncretic. The struggles of first-wave feminism continue even where legal rights have been accorded, but sexist or misogynist cultural practices persist, second-wave feminism continues among many men and women both who reject the constructivist claims of third-wave feminism, and third-wave feminism continues to battle essentialist notions that would treat any woman who rejects emotional engagement for objective analysis as something other than a *real* woman.

Miriam's feminism finds its first full expression in her frustration with working in a dental office in *The Tunnel*, and the liberty she discovers in becoming a New Woman: walking the city at night, smoking cigarettes, riding a bicycle. As Miriam gradually builds her confidence to begin writing, she also develops an awareness of herself as a woman in a world that treats women differently from men, and finds her voice in challenging that world. By dint of her education and reading, as well as her temperamental antipathy towards anyone—man or woman—who condescends to her, Miriam grows to assert her independence and, as she is a woman, thus to assert a feminist consciousness as well.

Key to this emerging consciousness is Miriam's complex impatience with the entire sex-gender system. The only thing that irritates her more than a condescending man is a simpering woman, and both drive her to fits of rage at times. But Miriam is not simply a misanthrope. Rather, she objects to how gender roles lead men and women to behave in ways she takes to be unnatural, denying their human connection in accordance with the demands made upon them to play a part. When men feel they must explain, guard, protect, or educate her, Miriam bristles: "Men are simply paltry and silly—all of them" (p. 243). Perhaps even more, she rages when women smile insincerely, make cutting comments, play up to men by tearing other women down, or stand in judgement of one another: "outwardly a girl with blowy hair and a wavy hat, smiling in boats, understanding botany and fishing ... inwardly a designing female, her mind lit by her cold intellectual 'ethical'—hooooo—the very *sound* of the word—'ethical Pantheism'; cool and secret and hateful. 'Rather a nice little thing'; 'pretty green dress'; *nice!*" (p. 241). Gender conventions and how they pervert free, open human interaction are the culprit for Miriam, and she is an unforgiving critic of them. At the same time, in her commitment to writing feminine consciousness, Richardson often gave in to a tendency to essentialize, with comments suggesting women constitute "the synthetic principle of human life," while men have a "mental tendency to departmentalize, to analyze, to separate single things from their flowing environment" ("Comments," *Dental Record* 1916). She also remarked that a woman's mind "is capable of being all over the place and in all camps at once" ("Leadership," p. 347), suggesting a kind of fluidity and inconstancy that might well play into gender stereotypes, though Elaine Showalter has argued conversely that Richardson's refusal to structure consciousness in the novel bespeaks a more principled refusal to impose a pattern or system on any sort of being.

In this respect, Miriam has a great deal in common with Richardson, but Richardson has one more arrow to her quiver than Miriam does (at least until the final chapter-volume, *March Moonlight*): she is a writer of experimental, innovative, and challenging prose that strives to produce "the feminine equivalent to the current masculine realism" (Foreword, p. 375). Richardson wanted to get at women's experience of modernity through experimental means, by developing a style that would reflect the way she thought women's minds worked, and the particular concerns they encountered in the world. Richardson saw the literary and artistic tradition as male-dominated, and like Woolf and many other female modernists, wanted to separate herself from that tradition by creating a new one. She felt women were less successful in the world because they had not been afforded the same opportunities as men, rather than that they were inherently unable to measure up. She makes this clear in many of her essays, including "Talent and Genius" (1923), and "The Reality of Feminism" (1917), where she anticipates Woolf's *A Room of One's Own* (1929) and *Three Guineas* (1938) in suggesting that women can perform the same tasks and have the same creativity as men, so long as they have financial and personal autonomy. Richardson argues, much like Woolf, that women's "financial independence must be secured" before they can do much in the public world ("The Reality of Feminism," p. 353). Previous female writers who had met with success, Richardson thought, were just writing as men, with what she perceived as male language. Richardson felt that language was a male construct that women had been forced to use. However, because the woman writer had only these words to work with, women's art shouldn't be about the words, but about creating atmosphere. In *Revolving Lights* (1923), Miriam, at that point a budding writer, acts as a conduit for this notion:

It's as big an art as any other. Most women work at it the whole of the time. Not one man in a million is aware of it. It's like air within the air. It may be deadly. Cramping and awful, or simply destructive, so that no life is possible without it. So is the bad art of men. At its best it is absolutely life-giving. And not soft. Very hard and stern and austere in its beauty. And like mountain air. A woman's way of 'being' can be discovered in the way she pours out tea.... I feel the atmosphere created by the lady of the house as soon as I get on to the door step. (257)

As is so often the case with modernism, this aesthetic expression anticipates later theoretical developments, in this case along key lines of feminist scholarship. For example, Richardson here anticipates Elaine Showalter's claim that the female tradition of the novel up to the twentieth century was fraught with problems because many early female novelists were either imitative of the male tradition or were simply reinscribing myths of femininity. She also anticipates the more radical claims of Hélène Cixous, Julia Kristeva, and Luce Irigaray, who argue that the syntax, grammar, and structure of prose are gendered masculine and make it impossible to express women's experience. As Richardson herself put it, "Feminine prose, as Charles Dickens and James Joyce have delightfully shown themselves to be aware, should properly be unpunctuated, moving from point to point without formal obstructions" (Foreword, p. 377). From such a view, rule-bound writing is essentially masculine; for women it is akin to speaking a second language, a foreign tongue, all the time. Richardson articulates this perspective precisely in the *The Tunnel*: "In speech with a man a woman is at a disadvantage—because they speak different languages. She may understand his. Hers he will never speak nor understand. In pity, or from other motives, she must therefore, stammeringly, speak his. He listens and is flattered and thinks he has her mental measure when he has not touched even the fringe of her consciousness...." (p. 247). Hélène Cixous will term the mode of writing that *can* and does articulate this women's language *écriture féminine* (about which more below). *Écriture féminine* serves for Cixous as a means of expressing feminine experience by exuberantly writing the female body into literature, and shares a great deal with Kristeva's insistence on the semiotic elements of writing that disrupt the masculine symbolic with feminine rhythms, flows, and pulsions. Both are anticipated, in theory and practice, by Richardson's attempt to discover a feminine style, as early as 1912.

Style

Given the history of Western aesthetics, in which male subjectivity has so easily been universalized and female subjectivity correspondingly marginalized or erased, it was perhaps inevitable that Richardson's focus on women's experience would be contained and personalized, whereas Joyce's and Proust's experiments could more easily (though not without hiccups) be generalized. Indeed, J.M. Murry put his finger on this distinction as early as 1922 in "The Break Up of the Novel," where he claimed that Richardson's "insistence upon the immediate consciousness as reality" is unlike Proust's and Joyce's in that it is "instinctive and irrational; it has a distinctly feminine tinge" (*Pointed Roofs*, p. 230). Nonetheless, Murry did link Joyce and Proust with Richardson in broader terms, writing that *Pilgrimage* "attempts to record immediately the growth of a consciousness. Immediately; without any effort at mediation by means of an interposed plot or story" (*Pointed Roofs*, p. 230) Joyce, Proust, and Richardson were "trying to present the content of their consciousness as it was before it had been re-shaped in obedience to the demands of practical life; they were exploring the strange limbo where experiences once conscious face into unconsciousness" (*Pointed Roofs*, p. 230). The style of *Pilgrimage* is characterized above all else by its subjectivity, leading Murry to surmise that Richardson, along with some of her contemporaries, was suggesting that the truth is subjective: "All that we can know is our own experience," wrote Murry, "and the closer we keep to the immediate quality of that experience, the nearer we shall be to truth" (*Pointed Roofs*, p. 230). Murry's ventriloquism here, speaking in the place of writers such as Richardson, is not far off, though it leans perhaps too heavily on the straw-man of relativism. Richardson, at least, is not "trying to present the content of [her] consciousness as it was before it had been re-shaped," but to stage the process by which thought itself is shaped in the constant dialectic between object and subject. Or, to be even more precise, she is illustrating the extent to which the subject/object binary is itself illusory, with each shaping the other in a constant, ever-evolving set of relations whose truth lies only in becoming.

Perhaps the most effective means of rendering the immediacy of experience is through stream of consciousness. The expression "stream of consciousness" comes from the psychology of William James,[1] who described consciousness in these terms, as opposed

---

1 William James (1842-1910), American psychologist and philosopher. James's theories of consciousness, religious experience, and pragmatism

to a succession of states or points on a line. In literary critical terms, stream of consciousness is the technique of rendering in prose, with as little syntactical, grammatical, or punctuational ordering as necessary, the contents of a character's consciousness. Logic often disappears in favour of association, or what Jean-Paul Sartre called "emotional constellations" (268). Similar techniques include the interior monologue, in which a character's internal self-talk is rendered for the reader, and free indirect discourse, in which a character's consciousness focalizes the narrative and colours it with his or her perspective. In truth, *Pilgrimage* exemplifies interior monologue and free indirect discourse much more often than it does stream of consciousness, though only the latter term was in common use during Richardson's writing career.

One of the most curious facts about these techniques is that they are so frequently dated as originating much later than they actually did. Though Proust, Joyce, and Woolf certainly made use of them, none of them originated them. In fact, the term "stream of consciousness" was first applied to a literary technique by May Sinclair in a 1918 review of the first three volumes of *Pilgrimage*: "there is no drama, no situation, no set scene. Nothing happens. It is just life going on and on. It is Miriam Henderson's stream of consciousness going on and on. And in neither is there any grossly discernible beginning or middle or end" (*Pointed Roofs*, p. 238). Richardson rejected the stream of consciousness label throughout her life, taking writerly issue with it as a bad metaphor, calling it "death-dealing" and "inane," setting it among the "formulae devised to meet the exigencies of literary criticism" (Foreword, p. 377). Richardson did not see consciousness as a stream exactly, but something more spatial, with depth as well as movement. The temporal analogy of the stream, she felt, sacrificed this depth to the narrative of progress. As an alternative, she suggested "fountain of consciousness," although she failed to find even that figure entirely satisfactory (Letter to Shiv Kumar, 10 August 1952).

As Sinclair's borrowing from William James indicates, changes in the understanding of human psychology at the turn of the twentieth century played a significant role in modernist experiments with narrative technique, representation, and novelistic form. James famously also influenced Gertrude Stein, who studied with him before going on to write such cutting-edge works

profoundly influenced many early twentieth-century writers and artists, as well as other philosophers and psychologists.

as *Three Lives* (1909), *The Making of Americans* (1925), and *The Autobiography of Alice B. Toklas* (1933). Sigmund Freud is another important figure for his innovative ideas about the unconscious, sexuality, and hidden instinctual impulses behind common practices, what he called "the psychopathology of everyday life." Henri Bergson (1859-1941), as well, theorized subjectivity in relationship to time, arguing that a concept of duration, or *durée*, more accurately captured human experience of temporality than standardized clock time (see Bergson, *Pointed Roofs*, pp. 223-29).

These shifts in psychological theory drove a parallel turn in the arts towards subjectivity, interiority, perception, and experience as the objects of artistic representation. Turning away from the realist impulse to describe objective reality accurately, or the naturalist determination to capture the objective operations of a universe independent of human experience, modernist writers and artists sought instead to validate and render as accurately as possible the immediate truth of human experience. Impressionism in painting is a fine example: rather than attempt to paint with photographic accuracy, the impressionists sought instead to capture the subjective experience of the objects they painted. Still lives, landscapes, and crowd scenes were increasingly rendered in terms of how they were perceived and felt by the recording observer rather than how they might be objectively captured. Impressionist paintings thus render objects such as crowds with blurry outlines, flashes or blotches of colour, haze, and implied movement. The objective is to capture the fleeting experience of light, movement, and shape as it happens, rather than retroactively, to give it clarity, definition, and certainty. For modernist aesthetics, to impose order and hierarchy on the chaos of perception was to falsify it, to add layers of distance between the phenomenon and its perceiver, and thus to rob the experience—and thus human being itself—of its authenticity.

Many key modernist writers articulated this new approach in their own writing about their practice. Virginia Woolf, in "Modern Novels" (1919), writes,

> The mind, exposed to the ordinary course of life, receives upon its surface a myriad impressions—trivial, fantastic, evanescent, or engraved with the sharpness of steel. From all sides they come, an incessant shower of innumerable atoms, composing in their sum what we might venture to call life itself; and to figure further as the semi-transparent envelope, or luminous halo, surrounding us from the beginning of con-

sciousness to the end. It is not perhaps the chief task of the novelist to convey this incessantly varying spirit with whatever stress or sudden deviation it may display, and as little admixture of the alien and external as possible?[1]

Equally, Ezra Pound, in outlining "A Few Don'ts from an Imagiste" (1913), urges poets to adhere to the concrete dimension of human experience rather than poetic traditions of metaphor and intellectualism. He provides perhaps the most succinct example of his method in the poem "In a Station of the Metro": "The apparition of these faces in the crowd; / Petals on a wet, black bough" (35). T.S. Eliot, in his introduction to Djuna Barnes's *Nightwood* (1936), notes that the application of these innovations leads inevitably to prose that reads as verse, just as Pound's "Jefferson" Cantos simply transcribe prose into verse form. This sort of borrowing and cross-application of method leads most famously to literary impressionism, first explicated as a method by Ford Madox Ford in his analysis of Joseph Conrad's technique ("On Impressionism" 1914). More abstractly, though, it also underwrites Gertrude Stein's updating of the Latin prescription, "*ut pictura poesis*"[2] (from Horace's *Ars Poetica*), in her own "Composition as Explanation" (1925). There, Stein writes,

> The only thing that is different from one time to another is what is seen and what is seen depends upon how everybody is doing everything. This makes the thing we are looking at very different and this makes what those who describe it make of it, it makes a composition, it confuses, it shows, it is, it looks, it likes it as it is, and this makes what is seen as it is seen. Nothing changes from generation to generation except the thing seen and that makes a composition. (422)

That is, Stein regards the experience of time as an arrangement that pertains to the perceiver. She relates the composition of a particular historical moment to the composition of a painting or photograph, but also to the form and alignment of the various parts of a literary work. Having overturned the realist obsession with plot, linearity, character development, and moral outcomes, modernist literature must be understood as itself striving for an

---

1 Virginia Woolf, "Modern Novels," *Times Literary Supplement* (10 April 1919).
2 "As is painting so is poetry."

immediacy of experience. A novel is not to be read and gradually discovered chapter by chapter, but experienced as a whole whose parts relate in myriad ways without necessarily following logically, temporally, or structurally. It must be experienced as a painting is, as a whole whose parts interrelate through proximity, thematic coherence, aesthetic effect, suggestion, and association. *Ut pictura poesis* is thus made new,[1] offering a long-standing ratification of the wholesale remaking of literary representation.

In what might seem a paradox, the commitment to heightened verisimilitude—to a more accurate rendering of human experience and consciousness—typical of modernism and certainly of *Pilgrimage*, led writers to evolve techniques devoted to making the familiar strange. Russian literary critic Viktor Shklovsky, in his "Art as Technique" (1917) called this process defamiliarization, and suggested that if art were to be true to the realities of human experience, it must first disrupt our easy, habitual comprehension of the everyday world:

> art exists that one may recover the sensation of life; it exists to make one feel things, to make the stone stony. The purpose of art is to impart the sensation of things as they are perceived and not as they are known. The technique of art is to make objects "unfamiliar," to make forms difficult, to increase the difficulty and length of perception because the process of perception is an aesthetic end in itself and must be prolonged. Art is a way of experiencing the artfulness of an object: the object is not important. (11)

Pilgrimage presents an early and uniquely sustained experiment with these principles, through a variety of technical and formal elements. *Pilgrimage*'s close focus on Miriam Henderson's consciousness is itself an artistic feat of endurance and rigour, locked in a close dance with innovations in literary treatment that would become hallmarks of modernist literary practice.

Perhaps the most characteristically experimental aspect of *Pilgrimage* is its commitment to a single point of view for all thirteen chapter-volumes. Though there are parts of the narrative in the third-person, nothing of any consequence is relayed to readers other than through Miriam's consciousness. The point of view of

---

1   "Make it new!" is Ezra Pound's imperative for modernism, most famously articulated in his Canto XV. If modernism has a slogan, this is it.

the novel is exclusively her own. We are not told about other characters' motives or thoughts, and can only deduce them from Miriam's observations and reactions. Likewise, we only get to know the other characters, and the settings, through Miriam's impressions of them. When she first visits her old friend Alma and her husband Hypo, Miriam's impressions of the bedroom assigned to her capture vastly more than simply what it looks like:

> The strange shock of the bedroom, the strange new thing springing out from it ... the clear soft bright tones, the bright white light streaming through the clear muslin, the freshness of the walls ... the flattened dumpy shapes of dark green bedroom crockery gleaming in a corner; the little green bowl standing in the middle of the white spread of the dressing-table cover ... wild violets with green leaves and tendrils put there by somebody, with each leaf and blossom standing separate ... touching your heart; joy, looking from the speaking pale mauve little flowers to the curved rim of the green bowl and away to the green crockery in the corner; again and again the fresh shock of the violets. (p. 154)

The prose itself here captures the vague gestures of impressionism, and the emotions inextricably bound up with the colours, placements, and shapes of the furnishings make the description as much a record of Miriam's impressions as of the room itself.

This emphasis on impression ties Richardson's technique to that of literary impressionism, particularly when she records Miriam's experience of London, the English countryside, or a crowded room of people. Richardson also relies heavily upon free indirect discourse to colour the third-person narration with Miriam's characteristic perspective. The slippage from free indirect discourse to interior monologue can be difficult to detect, so that we at times find ourselves moving from one narrative voice to another, and inside Miriam's head, with little notice: "From above came the tap-tap of a door swinging gently in a breeze and behind the sound was a soft faint continuous murmur. She ran up the short twisting flight of bare stairs into a blaze of light. Would her room be a bright suburban bedroom? Had it been a dull day when she first called? The skylight was blue and gold with light, its cracks threads of bright gold" (p. 56). As Miriam first discovers her room in Mrs Bailey's house, the narrative moves rapidly through an objective perspective coloured with Miriam's impressions, to free indirect discourse in the questions posed, and back to coloured narration in the final line. Throughout, because the narrative is always focalized through Miriam's consciousness, we are never free of her impressions, and thus always susceptible to her moods, errors, and assumptions.

Finally, Richardson's innovative use of stream of consciousness at times threatens to overwhelm readers who are trying to make sense of events. Stream of consciousness mimics the immediacy of experience itself in forcing us to ride the wave of stimulus or experience, only making sense of it after the fact—sometimes long after, when we have finally been given enough information to understand. To quote Sartre again, it affords a "vision of the world [that] can be compared to that of a man sitting in an open car and looking backwards. At every moment, formless shadows, flickerings, faint tremblings and patches of light rise up on either side of him, and only afterwards, when he has a little perspective, do they become trees and men and cars" (267). Moreover, as *Pilgrimage* progresses we learn that we cannot always trust Miriam's interpretations or impressions of her experiences; not only can it be difficult to figure out *what* is happening, it can be difficult to understand *why* it is happening. On her final morning at a country house, Miriam is absorbed in considering both her own ignorance of what others think and their ignorance of her own state of mind:

> They knew one liked some things better than others; or suddenly liked everything very much indeed ... she said you were apathetic ... what does that mean? ... what did she mean? ... with her, one could see nothing and sat waiting ... I said I don't think so, I don't think she is apathetic at all. Then they understood when one sat in a heap.... They had been pleased this morning because of one's misery at going away. They did not know of the wild happiness in the garden before breakfast. (p. 275)

This passage comes at the very beginning of a chapter, and lacks sufficient context to make immediate sense; the best we can do is follow Miriam's line of thought and guess at what has happened. Add to this the challenge of figuring out why Miriam feels as she does, and the "collaborative reader" Richardson posited as the ideal becomes a necessity.

Only through reading and re-reading the books can we piece together the story, by recognizing Miriam's later reflections on current events and putting them together into a kind of collage of consciousness. Richardson's play with point of view and narrative perspective thus manages to make the everyday unfamiliar, at times radically so, in ways that other writers such as Joyce, Woolf, Ford, Elizabeth Bowen, William Faulkner, and Mary Butts will adopt, develop and refine.

A hallmark of stream of consciousness, free indirect discourse, and interior monologue is non-standard use of writing conventions such as grammar, syntax, and punctuation. The final chapter of Joyce's *Ulysses* is famous for its lack of punctuation and the inclusion of only eight section-breaks in nearly fifty pages of dense prose. Richardson innovates some of these elements in her effort to capture in words the immediate, flowing, fragmented, and often disjointed features of thought. To achieve a flow akin to consciousness, to being along for the ride in someone's head, Richardson experimented with grammar and punctuation. Much of *Pilgrimage* is characterized by extensive use of dashes, ellipses, long sentences and sentence fragments. In "About Punctuation" (1924), Richardson suggests that modern literature needs to do away with regulated punctuation. A text without punctuation, save for periods, may be difficult to follow, but she thought readers would get used to it as they went along. Readers would find themselves "*listening*. Reading through the ear as well as through the eye" ("About," p. 339 this edition). To Richardson, experimentation with the comma was paramount in conveying the leaping, running-on nature of thought, as demonstrated in the following passage:

> In the instant before her mind had slid back, and she had listened to the muffled footsteps thudding along the turf of the low cliff above her head, waiting angrily and anxiously for further disturbance, she had been perfectly alive, seeing; perfect things all round her, no beginning or ending ... there had been moments like that, years ago, in gardens, by seas and cliffs. (p. 249)

The punctuation in this passage captures the movement of Miriam's thoughts as full sentences would not, and render the fragmentary nature of how they occur to her, often flitting away or being chased aside by the next thought.

Consequent upon this approach to rendering human consciousness is a certain sacrifice of structure. Aside from the fact of time progressing, *Pilgrimage* affords almost no milestones by which to assess where one is in the text. Time is certainly not divided up and marked the way it is in realist novels, or even those of Woolf and Joyce. We often don't even know what year it is, and unless a reader is familiar with London it can be a challenge to understand where one is as well. For, of course, just as we do not habitually think about where we are in our lives or in terms of episodes in them, so Miriam does not often meditate upon where she is in the narrative of *Pilgrimage*. And, with the narrative largely confined to Miriam's consciousness, there is not much chance for a narrator to intervene with extra-diegetic markers that will help to orient the reader. To employ an old distinction, there is much story in *Pilgrimage*, but not much plot: we are told what happens, though not in any orderly—or retroactively ordered—way. We leap about in time according to the whims of Miriam's consciousness, and the whole only begins to take shape, as Stein indicates is appropriate, when we have reached the end and can see it entire. Richardson's innovation here is perhaps even more radical than that of Joyce, whose masterpiece *Ulysses* is at least nominally structured around episodes of Homer's *Odyssey* and restricted to a single day. Similarly, Richardson's novels lack a moment of epiphany, as in the works of Joyce, Woolf, or Katherine Mansfield. All of the very brief Chapter VII in *The Tunnel*, for example, presents as profoundly enigmatic unless the reader has managed to figure out that it concerns Miriam's memory of her mother's recent death, following a period of mental illness. Without that knowledge, Miriam's intense moment of recollection and fear of madness remains inaccessible to readers, and deprives them of the sort of insight furnished by conventional epiphanies. Enter the collaborative reader.

This need to wait for insight, to put one's questions or perplexity on hold perhaps indefinitely before understanding, goes by the name of *delayed decoding*. First applied by Ian Watt to Joseph Conrad's tendency to render unexpected events first in terms of a character's experience of them, and only later naming the events (e.g., a ship exploding is narrated first as a crazy upheaval of the deck, a blow to the head, and noise, then later on recounted as an explosion), the term delayed decoding applies equally well to Richardson's tendency to narrate events by examining their epiphenomena in Miriam's consciousness. Miriam's outrage with Dr. Hancock at the opening of Chapter XX is a case in point: without informing the reader about the nature of Miriam's feelings for Dr. Hancock, the details of her visit to his family, or the outcome of his consultations with his sisters, the narrative gives the reader only Miriam's sense of injury and outrage. Only as more bits of information are provided, innocuously, often hidden in amongst other happenings, is the reader able to decipher or reconstruct events to account for the results they produce. It's a technique that inverts causality as we traditionally find it in narrative, placing effects first and leaving causes for later accounting, if at all. In this, it is much truer of course to the great majority of human experience, if equally estranging in a narrative context where we have grown accustomed to being told stories from the end, as it were, when events can be placed into their proper sequence and importance. Richardson uses this technique to enormous effect throughout *Pilgrimage*, allowing us to experience rather than simply be told about Miriam's misunderstandings, errors, misattributions, and so forth. It also, however, allows us more direct access to her moments of rapture, enjoyment, and pleasure. When Miriam rhapsodizes over some overheard piano music, we are often treated to her rhapsody first, and only later to its cause. The effect is much like suddenly feeling happy, and only afterwards coming to realize it is because one has heard a familiar voice or smelled a pleasant smell.

Contemporary Reactions

Because it was the fourth installment in the *Pilgrimage* series, *The Tunnel* did not initially bewilder its readers as *Pointed Roofs* had four years earlier. Appearing in 1919, it followed or is contemporaneous with several key modernist experimental works, including the first volume of Proust's *A la recherche du temps perdu* (1913), Joyce's *A Portrait of the Artist as a Young Man* (1916), and May Sinclair's *Mary Olivier: A Life* (1919). All of these novels, and many more that would follow in their wake, challenge the very notion of what a novel is, how stories ought to be told, whether novels should have stories at all, and how human consciousness ought to be understood. Readers had begun to get the hang of reading such works, so *The Tunnel* had a somewhat more indulgent reception than its predecessor chapter-volumes had, even provoking Virginia Woolf to grudging respect. Nonetheless, some critics continued to take issue with both the method and the matter of *The Tunnel*.

Method

Richardson's intense focus on Miriam Henderson's internal life, her consciousness and perceptions, means that there is little in the way of a readily recognizable narrative arc to the chapter-volumes. Episodes occur, often so mutedly that their import can be missed altogether, and the larger shape of the narrative is nowhere near as apparent as it is with nineteenth-century novels such as those by Dickens, Gaskell, Austen, the Brontës, or Eliot. Instead, readers must attend to the method by which the tale is told. As Virginia Woolf put it, "It is a method that demands attention, as a door whose handle we wrench ineffectively calls our attention to the fact that it is locked" ("Review of *The Tunnel*," p. 325). Woolf, who would go on herself to experiment with narrative technique and novelistic form over the coming decades, confessed to disappointment with Richardson's method, arguing that it hews too much to the surface of things and fails to reach to the meaningful depths of daily life: "we cannot deny a slight sense of disappointment.... Things look much the same as ever. It is certainly a very vivid surface. The consciousness of Miriam takes the reflection of a dentist's room to perfection" (p. 327). At the same time, she allows that *The Tunnel*, at least, is "better in its failure than most books in their success" (p. 327). She recognizes the ambition of Richardson's narrative experiments, and celebrates it even as she detects a failure of execution. John Rodker was somewhat less generous, noting that what had been in *Pointed Roofs* "a bright and not unoriginal conception [is] becoming thickened to the diameter of a hawser" (p. 328). By contrast, Olive Heseltine saw *The Tunnel* as "simply life. Shapeless, trivial, pointless, boring, beautiful, curious, profound. And above all, absorbing" (562; qtd by McCracken, n.p.). She finds it "forty times more interesting than *Pointed Roofs*," sees "no reason why [the] chronicle should ever stop," and "hopes it never will" (565; qtd. by McCracken n.p.). Likewise, Babette Deutsch, pairing *The Tunnel* with May Sinclair's *Mary Olivier: A Life*, found in both novels "that element of 'return' to a transcendent reality which is reminiscent of poetry, that sensitive appreciation which makes for living prose" (441). Sinclair herself praised Richardson: "Miss Richardson has only imposed on herself the conditions that life imposes on all of us. And if you are going to quarrel with those conditions you will not find her novels satisfactory. But your satisfaction is not her concern" (xxx). She goes on to recommend *Pilgrimage* as a triumph of the sensual and mindfulness in novelistic art: "It is as if no other writers had ever used their senses so purely and with so intense a joy in their use" (p. 239).

Matter

Sinclair's sense that everyday life is the matter of *Pilgrimage*, and that its depiction of it in fine detail is its strength, led her to concur with Katherine Mansfield in criticizing it for a failure to be selective in subject matter: "everything being of equal importance to her, it is impossible that everything should not be of equal unimportance" (p. 331). Mansfield continues, writing that Richardson possesses a remarkable ability to record and reconstruct otherwise unremarkable moments in complete detail: "Anything that goes into her mind she can summon forth again, and there it is, complete in every detail, with nothing taken away from it—and nothing added. This is a rare and interesting gift, but we should hesitate before saying it was a great one" (p. 327). Perhaps uncharitably, this impatience with Richardson's unprecedented concentration on the very aspects of life so often deemed unworthy of attention let alone artistic representation led to the charge of narcissism: "Miss Richardson has a passion for registering every single thing that happens in the clear, shadowless country of her mind. One cannot imagine her appealing to the reader or planning out her novel; her concern is primarily, and perhaps ultimately, with herself" (p. 329). With this claim, Mansfield helps establish the vein of criticism that will prove so abundant for future critics of many other modernist novelists in addition to Richardson: narrative experimentation is self-indulgent, masturbatory, narcissistic, bourgeois, ahistorical, unethical, and anti-social.

Envy

Of course, such a criticism smacks as well of resentment, whether of the justified class-based sort that would inform later Marxist critiques of modernist experimentation or of the less noble professional sort that sees artists ignore or attack other artists out of a sense of their own fragile value. Notoriously, Virginia Woolf and Katherine Murry (née Mansfield, J. Middleton's wife) discussed Richardson at least once, and in disapproving tones. Woolf's diary entry for 22 March 1919 notes that when she last saw Murry she "flung down her pen & plunged, as if we'd been parted for 10 minutes, in to the question of Dorothy Richardson; & so on with the greatest freedom & animation on both sides until I had to catch my train" (*The Diary of Virginia Woolf* I: 257). That this conversation was not full of praise one may deduce from the diary entry of only ten months later, in which Woolf tellingly writes "Today, bearing K[atherine] M[urry] in mind, I refused to do Dorothy Richardson for the Supt.[1] The truth is that when I looked at it, I felt myself looking for faults; hoping for them. And they would have bent my pen, I know. There must be an instinct of self-preservation at work. If she's good then I'm not" (*The Diary of Virginia Woolf* I: 314). Scarcely three months later Woolf again damns Richardson (this time along with Joyce) for her reliance upon "the damned egotistical self" (*The Diary of Virginia Woolf* II: 14). And, on 21 February 1921, she reveals a pettiness one does not often associate with her, recording another refusal to review Richardson's work: "Massingham would be grateful if I would review D. Richardson for him. This amuses & slightly gratifies me—especially as I refuse" (*The Diary of Virginia Woolf* II: 93).[2]

That so great a talent as Virginia Woolf felt envious of Richardson, to the point of being unable to be objective in assessing her achievement, speaks more eloquently for the real value of her innovation than could any number of encomia. Unfortunately, Richardson's commitment to her method, and to the grand vision of *Pilgrimage*, meant that subsequent chapter-volumes after *The Tunnel* were reviewed less and less often, and with less and less praise. It seemed to many that she was simply doing the same thing over and over again. By the time she died in 1957, Richardson's works were little-known and had to wait until the 1970s for rediscovery. Only in 1973 was Richardson's literary executor, Rose Odle, able to have a biography of Richardson completed by Gloria Fromm. Three years later, Thomas Staley's 1976 study of Richardson reintroduced her to the academic world, spawning a steady trickle of studies that has become more of a freshet since Bonnie Kime Scott's (ed.) anthology *The Gender of Modernism* appeared in 1990. As modernist studies have been expanded and revived at the turn of this century, Richardson's star has been steadily on the rise, and we look forward to a great many more readers, students, and scholars of her work in the decades to come.[3]

Stephen Ross

---

1   That is, the *Times Literary Supplement*.

2   Woolf declined to review either *Interim* (1920) or *Deadlock* (1921). She had previously reviewed *The Tunnel*. Massingham: Henry William Massingham (1860-1924), journalist and newspaper editor.

3   For example, *The Collected Letters of Dorothy Richardson* are at last being published by The Richardson Project, beginning in 2015. See <http://dorothyrichardson.org/Editions/Letters.html> for details on the project's progress.

Works Cited

Alighieri, Dante. *The Divine Comedy*. New York: Penguin, 2013.

Benstock, Shari. *Women of the Left Bank: Paris, 1900-1940*. Austin: U of Texas P, 1986.

Bergson, Henri. "Duration" (1907). Trans. Arthur Mitchell. In Richard Ellmann and Charles Fiedelson, eds. *The Modern Tradition: Backgrounds of Modern Literature*. New York: Oxford UP, 1965. 723-30. Reprinted in Stephen Ross and Tara Thomson, eds. Dorothy Richardson, *Pointed Roofs*. Peterborough: Broadview P, 2014. 223-28.

Bluemel, Kristin. *Experimenting on the Borders of Modernism: Dorothy Richardson's Pilgrimage*. Athens, GA: U of Georgia P, 1997.

Cixous, Hélène. "The Laugh of the Medusa." *Signs* 1.4 (Summer 1976): 875-93.

Deutsch, Babette. "Freedom and the Grace of God." *Dial* 67 (15 November 1919): 441-42.

Eliot, T.S. Introduction to Djuna Barnes, *Nightwood*. New York: New Directions, 1996 (1936).

Ford (Hueffer), Ford Madox. "On Impressionism." *Poetry and Drama* 2.6 (June-December 1914): 167-75 (first article) and 323-34 (second article).

Friedman, Susan Stanford. "Definitional Excursions: The Meanings of Modern/Modernity/Modernism." *Modernism/Modernity* 8.3 (September 2001): 493-513.

Fromm, Gloria. *Dorothy Richardson: A Biography*. Chicago: U of Illinois P, 1977.

Hanscombe, Gillian. *The Art of Life: Dorothy Richardson and the Development of Feminine Consciousness*. London: P. Owen, 1982.

Hardy, Thomas. *Tess of the D'Urbervilles*. Ed. Scott Elledge. New York: W.W. Norton, 1991.

Heseltine, Olive. "Life. *The Tunnel*." *Everyman* [London], 22 March 1919: 562, 565.

Horace. "Ars Poetica." Trans. D.A. Russell. *The Norton Anthology of Theory and Criticism*. Gen. Ed. Vincent B. Leitch. New York: W.W. Norton, 2010 (2nd ed.). 122-33.

Irigaray, Luce. *This Sex Which Is Not One*. Ithaca, NY: Cornell UP, 1985.

James, William. "Stream of Consciousness," *Psychology*. Cleveland and New York: World, 1892: 151-75. Reprinted in Stephen Ross and Tara Thomson, eds. Dorothy Richardson, *Pointed Roofs*. Peterborough: Broadview P, 2014. 219-22.

Kristeva, Julia. *The Revolution in Poetic Language*. New York: Columbia UP, 1984.

McCracken, Scott. <http://www.dorothyrichardson.org>. Accessed 20 January 2014.

Murry, John Middleton. "The Break-Up of the Novel" *Yale Review* 12 (October 1922): 288-304.

Olson, Liesl. *Modernism and the Ordinary*. New York: Oxford UP. 2009.

Pound, Ezra. "Canto XV." In *The Cantos of Ezra Pound*. New York: New Directions, 1993. 64-67.

——. "A Few Don'ts from an Imagiste." *Poetry* (March 1913): 200-06.

——. "In a Station of the Metro." *Selected Poems of Ezra Pound*. New York: New Directions, 1957. 35.

Richardson, Dorothy. "About Punctuation." *Adelphi* 1 (April 1924): 990-96. Reprinted in this edition, pp. 339-44.

——. "Comments by a Layman." *The Dental Record* 36 (1916):141.

——. *Dawn's Left Hand*. London: Duckworth, 1931.

——. Foreword. *Pilgrimage*. Collected Edition. London: J.M. Dent, 1938. 9-12. Reprinted in this edition, pp. 374-78.

——. "Leadership in Marriage." *New Adelphi* 2 (June-August 1929): 345-48.

——. "Letter to Shiv Kumar, 10/08/1952," Dorothy Richardson Collection. General Collection, Beinecke Rare Book and Manuscript Library, Yale University.

——. *March Moonlight*. New York: Random House, 1967.

——. *Pointed Roofs*. Ed. Stephen Ross and Tara Thomson. Peterborough: Broadview P, 2014.

——. "The Reality of Feminism." *The Ploughshare* 2 (September 1917): 241-46. Reprinted in this edition, pp. 348-57.

——. *Revolving Lights*. London: Duckworth, 1923.

——. "Talent and Genius: Is Not Genius Far More Common than Talent?" *Vanity Fair* 21 (October 1923): 118; 120. Reprinted in this edition, pp. 357-62.

Sartre, Jean-Paul. "On 'The Sound and the Fury': Time in the Work of Faulkner." In David Minter, ed. *The Sound and the Fury*. 2nd ed. New York: W.W. Norton, 1994 (1947). 265-71.

Scott, Bonnie Kime. Introduction. In Bonnie Kime Scott, ed. *The Gender of Modernism: A Critical Anthology*. Blooomington and Indianapolis: Indiana UP, 1990. 1-18.

Shklovsky, Viktor. "Art as Technique" (1917). In Richard J. Lane, ed. *Global Literary Theory: An Anthology*. New York: Routledge, 2013. 7-20.

Showalter, Elaine. *A Literature of Their Own*. Princeton: Princeton UP, 1977.

Sim, Lorraine. *Virginia Woolf: The Patterns of Ordinary Experience*. London: Ashgate, 2010.

Sinclair, May. *Mary Olivier: A Life*. New York: NYRB Classics, 2002.

——. "The Novels of Dorothy Richardson." *The Little Review* 5.12 (April 1918): 3-11.

Staley, Thomas. *Dorothy Richardson*. Boston: Twayne, 1976.

Stein, Gertrude. "Composition as Explanation." In Vassiliki Kolocotroni et al., eds. *Modernism: An Anthology of Sources and Documents.* Chicago: U of Chicago P, 1998. 421-25.

Walpole, Hugh. "Realism and the New English Novel." *Vanity Fair* 20 (March 1923): 34, 112. Reprinted in Stephen Ross and Tara Thomson, eds. *Dorothy Richardson, Pointed Roofs.* Peterborough: Broadview P, 2014. 233-36.

Watt, Ian. *Conrad in the Nineteenth Century.* Berkeley: U of California P, 1979.

Winning, Joanne. *The Pilgrimage of Dorothy Richardson.* Madison: U of Wisconsin P, 2000.

Woolf, Virginia. "Diary Entry for 22 March 1919." *The Diary of Virginia Woolf. Volume I: 1915-1919.* Ed. Anne Olivier Bell. London: Hogarth P, 1977. 257-58.

——. "Diary Entry for 28 November 1919." *The Diary of Virginia Woolf. Volume I: 1915-1919.* Ed. Anne Olivier Bell. London: Hogarth P, 1977. 314-15.

——. "Diary Entry for 26 January 1920." *The Diary of Virginia Woolf. Volume II: 1920-1924.* Ed. Anne Olivier Bell. London: Hogarth P, 1978. 14-15.

——. "Diary Entry for 21 February 1921." *The Diary of Virginia Woolf. Volume II: 1920-1924.* Ed. Anne Olivier Bell. London: Hogarth P, 1978. 93-94.

——. "Modern Novels." *The Times Literary Supplement* (10 April 1919).

——. *A Room of One's Own.* Peterborough: Broadview P, 2001.

——. *Three Guineas.* Peterborough: Broadview P, 2012.

——. "The Tunnel [review]." *Times Literary Supplement*, 13 February 1919, p. 81. Reprinted in this edition, pp. 325-27.

Dorothy Richardson: A Brief Chronology

1873   Dorothy Miller Richardson is born at Abingdon.
1890   Father's financial troubles mean she must go to work as a governess to support herself.
1893   Father declares bankruptcy.
1895   Ceases work as a governess to care for her mentally ill mother.
1895   Mother commits suicide.
1895   H.G. Wells's *The Time Machine* published.
1896   Moves to London to work as a receptionist and assistant at a dental office in Harley Street.
1896   Meets H.G. Wells.
1896   Wells's *The Island of Dr. Moreau* published.
1898   Wells's *The War of the Worlds* published.
1903   Women's Social and Political Union formed, led by Emmeline Pankhurst, to promote the cause of women's suffrage.
1903   Henry James's *The Ambassadors* published.
1905   Begins an affair with Wells.
1906   Begins publishing articles, reviews, stories, poems, and translations, often in dental journals.
1907   Pregnancy by Wells ends in a miscarriage.
1909   Wells's *Ann Veronica* published.
1912   Begins work on *Pointed Roofs*.
1912   May Sinclair publishes *Feminism*, a suffragist pamphlet.
1914   World War I begins.
1914   Publishes *The Quakers Past and Present* and *Gleanings from the work of George Fox*.
1915   *Pointed Roofs*.
1916   *Backwater*.
1917   *Honeycomb*.
1917   Marries Alan Odle; they begin spending summers in London and winters in Cornwall.
1918   May Sinclair refers to Richardson's writing as "stream of consciousness."
1918   World War I ends.
1919   *The Tunnel*.
1919   Sinclair's *Mary Olivier: A Life* published.
1919   *Interim* serialized in *The Little Review*, alongside *Ulysses*.
1920   *Interim*.

1921   *Deadlock.*
1922   Publication of Marcel Proust's *A la recherche du temps perdu* in English, Katherine Mansfield's *The Garden Party: and Other Stories*, James Joyce's *Ulysses*, Virginia Woolf's *Jacob's Room*, Sinclair's *Life and Death of Harriet Frean*, and T.S. Eliot's *The Waste Land.*
1923   *Revolving Lights.*
1925   *The Trap.*
1925   Virginia Woolf's *Mrs Dalloway* published.
1927   *Oberland.*
1927   Woolf's *To the Lighthouse* published.
1928   Women receive the vote in England on same terms as men.
1928   Radclyffe Hall's *The Well of Loneliness* published.
1929   "Black Tuesday" crash on Wall Street sets off the Great Depression of the 1930s.
1930   *John Austen and the Inseparables.*
1931   *Dawn's Left Hand.*
1931   Woolf's *The Waves* published.
1933   Adolph Hitler becomes Chancellor of Germany.
1935   *Clear Horizon.*
1936   Onset of Spanish Civil War (which ends in 1939).
1936   Djuna Barnes's *Nightwood* published.
1937   Nazis bomb the Spanish town of Guernica, inaugurating age of Total War.
1938   Collected *Pilgrimage* published in 4 vols. (including first publication of *Dimple Hill*).
1939   World War II begins.
1945   World War II ends.
1946   Three sections of *March Moonlight* published in *Life and Letters.*
1948   Odle dies.
1954   Moves into a nursing home.
1957   Richardson dies.
1967   J.M. Dent reprints the collected *Pilgrimage* in 4 vols., including *March Moonlight.*
1979   Virago reprints the collected *Pilgrimage* in 4 vols.
1989   *Journey to Paradise: Short Stories and Autobiographical Sketches.*

A Note on the Text

For our edition we have taken the Collected Edition of 1938 (reprinted in 1967) as the authoritative version of the text, though we have corrected obvious printing errors. George H. Thomson's charting of the variants between the 1st British and American editions, and the Collected Edition, suggests a troubled publication history, in which none of the published texts precisely reflects Richardson's intent. A number of typographical errors are noted between the manuscript and the first editions. In addition, Gerald Duckworth and Company, the press that published the first edition, wanted to regularize the punctuation somewhat to make it more accessible to readers—a move the author unsuccessfully resisted. Richardson corrected some of these errors and changes for the Collected Edition, but missed quite a few as well, as she appears to have been working from the Duckworth proofs themselves, rather than her own manuscripts. In addition, Richardson herself made some new revisions, especially to the punctuation, for the Collected Edition, which we have preserved in this edition. Richardson's changes were not substantial in terms of plot or character, but instead focussed on errors that she says (in her letters) she failed to catch in the first round of publication. However, there are typographical errors evident in the Collected Edition as well, which we have also corrected.

THE TUNNEL

TO
M.K.[1]

---

1 Margaret Kennedy (married name Margaret Davies, Lady Davies) (1896-1967). A novelist and playwright active from 1922 until her death, Kennedy is best known for *A Constant Nymph* (1924), the stage adaptation of which (with Basil Dean [1888-1978]) was a huge success, starring Noël Coward (1899-1973) (later replaced by Sir John Gielgud [1904-2000]) and Edna Best (1900-74).

CHAPTER I

Miriam paused with her heavy bag dragging at her arm. It was a disaster. But it was the last of Mornington Road.[1] To explain about it would be to bring Mornington Road here.

"It doesn't matter now," said Mrs Bailey[2] as she dropped her bag and fumbled for her purse.

"Oh, I'd better settle it at once or I shall forget about it. I'm so glad the things have come so soon."

When Mrs Bailey had taken the half-crown[3] they stood smiling at each other. Mrs Bailey looked exactly as she had done the first time. It was exactly the same; there was no disappointment. The light coming through the glass above the front door made her look more shabby and worn. Her hair was more metallic. But it was the same girlish figure and the same smile triumphing over the badly fitting teeth. Miriam felt like an inmate returning after an absence. The smeariness of the marble-topped hall table did not offend her. She held herself in. It was better to begin as she meant to go on. Behind Mrs Bailey the staircase was beckoning. There was something waiting upstairs that would be gone if she stayed talking to Mrs Bailey.

Assuring Mrs Bailey that she remembered the way to the room, she started at last on the journey up the many flights of stairs. The feeling of confidence that had come the first time she mounted them with Mrs Bailey returned now. She could not remember noticing anything then but a large brown dinginess, one rich warm even tone everywhere in the house; a sharp contrast to the cold, harshly lit little bedroom in Mornington Road. The day was cold. But this house did not seem cold and, when she rounded the first flight and Mrs Bailey was out of sight, the welcome of the place fell upon her. She knew it well, better than any place she had known in all her wanderings—the faded umbers and browns of the stair carpet, the gloomy heights of

---

1   A London road, situated northeast of Regent's Park. Though it seems she is referring to a location from an earlier volume, this is its first actual mention in the *Pilgrimage* series. Miriam's stay at Mornington Road would have occurred in between *Honeycomb* (vol. 3) and *The Tunnel*.

2   Real life counterpart was Mrs. K. Baker (Fromm, 27).

3   A British coin worth one eighth of a pound, or two and a half shillings. Before 1970, the British currency did not operate on a decimal currency, and the half-crown was equivalent to thirty pennies. A half-crown then would be worth about £8.50 today.

wall, a patternless sheen where the staircase lights fell upon it and, in the shadowed parts, a blurred scrolling pattern in dull madder[1] on a brown background; the dark landings with lofty ceilings and high dark polished doors surmounted by classical reliefs in grimed plaster, the high staircase windows screened by long smoke-grimed lace curtains. On the third landing the ceiling came down nearer to the tops of the doors. The light from above made the little grained doors stare brightly. Patches of fresh brown and buff shone here and there in the threadbare linoleum. The cracks of the flooring were filled with dust and dust lay along the rim of the skirting. Two large tin trunks standing one upon the other almost barred the passage way. It was like a landing in a small suburban lodging-house, a small silent, afternoon brightness, shut in and smelling of dust. Silence flooded up from the lower darkness. The hall where she had stood with Mrs Bailey was far away below, and below that were basements deep in the earth. The outside of the house, with its first-floor balcony, the broad shallow flight of steps leading to the dark green front door, the little steep flight running sharply down into the railed area, seemed as far away as yesterday.

The little landing was a bright plateau. Under the skylight, shut off by its brightness from the rest of the house, the rooms leading from it would be bright and flat and noisy with light compared with the rest of the house. From above came the tap-tap of a door swinging gently in a breeze and behind the sound was a soft faint continuous murmur. She ran up the short twisting flight of bare stairs into a blaze of light. Would her room be a bright suburban bedroom? Had it been a dull day when she first called? The skylight was blue and gold with light, its cracks threads of bright gold. Three little glaring yellow-grained doors opened on to the small strip of uncovered dusty flooring; to the left the little box-loft, to the right the empty garret behind her own and, in front of her, her own door ajar; tapping in the breeze. The little brass knob rattled loosely in her hand and the hinge ran up the scale to a high squeak as she pushed open the door, and down again as it closed behind her neatly with a light wooden sound. The room was half dark shadow and half brilliant light.

She closed the door and stood just inside it looking at the room. It was smaller than her memory of it. When she had stood

---

1 A shade of blue.

in the middle of the floor with Mrs Bailey, she had looked at nothing but Mrs Bailey, waiting for the moment to ask about the rent. Coming upstairs she had felt the room was hers and barely glanced at it when Mrs Bailey opened the door. From the moment of waiting on the stone steps outside the front door, everything had opened to the movement of her impulse. She was surprised now at her familiarity with the detail of the room ... that idea of visiting places in dreams. It was something more than that ... all the real part of your life has a real dream in it; some of the real dream part of you coming true. You know in advance when you are really following your life. These things are familiar because reality is here. Coming events cast *light*. It is like dropping everything and walking backwards to something you know is there. However far you go out, you come back.... I am back now where I was before I began trying to do things like other people. I left home to get here. None of those things can touch me here.

... The room asserted its chilliness. But the dark yellow graining of the wall-paper was warm. It shone warmly in the stream of light pouring through the barred lattice window. In the further part of the room, darkened by the steep slope of the roof, it gleamed like stained wood. The window space was a little square wooden room, the long low double lattice breaking the roof, the ceiling and walls warmly reflecting its oblong of bright light. Close against the window was a firm little deal table[1] covered with a thin, brightly coloured printed cotton table-cloth. When Miriam drew her eyes from its confusion of rich fresh tones, the bedroom seemed very dark. The bed, drawn in under the slope, showed an expanse of greyish white counterpane, the carpet was colourless in the gloom. She opened the door. Silence came in from the landing. The blue and gold had gone from the skylight. Its sharp grey light shone in over the dim colours of the threadbare carpet and on to the black bars of the little grate and the little strip of tarnished yellow-grained mantelpiece, running along to the bedhead where a small globeless[2] gas bracket stuck out at an angle over the head of the bed. The sight of her luggage

---

1 A table made of soft wood, typically pine. Common because deal pine was cheap, though of reasonable quality. Deal tables were not typically polished or stained the assumption was that they would be ruined by food stains anyway.

2 Before electric lighting, gas was used to light rooms with an open flame, often diffused with a glass shade (though not here).

piled up on the other side of the fireplace drew her forward into the dimness. There was a small chest of drawers, battered and almost paintless, but with two long drawers and two small ones and a white cover on which stood a little looking-glass framed in polished pine ... and a small yellow wardrobe with a deep drawer under the hanging part, and a little drawer in the rickety little washstand and another above the dusty cupboard of the little mahogany sideboard. I'll paint the bright part of the ceiling; scrolls of leaves.... Shutting the quiet door she went into the brilliance of the window space. The outside world appeared; a long row of dormer windows and the square tops of the larger windows below them, the windows black or sheeny grey in the light, cut out against the dinginess of smoke-grimed walls. The long strip of roof sloping back from the dormers was a pure even dark grey. She bent to see the sky, clear soft heavy grey, striped by the bars of her window. Behind the top rim of the iron framework of the bars was a discoloured roll of window blind. Then the bars must move.... Shifting the table she pressed close to the barred window. It smelt strongly of rust and dust. Outside she saw grey tiles sloping steeply from the window to a cemented gutter, beyond which was a little stone parapet about two feet high. A soft wash of madder lay along the grey tiles. There must be an afterglow somewhere, just out of sight. Her hands went through the bars and lifted the little rod which held the lattice half open. The little square four-paned frame swung free and flattened itself back against the fixed panes, out of reach, its bar sticking out over the leads. Drawing back grimed fingers and wrists striped with grime, she grasped the iron bars and pulled. The heavy framework left the window frame with a rusty creak and the sound of paint peeling and cracking. It was very heavy, but it came up and up until her arms were straight above her head, and looking up she saw a stout iron ring in a little trapdoor in the wooden ceiling and a hook in the centre of the endmost bar in the iron framework.

Kneeling on the table to raise the frame once more and fix it to the ceiling, she saw the whole length of the top row of windows across the way and wide strips of grimy stucco placed across the house fronts between the windows.

The framework of the freed window was cracked and blistered, but the little square panes were clean. There were four little windows in the row, each with four square panes. The outmost windows were immovable. The one next to the open one had lost its bar, but a push set it free and it swung wide. She leaned out, holding back from the dusty sill, and met a soft fresh breeze streaming straight in from the west. The distant murmur of traffic changed into the clear plonk plonk and rumble of swift vehicles. Right and left at the far end of the vista were glimpses of bare trees. The cheeping of birds came faintly from the distant squares and clear and sharp from neighbouring roofs. To the left the trees were black against pure grey, to the right they stood spread and bunched in front of the distant buildings blocking the vista. Running across the rose-washed façade of the central mass she could just make out "Edwards's Family Hotel" in large black letters. That was the distant view of the courtyard of Euston Station[1].... In between that and the square of trees ran the Euston Road, by day and by night, her unsleeping guardian, the rim of the world beyond which lay the northern suburbs, banished.[2]

From a window somewhere down the street out of sight came the sound of an unaccompanied violin, clearly attacking and dropping and attacking a passage of half a dozen bars. The music stood serene and undisturbed in the air of the quiet street. The man was following the phrase, listening; strengthening and clearing it, completely undisturbed and unconscious of his surroundings. "Good heavens," she breathed quietly, feeling the extremity of relief, passing some boundary, emerging strong and equipped in a clear medium.... She turned back into the twilight of the room. Twenty-one and only one room to hold the richly renewed consciousness, and a living to earn, but the self that was with her in the room was the untouched tireless self of her seventeenth year and all the earlier time. The familiar light moved within the twilight, the old light.... She might as well wash the grime from her wrists and hands. There was a scrap of soap in the soap dish, dry and cracked and seamed with dirt. The washstand rocked as she washed her hands; the toilet things did not match, the towel-horse held one small thin face-towel and fell sideways against the wardrobe as she drew off the towel. When the gas was on she would be visible from the opposite dormer window. Short skimpy faded Madras muslin[3] curtains screened a few inches of the

---

1 Euston Railway Station (opened 1837), the first inter-city railway station in London. The Euston Tube station didn't open until 1907, as part of the City and South London Railway, which became the City Line.

2 In *Backwater* (*Pilgrimage* vol. 2), Miriam teaches at a boarding school called Wordsworth House, in Banbury Park (the fictional version of the real Finsbury Park), north of London.

3 A light weight cotton fabric, with patterned texture and designs. The name refers to the Indian city of Madras.

endmost windows and were caught back and tied up with tape.[1] She untied the tape and disengaged with the curtains a strong smell of dust. The curtains would cut off some of the light. She tied them firmly back and pulled at the edge of the rolled up blind. The blind, streaked and mottled with ironmould,[2] came down in a stifling cloud of dust. She rolled it up again and washed once more. She must ask for a bath towel and do something about the blind, sponge it or something; that was all.

A light had come in the dormer on the other side of the street. It remained unscreened. Watching carefully she could see only a dim figure moving amongst motionless shapes. No need to trouble about the blind. London could come freely in day and night through the unscreened happy little panes; light and darkness and darkness and light.

London, just outside all the time, coming in with the light, coming in with the darkness, always present in the depths of the air in the room.

The gas flared out into a wide bright flame. The dingy ceiling and counterpane turned white. The room was a square of bright light and had a rich brown glow, shut brightly in by the straight square of level white ceiling and thrown up by the oblong that sloped down, white, at the side of the big bed almost to the floor. She left her things half unpacked about the floor and settled herself on the bed under the gas jet with *The Voyage of the Beagle*.[3] Unpacking had been a distraction from the glory, very nice, getting things straight. But there was no *need* to do anything or think about anything ... ever, here. No interruption, no one watching or speculating or treating one in some particular way that had to be met. Mrs Bailey did not speculate. She knew, everything. Every evening here would have a glory, but not the same kind of glory. Reading would be more of a distraction than

---

1   That is, ribbon.
2   Rust or ink stains.
3   An 1839 book by English naturalist Charles Darwin (1809-82), alternately titled *Journals and Remarks*. This title refers to his second journey on the *HMS Beagle* through the Galapagos Islands, while he was developing his theory of evolution.

unpacking. She read a few lines. They had a fresh attractive *meaning*. Reading would be real. The dull adventures of the *Beagle* looked real, coming along through reality. She put the book on her knee and once more met the clear brown shock of her room.

The carpet is awful, faded and worn almost to bits. But it is right, in this room.... This is the furnished room; one room. I have come to it. "You could get a furnished room at about seven shillings[1] rental." The awful feeling, no tennis, no dancing, no house to move in, no society.[2] The relief at first when Bennett[3] found those people ... maddening endless roads of little houses in the east wind ... their kind way of giving more than they had undertaken, and smiling and waiting for smiles and dying all the time in some dark way without knowing it; filling the rooms and the piano and the fern on the serge table-cloth and the broken soap-dish in the bathroom until it was impossible to read or think or play because of them, the feeling of them stronger and stronger till there was nothing but crying over the trays of meals and wanting to scream. The thought of the five turnings to the station, all into long little roads looking alike and making you forget which was which and lose your way, was still full of pain ... the relief of moving to Granville Place[4] still a relief, though it felt a mistake from the first. Mrs Corrie's[5] old teacher liking only certain sorts of people knew it was a mistake, with her peevish

---

1 A shilling is a British coin. Twenty shillings made one pound. This rental rate would be about £23.80 in today's currency. The line here is unattributed, and serves as a generic bit of advice.
2 Miriam's father, like Dorothy Richardson's, was a wealthy gentleman who went bankrupt, forcing his daughters to move away from home. Miriam chose to support herself, beginning with a stint in Germany as a teacher in a boarding school (*Pointed Roofs*, *Pilgrimage* vol. 1), but her three sisters followed the more conventional path at the time, two of them marrying and one becoming a governess. Miriam reflects frequently on the embarrassment and difficulties of being *déclassée*, essentially stripped of her comfortable social position in a class-based English society.
3 Bennett Brodie, husband of Miriam's sister Sarah.
4 A central London street near Hyde Park, one block north of Oxford Street.
5 Miriam's employer in *Honeycomb* (*Pilgrimage* vol. 3), for whom she worked as a governess.

silky old face and her antique brooch. But it had been the beginning of London.... Bond Street[1] that Sunday morning in the thick fog; these sudden pictures gleaming in a window, filmy ... von Hier.[2] Adelina Compayne, hanging out silk stockings on the top balustrade. "I *love* cawfy" ... that was the only real thing that had been said downstairs. There was no need to have been frightened of these two women in black silk evening dress. None of these clever things were real. They said young Asquith[3] is a really able man, to hide their thoughts. The American Academy[4] pupils talked together to keep everybody off, except when they made their clever jokes ... "if any one takes that top bit there'll be murder, Miss Spink." When they went out of the room, they looked silly. The young man was real somewhere else.

The little man talking about the wonders of the linotype[5] in the smoking-room.... How did I get into the smoking-room? Someone probably told Miss Spink I talked to him in the smoking-room and smoked a cigarette.[6] Perhaps his wife. If they could have seen. It was so surprising to hear anybody suddenly talking. Perhaps he began in the hall and ushered me into the smoking-room. There was no one there and I can't remember anything about the linotype, only the quiet and the talking face and suddenly feeling in the heart of London. But it was soon after

---

1   A central London street noted for its fashionable shops. Also the location of the prestigious Sotheby's auction house and the Fine Art Society.

2   German: from here on.

3   Herbert Henry Asquith (1852-1928), British Prime Minister 1908-16. In 1896, when this novel is set, Asquith was a Liberal MP who had served as Home Secretary (1892-94). He was regarded as an innovative political thinker; however, after his term as Secretary, his career did not progress much until after the turn of the twentieth century.

4   Reference to American expats studying in London, likely at the Royal Academy of Arts, situated at this time in Piccadilly Circus, just southeast of the area Miriam has been describing. The Academy was a highly influential training ground for young artists in the mid-Victorian period; however, by around the turn of the twentieth century, modern artists and thinkers regarded its methods as conservative, largely focused on classicism and realism.

5   An early type-setting machine invented in 1894. It was the industry standard for newspapers in the late 1800s through to the mid-twentieth century. Linotype allowed for more efficient printing, thus dramatically increasing the size of newspapers.

6   It was uncommon, and somewhat scandalous, for a woman to smoke regularly at this time.

that they all began being stand-offish; before Mr Chamberlayne came; before Adela began playing Esther Summerson[1] at the Kennington.[2] They approved of my going down to fetch her, until he began coming too. The shock of seeing her clumsy heavy movements on the stage and her face looking as though it were covered with starch.... I can *think* about it all, here, and not mind.

She *was* beautiful. It was happiness to sit and watch her smoking so badly, in bed, in the strip of room, her cloud of hair against the wall in the candlelight, two o'clock ... the Jesuit[3] who had taught her chess ... and Michael Somebody, the little book *The Purple Pillar.*[4] He was an *author* and he wanted to marry her and take her back to Ireland. Perhaps by now she was back from America and had gone, just out of kindness. She was strong and beautiful and good, sitting up in her chemise, smoking.... I've got that photograph of her as Marcia[5] somewhere. I must put it up. Miss Spink was surprised that last week, the students getting me into their room ... the dark clean shining piano, the azaleas and the muslin-shaded[6] lamp, the way they all sat in their evening dresses, lounging and stiff, with stiff clean polished hair.... "Miss Dust here's going to be the highest soprano in the States." ...

---

1 The heroine of Charles Dickens's (1812-70) novel *Bleak House* (1853), which was adapted as a play a number of times throughout the late 19th century.

2 A suburban London theatre. This appears to be an incongruity in Richardson's reconstruction of Miriam's timeline, as the Kennington did not open until 1898, and was originally called the Princess of Wales Theatre.

3 A member of the Roman Catholic religious order The Society of Jesus. Founded in 1540 by Saint Ignatius of Loyola, the order takes a quasi-military approach to evangelism, its founding document beginning, "Whoever desires to serve as a soldier of God."

4 Unidentified, but possibly "a playful glance towards H.G. Wells's short story 'The Purple Pileus' (1896) in *The Plattner Story, and Others* (London: Methuen, 1897)." George Thomson, *Notes on "Pilgrimage": Dorothy Richardson Annotated* Greensboro, SC: ELT P, 1999), 72-73.)

5 Unidentified, but possibly Marcia Aurelia Ceionia Demetrias, mistress and assassin of Roman Emperor Commodus (182-93 CE), who famously influenced Commodus in his leniency towards Christians. Creating tableaux vivants was a popular pastime in the nineteenth century (we see Miriam lead students in it in *Pointed Roofs*) and historical figures often provided the material for copy.

6 A woven cotton fabric, usually white.

"None of that, Miss Thicker." ... "When she caught that top note and the gold medal she went right up top, to stay there, that minute."

She was surprised when Mrs Potter took me to hear Melba.[1] I heard Melba. I don't remember hearing her. English opera houses are small; there are fine things all over the world. If you see them all you can compare one with the other; but then you don't see or hear anything at all. It seems strange to be American and at the same time stout and middle-aged. It would have got more and more difficult with all those people. The dreadful way the Americans got intimate and then talked or hinted openly, everywhere, about intimate things. No one knew how intimate Miss O'Veagh was. I shall remember. There is something about being Irish Roman Catholic that makes *happiness*. She did not seem to think the George Street[2] room awful. She was *surprised* when I talked about the hole in the wall and the cold and the imbecile servant and the smell of ether. "We are brought up from the first to understand that we must never believe anything a man says." She *came* and sat and talked and wrote after she had gone ... "good-bye—sweet blessed little rose of Mary."[3] ... she tried to make me think I was young and pretty. She was sorry for me without saying so.

I should never have gone to Mornington Road unless I had been nearly mad with sorrow ... if Miss Thomas disapproved of germs and persons who let apartments why did she come and take a room at George Street? She must have seen she drove me nearly mad with sorrow. The thought of Wales full of Welsh people[4] like her, makes one mad with sorrow.... Did she think I could get to know her by hearing all her complaints? She's somewhere now, sending someone mad.

I was mad already when I went to Mornington Road.

"You'll be all right with Mrs Swanson ..." the awful fringes, the *horror* of the ugly clean little room, the horror of Mrs Swanson's heavy old body moving slowly about the house, a heavy dark

---

1   Dame Nellie Melba (1861-1931), an Australian soprano who became a successful opera singer in Europe in the late nineteenth century.

2   A London street just north of Hyde Park.

3   The Virgin Mary has a central role in the Roman Catholic church. She is worshipped as the mother of God, and many blessing and prayers invoke her name.

4   Though Wales has its own language, and a national identity, it was officially taken over by England in the sixteenth century, and remains part of the United Kingdom.

mountain, fringes, bulges, slow dead eyes, slow dead voice, slow grimacing evil smile ... housekeeper to the Duke of Something and now moving slowly about, heavy with disapproval. She thought of me as a business young lady.

Following advice is certain to be wrong. When you don't follow advice there may be awful things. But they are not arranged beforehand. And when they come you do not know that they are awful until you have half got hold of something else. Then they change into something that has not been awful. Things that remain awful are in some way not finished.... Those women are awful. They will get more and more awful, still disliking and disapproving till they die. I shall not see them again.... I will never again be at the mercy of such women or at all in the places where they are. That means keeping free of all groups. In groups sooner or later one of them appears, dead and sightless and bringing blindness and death ... although they seem to like brightness and children and the young people they approve of. I run away from them because I must. They kill me. The thought of their death is awful. Even in heaven no one could explain anything to them, if they remain as they are. Wherever people advise you to go there is in the end one of those women....

When she turned out the gas the window spaces remained faintly alight with a soft light like moonlight. At the window she found a soft bluish radiance cast up from below upon the opposite walls and windows. It went up into the clear blue darkness of the sky.

When she lay down the bed smelt faintly of dust. The air about her head under the sharply sloping ceiling was still a little warm with the gas. It was full of her untrammelled thoughts. Her luggage was lying about, quite near. She thought of washing in the morning in the bright light on the other side of the room ... leaves crowding all round the lattice and here and there a pink rose ... *several pink roses* ... the lovely air chilling the water ... the basin quite up against the lattice ... dew splashing off the rose bushes in the little garden almost dark with trellises and trees, crowding with Harriett[1] through the little damp stiff gate, the sudden lineny smell of Harriett's pinafore and the thought of

---

1   The youngest of Miriam's three sisters.

Harriett in it, feeling the same, sudden bright sunshine, two shouts, great cornfields going up and up with a little track between them ... up over Blewburton[1] ... *Whittenham Clumps.*[2] Before I saw Whittenham Clumps I had always known them. But we saw them before we knew they were called Whittenham Clumps. It was a surprise to know anybody who had seen them and that they had a name.

St Pancras[3] bells were clamouring in the room; rapid scales, beginning at the top, coming with a loud full thump on to the fourth note and finishing with a rush to the lowest which was hardly touched before the top note hung again in the air, sounding outdoors clean and clear while all the other notes still jangled together in her room. Nothing had changed. The night was like a moment added to the day; like years going backwards to the beginning; and in the brilliant sunshine the unchanging things began again, perfectly new. She leaped out of bed into the clamorous stillness and stood in the window rolling up the warm hair that felt like a shawl round her shoulders. A cup of tea and then the bus to Harriett's. A bus somewhere just out there beyond the morning stillness of the street. What an *adventure* to go out and take a bus without having to face anybody. They were all out there, away somewhere, the very thought and sight of them, disapproving and deploring her surroundings. She listened. There they were. There were their very voices, coming plaintive and reproachful with a held-in indignation, intonations that she knew inside and out, coming on bells from somewhere beyond the squares—another church. She withdrew the coloured cover and set her spirit lamp[4] on the inkstained table. Strong bright light was standing outside the window. The clamour of the bells had ceased. From far away down in the street a loud hoarse voice came thinly up. *"Referee—Lloyd's—*

---

1 Blewburton Hill is the site of an ancient iron age fort in Oxfordshire.
2 Richardson misremembers or changes the spelling from Wittenham to Whittenham. Also, one of the hills that make up the "clump" was an Iron Age fort, with ditches and earthworks. (Thanks to Scott McCracken for his insight on this point.) The "clumps" are a set of hills in Oxfordshire, in the Thames Valley.
3 One of the prominent old churches in London, on Euston Road. An "Old Church" stood on the site since ancient times, then "St Pancras New Church" was built on the site in the early 1920s.
4 A lamp that burns liquid fuel, often alcohol.

Sunday Times—People[1]—pypa...."[2]A front door opened with a loud crackle of paint. The voice dropped to speaking tones that echoed clearly down the street and came up clear and soft and confidential. *"Referee? Lloyd's?"* The door closed with a large firm wooden sound and the harsh voice went on down the street.

St Pancras bells burst forth again. Faintly interwoven with their bright headlong scale were the clear sweet delicate contralto of the more distant bells playing very swiftly and reproachfully a five-finger exercise in a minor key. That must be a very high-Anglican[3] church; with light coming through painted windows on to carvings and decorations.

As she began on her solid slice of bread and butter, St Pancras[4] bells stopped again. In the stillness she could hear the sound of her own munching. She stared at the surface of the table that held her plate and cup. It was like sitting up to the nursery table. "How frightfully happy I am," she thought with bent head. Happiness streamed along her arms and from her head. St Pancras bells began playing a hymn tune, in single firm beats with intervals between that left each note standing for a moment gently in the air. The first two lines were playing carefully through to the distant accompaniment of the rapid weaving and interweaving in a regular unbroken pattern of the five soft low contralto bells of the other church. The third line of the hymn ran through Miriam's head, a ding-dong to and fro from tone to semitone. The bells played it out, without the semitone, with a perfect, satisfying falsity. Miriam sat hunched against the table listening for the ascending stages of the last line. The bells climbed gently up, made a faint flat dab at the

---

1   All Sunday newspapers. *The Sunday Referee* (1877-1939) reported mainly on sports news. *Lloyd's News* (1842-1931) was a moderately liberal publication. *The Sunday Times* (founded 1822) is a major publication still in circulation. At the time this novel is set, it was edited by Rachel Beer (1858-1927, née Sassoon), the first female editor of a national newspaper. *People* (founded 1881) is a tabloid still in circulation.
2   Cockney pronunciation of "people."
3   High Anglicanism is the strain of Anglicanism most closely related to Roman Catholicism. Anglicanism is the religious practices of the Church of England and its sister churches. (Thanks to Scott McCracken for his help with this information.)
4   See p. 66, note 3.

last top note, left it in the air askew above the decorous little tune and rushed away down their scale as if to cover the impropriety. They clamoured recklessly mingling with Miriam's shout of joy as they banged against the wooden walls of the window space.

CHAPTER II

"Been to church?" said Gerald,[1] digging his shoulders into his chair.

"No. Have you?"

"We've not been for weeks.... Everybody thinks us awful heathens."

"P'raps you are."

"It's Curls. She says she's hanged if she's going any more."

"I can't stand the vicar," said Harriett. "He doesn't believe a word he says."

Fancy Harriett! ...

"Besides, what's the good?"

"Oh, there you are."

"There's nothing the matter with church once in a way to my way of thinking, if it's a decent high musical service."[2]

"Even Eve[3] hardly ever goes now—and nobody could possibly be more goody than she is."

This was disquieting. It was one thing to be the agnostic[4] of the family—but Eve and Harriett. Miriam pondered resentfully while Gerald smoked and flicked his clothing and Harriett sat upright and pursed and untroubled in her great chair. She wondered whether she ought to say something about Unitarianism.[5] But after all there might not be anything in it, and they might not feel the relief of the way it cleared up the trouble about Christ. Besides there was no worry here in the room. A discussion would lead nowhere. They could all three look at each other if they wanted to, and laugh everything off. In the middle of a sleepy Sunday afternoon, with nothing to do, sitting in three huge chairs and looking at each other, they were all right. Harriett's strength and scorn were directed against everything in the world, but not against herself ... never against herself. Harriett often thought her grumpy and ill-tempered, but she approved of her. She was approving now.

---

1 Gerald Ducayne, Harriett's husband, whom she marries in *Honeycomb* (*Pilgrimage* vol. 3).

2 That is, a service in the High Anglican style, very similar to Catholic mass.

3 The second oldest of Miriam's sisters.

4 Someone who believes that we lack sufficient knowledge or capacity to know with certainty whether a God exists.

5 A Christian sect that rejects the divinity of Jesus Christ and the doctrine of the Trinity, or God as the Father, the Son, and the Holy Ghost.

"After all, Frills, it's good form to go," Gerald said idly. "Go on. Smart people go to show their clothes."

"Well, we've shown ours."

Harriett flew out of her chair and daintily kicked him.

He grabbed and missed and sank back wailing, his face hidden in a cushion. Her dainty foot flew out once more and he smothered a shriek.

"Shut up," said Harriett curling herself up in her chair.

Gerald wailed on.

"Do we smoke in here?" said Miriam, wanting the scene to drop or change while it was perfect. She would tell them now about her change of lodgings.

"Yes," said Harriett absently, with an eye on Gerald.

"I've changed my diggings,"[1] began Miriam formally, fumbling for her packet of cigarettes. Harriett was hurling a cushion. Gerald crumpled into the depths of his chair and sobbed aloud, beating with his arms.

"Stop it, silly," piped Harriett, blushing.

"I've changed my diggings," repeated Miriam uncomfortably. Harriett's face flashed a response. Gerald's loud wailings were broken by beseeching cries. Masquerade, but real, absolutely real and satisfying. Miriam answered them from some far deep in herself as if they were her own cries. Harry was embarrassed. Her bright strength was answering. She was ashamed at being seen answering.

Miriam got up conversationally and began looking about for matches in the soft curtained drawing-room light. There were swift movements and Harriett's voice busily chiding. When she turned Gerald was sitting on the floor at Harriett's knee, beating it gently with his head.

"Got a match, G?" she said, seeing in imagination the flare of the match in the soft greenish glare of the room. There was bright light all round the house and a glare of brightness in the garden, beyond the curtains. "Rather," said Gerald, "dozens." He sat up and handed out a box. Leaning back against Harriett's knee he began intoning a little poem of appeal. There was a ring at the front door bell. Miriam got herself to the piano, putting cigarettes and matches behind a vase on the mantelshelf. "That's old Tremayne," said Gerald cheerfully, shooting his linen and glancing in the strip of mirror in the overmantel. The door opened admitting the light from the hall. The curtains at the open french

---

1 Slang term for where one lives; also, "digs."

windows swayed forward, flooding the room with the bright garden light. Into the brightness stepped Mr Tremayne, grey-clad and with a pink rose in his buttonhole.

Over tea they heard the story of his morning and how it had been interrupted by the man on the floor above who had come down in his dressing-gown to tell him about a birthday party ... the two men sitting telling each other stories about drinks and people seeing each other home. After tea he settled back easily in his chair and went on with his stories. Miriam found it almost impossible to follow him. She grew weary of his bantering tone. It smeared over everything he touched and made him appear to be saying one thing over and over again in innuendo. Something he could not say out and could never get away from. He made little pauses and then it gleamed horribly about all his refinement of dress and bearing and Gerald laughed encouragingly and he went on, making a story that was like a play, that looked like life did when you looked at it, a maddening fussiness about nothing and people getting into states of mind. He went on into a story about business life ... people getting the better of each other. It made her feel sick with apprehension. Anybody in business might be ruined any minute, unless he could be sure of getting the better of someone else. She had never realized that before.... It pressed on her breathing and made her feel that she had had too much tea.... She hated the exponent sitting there so coolly. It made the cool green-lit afternoon room an island amongst horrors. But it was that to him too ... he felt the need of something beyond the everlasting innuendo of social life and the everlasting smartness of business life. She felt it was true that he spent Sunday mornings picking out hymn tunes with one finger, and liked "Sabbath music" and remembered the things his mother used to play to him. He wanted a home, something away from business life and away from social life. He saw her as a woman in a home, nicely dressed in a quiet drawing-room, lit by softly screened clear fresh garden daylight.... "Business is business...." "Man's love is of man's life a thing apart—'tis woman's whole existence."[1] Byron did not know what he was saying when he wrote it in his calm patronizing way. Mr Tremayne would admire it as a "great truth"—thinking it like a man in the way Byron thought it. What a hopeless thing a man's consciousness was. How awful to have nothing but a man's consciousness. One could

---

1 A line from English Romantic poet Lord Byron's (1788-1824) long poem "Don Juan" (1818-23), published in segments, or Cantos.

test it so easily if one were a little careful, and know exactly how it would behave....

Opening a volume of Mendelssohn[1] she played, from his point of view, one of the *Songs without Words* quietly into the conversation. The room grew still. She felt herself and Mr Tremayne as duplicates of Harriett and Gerald, only that she was a very religious, very womanly woman, the ideal wife and mother and he was a bad fast man who wanted to be saved. It was such an easy part to play. She could go on playing it to the end of her life, if he went on in business and made enough money, being a "gracious silence," taking an interest in his affairs, ordering all things well, quietly training the servants, never losing her temper or raising her voice, making the home a sanctuary of rest and refreshment and religious aspiration, going to church.... She felt all these things expressing themselves in her bearing. At the end of her piece she was touched to the heart by the look of adoration in his eyes, the innocent youthfulness shining through his face. There was something in him she could have and guard and keep if she chose. Something that would die if there were no woman to keep it there. There was nothing in his life of business and music halls to keep it there, nothing but the memory of his mother and he joined her on to that memory. His mother and his wife were sacred ... apart from life. But he could not be really happy with a woman unless he could also despise her. Any interest in generalities, any argument or criticism or opposition would turn him into a towering bully. All men were like that in some way. They had each a set of notions and fought with each other about them, whenever they were together and not eating or drinking. If a woman opposed them they went mad. He would like one or two more Mendelssohns and then supper. And if she kept out of the conversation and listened and smiled a little, he would go away adoring. She played the Duetto;[2] the chords made her think of Beethoven[3] and play the last page carelessly and glance at Harriett. Harriett had felt her response to the chords and knew she was getting away from Mendelssohn. Mr

---

1 Felix Mendelssohn (1809-47), a German romantic composer. His famed *Songs without Words* is a series of musical pieces consisting of eight cycles of six songs each.

2 Opus 38 Number 6 of *Songs without Words*, so titled because it represented two melodies for two singers.

3 Ludwig van Beethoven (1770-1827), German classical and romantic composer.

Tremayne had moved to a chair quite close to the piano, just behind her. She found the Beethoven and played the first movement of a sonata. It leapt about the piano breaking up her pose, using her body as the instrument of its gay wild shapeliness, spreading her arms inelegantly, swaying her, lifting her from the stool with the crash and vibration of its chords.... "Go on," said Harriett when it came to an end. The *Largo*[1] came with a single voice, deep and broad and quiet; the great truth behind the fuss of things. She felt her hearers grow weary of its reiterations and dashed on alone recklessly into the storm of the last movement. Through its tuneless raging, she could hear the steady voice and see the steady shining of the broad clear light. Daylight and gaiety and night and storm and a great song and truth, the great truth that was bigger than anything. Beethoven. She got up, charged to the fingertips with a glow that transfigured all the inanimate things in the room. The party was wrecked ... a young lady who banged the piano till her hair nearly came down.... Mr Tremayne had heard nothing but noise.... His eyes smiled, and his uneasy mouth felt for compliments.

"Why didn't you ask him to supper, La Fée?"[2]
"The Bollingdons are coming round, silly."
"Well?"
"With one small chicken and a blancmange."[3]
"Heaven help us."
When they sat down to play halfpenny nap[4] after supper, Miriam recovered her cigarette from its hiding-place. She did not know the game. She sat at Harriett's new card-table wrapped in the unbroken jesting of the Bollingdons and the Ducaynes, happily learning and smoking and feeling happily wicked. The Bollingdons taught her simply, with a complete trustful friendliness, Mrs Bollingdon leaning across in her pink satin blouse, her

---

1 A largo is a piece of music played at a very slow tempo. That this one comes after the end of the first movement, and builds into a "storm," suggests that Miriam is playing Beethoven's *Sonata* Opus 31, whose second movement (a largo) begins with the same chord that ends Mendelssohn's Duetto.

2 French: the fairy.

3 An English dessert, somewhat like pudding, usually made with milk or cream, sugar, a thickener, and sometimes flavoured with almonds.

4 A card game, usually involving gambling.

clear clean bulging cheeks and dark velvet hair, like a full-blown dark rose. Between the rounds they poured out anecdotes of earlier nap parties, all talking at once. The pauses at the fresh beginnings were full of the echoes of their laughter. Miriam, in the character of the Honourable Miss Henderson, had just accepted Lord Bollingdon's invitation to join the Duke and Duchess of Ducayne and himself and Lady Bollingdon, in an all-day party to Wembley Park[1] in a break[2] and four on Easter Monday, and had lit a second cigarette and accepted a small whisky and soda when Mr Grove[3] was announced. Harriett's face flushed jocular consternation.

When the party subsided after Mr Grove's spasmodic hand-shakings, Miriam got herself into a chair in a far corner, smoking her cigarette with burning cheeks. Sitting isolated with her cigarette and her whisky while he twice sent his low harsh clearly murmuring voice into the suddenly empty air to say that he had been to evensong[4] at the Carmelites[5] and was on his way home, she examined the relief in his presence and the nature of her farewell. Mr Bollingdon responded to him, remarking each time on the splendour of the evening.

Strolling home towards midnight along the narrow pavement of Endsleigh Gardens,[6] Miriam felt as fresh and untroubled as if it were early morning. When she had got out of her Hammer-smith omnibus[7] into the Tottenham Court Road,[8] she had found that the street had lost its first terrifying impression and had become part of her home. It was the borderland of the part of

---

1 An area in northwest London.

2 An open horse-drawn carriage, here drawn by four horses.

3 A character from *Honeycomb* (*Pilgrimage* vol. 3) who shows a romantic interest in Miriam.

4 Evening prayer in the Anglican church.

5 Members of the Roman Catholic Order of the Brothers of Our Lady of Mount Carmel, likely founded in the twelfth or early thirteenth century. The Carmelite order is primarily devoted to contemplation, broadly construed to include prayer, service, and community.

6 An area in London's Bloomsbury neighbourhood, where Miriam lives. Richardson lived in Bloomsbury from 1896 until the early 1900s.

7 Hammersmith is a rail, tube, and bus station in London. The omnibus was an early twentieth century form of public transit, later shortened to "bus." Most were run by the London General Omnibus Company (1855-1933).

8 A major road in London. Its south end is near the British Museum, in Bloomsbury.

London she had found for herself; the part where she was going to live, in freedom, hidden, on her pound a week. It was all she wanted. That was why she was young and glad; that was why fatigue had gone out of her life. There was nothing in the world that could come nearer to her than the curious half twilight half moonlight effect of lamplit Endsleigh Gardens opening out of Gower Place;[1] its huge high trees, their sharp shadows on the little pavement running by the side of the railings, the neighbouring gloom of the Euston Road dimly lit by lamps standing high in the middle of the roadway at long intervals, the great high quiet porched houses, black and still, the shadow mass of St Pancras church, the great dark open space in front of the church, a shadowy figure-haunted darkness with the vague stream of the Euston Road running to one side of it and the corridor of Woburn Place[2] opening on the other. The harsh voice of an invisible woman[3] sounded out from it as she turned off into her own street.... "Dressed up—he was—to the bloody death...." The words echoed about her as she strolled down the street controlling her impulse to flinch and hurry. The woman was there, there and real, and that was what she had said. Resentment was lurking about the street. The woman's harsh voice seemed close. Miriam pictured her glaring eyes. There was no pretence about her. She felt what she said. She belonged to the darkness about St Pancras church ... people had been garrotted in that part of the Euston Road not so very long ago[4].... Tansley Street[5] was a soft grey gloaming after the darkness. When she rattled her key into the keyhole of number seven, she felt that her day was beginning. It would be perpetually beginning now. Nights and days were all one day; all hers, unlimited. Her life and work at Wimpole Street[6] were something extra, thrown in with her own

---

1 A London street, just off Euston Road.

2 A London street, in the Bloomsbury neighbourhood, named after Woburn Abbey.

3 This would have been a prostitute, as women were otherwise rarely hanging around in the street at midnight.

4 This refers to the "London Garrotting Scare" of 1862, during which there was a sharp rise in people being robbed and garrotted. Garrotting is strangling, usually with a wire or cord.

5 The fictional street Miriam lives on.

6 The street where Miriam works in a dentist's office. Wimpole Street was a well-known strip of professional and medical offices. Richardson herself worked in a similar office on Harley Street, another major professional thoroughfare, running parallel to Wimpole Street.

life of endless day. Sarah[1] and Harriett, their lives and friends, her own friends, the Brooms,[2] the girls in Kenneth Street,[3] all thrown in. She lit her table lamp and the gas and two candles, making her little brown room brilliant under a brilliant white ceiling, and sat down, eager to tell someone of her wealth and freedom.

Someone must know she was in London, free, earning her own living. Lilla?[4] She would not see the extraordinary freedom; earning would seem strange and dreadful to her ... someone who would understand the extraordinary freedom.... Alma.[5] *Alma!* Setting forth the London address in a heavy careless hand at the head of a post card, she wrote from the midst of her seventeenth year, "Dear A. Where are you?"

Walking home along the Upper Richmond Road; not liking to buy sweets; not enjoying anything to the full—always afraid of her refinements; always in a way wanting to be like her; wanting to share her mysterious knowledge of how things were done in the world and the things one had to do to get on in some clever world where people were doing things. Never really wanting it, because the mere thought took the beauty from the syringa[6] and made it look sad. Never being able to explain why one did not want to do reasonable clever things in a clever brisk reasonable way; why one disliked the way she went behaving up and down the Upper Richmond Road, with her pretty neat brisk bustling sidling walk, keeping her secret with a sort of prickly brightness. The Upper Richmond Road was heaven, pure heaven; smelling of syringa. She liked flowers but she did not seem to know.... *Syringa.* I had forgotten. That is one of the things I have always wanted to stop and remember.... What was it all about? What was she doing now? Anyhow the London post card would be an answer. A letter, making her see

1 Miriam's oldest sister.

2 Grace Broom is a student at the boarding school where Miriam works in *Backwater* (*Pilgrimage* vol. 3). She regularly visits with the Broom family when Grace becomes ill.

3 Miriam's friends, Mag and Jan, whom readers meet later in this novel.

4 Miriam's school friend, whom she references occasionally in earlier volumes of *Pilgrimage*.

5 Another of Miriam's school friends.

6 A flowering shrub, with flowers typically light purple.

Germany[1] and bits of Newlands[2] and what life was now would answer everything, all her snubs and cleverness and bring back the Upper Richmond Road and make it beautiful. She will know something of what it was to me then. Perhaps that was why she liked me, even though she thought me vulgar and very lazy and stupid. ¯

---

1 Miriam lives in Hanover, Germany in *Pointed Roofs* (*Pilgrimage* vol. 1), where she works as a teacher and governess in a boarding school.

2 An area of southeastern London, where Miriam lives and works as a governess in *Honeycomb* (*Pilgrimage* vol. 3).

CHAPTER III

There was a carriage at the door. West-end people, after late nights, managing to keep nine o'clock appointments—in a north wind. Miriam pressed the bell urgently. The scrubbed chalky mosaic and the busy bright brass plate reproached her for her lateness during the long moment before the door was opened.... It must be someone for Mr Orly; an appointment made since last night; that was the worst of his living in the house. He was in his surgery now, with the patient. The nine-fifteen patient would come almost at once. He would discover that his charts were not out before there was any chance of getting at his appointment book.... As the great door swung open she saw Mr Hancock turn the corner of the street, walking very rapidly before the north wind.... Mr Orly's voice was sounding impatiently from the back of the hall.... "Where's Miss Hends? ... Oh—here y'are Miss Hends, I say, call up Chalk for me will ya, get him to come at once, I've got the patient waiting." His huge, frock-coated form swung round into his surgery without waiting for an answer. Miriam scurried through the hall past Mr Leyton's open surgery door and into her room. Mr Leyton[1] plunged out of his room as she was flinging down her things and came in briskly. "Morning, Pater,[2] got a gas case?"

"M'm," said Miriam. "I've got to call up Chalk and I haven't a second to do it."

"Why Chalk?" .

"Oh, I don't know. He said 'Chalk,'" said Miriam angrily, seizing the directory.

"I'll call him up if you like."

"You are a saint. Tell him to come at once—sooner," said Miriam, dabbing at her hair as she ran back through the hall and upstairs. As she passed the turn of the staircase, Mr Hancock was let in at the front door. She found his kettle furiously boiling on its wrought-iron stand near the chair. The stained-glass window just behind it was dim with steam. She lowered the gas, put a tumbler in the socket of the spittoon, lit the gas burner on the bracket table and swiftly pulled open its drawers one by one. The instruments were all right ... the

---

1 Mr. Leyton is the son of Mr. and Mrs. Orly, although it is unclear why he has a different last name.

2 Latin: father; common term of reference for the father of a family in Victorian England.

bottles—no chloroform,[1] the carbolic[2] bottle nearly empty and its label soaked and defaced. Gathering the two bottles in her hand, she turned to the instrument cabinet, no serviettes, no rubber dam,[3] clamps[4] not up from the workshop. The top of the cabinet still to be dusted. Dust and scraps of amalgam were visible about the surfaces of the paper lining the instrument drawers. No saliva tubes in the basin. She swung round to the bureau and hurriedly read through the names of the morning's patients. Mr Hancock came quietly in as she was dusting the top of the instrument cabinet by pushing the boxes and bottles of materials that littered its surface to the backmost edge. They were all lightly coated with dust. It was everlasting, and the long tubes and metal body of the little furnace were dull again. "Good morning," they said simultaneously, in even tones. There were sounds of letters being opened and the turning of the pages of the appointment book. The chain of Mr Hancock's gold pencil case rattled softly as he made notes on the corners of the letters.

"Did you have a pleasant week-end?"

"Very," said Miriam emphatically.

There was a squeak at the side of the cabinet. "Yes," said Miriam down the speaking tube[5].... "Thank you. Will you please bring up some tubes and serviettes?"

"Mr Wontner."

"Thank you...." "Mrs Hermann is 'frightfully shocked' at the amount of her account. What did we send it in for?"

"Seventy guineas.[6] It's a reduction, and it's two years' work for

---

1 Chloroform was used to render dental patients unconscious during operations.

2 Carbolic was used as a disinfectant.

3 The rubber dental dam is used to isolate a tooth that is being filled, to prevent contact with bacteria in the mouth.

4 Used to keep the mouth open during dental surgery and as a frame for the rubber dam.

5 Prior to the widespread adoption of telephones, a speaking tube was commonly used in nineteenth-century offices to communicate across rooms. It was typically made from cone-shaped devices connected by air tubes.

6 A guinea was a British coin, valued at 21 shillings. In 1816, the guinea was officially replaced by the pound sterling as the major unit of currency. People nonetheless continued to use the term to refer to 21 shillings. Seventy guineas is roughly equivalent to £5,000 in today's currency.

the whole family." The bell sounded again.... "Lady Cazalet has bad toothache and can you see her at once?"

"Con*found*.... Will you go down and talk to her and see if you can get one of the others to see her?"

"She won't."

"Well then, she must wait. I'll have Mr Wontner up." Miriam rang. Mr Hancock began busily washing his hands. The patient came in. He greeted him over his shoulder. Miriam gathered up the sheaf of annotated letters and the appointment book and ran downstairs. "Has Mr Leyton a patient, Emma?" "Miss Jones just gone in, miss. Oh, Emma, will you ask the workshop for Mr Hancock's rubber and clamps?" She rang through to Mr Leyton's room. "There's a patient of Mr Hancock's in pain, can you see them if I can persuade them?" she murmured. "Right, in ten minutes," came the answering murmur. Mr Hancock's bell sounded from her room. She went to his tube in the hall. "Can I have my charts?" Running into her room she hunted out the first chart from a caseful and ran upstairs with it. Mr Hancock's patient was sitting forward in the chair urging the adoption of the decimal system.[1] Running down again, she went into the waiting-room. The dark, Turkey-carpeted oak-furnished length seemed full of seated forms. Miriam peered and Lady Cazalet, with her hat already off, rose from the deep arm-chair at her side. "Can he see me?" she said in a clear trembling undertone, her dark eyes wide upon Miriam's. Miriam gazed deep into the limpid fear. What a privilege. How often Captain Cazalet must be beside himself with unworthiness. "Yes, if you can wait a little," she said dropping her eyes and standing with arms restrained. "I think it won't be very long," she added, lingering a moment as the little form relapsed into the chair.

"Lady Cazalet will wait until you can see her," she tubed up to Mr Hancock.

"Can't you make her see one of the others?"

"I'm afraid it's impossible; I'll tell you later."

"Well, I'll see her as soon as I can. I'm afraid she'll have to wait."

Miriam went back to her room to sort out the remaining charts. On her table lay a broken denture in a faded morocco case;[2] a strip of paper directed "five-thirty sharp," in Mr Orly's

---

1　The decimal system was an early name for the metric system. Official discussions around adopting it in the UK began in 1818, and the issue was debated in Parliament until finally adopted in 1965.

2　A solid, folding case, often lined with silk or velvet, and held closed with a hook. Morocco leather comes from the country of Morocco.

handwriting. Mr Leyton's door burst open. He came with flying coat-tails.

"'V' I got to see that patient of Mr Hancock's?" he asked breathlessly.

"No," said Miriam "she won't."

"Right," he said swinging back. "I'll keep Miss Jones on."

Mr Hancock's bell sounded again. Miriam flew to the tube.

"My clamps please."

"Oh yes," she answered, shocked, and hurried back to her room.

Gathering up the broken denture, she ran down the stone steps leading to the basement. Her cheap unyielding shoes clattered on the unyielding stones. The gas was on in the lunch room, Mrs Willis scrubbing the floor. The voices of the servants came from the kitchens in the unknown background. She passed the lunch room and the cellar and clamped on across the stone hall to the open door of the workshop.

Winthrop was standing at the small furnace in the box-lined passage way. It was roaring its loudest. Through its open door, the red light fell sharply on his pink-flushed face and drooping fair moustache and poured down over his white apron. "Good ph-[1]morning," he said pleasantly, his eye on the heart of the furnace, his foot briskly pumping the blower.

From the body of the room came sounds of tapping and whistling ... the noise of the furnace prevented their knowing that any one had come in.... Miriam drew near to the furnace, relieved at the shortness of her excursion. She stared at the tiny shape blazing red-gold at the heart of the glare. Winthrop gathered up a pair of tongs and drew the mould from the little square of light.[2] The air hissed from the bellows and the roaring of the flames died down. In a moment he was standing free with hot face and hot patient ironic eyes, gently taking the denture from her hands. "Good morning," said Miriam. "Oh, Mr Winthrop, it's a repair for Mr Orly. It's urgent. Can you manage it?" "It's ph—ph—sure to be urgent," said Winthrop examining the denture with a short-sighted frown. Miriam waited anxiously. The hammering and whistling had ceased. "It'll be all right, Miss ph-Henderson," said Winthrop encouragingly. She turned to the door.

---

1 Suggests Winthrop has a mild stutter.
2 At this time, dental implements were being made by hand in the dentistry office itself.

The clamps.... Gathering herself together, she went down the passage and stood at the head of the two stone steps leading down into the body of the room. A swift scrubbing of emery paper[1] on metal was going on at the end of the long bench, lit by a long skylight, from which the four faces looked up at her with a chorus of good mornings in response to her greeting. "Are Mr Hancock's clamps ready?" she asked diffidently. "Jimmy ..." The figure nearest to her glanced down the row of seated forms. The small bullet-headed boy at the end of the bench scrubbed vigorously and ironically with his emery stick. "He won't be a minute, Miss Henderson," said the near pupil comfortingly.

Miriam observed his spruce grey suit curiously masked by the mechanic's apron, the quiet controlled amused face, and felt the burden of her little attack as part of the patient prolonged boredom of his pupillage. The second pupil, sitting next to him, kept dog-like sympathetic eyes on her face, waiting for a glance. She passed him by, smiling gently in response without looking at him while her eyes rested upon the form of the junior mechanic, whose head was turned in the direction of the scrubbing boy. The head was refined, thin and clear cut, thatched with glossy curls. Its expression was servile—the brain eagerly seeking some flowery phrase—something to decorate at once the occasion and the speaker, and to give relief to the mouth strained in an arrested, obsequious smile. Nothing came and the clever meticulous hands were idle on the board. It seemed absurd to say that Mr Hancock was waiting for the clamps while Jimmy was scrubbing so busily. But they had obviously been forgotten. She fidgeted.

"Will somebody send them up when they're done?"

"Jimmy, you're a miserable sinner, hurry up," said the senior pupil.

"They're done," said Jimmy in a cracked bass voice. "Thank goodness," breathed Miriam, dimpling. Jimmy came round and scattered the clamps carefully into her outstretched hand, with downcast eyes and a crisp dimpling smile.

"Rule Bri*tann*ia,"[2] remarked the junior pupil, resuming his work as Miriam turned away and hurried along the passage and through the door held open for her by Winthrop. She flew up to Mr Hancock's room, three steps at a time, tapped gently at the

---

1   Used for sanding hard materials.
2   A popular, patriotic British song, dating from 1740 and usually associated with the Navy. It is considered a celebration of the British Empire.

door, and went in. He came forward across the soft grey green carpet to take the clamps and murmured gently, "Have you got my carbolic?"

Miriam looked out the remainder of the charts and went anxiously through the little pile of letters she had brought down from Mr Hancock's room. All but three were straightforward appointments to be sent. One bore besides the pencilled day and date the word "Tape" ... she glanced through it—it was from a university settlement worker, asking for an appointment for the filling of two front teeth.... She would understand increasing by one thickness per day until there were five, to be completed two days before the appointment falls due so that any tenderness may have passed off. Mrs Hermann's letter bore no mark. She could make a rough summary in Mr Hancock's phraseology. The third letter enclosed a printed card of appointment with Mr Hancock which she had sent without filling in the day and hour. She flushed. Mr Hancock had pencilled in the missing words. Gathering the letters together, she put them as far away as her hand would reach, leaving a space of shabby ink-stained morocco[1] clear under her hands. She looked blindly out of the window; hand-painted, they are hand-painted, forget-me-nots and gold tendrils softly painted, not shining, on an unusual shape, a merry Christmas. Melly Klismas. In this countree heapee lain, chiney man lun home again, under a red and green paper umbrella in the pouring rain, that was not a hand-painted one, but better, in some *strange* way, close bright colours drawing everything *in*; a shock. I stayed in there. There was something. Chinee man lun *home* again.[2] Her eye roamed over the table; everything but the newly-arrived letters shabby under the high wide uncurtained window. The table fitted the width of the window. There was something to be done before anything could be done. Everything would look different if something were done. The fresh letters could lie neatly on the centre of the table in the midst of something. They were on the address books,

---

1   See p. 80, note 2.

2   It appears that Miriam is observing something outside her window, but it is unclear what. Scholars have as yet been unable to find a reference for this quotation. However, it is clear that it reflects both an obsession with Eastern cultures that existed at this time, and the accompanying racism toward "Orientals."

spoiled by them. It would take years to check the addresses one by one till the old books could be put away. If the day-books were entered up to date, there would still be those, disfiguring everything. If everything were absolutely up to date, and all the cupboards in perfect order and the discounts and decimals always done in the depot-books to time, there would be time to do something. She replaced the letters in the centre of the table and put them back again on the address books. His nine-forty-five patient was being let in at the front door. In a moment his bell would ring and something must be said about the appointment card. "Mr Orly?" A big booming elderly voice, going on heavily murmuring into the waiting-room. She listened tensely to the movements of the servant. Was Mr Orly in "the den" or in his surgery? She heard the maid ring through to the surgery and wait. No sound. The maid came through her room and tapped at the door leading from it. "*Come* in," sang a voice from within, and Miriam heard the sound of a hammer on metal as the maid opened the door. She flew to the surgery. Amidst the stillness of heavy oak furniture and dark Turkey carpet floated in the confirming smell. There it was, all about the spittoon and the red-velvet-covered chair and the bracket table, a horrible confusion—and blood stains, blood-clotted serviettes, forceps[1] that made her feel sick and faint. Summoning her strength, she gathered up the serviettes and flung them into a basket behind the instrument cabinet. She was dabbing at the stains on the American cloth cover of the bracket when Mr Orly came swinging in, putting on his grey frock-coat and humming *Gunga Din*[2] as he came. "Regular field day," he said cheerfully. "I shan't want those things—just pop 'em out of sight." He turned up the cupboard gas and in a moment a stream of boiling water hissed down into the basin filling the room with steam. "I say, has this man got a chart? Don't throw away those teeth. Just look at this—how's that for twisted? Just look here." He took up an object to which Miriam forced reluctant eyes, grotesquely formed fangs protruding from the enclosing blades of a huge forceps. "How's that, eh?" Miriam made a sympathetic sound.

---

1 A strong tool used to grasp objects; in this case, probably used for extracting teeth.

2 An 1892 poem by Rudyard Kipling (1865-1936) about an Indian water-carrier who is killed bringing water to English soldiers. It was set to music by popular composer Gerald Francis Cobb between 1892 and 1897.

Gathering the many forceps he detached their contents, putting the relic into a bottle of spirit and the rest into the hidden basket. The forceps went head first into a jar of carbolic and Miriam breathed more freely. "I'll see to those. I say, has this man got a chart?" "I'll see," said Miriam eagerly making off with the appointment book. She returned with the chart. Mr Orly hummed and looked. "Right. Tell 'em to send him in. I say, 'v' I got any gold and tin?"[1] Miriam consulted the box in a drawer in the cabinet. It was empty. "I'm afraid you haven't," she said guiltily. "All right, I'll let y' know. Send 'im in," and he resumed *Gunga Din* over the wash-hand basin. Mr Hancock's bell was ringing in her room and she hurried off, with a sign to the little maid waiting with raised eyebrows in the hall. Darting into her room, she took the foils from the safe, laid them on a clean serviette amongst the litter on her table, and ran upstairs. Mr Leyton opened his door as she passed: "I say, can you feed for me," he asked breathlessly, putting out an anxious head. "I'll come down in a minute," promised Miriam from the stairs. Mr Hancock was drying his hands. He sounded his bell as she came in. The maid answered. "I'm so sorry," began Miriam. "Show up Mr Green," said Mr Hancock down the speaking-tube. "You remember there's Lady Cazalet?" said Miriam relieved and feeling she was making good her carelessness in the matter of the appointment card.

"Oh, con*found*." He rang again hurriedly. "Show up Lady Cazalet." Miriam swept from the bracket table the litter of used instruments and materials, disposing them rapidly on the cabinet, into the sterilizing tray, the waste basket and the wash-hand basin, tore the uppermost leaf from the headrest pad, and detached the handpiece from the arm of the motor drill while the patient was being shown upstairs. Mr Hancock had cleared the spittoon, set a fresh tumbler, filled the kettle and whisked the debris of amalgam[2] and cement from the bracket table before he began the scrubbing and cleansing of his hands, and when the patient came in Miriam was in her corner reluctantly handling the instruments, wet with the solution that crinkled her finger-tips and made her skin brittle and dry. Everything was in its worst state. She began the business of drying and

---

1 Fillings then were most commonly gold, but tin was often used as a substitute.
2 Another material for filling teeth, though used less frequently at this time than gold and tin.

cleansing, freeing fine points from minute closely adhering fragments, polishing instruments on the leather pad, repolishing them with the leather, scraping the many little burs with the fine wire brush, scraping the clamps, clearing the obstinate amalgam from slab and spatula. The tedium of the long series of small, precise, attention-demanding movements was aggravated by the prospect of a fresh set of implements already qualifying for another cleansing; the endless series to last as long as she stayed at Wimpole Street ... Were there any sort of people who could do this kind of thing patiently, without minding? ... the evolution of dentistry was wonderful, but the more perfect it became the more and more of this sort of thing there would be ... the more drudgery workers, at fixed salaries ... it was only possible for people who were fine and nice ... there must be, everywhere, women doing this work for people who were not nice. They *could* not do it for the work's sake. Did some of them do it cheerfully, as unto God? It was wrong to work unto man. But could God approve of this kind of thing? ... was it right to spend life cleaning instruments? ... the blank moment again, of gazing about in vain for an alternative ... all work has drudgery. That is not the answer.... Blessed be Drudgery,[1] but that was housekeeping, not someone else's drudgery.... As she put the things back in the drawers, every drawer offered tasks of tidying, replenishing, and repapering of small boxes and grooves and sections. She had remembered to bring up Lady Cazalet's chart. It looked at her, propped against the small furnace. Behind it were the other charts for the day, complete. The drug bottles were full, there was plenty of amadou[2] pulled soft and cut ready for use, a fair supply of both kinds of Japanese paper.[3] None of the bottles and boxes of stopping materials were anywhere near running short and the gold drawer was filled. She examined the drawers that held the less frequently used fittings and materials, conducting her operations noiselessly, without impeding Mr Hancock's perpetual movements to and fro between the chair and the instrument cabinet. Meanwhile the dressing of Lady Cazalet's painful tooth went quietly on and Mr Leyton was waiting, hoping for her assis-

---

1 The title of an 1890 pamphlet by Unitarian pastor William C. Gannett (1840-1923) on the value of hard work.
2 Highly absorbent natural sponge material derived from bracket fungi.
3 Very fine tissue paper.

tance downstairs. There was no excuse for waiting upstairs any longer. She went to the writing table and hung over the appointment book.

It was a busy day. Mr Hancock would hardly have half an hour for lunch.... She examined the names carefully, one by one, and wrote against one "Ask address," underlined, and against another "Inquire for brother—ill." Lady Cazalet drew a deep sigh ... she had been to other dentists. But perhaps they were good ones. Perhaps she was about thirty ... had she ever gone through a green baize door and seen a fat common little man with smooth sly eyes standing waiting for her in a dark stuffy room smelling of creosote?[1] Even if she had always been to good ones, they were not Mr Hancock. They were dentists. Cheerful ordinary men with ordinary voices and laughs, thinking about all manner of things. Or apparently bland, with ingratiating manners. Perhaps a few of them, some of his friends and some of the young men he had trained, were something like him. Interested in dentistry and the way it was all developing, some of them more enthusiastic and interested in certain special things than he was. But no one could be quite like him. No other patients had the lot of his patients. No other dentist was so completely conscious of the patient all the time, as if he were in the chair himself. No other dentist went on year after year remaining sensitive to everything the patient had to endure. No one else was so unsparing of himself ... children coming eagerly in for their dentistry, sitting in the chair with slack limbs and wide open mouths and tranquil eyes ... small bodies braced and tense, fat hands splayed out tightly on the too-big arms of the chair, in determination to bear the moment of pain bravely for him.... She wandered to the corner cupboard and opened it and gazed idly in. But none of them knew what it cost.... "I think you won't have any more pain with that; I'll just put in a dressing for the present"—she was Lady Cazalet again, without toothache, and that awful feeling that you know your body won't last ... they did not know what it cost. What always doing the best for the patient *meant*. Perhaps they knew in a *way*; or knew something and did not know what it was ... there would be something different in Mr Hancock's expression, especially in the three-quarters view when his face

---

1 An antiseptic and anaesthetic, used by dentists in the nineteenth century to sterilize teeth and numb the pain of toothaches.

was turned away towards the instrument cabinet, if he saved his nerves and energy and money by doing things less considerately, not perpetually having the instruments sharpened and perpetually buying fresh outfits of sharp burs. The patient would suffer more pain ... a dentist at his best ought to be more delicately strong and fine than a doctor ... like a fine engraving ... a surgeon working amongst live nerves ... and he would look different himself. It was *in* him. It was keeping to that, all day, and every day, choosing the best difficult tiresome way in everything that kept that radiance about him when he was quietly at work ... I mustn't stay here thinking these thoughts ... it's that evil thing in me, keeping on and on, always thinking thoughts, nothing getting done ... going through life like—a stuck pig. If I went straight on, things would come like that just the same in flashes—bang, bang, in your heart, everything breaking into light just in front of you, making you almost fall off the edge into the expanse coming up before you, flowers and light stretching out. Then you shut it down, letting it go through you with a leap that carries you to the moon—the sun, and makes you bump with life like the little boy bursting out of his too small clothes and go on choking with song to do the next thing deftly. That's right. Perhaps that is what they all *do*? Perhaps that's why they won't stop to remember. Do you realize? Do you realize you're in Brussels?[1] Just *look* at the white houses there, with the bright green trees against them in the light. It's the *air*, the clearness. Sh—If they hear you, they'll put up the rent. They were just Portsmouth[2] and Gosport[3] people, staying in Brussels and fussing about Portsmouth and Gosport and aunt this and Mr that.... I shan't realize Brussels and Belgium for years because of that. They hated and killed me because I was like that.... I must be like that ... something comes along, *golden*, and presently there is a thought. I can't be easy till I've said it in my mind, and I'm sad till I have said it somehow ... and sadder when I have said it. But nothing gets done. I must stop thinking, from now, and be fearfully efficient.[4] Then people will understand and

---

1 Miriam here recalls a visit to Brussels, which does not occur in the volumes of *Pilgrimage*; however, she refers to memories of it a number of times throughout the series.
2 A town on the southern coast of England.
3 Another town on the southern coast of England, just across an inlet from Portsmouth.
4 The idea of efficiency developed out of the Industrial Revolution in Britain, and became more widespread in the nineteenth century, as the nation wanted to improve the administrative and economic functioning

like me. They will hate me too, because I shall be absurd, I shan't be really in it. Perhaps I shall. Perhaps I shall get in. The wonder is they don't hate me more. There was a stirring in the chair and a gushing of fresh water into the tumbler. *Why* do I meet such nice people? One after another. "There," said Mr Hancock, "I don't think that will trouble you any more. We will make another appointment." Miriam took the appointment book and a card to the chair-side and stayed up-stairs to clear up.

When she reached the hall Mr Orly's door was standing wide. Going into the surgery she found the head parlourmaid rapidly wiping instruments with a soiled serviette. "Is it all right, James?" she said vaguely, glancing round the room.

"Yes, miss," answered James briskly emptying the half-filled tumbler and going on to dry and polish it with the soiled serviette ... the housemaid spirit ... the dry corner of a used serviette probably appeared to James much too good to wipe anything with. Telling her would not be any good. She would think it a waste of time.... Besides, Mr Orly himself would not really mind; and the things were "mechanikly clean" ... that was a good phrase of Mr Leyton's ... with his own things always soaking, even his mallets, until there was no polish left on the handles; and his nail-brush in a bath of alcohol.... Mr Orly came in, large and spruce. He looked at his hands and began combing his beard, standing before the overmantel. "Hancock busy?"

"Frightfully busy."

Miriam looked judicially round the room. James hovered. The north wind howled. The little strip of sky above the outside wall that obscured the heavily stained glass of the window seemed hardly to light the room and the little light there was was absorbed by the heavy dull oak furniture and the dark heavy Turkey carpet and dado[1] of dull red and tarnished gold.

"It *is* dark for April," murmured Miriam. "I'll take away your gold and tin box if I may."

"Thank ye," said Mr Orly nervously, wheeling about with a harsh sigh to scan the chair and bracket-table; straightening his

---

of the British Empire. The Efficiency Movement gained traction in Britain in the early twentieth century, focusing on modernization, eliminating waste, and increasing people management.

1　The lower part of a wall, between the baseboard and the chair-rail or dado-rail.

waistcoat and settling his tie. "I got through without it—used some of that new patent silicate[1] stuff of Leyton's. All right—show in the countess."

James disappeared. Miriam secured the little box and made off. On her table was a fresh pile of letters, annotated in Mr Orly's clear stiff upright rounded characters. She went hurriedly through them. Extricating her blotter she sat down and examined the inkstand. Of course one of her pens had been used and flung down still wet with its nib resting against the handle of the other pens.... Mr Leyton ... his gold filling; she ought to go in and see if she could help ... perhaps he had finished by now. She wiped away the ink from the nib and the pen-handles.

Tapping at Mr Leyton's door, she entered. He quickly turned a flushed face, his feet scrabbling noisily against the bevelled base of the chair with the movement of his head. "Sawl right Miss Henderson. I've finished. 'V' you got any emery strips?—mine are all worn out."

Back once more in her room she heard two voices talking both at once excitedly in the den. Mrs Orly had a morning visitor. She would probably stay to lunch. She peered into the little folding mirror hanging by the side of the small mantelpiece and saw a face flushed and animated so far. Her hair was as unsatisfactory as usual. As she looked she became conscious of its uncomfortable weight pinned to the back of her head and the unpleasant warm feeling of her thick fringe. By lunch-time her face would be strained and yellow with sitting at work in the cold room with her feet on the oilcloth under the window. She glanced at the oil-lamp standing in the little fireplace, its single flame glaring nakedly against the red-painted radiator. The telephone bell rang.[2] Through the uproar of mechanical sounds that came to her ear from the receiver she heard a far-off faint angry voice in incoherent reiteration. "Hallo, hallo," she answered encouragingly. The voice faded but the sounds went on, punctuated by a sharp angry popping. Mr Orly's door opened and his swift heavy tread came through the hall. Miriam looked up apprehensively,

---

1 Silicate cement was used for fillings in the nineteenth and early twentieth centuries.

2 Telephones were not owned by private residences until the early twentieth century. In the late nineteenth century, the telephone (patented by Alexander Graham Bell in 1876) was largely considered a business tool and was occasionally used in offices.

saying "Hallo" at intervals into the angry din of the telephone. He came swiftly on humming in a soft light baritone, his broad forehead, bald rounded crown, and bright fair beard shining in the gloom of the hall. A crumpled serviette swung with his right hand. Perhaps he was going to the workshop. The door of the den opened. Mrs Orly appeared and made an inarticulate remark abstractedly, and disappeared. "Hallo, hallo," repeated Miriam busily into the telephone. There was a loud report and the thin angry voice came clear from a surrounding silence. Mr Orly came in on tiptoe, sighed impatiently and stood near her, drumming noiselessly on the table at her side. "Wrong number," said Miriam, "will you please ring off?"

"What a lot of trouble they givya," said Mr Orly. "I say, what's the name of the American chap Hancock was talking about at lunch yesterday?"

Miriam frowned.

"Can y' remember? About sea-power."

"Oh," said Miriam relieved. "Mahan."[1]

"Eh?"

"Mahan. May-ann."

"That's it. You've got it. Wonderful. Don't forget to send off Major Moke's case sharp, will ye?"

Miriam's eyes scanned the table and caught sight of a half-hidden tin box.

"No. I'll get it off."

"Right. It's in a filthy state, but there's no time to clean it."

He strode back through the hall murmuring "Mahan." Miriam drew the tin from its place of concealment. It contained a mass of dirty cotton-wool upon which lay a double denture coated with tartar and joined by tarnished gold springs. "Eleven-thirty, sharp," ran the instruction on an accompanying scrap of paper. No address. The name of the patient was unfamiliar. Mrs Orly put her head through the door of the den.

"What did Ro want?"

Miriam turned towards the small sallow eager face and met the kind sweet intent blue glint of the eyes. She explained, and Mrs Orly's anxious little face broke into a smile that dispelled the lines on the broad strip of low forehead leaving it smooth and sallow under the smoothly brushed brown hair.

---

1 Alfred Thayer Mahan (1840-1914), an American Navy officer. His influential idea of "sea power" suggested that the most powerful nations would be those with the strongest naval presence.

"How funny," said Mrs Orly hurriedly. "I was just comin' out to ask you the name of that singer. You know. Mark something. Marksy...."

"Mar-kaysie,"[1] said Miriam.

"That's it. I can't think how you remember." Mrs Orly disappeared and the two voices broke out again in eager chorus. Miriam returned to her tin. Mastering her disgust she removed the plate from the box, shook the cotton-wool out into the paper-basket, collected fresh wool, packing paper, sealing-wax, candle and matches and set to work to make up the parcel. She would have to attack the workshop again, and get them to take it out. Perhaps they would know the address. When the case was half packed she looked up the patient's name in the ledger. Five entries in about as many years—either repairs or springs—how simple dentistry became when people had lost all their teeth. There were two addresses, a town and a country one, written in a long time ago in ink; above them were two in pencil, one crossed out. The newest of the address books showed those two addresses, one in ink, neither crossed out. What had become of the card and letter that came with the case? In the den with Mrs Orly and her guest....

Footsteps were coming neatly and heavily up the basement stairs. Winthrop. He came in smiling, still holding his long apron gathered up to free his knees. "Ph—ph—Major Moke's case ready?" he whispered cheerfully.

"Almost—but I don't know the address."

"It's the ph—ph—*Buck*inham Palace Otel. It's to go by hand."

"Oh, thank goodness," laughed Miriam sweeping the scissors round the uneven edge of the wrapping-paper.

"My *word*," said Winthrop, "What an eye you've got, I couldn't do that to ph-save melife, and I'm supposed to be a ph-mechanic."

"Have I?" said Miriam surprised. "I shan't be two minutes; it'll be ready by the time anybody's ready to go. But the letters aren't."

"All right. I'll send up for them when we go out to lunch," said Winthrop consolingly, disappearing.

Miriam found a piece of fine glazed green twine in her string

---

1   Likely a member of the Marchesi family (Salvatore, Mathilde, and Blanche). Salvatore and Mathilde were singers and teachers; their daughter Blanche had a successful singing career in London in the early years of the twentieth century.

box and tied up the neat packet—sealing the ends of the string with a neat blob on the upper side of the packet, and the folded paper at each end. She admired the two firmly flattened ends of string close together. Their free ends united by the firm red blob were a decorative substitute for a stamp on the white surface of the paper. She wrote in the address in an upright rounded hand with firm rotund little embellishments. Poring over the result she examined it at various distances. It was delightful. She wanted to show it to someone. It would be lost on Major Moke. He would tear open the paper to get at his dreadful teeth. Putting the stamps on the label, she regretfully resigned the packet and took up Mr Orly's day-book. It was in arrears—three, four days not entered in the ledger. "Major Moke repair—one guinea,"[1] she wrote. Mr Hancock's showing-out bell rang. She took up her packet and surveyed it upside down. The address looked like Chinese. It was really beautiful ... but handwriting was doomed ... shorthand[2] and typewriting[3] ... she ought to know them, if she were ever to make more than a pound a week[4] as a secretary ... awful. What a good thing Mr Hancock thought them unprofessional ... yet there were already men in Wimpole Street who had their correspondence typed. What did he mean by saying that the art of conversation was doomed? He did not like conversation. Jimmy came in for the parcel and scuttled downstairs with it. Mr Hancock's patient was going out through the hall. He had not rung for her to go up. Perhaps there was very little to clear and he was doing it himself.

He was coming downstairs. Her hands went to the pile of letters and busily sorted them. Through the hall. In here. Leisurely. How are you getting on? Half amused. Half solicitous. The first weeks. The first day. She had only just come. Perhaps there would be the hand on the back of the chair again, as before he discovered the stiffness like his own stiffness. He was coming

---

1 See p. 79, note 6.
2 An abbreviated symbolic writing method that allows for very fast writing, as is essential when taking dictation.
3 Invented in the 1860s, typewriters quickly became indispensable for professional and business communication. Typists were almost exclusively women, and learning to type presented one of the very few opportunities for unmarried women to earn a living.
4 Miriam's salary is roughly equivalent to £68 per week in today's currency.

right round to the side of the chair into the light, waiting, without having said anything. She seemed to sit through a long space waiting for him to speak, in a radiance that shaped and smoothed her face as she turned slowly and considered the blunted grave features, their curious light, and met the smiling grey eyes. They were not observing the confusion on the table. He had something to say that had nothing to do with the work. She waited startled into an overflowing of the curious radiance, deepening the light in which they were grouped. "Are you busy?" "No," said Miriam in quiet abandonment. "I want your advice on a question of decoration," he pursued, smiling down at her with the expression of a truant schoolboy and standing aside as she rose. "My patient's put off," he added confidentially, holding the door wide for her. Miriam trotted incredulously upstairs in front of him and in at the open surgery door and stood contemplating the room from the middle of the great square of soft thick grey-green carpet, with her back to the great triple window and the littered remains of a long sitting.

Perhaps a question of decoration meant altering the positions of some of the pictures. She glanced about at them, enclosed in her daily unchanging unsatisfying impressions—the green landscape plumy with meadow-sweet, but not letting you through to wander in fields, the little soft bright colour painting of the doorway of St Mark's—San Marco,[1] painted by an Englishman, with a procession going in at the door and beggars round the doorway, blobby and shapeless like English peasants in Italian clothes ... bad ... and the man had worked and studied and gone to Italy and had a name and still worked and people bought his things ... an engraving very fine and small of a low bridge in a little town, quiet, sharp cheering lines; and above it another engraving, a tiresome troubled girl, all a sharp film of fine woven lines and lights and shadows in a rich dark liny filmy interior, neither letting you through nor holding you up, the girl worrying there in the middle of the picture, not moving, an obstruction ... Maris[2] ... the two little watercolours of Devonshire, a boat with a brown sail and a small narrow piece of a street zigzagging sharply up between crooked houses, by a Londoner—just to say how crooked everything was ... that thing in this month's *Studio*[3] was

---

1 St. Mark's Basilica in Venice, Italy.
2 Could refer to any of three Dutch brothers, all painters: Jacob (1837-99), Willem (1844-1910), and Matthijs (1839-1917) Maris.
3 *The Studio* (founded 1893), a monthly magazine of decorative and fine arts, was a proponent of the Arts and Crafts movement (late nineteenth

better than any of these ... her heart throbbed suddenly as she thought of it ... a narrow sandy pathway going off, frilled with sharp greenery; far into a green wood.... Had he seen it? The *Studios* lay safely there on the polished table in the corner, the disturbing bowl of flowers from the country, the great pieces of pottery, friends, warm and sympathetic to touch, never letting you grow tired of their colour and design ... standing out against the soft dull gold of the dado and the bold soft green and buff of the wall-paper. The oil painting of the cousin was looking on a little superciliously ... centuries of "fastidious refinement" looking forth from her child's face. If she were here, it would be she would be consulted about the decoration; but she was away somewhere in some house, moving about in a dignified way under her mass of gold hair, saying things when speech became a necessity in the refined fastidious half-contemptuous tone, hiding her sensitive desire for companionship, contemptuous of most things and most people. To-day she had an interested look, she was half jealously setting standards for him all the time.... Miriam set her aside. The Chinese figures staring down ferociously from the narrow shelf running along the base of the high white frieze were more real to her. They belonged to the daily life here, secure from censure.

From the brown paper wrappings emerged a large plaque of Oriental pottery. Mr Hancock manœuvred it upright, holding it opposite to her on the floor, supported against his knees. "There—what do you think of that?" he murmured bending over it. Miriam's eyes went from the veinings on his flushed forehead to the violent soft rich red and blue and dull green covering the huge concave disk from side to side. It appeared to represent a close thicket of palm fronds, thin flat fingers, superimposed and splaying out in all directions over the deep blue background. In the centre appeared the head and shoulders of an enormous tiger, coming sinuously forward, one great paw planted on the greenery near the foremost middle edge of the plaque.

"M'm," said Miriam staring.

Mr Hancock rubbed the surface of the plaque with his forefinger. Miriam came near and ran her finger down across the rich smooth reliefs.

"Where shall I put it?" said Mr Hancock.

---

century), which used romantic, medieval, and organic motifs, particularly for interior design.

"I should have it somewhere on that side of the room, where the light falls on it."

Mr Hancock raised the plaque in his arms and walked with it to the wall raising it just above his head and holding it in place between the two pictures of Devonshire. They faded to a small muddled dinginess, and the buff and green patterning of the wall-paper showed shabby and dim.

"It looks somehow too big or too small or something.... I should have it down level with the eyes, so that you can look straight into it."

Mr Hancock carefully lowered it.

"Let me come and hold it so that you can look," said Miriam advancing.

"It's too heavy for you," said Mr Hancock, straining his head back and moving it from side to side.

"I believe it would look best," said Miriam, "across the corner of the room as you come in—where the corner cupboard is—I'm sure it would," she said eagerly and went back to the centre of the carpet.

Mr Hancock smiled towards the small oak cupboard fixed low in the angle of the wall.

"We should have to move the cupboard," he said dubiously and carried the heavy plate to the indicated place.

"That's simply lovely," said Miriam in delight as he held the plaque in front of the long narrow facade of black oak.

Mr Hancock lowered the plaque to the floor and propped it crosswise against the angle.

"It would be no end of a business fixing it up," he murmured crossing to her side. They stood looking at the beautiful surface; blurred a little in the light by its backward tilt. They gazed fascinated as the plaque slid gently forward and fell heavily, breaking into two pieces.

They regarded one another quietly and went forward to gather up the fragments. The broken sides gritted together as Miriam held hers steady for the other to be fitted to it. When they were joined the crack was hardly visible.

"That'll be a nice piece of work for Messrs Nikkoo," said Mr Hancock with a little laugh, "we'd better get it in back behind the sofa for the present." They spread the brown paper over the brilliant surfaces and stood up. Miriam's perceptions raced happily along. How had he known that she cared for things? She was not sure that she did ... not in the way that he did.... How did he know that she had noticed any of his things? Because she had blurted out "Oh what a perfectly lovely picture," when he showed her the painting of his sister? But that was because he admired his sister and her brother had painted the picture and he admired them both and she had not known about this when she spoke.

"Did you see this month's *Studio*?" she asked shyly.

He turned to the table and took up the uppermost of the pile.

"There's a lovely green picture," said Miriam, "at least I like it."

Mr Hancock turned pages ruminatively.

"Those are good things," he said flattening the open page.

"Japanese Flower Decorations,"[1] read Miriam looking at the reproduced squares of flowering branches arranged with a curious naturalness in strange flat dishes. They fascinated her at once—stiff and real, shooting straight up from the earth and branching out. They seemed coloured. She turned pages and gazed.

"How nice and queer."

Mr Hancock bent smiling. "They've got a whole science of this, you know," he said; "it takes them years to learn it; they apprentice themselves and study for years...."

Miriam looked incredulously at the simple effects—just branches placed "artistically" in flat dishes and fixed somehow at the base amongst little heaps of stones.

"It looks easy enough."

Mr Hancock laughed. "Well—you try. We'll get some broom or something, and you shall try your hand. You'd better read the article. Look here—they've got names for all the angles.... 'Shin,'" he read with amused admiring delight, "'sho-shin'[2] ... there's no end of it."

Miriam fired and hesitated. "It's like a sort of mathematics.... I'm no good at mathematics."

"I expect you could get very good results ... we'll try. They carry it to such extraordinary lengths because there's all sorts of social etiquette mixed up with it—you can't have a branch pointing at a guest for instance—it would be rude."

---

1 Ikebana, the Japanese art of flower arrangement, is an ancient and spiritual practice whose significance extends well beyond simple interior decoration.

2 These names do not actually refer to the angles of the flowers, but designate individual stems, "shin" being the primary stem, and "shoshin" the secondary. In the Rikka style of Ikebana, the most formal style dating from the sixteenth century, nine stems are used to represent nine different aspects of nature, and their harmonious positioning is meant to be a Buddhist expression of the natural world.

"No wonder it takes them years," said Miriam.

They laughed together, moving vaguely about the room.

Mr Hancock looked thoughtfully at the celluloid tray of hairpins on the mantelshelf, and blew the dust from it ... there was something she remembered in some paper, very forcibly written, about the falsity of introducing single specimens of Japanese art, the last results of centuries of an artistic discipline, that was it, that had grown from the life of a secluded people living isolated in a particular spot under certain social and natural conditions, into English household decoration.... *Gleanings in Buddha Fields*,[1] the sun on rice-fields ... and Fujiyama—Fuji-no-San,[2] in the distance ... but he did not like Hearn—"there's something in the chap that puts me off" ... puts off—what a good phrase ... "something sensuous in him" ... but you could never forget *Buddha Fields*. It made you know you were in Japan, in the picture of Japan ... and somebody had said that all good art, all great art, had a sensuous element ... it was dreadful, but probably true ... because the man had observed it and was not an artist, but somebody looking carefully on. Mr Hancock, Englishman, was "put off" by sensuousness, by anybody taking a delight in the sun on rice fields and the gay colours of Japan ... perhaps one ought to be "put off" by Hearn ... but Mr Hancock liked Japanese things and bought them and put them in with his English things, that looked funny and tame beside them. What he did not like was the expression of delight. It was queer and annoying somehow ... especially as he said that the way English women were trained to suppress their feelings was bad. He had theories and fixed preferences and yet always seemed to be puzzled about so many things.

"D'you think it right to try to introduce single pieces of Japanese art into English surroundings?" she said tartly, beginning on the instruments.

"East is East and West is West and never the twain can meet?"[3]

"That's a dreadful idea—I don't believe it a bit."

Mr Hancock laughed. He believed in those awful final dreary-

---

1   An 1897 book by Lafcadio Hearn (1850-1904), a Greek-Irish writer who lived in Japan and wrote numerous books about Japanese culture and aesthetics for Western audiences.

2   The two Japanese names for Mount Fuji, the tallest mountain (and volcano) in Japan.

3   Hancock slightly misquotes the opening line of Rudyard Kipling's 1889 poem "The Ballad of East and West": "Oh, East is East and West is West, and never the twain shall meet."

weary things ... some species are so widely differentiated that they cannot amalgamate—awful ... but if one said that he would laugh and say it was beyond him ... and he liked and disliked without understanding the curious differences between people—did not know why they were different—they put him off or did not put him off and he was just. He liked and reverenced Japanese art and there was an artist in his family. That was strange and fine.

"I suppose we ought to have some face-powder here," mused Mr Hancock.

"They'll take longer than ever if we do."

"I know—that's the worst of it; but I commit such fearful depredations ... we want a dressing-room ... if I had my way we'd have a proper dressing-room downstairs. But I think we must get some powder and a puff.... Do you think you could get some ...?" Miriam shrank. Once in a chemist's shop, in a strong Burlington Arcade[1] west-end mood, buying some scent, she had seized and bought a little box ... La Dorine de Poche ... Dorin, Paris[2] ... but that was different to asking openly for powder and a puff ... la Dorine de Dorin, Paris was secret and wonderful.... "I'll try," she said bravely and heard the familiar little sympathetic laugh.

Lunch would be ready in a few minutes and none of the letters were done. She glanced distastefully at the bold handwritings, scrawling, under impressive stamped addresses with telephone numbers, and names of stations and telegraphic addresses, across the well-shaped sheets of expensive notepaper, to ask in long, fussy, badly-put sentences for expensive appointments. Several of the signatures were unfamiliar to her and must be looked up in the ledger, in case titles might be attached. She glanced at the dates of the appointments—they could all go by the evening post. What a good thing Mr Hancock had given up overlooking the correspondence. Mrs Hermann's letter he should see ... but that could not anyhow have been answered by return. The lunch-bell rang.... Mr Orly's letters! There was probably a telegram or some dreadful urgent thing about one or other of them that ought to have been dealt with. With beating heart she fumbled them through—each one bore the word "Answered" in Mrs Orly's fine pointed hand. Thank goodness. Opening a drawer she crammed

---

1 A covered shopping arcade in London, primarily for jewelry and fashionable items.

2 Brand name of a fashionable powder box, or compact, made by the Paris company, Dorin.

them into a crowded clip ... at least a week's addresses to be checked or entered.... Mr Hancock's unanswered letters went into the same drawer, leaving her table fairly clear. Mr Leyton's door burst open, he clattered down the basement stairs. Miriam went into his room and washed her hands in the corner basin under the patent unleaking taps. Everything was splashed over with permanganate of potash.[1] The smell of the room combined all the dental drugs with the odour of leather—a volunteer officer's accoutrements lay in confusion all over on the secretaire.[2] Beside them stood an open pot of leather polish. Mr and Mrs Orly passed the open door and went downstairs. They were alone. The guest had gone.

"Come and share the remains of the banquet, Miss Hens'n."

"*Do* have just a bit of somethin', Ro darling, a bit of chicking or somethin'."

"Feeling the effects?" remarked Mr Leyton cheerfully munching. "I've got a patient at half past," he added, nervously glancing up as if to justify his existence as well as his remark. Miriam hoped he would go on; perhaps it would occur to Mrs Orly to ask him about the patient.

"*You*'d feel the effects, my boy, if you hadn't had a wink the whole blessed night."

"Hancock busy, Miss Hens'?" Miriam glanced at the flushed forehead and hoped that Mr Orly would remain with his elbows on the table and his face hidden in his hands. She was hungry, and there would be no peace for anybody if he were roused.

"Too many whiskies?" inquired Mr Leyton cheerfully, shovelling salad on to his plate.

"Too much whisking and frisking altogether, captain," said Mr Orly incisively, raising his head.

Mrs Orly flushed, and frowned at Mr Orly.

"Don't be silly, Ley—you know how father hates dinner parties."

Mr Orly sighed harshly, pulling himself up as Miriam began a dissertation on Mr Hancock's crowded day.

"Ze got someone with him now?" put in Mrs Orly perfunctorily.

"Wonderful man," sighed Mr Orly harshly, glancing at his son.

---

1 Another disinfectant used by dentists in the nineteenth century. Now called potassium permanganate, it is still widely used, particularly in water treatment.

2 A narrow desk with drawers and a surface for writing and organizing correspondence.

"Have a bit of chicking, Ro."

"No, my love, no, not all the perfumes of Araby—not all the chickens of Cheshire. Have some pâté, Miss Hens'—No? despise pâté?"

A maid came briskly in and looked helpfully round.

"Who's your half-past-one patient, Ley?" asked Mrs Orly nervously.

"Buck," rapped Mr Leyton. "We going to wait for Mr Hancock, Mater?"[1]

"No, of course not. Keep some things hot, Emma, and bring in the sweets."

"Have some more chicken, Miss Hens'. Emma!"—he indicated his son with a flourish of his serviette—"wait upon Mr Leyton, serve him speedily."

Emma, arrested, looked helpfully about, smiled in brisk amusement, seized some dishes, and went out.

Mrs Orly's pinched face expanded. "Silly you are, Ro." Miriam grinned, watching dreamily. Mr Leyton's flushed face rose and dipped spasmodically over the remains of his salad.

"Bucking for Buck"—laughed Mr Orly in a soft falsetto.

"Ro, you *are* silly, who's Buck, Ley?"

"Don't question the officer, Nelly."

"Ro, you *are* absurd," laughed Mrs Orly.

"Help the *jellies*,[2] dearest," shouted Mr Orly in a frowning whisper. "Have some jelly, Miss Hens'. It's all right, Ley ... glad you so busy, my son. How many did you have this morning?" Mopping his brow and whisking his person with his serviette, he glanced sidelong.

"Two," said Mr Leyton, noisily spooning up jelly. "Any more of that stuff, mater? how about Hancock?"

"There's plenty here," said Mrs Orly helping him. Miriam laboured with her jelly and glanced at the dish. People wolfed their food. It would seem so conspicuous to begin again when the fuss had died down; with Mr Orly watching as if feeding were a contemptible self-indulgence.

"Had a beastly gold case[3] half the morning," rapped Mr Leyton and drank, with a gulp.

---

1 Latin: mother; common term of reference for the mother of a family in Victorian England.

2 Possibly a gelatin-based dessert, but given the presence of pâté here, more likely a savoury gelatin of the sort that typically accompanies pâtés and headcheeses.

3 That is, a tooth that required capping with gold amalgam.

"Get any help?" said Mr Orly, glancing at Miriam.

"No," said Mr Leyton in a non-committal tone, reaching across the table for the cheese.

"Hancock too busy?" asked Mr Orly. "Have some more jelly, Miss Hens'n."

"No thank you," said Miriam.

"A bit of cheese; a fragment of giddy Gorgonzola."

"No thanks."

Mrs Orly brushed busily at her bodice, peering down with indrawn chin. The room was close with gas. If Mr Hancock would only come down, and give her the excuse of attending to his room.

"What you doing s'aafnoon?" asked Mr Leyton.

"I, my boy, I don't know," said Mr Orly with a heavy sigh, "string myself up, I think."

"You'd much better string yourself round the Outer Circle[1] and take Lennard's advice."

"Good advice, my boy—if we all took good advice ... eh, Miss Hens'n? I've taken twenty grains of phenacetin[2] this morning."

"Well, you go and get a good walk," said Mr Leyton clattering to his feet. "'Scuse me, mater."

"Right, my boy! Excellent! A Daniel come to judgment![3] All right, Ley—get on with you. Buck up and see Buck. Oh-h-h, my blooming head. Excuse my language Miss Hens'n. Ah! Here's the great man. Good morning Hancock. How are you? D'they know you're down?"

Mr Hancock murmured his greetings and sat down opposite Miriam with a grave preoccupied air.

"Busy?" asked Mr Orly turning to face his partner.

"Yes—fairly," said Mr Hancock pleasantly.

"Wonderful man.... Ley's gone off like a bee in a gale. D'they know Hancock's down, Nelly?"

---

1   The outer ring road around Regent's Park.

2   An analgesic, introduced in 1887. A reasonable dose would have been between 10 and 30 grains per 24 hours.

3   From Shakespeare's *The Merchant of Venice* IV.i. The phrase is commonly used to describe a judicious judgement, derived from the biblical book of Daniel, likely 5:14: "I have even heard of thee, that the spirit of the gods is in thee, and that light and understanding and excellent wisdom is found in thee" (King James Version). Daniel, a biblical prophet, was an advisor to the Babylonian court, interpreting dreams and visions for the kings. This seems simply a loose reference to his son's offering him advice.

Miriam glanced at Mr Hancock, wishing he could lunch in peace. He was tired. Did he too feel oppressed with the gas and the pale madder[1] store cupboards? ... glaring muddy hot pink?

"I've got a blasted head[2] on ... excuse my language. Twenty of 'em, twenty to dinner."

"Oh, yes?" said Mr Hancock shifting in his chair and glancing about.

"*Nelly!* D'they know he's down? Start on a pâté, Hancock. The remains of the banquet."

"Oh ... well, thanks."

"You never get heads, do ye?"

Mr Hancock smiled, and began a murmuring response as he busied himself with his pâté.

"Poor Ro, he's got a most awful head.... How's your uncle, Mr Hancock?"

"Oh—thank you.... I'm afraid he's not very flourishing."

"He's better than he used to be, isn't he?"

"Well—yes, I think perhaps on the whole he is."

"You ought to have been there, Hancock. Cleave came. He was in no end of form. Told us some fine ones. Have a biscuit and butter Miss Hens'n."

Miriam refused and excused herself.

On her way upstairs she strolled into Mr Leyton's room. He greeted her with a smile—polishing instruments busily.

"Mr Hancock busy?" he asked briskly.

"M'm."

"You busy? I say, if I have Buck in will you finish up these things?"

"All right, if you like," said Miriam, regretting her sociable impulse. "Is Mr Buck here?" She glanced at the appointment book.

"Yes, he's waiting."

"You haven't got anybody else this afternoon," observed Miriam.

"I know. But I want to be down at headquarters by five in full kit if I possibly can. Has the pater got anybody?"

"No. The afternoon's marked off—he's going out, I think. Look here, I'll clear up your things afterwards, if you want to go out. Will you want all these for Mr Buck?"

"Oh—all right, thanks; I dunno. I've got to finish him off this afternoon and make him pay up."

---

1 See p. 56, note 1.
2 Headache.

"Why pay up? Isn't he trustworthy?"

"Trustworthy? A man who's just won three hundred pounds on a horse and chucked his job on the strength of it."

"What a fearfully insane thing to do."

"Lost his head."

"Is he very young?"

"Oo—'bout twenty-five."

"H'm. I spose he'll begin the rake's progress."[1]

"That's about it. You've just about hit it," said Mr Leyton with heavy significance.

Miriam lingered.

"I boil every blessed thing after he's been ... if that's any indication to you."

"*Boil* them!" said Miriam vaguely distressed and pondering over Mr Leyton standing active and aseptic between her and some horror ... something infectious ... it must be that awful mysterious thing ... how awful for Mr Leyton to have to stop his teeth.

"Boil 'em," he chuckled knowingly.

"Why on earth?" she asked.

"Well—there you are," said Mr Leyton—"that's all I can tell you. I *boil* 'em."

"Crikey," said Miriam half in response and half in comment on his falsetto laugh, as she made for the door. "Oh, but I say, I don't understand your boiling apparatus, Mr Leyton."

"All right, don't you worry. I'll set it all going and shove the things in. You've only to turn off the gas and wipe 'em. I dare say I shall have time to do them myself."

When she had prepared for Mr Hancock's first afternoon patient Miriam sat down at her crowded table in a heavy drowse. No sound came from the house or from the den. The strip of sky above the blank wall opposite her window was an even cold grey. There was nothing to mark the movement of the noisy wind. The room was cold and stuffy. Shivering as she moved, she glanced round at the lamp. It was well trimmed. The yellow flame was at its broadest. The radiator glared. The warmth did not reach her. She was cold to the waist, her feet without feeling, on the strip of linoleum; her knees protruding into the window space felt as if

---

1   *A Rake's Progress* is a series of eight paintings (1732-33) by William
    Hogarth (1697-1764) illustrating the decline of Tom Rakewell, the son
    of a rich merchant who squanders all his money on various pleasures
    and ends up in prison.

they were in cold water. Her arms crept and flushed with cold at every movement, strips of cold wrist disgusted her, showing beyond her skimpy sleeves and leading to the hopelessness of her purplish red hands swollen and clammy with cold. Her hot head and flushed cheeks begged for fresh air. Warm rooms, with carpets and fires; an even, airy warmth.... There were people who could be in this sort of cold and be active, with cool faces and warm hands, even just after lunch. If Mr Leyton were here he would be briskly entering up the books—perhaps with a red nose; but very brisk. He was finishing Buck off; briskly, not even talking. Mr Hancock would be working swiftly at well-up-to-date accounts, without making a single mistake. Where had he sat doing all those pages of beautiful spidery book-keeping? Mr Orly would be rushing things through. What a drama. He knew it. He *knew* he had earned his rest by the fire ... doing everything, making and building the practice ... people waiting outside the surgery with basins for him to rush out and be sick. Her sweet inaccurate help in the fine pointed writing on cheap paper ... the two cheap rooms they started in.... *The Wreck of the "Mary Gloucester"*[1] ... "and never a doctor's brougham to help the missis unload." They had been through everything together ... it was all there with them now ... rushing down the street in the snow without an overcoat to get her the doctor. They were wise and sweet; in life and wise and sweet. They had gone out and would be back for tea. Perhaps they had gone out. Everything was so quiet. Two hours of cold before tea. Putting in order the materials for the gold and tin she propped her elbows on the table and rested her head against her hands and closed her eyes. There was a delicious drowsiness in her head, but her back was tired. She rose and wandered through the deserted hall into the empty waiting-room. The clear blaze of a coal fire greeted her at the doorway and her cold feet hurried in on to the warm Turkey carpet. The dark oak furniture and the copper bowls and jugs stood in a glow of comfort. From the centre of the great littered table a bowl of daffodils asserted the movement of the winter and pointed forward and away from the winter stillness of the old room. The long faded rich crimson rep[2] curtains obscured half the width of each high window, and the London light, screened by the high opposing houses, fell dimly on

---

1 Rudyard Kipling's poem "The Mary Gloster," about a shipping man who makes a number of bad investments and whose wife dies in the wreck of one of his ships. The subsequent quotation is a line from the poem.

2 Fabric of silk, wool, or cotton usually corded or ribbed.

the dingy books and periodicals scattered about the table. Miriam stood by the mantelpiece, her feet deep in the black sheepskin rug, and held out her hands towards the fire. They felt cold again the instant she withdrew them from the blaze. The hall clock gonged softly twice. The legal afternoon had begun. Any one finding her in here now would think she was idling. She glanced at the deep dark shabby leather arm-chair near by and imagined the relief that would come to her whole frame, if she could relax into it for five undisturbed minutes. The ringing of the front door bell sent her hurrying back to her room.

The sound of reading came from the den—a word-mouthing, word-slurring monotonous drawl—thurrah-thurrah-thurrah; thurrah thurrah ... a single beat, on and on, the words looped and forced into it without any discrimination, the voice dropping uniformly at the end of each sentence ... *thrah*.... An Early Victorian voice, giving reproachful instruction to a child ... a class of board-school children reciting.... Perhaps they had changed their minds about going out.... Miriam sat with her hands tucked between her knees, musing, with her eyes fixed on the thin sheets of tin and gold ... extraordinary to read any sort of text like that ... but there was something in it, something nice and good ... listening carefully you would get most of the words. It would be better to listen to than a person who read with intelligent modulations, as if they had written the thing themselves; like some men read ... and irritatingly intelligent women ... who knew they were intelligent. But there ought to be clear ... enunciation. Not expression—that was like commenting as you read; getting at the person you were reading to ... who might not want to comment in the same way. Reading, with expression, really hadn't any expression. How wonderful—of course. Mrs Orly's reading had an expression; a shape. It was exactly like the way they looked at things; exactly; everything was there; all the things they agreed about, and the things he admired in her ... things that by this time she knew he admired.... She was conscious of these things ... that was the difference between her and her sister, who had exactly the same things but had never been admired ... standing side by side exactly alike, the sister like a child—clear with a sharp fresh edge; Mrs Orly with a different wisdom ... softened and warm and blurred ... conscious, and always busy distracting your attention, but with clear eyes like a child, too.

Presently the door opened quietly and Mrs Orly appeared in the doorway. "Miss Hens'n," she whispered urgently. Miriam turned to meet her flushed face. "Oh, Miss Hens'n," she pursued absently, "if Mudie's[1] send, d'you mind lookin' and choosin' us something nice?"

"Oh," said Miriam provisionally with a smile.

Mrs Orly closed the door quietly and advanced confidently with deprecating bright wheedling eyes. "Isn't it tahsome," she said conversationally. "Ro's asleep and the carriage is comin' round at half past. Isn't it tahsome!"

"Can't you send it back?"

"I want him to go out; I think the drive will do him good. I say, d'you mind just lookin'—at the books?"

"No, I will; but how shall I know what to keep? Is there a list?"

Mrs Orly looked embarrassed. "I've got a list somewhere," she said hurriedly, "but I can't find it."

"I'll do my best," said Miriam.

"*You* know—anythin' historical ... there's one I put down, *The Sorrows of a Young Queen.*[2] Keep that if they send it and anything else you think."

"Is there anything to go back?"

"Yes, I'll bring them out. We've been reading an awful one—awful."

Miriam began fingering her gold-foil. Mrs Orly was going to expect her to be shocked....

"By that awful man Zola...."[3]

"Oh, yes," said Miriam, dryly.

"Have you read any of his?"

"Yes," said Miriam carefully.

"*Have* you? Aren't they shockin'?"

"Well I don't know. I thought *Lourdes*[4] was simply wonderful."

"Is that a nice one—what's it about?"

"Oh you know—it's about the Madonna of Lourdes,[5] the mir-

---

1 Mudie's Lending Library, founded in 1840 by Charles Edward Mudie (1818-90), remained open until the 1930s.

2 Richardson is conflating the title of Johan Wolfgang von Goethe's *The Sorrows of Young Werther* (1774) with J.M. Synge's play *Deirdre of the Sorrows*. This play, based on Irish myth, was first performed at the Abbey Theatre in 1910.

3 Émile Zola (1840-1902), a naturalist or decadent French writer, whose work often dealt with scandalous topics such as alcoholism and prostitution.

4 Zola's 1894 novel, one of three in a series called *Les Trois Villes*.

5 Beginning with Saint Bernadette Soubirous's experience in 1858, the city of Lourdes has been the site of several apparitions of the Virgin Mary. The shrine there remains a popular pilgrimage destination for devout Roman Catholics.

acles, in the south of France. It begins with a crowded trainload of sick people going down through France on a very hot day ... it's simply stupendous ... you feel you're in the train, you go through it all"—she turned away and looked through the window overcome ... "and there's a thing called *Le Rêve*,"[1] she went on incoherently with a break in her voice, "about an embroideress and a man called Félicien—it's simply the most *lovely* thing."

Mrs Orly came near to the table.

"You understand about books, don't you," she said wistfully.

"Oh, no," said Miriam. "I've hardly read anything."

"I wish you'd put those two down."

"I don't know the names of the translations," announced Miriam conceitedly.

A long loud yawn resounded through the door.

"Better, boysie?" asked Mrs Orly turning anxiously towards the open door.

"Yes, my love," said Mr Orly cheerfully.

"I *am* glad, boy—I'll get my things on—the carriage'll be here in a minute."

She departed at a run and Mr Orly came in and sat heavily down in a chair set against the slope of the wall close by and facing Miriam.

"Phoo," he puffed, "I've been taking phenacetin all day; you don't get heads, do you?"

Miriam smiled and began preparing a reply.

"How's it coming in? Totting up, eh?"

"I think so," said Miriam uneasily.

"What's it totting up to this month? Any idea?"

"No; I can see if you like."

"Never mind, never mind.... Mrs O.'s been reading ... phew! You're a lit'ry young lady—d'you know that French chap—Zola—Emmil Zola——" Mr Orly glanced suspiciously.

"Yes," said Miriam.

"Like 'im?"

"Yes," said Miriam firmly.

"Well—it's a matter of taste and fancy," sighed Mr Orly heavily. "Chacun à son goût[2]—shake an ass and go, as they say. One's enough for me. I can't think why they do it myself—sheer,

---

1 An 1888 Zola work from the 20-novel cycle *Les Rougon-Macquart*, which follows the lives of a fictional family in nineteenth-century France.

2 French: To each his own taste.

well to call a spade a spade sheer bestiality those French writers
—don't ye think so, eh?"

"Well no. I don't think I can accept that as a summary of
French literature."

"Eh, well, it's beyond me. I suppose I'm not up to it. Behind
the times. Not cultured enough. Not cultured enough I guess.
Ready dearest?" he said, addressing his wife and getting to his
feet with a groan. "Miss Hens'n's a great admirer of Emmil
Zola."

"She says some of his books are pretty, didn't you, Miss
Hens'n? It isn't fair to judge from one book, Ro."

"No, my love, no. Quite right. Quite right. I'm wrong—no
doubt. Getting old and soft. Things go on too fast for me."

"Don't be so silly, Ro."

Drowsily and automatically Miriam went on rolling tin and
gold—sliding a crisp thick foil of tin from the pink-tissue-paper-
leaved book on to the serviette ... a firm metallic crackle ... then
a silent layer of thin gold ... then more tin ... adjusting the three
slippery leaves in perfect superposition without touching them
with her hands, cutting the final square into three strips, with the
long sharp straight-bladed scissors—the edges of the metal
adhering to each other as the scissors went along—thinking again
with vague distant dreamy amusement of the boy who cut the
rubber tyre to mend it—rolling the flat strips with a fold of the
serviette, deftly, until they turned into neat little twisted crinkled
rolls—wondering how she had acquired the knack. She went on
and on lazily, unable to stop, sitting back in her chair and working
with outstretched arms, until a small fancy soap box was filled
with the twists—enough to last the practice for a month or two.
The sight filled her with a sense of achievement and zeal. Putting
on its lid, she placed the soap box on the second chair. Lazily, stu-
pidly, longing for tea—all the important clerical work left
undone, Mr Orly's surgery to clear up for the day—still, she was
working in the practice. She glanced approvingly at the soap box
... but there were ages to pass before tea. She did not dare to look
at her clock. Had the hall clock struck three? Bending to a drawer
she drew out a strip of amadou—offended at the sight of her red
wrist coming out of the harsh cheap black sleeve and the fingers
bloated by cold. They looked lifeless; no one else's hands looked
so lifeless. Part of the amadou was soft and warm to her touch,
part hard and stringy. Cutting out a soft square, she cut it rapidly
into tiny cubes, collecting them, in a pleasant flummery heap on

the blotting paper—Mr Hancock should have those; they belonged to his perfect treatment of his patients; it was quite just. Cutting a strip of the harsher part, she pulled and teased it into comparative softness and cut it up into a second pile of fragments. Amadou, gold, and tin ... Japanese paper?[1] A horrible torpor possessed her. Why did one's head get into such a hot fearful state before tea? ... grey stone wall and the side of the projecting glass-roofed peak of Mr Leyton's surgery ... grey stone wall ... wall ... railings at the top of it ... cold—a cold sky ... It was their time—nine to six—no doubt those people did best who thought of nothing during hours but the work—cheerfully—but they were always pretending—in and *out* of work hours they pretended. There was something wrong in them and something wrong in the people who shirked. "La—te—ta—te—te—ta," she hummed, searching her table for relief. Mr Hancock's bell sounded and she fled up to the warmth of his room. In a moment Mudie's cart came and the maid summoned her. There was a pile of books in the hall.... She glanced curiously at the titles, worried with the responsibility—*The Sorrows*—that was all right. *Secrets of a Stormy Court*[2] ... that was the sort of thing ... "you can't make a silk purse out of a sow's ear"[3] ... one day she must explain to Mr Orly that that was really "sousière" a thing to hold halfpence. *My Reminiscences* by Count de Something.[4] Perhaps that was one they had put down. The maid presented the volumes to be returned. Taking them, Miriam asked her to ask Mr Hancock if he had anything to change. *Cock Lane and Common Sense*[5] she read ... there was some sort of argument in that ... the "facts" of some case ... it would sneer at something, some popular idea ... it was probably by some doctor or scientific man ... but that was not the book.... *The Earth*[6] ... Émile Zola. She flapped the book

---

1 See p. 86, note 3.
2 *The Sorrows* is likely *The Sorrows of Young Werther* (1774) by Goethe. *Secrets of a Stormy Court* has not been identified.
3 A proverb dating back to the sixteenth century, though usually attributed to author Jonathan Swift (1667-1745), suggesting that one cannot make something fine without the right material. Miriam thinks to herself that it is actually based on a mis-hearing of the French "sousière."
4 Probably an English translation of *Mes Souvenirs* (1904) by Gustave Armand Henri, comte de Reiset (1821-1905).
5 An anthropological book by Andrew Lang, published in 1894, about folklore and the occult.
6 *La Terre* (*The Earth*) is an 1887 Zola novel, the fifteenth in the Rougon-Macquart series.

open and hurriedly read a few phrases. The hall pulsated curiously. She flushed all over her body. "There's nothing for Mr Hancock, miss." "All right; these can go and these are to be kept," she said indistinctly. Wandering back to her room she repeated the phrases in her mind in French. They seemed to clear up and take shelter—somehow they were terse and acceptable and they were secret and secure—but English people ought not to read them; in English. It was—outrageous. Englishmen. The Frenchman had written them simply ... French logic ... Englishmen were shy and suggestive about these things—either that or breezy ... "filth," which was almost worse. The Orlys ought not to read them at all ... it was a good thing the book was out of the house ... they would forget. But she would not forget. Her empty room glanced with a strange confused sadness; the clearing up upstairs was not quite done; but she could not go upstairs again yet. Three-fifteen; the afternoon had turned; her clock was a little slow, too. The warm, quiet, empty den was waiting for the tea-tray. Clearing the remnants from her table, she sat down again. The heavy stillness of the house closed in.... She opened the drawer of stationery. Various kinds of notepaper lay slid together in confusion; someone had been fumbling there. The correspondence cards propped against the side of the drawer would never stay in their proper places. With comatose meticulousness she put the whole drawer in order, replenishing it from a drawer of reserve packets, until it was so full that nothing could slide. She surveyed the result with satisfaction; and shut the drawer. She would tidy one drawer every afternoon.... She opened the drawer once more and looked again. To keep it like that, would mean, never using the undermost cards and notepaper. That would not do ... change them all round sometimes. She sat for a while inertly, and presently lazily roused herself with the idea of going upstairs. Pausing in front of a long three-shelved whatnot[1] filling the space between the door and the narrow many-drawered specimen case that stood next her table, she idly surveyed its contents. Nothing but piles of *British Dental Journals*, *Proceedings of the Odontological Society*, circulars from the dental manufacturing companies. Propping her elbows on the upper shelf of the whatnot she stood turning leaves.

"Tea up?"

"Don't know," said Miriam irritably, passing the open door.

---

1 A narrow shelving unit, with pillars supporting a series of shelves.

He could see she had only just come down and could not possibly know. The soft jingling of the cups shaken together on a tray by labouring footsteps came from the basement stairs. Mr Leyton's hurried clattering increased. Miriam waited impatiently by her table. The maid padded heavily through, swinging the door of the den wide with her elbow. When she had retired, Miriam sauntered, warm and happy almost before she was inside the door, into the den. With her eyes on the tea-tray she felt the afternoon expand.... "There's a Burma girl a settin' and I know she thinks of me." ... "Come you *back*, you British soldier, come you *back* to Mandalay."[1] Godfrey's tune was much the best; stiff, like the words, the other was only singsong. Pushing off the distraction she sat down near the gently roaring blaze of the gas fire in a low little chair, upholstered in cretonne[2] almost patternless with age. The glow of the fire went through and through her. If she had tea at once, everything would be richer and richer, but things would move on and, if they came back, she would have finished and would have to go. The face of the railway clock fixed against the frontage of the gallery at the far end of the room said four-fifteen. They had evidently ordered tea to be a quarter of an hour late and might be in any minute ... this curious feeling that the room belonged to her more than to the people who owned it, so that they were always intruders.... Leaving with difficulty the little feast untouched ... a Dundee cake from Buszard's[3] ... she browsed rapidly, her eyes roaming from thing to thing ... the shields and assegais[4] grouped upon the raised dull gold papering of the high opposite wall, the bright beautiful coloured bead skirts spread out amongst curious carved tusks and weapons, the large cool placid gold Buddha reclining below them with his chin on his hand and his elbow on a red velvet cushion, on the Japanese cabinet; the Japanese cupboard fixed above Mrs Orly's writing table, the fine firm carved ivory on its panels; the tall vase of

---

1   From the poem "Mandalay," by Rudyard Kipling, first published in
    Barrack-Room Ballads, and Other Verses (1892).
2   A strong white fabric, often printed with patterns.
3   Buszard's was a famed London cake shop on Oxford Street, specializing
    in wedding cakes. Dundee cake is a traditional Scottish fruit cake.
4   Slender, iron-tipped spears of hard wood. "Originally the name of a
    Berber weapon adopted by the Moors, but extended by the Portuguese
    to the light javelins of African peoples in general. Most commonly
    applied to the spears of the indigenous African peoples of South Africa"
    (*OED*).

Cape gooseberries[1] flaring on the top of the cottage piano under the shadow of the gallery; the gallery with its upper mystery, the happy clock fastened against its lower edge, always at something after four, the door set back in the wall, leading into her far-away midday room, the light falling from the long high frosted window along the confusion of Mr Orly's bench, noisy as she looked at it with the sound of metal tools falling with a rattle, the drone and rattle of the motor lathe, Mr Orly's cheerful hummings and whistlings. Mr Orly's African tobacco pouch bunched underneath the lamp on the edge of the bench near the old leather arm-chair near to the fire, facing the assegais; the glass-doored bookcase on either side of the fire-place, the strange smooth gold on the strips of Burmese wood fastened along the shelves, the clear brown light of the room on the gold, the curious lettering sweeping across the gold.[2]

"Tea? Good."

Mr Leyton pulled up a chair and plumped into it digging at his person and dragging out the tails of his coat with one hand, holding a rumpled newspaper at reading length. When his coat-tails were free he scratched his head and scrubbed vigorously at his short brown beard.

"You had tea?" he said to Miriam's motionlessness, without looking up.

"No—let's have tea," said Miriam. Why should he assume that she should pour out the tea....

"I *say*, that's a *nasty* one," said Mr Leyton hysterically and began reading in a high hysterical falsetto.

Miriam began pouring out. Mr Leyton finished his passage with a little giggling shriek of laughter and fumbled for bread and butter with his eyes still on the newspaper. Miriam sipped her hot tea. The room darkled in the silence. Everything intensified. She glanced impatiently at Mr Leyton's bent unconscious form. His shirt and the long straight narrow ends of his tie made a bulging curve above his low-cut waistcoat. The collar of his coat stood away from his bent neck and its tails were bunched up round his hips. His trousers were so hitched up that his bent knees strained against the harsh crude Rope Brothers cloth.[3] The ends of his

---

1 Not the same as a typical gooseberry, but more like a tomato. Native to South America, they were cultivated in England from the eighteenth century.

2 The room is jammed with artifacts that evince British imperialism, as does tea itself.

3 Unidentified.

trousers peaked up in front, displaying loose rolls of black sock and the whole of his anatomical walking-shoes. Miriam heard his busily masticating jaws and dreaded his operations with his tea-cup. A wavering hand came out and found the cup and clasped it by the rim, holding it at the edge of the lifted newspaper. She busied herself with cutting stout little wedges of cake. Mr Leyton sipped, gasping after each loud quilting gulp; a gasp, and the sound of a moustache being sucked. Mr Hancock's showing-out bell rang. Mr Leyton plunged busily round, finishing his cup in a series of rapid gulps. "Kike?"[1] he said.

"M'm," said Miriam, "jolly kike—did you finish Mr Buck?"

"More or less——"

"Did you boil the remains?"

"Boiled every blessed thing—and put the serviette in k'bolic."

Miriam hid her relief and poured him out another cup.

Mr Hancock came in through the open door and quickly up to the tea-tray. Pouring out a cup he held the teapot suspended. "Another cup?"

"No, thanks, not just at present," said Miriam getting to her feet with a morsel of cake in her fingers.

"Plenty of time for my things," said Mr Hancock sitting down in Mr Orly's chair with his tea; his flat compact slightly wrinkled and square-toed patent leather shoes gleamed from under the rims of his soft, dark grey, beautifully cut trousers with a pleasant shine as he sat back comfortable and unlounging, with crossed knees in the deep chair.

Mr Leyton had got to his feet.

"Busy?" he said rapidly munching. "I say, I've had that man Buck this afternoon."

"Oh yes," said Mr Hancock brushing a crumb from his knee.

"*You* know—that case I told you about."

"Oh yes?" said Mr Hancock with a clear glance and a slight tightening of the face.

Miriam made for the door. Mr Hancock was not encouraging the topic. Mr Leyton's cup came down with a clatter. "I'm fearfully rushed," he said. "I must be off." He caught Miriam up in the hall. "I say, tea must have been fearfully late. I've got to get down to headquarters by five *sharp*."

"You go on first," said Miriam standing aside.

Mr Leyton fled up through the house three steps at a time.

---

1 "Cake" in Mr. Leyton's heavily-accented English.

When she came down again intent on her second cup of tea in the empty brown den, a light had been switched on, driving the dark afternoon away. The crayon drawings behind the piano shone out on the walls of the dark square space under the gallery as she hesitated in the doorway. There was someone in the dim brightness of the room. She turned noiselessly towards her table.

"Come and have some more tea, Miss Hens'n."

Miriam went in with alacrity. The light was on in the octagonal brass-framed lantern that hung from the skylight and shed a soft dim radiance through its old glass. Mrs Orly, still in her bonnet and fur-lined cape, was sitting drinking tea in the little old cretonne chair. She raised a tired flushed face and smiled brightly at Miriam as she came down the room.

"I'm dying for another cup; I had to fly and clear up Mr Hancock's things."

"Mr Hancock busy? Have some cake, it's rather a nice one." Mrs Orly cut a stout little wedge.

Clearing away the newspaper, Miriam took possession of Mr Leyton's chair.

Mr Orly swung in shutting the door behind him and down the room, peeling off his frock coat as he came.

"Tea, darling?"

"Well, m' love, since you're so pressing."

Mr Orly switched on the lamp on the corner of the bench and subsided into his chair, his huge bulk poised lightly and alertly, one vast leg across the other knee.

"'Scuse my shirt-sleeves, Miss Hens'n. I say, I've got a new song—like to try it presently, or are ye too busy?"

Poised between the competing interests of many worlds, Miriam basked in the friendly tones.

"Well, I *have* got rather a fearful lot of things to do."

"Come and try it now, d'ye mind?"

"Have your tea, Ro, darling."

"Right, my love, right, right, always right—Hancock busy?"

"Yes; he has two more patients after this one."

"Marvellous man."

"Mr Hancock never gets rushed or flurried, does he? He's always been the same ever since we've known him."

"He's very even and steady, outwardly," said Miriam indifferently.

"You think it's only outward?"

"Well, I mean he's really frightfully sensitive."

"Just so; it's his coolness carries him through, self-command,

I wish I'd got it."

"You'd miss other things, boysie; you can't have it both ways."

"Right, m' love—right. I don't understand him. D'you think any one does, Miss Hens'n—really, I mean? D'you understand him?"

"Well, you see I haven't known him very long——"

"No—but you come from the same district and know his relatives."

"The same Berkshire valley, and his cousins happened to be my people's oldest friends."

"Well, don't ye see, that makes all the difference.—I say, I heard a splendid one this afternoon. D'you think I could tell Miss Hens'n that one, Nelly?—you're not easily shocked, are you?"

"I've never been shocked in my life," said Miriam getting to her feet.

"Must ye go? Shall we just try this over?"

"Well, if it isn't too long."

"Stop and have a bit of dinner with us, can ye?"

Miriam made her excuse, pleading an engagement, and sat down to the piano. The song was a modern ballad with an easy impressive accompaniment, following the air. The performance went off easily and well, Mr Orly's clear trained baritone ringing out persuasively into the large room. Weathering a second invitation to spend the evening, she got away to her room.

Her mind was alight with the sense of her many beckoning interests, aglow with fullness of life. The thin piercing light cast upon her table by the single five-candle-power bulb, drawn low and screened by a green glass shade, was warm and friendly. She attacked her letters, dispatching the appointments swiftly and easily in a bold convincing hand, and drafted a letter to Mrs Hermann that she carried with a glow of satisfaction to Mr Hancock's room. When his room was cleared in preparation for his last patient, it was nearly six o'clock. She began entering his day-book in the ledger.[1] The boy coming up for the letters brought two dentures to be packed and dispatched by registered post from Vere Street[2] before six o'clock. "They'll be ready by the time you've got your boots on," said Miriam and packed her cases brilliantly in a mood of deft-handed concentration. Jimmy

---

1 The "day book" is a daily record of financial transactions, including receipts and payments.

2 A London street just off Oxford Street.

clattered up the stairs as she was stamping the labels. When he fled with them, she gave a general sigh and surveyed the balance of her day with a responsible cheerful wicked desperation; her mind leaping forward to her evening. The day books would not be done, even Mr Hancock's would have to go up unentered; she had not the courage to investigate the state of the cash book; Mr Leyton's room was ready for the morning; she ran through to Mr Orly's room and performed a rapid perfunctory tidying up; many little things were left; his depleted stores must be refilled in the morning; she glanced at his appointment book, no patient so far until ten. She left the room with her everyday guilty consciousness that hardly anything in it was up to the level of Mr Hancock's room ... look after Hancock, I'm used to fending for myself ... but he knew she did not do her utmost to keep the room going. There were times when he ran short of stores in the midst of a sitting. That could be avoided.

When Miriam entered his room at half past six, Mr Hancock was switching off the lights about the chair. A single light shone over his desk. The fire was nearly out.

"Still here?"

"Yes," said Miriam switching on a light over the instrument cabinet.

"I should leave those things to-night if I were you."

"It isn't very late."

She could go on, indefinitely, in this confident silence, preparing for the next day. He sat making up his daybook and would presently come upon Mrs Hermann's letter. As long as he was there, the day lingered. Its light had left the room. The room was colourless and dark except where the two little brilliant circles of light made bright patches of winter evening. Their two figures quietly at work meant the quiet and peace of the practice; the full, ended day, to begin again to-morrow in broad daylight in this same room. The room was full of their quiet continuous companionship. It was getting very cold. He would be going soon.

He stood up, switching off his light. "That will do excellently," he said with an amused smile, placing Mrs Hermann's letter on the flap of the instrument cabinet and wandering into the gloomy spaces.

"*Well.* I'll say good night."

"Good night," murmured Miriam.

Leaving the dried instruments in a heap with a wash-leather flung over them she gathered up the books, switched the room into darkness, felt its promise of welcome, and trotted downstairs through the quiet house. The front door shut quietly on Mr Hancock as she reached the hall. She flew to get away. In five minutes the books were in the safe and everything locked up. The little mirror on the wall, scarcely lit by the single bulb over the desk just directed the angle of her hat and showed the dim strange eager outline of her unknown face. She fled down the hall past Mr Leyton's room and the opening to the forgotten basement, between the heavy closed door of Mr Orly's room and the quiet scrolled end of the balustrade and past the angle of the high dark clock staring with its unlit face down the length of the hall, between the high oak chest and the flat oak coffer confronting each other in the glooms thrown by Mrs Orly's tall narrow striped Oriental curtains; she saw them standing in straight folds, the beautiful height and straightness of their many-coloured stripes, as they must have been before the outside stripe of each had been cut and used as a tie-up; and was out beyond the curtains in the brightly-lit square facing the door. The light fell on the rich edge of the Turkey carpet and the groove of the bicycle stand. In the corner stood the blue and white pipe, empty of umbrellas. Her hand grasped the machine-turned edge of the small flat circular knob that released the door ... brahma;[1] that was the word, at last.... The door opened and closed with its familiar heavy wooden firmness, neatly, with a little rattle of its chain. Her day scrolled up behind her. She halted, trusted and responsible, for a long second, in the light flooding the steps from behind the door.

The pavement was under her feet and the sparsely lamplit night all round her. She restrained her eager steps to a walk. The dark houses and the blackness between the lamps were elastic about her.

---

1 Brahma, the Hindu god of creation. It remains unclear why Miriam is trying to remember him.

CHAPTER IV

When she came to herself she was in the Strand.[1] She walked on a little and turned aside to look at a jeweller's window and consider being in the Strand at night. Most of the shops were still open. The traffic was still in full tide. The jeweller's window repelled her. It was very yellow with gold, all the objects close together and each one bearing a tiny label with the price. There was a sort of commonness about the Strand, not like the cheerful commonness of Oxford Street, more like the City with its many sudden restaurants. She walked on. But there were theatres also, linking it up with the West End,[2] and streets leading off it where people like Bob Greville had chambers. It was the tailing off of the West End and the beginning of a deep dark richness that began about Holywell.[3] Mysterious important churches crowded in amongst little brown lanes ... the little dark brown lane.... She wondered what she had been thinking since she left Wimpole Street, and whether she had come across Trafalgar Square[4] without seeing it or round by some other way. They were *fighting*; sending out suffocation and misery into the surrounding air ... she stopped close to the two upright balanced threatening bodies, almost touching them. The men looked at her. "Don't," she said imploringly and hurried on trembling.... It occurred to her that she had not seen fighting since a day in her childhood when she had wondered at the swaying bodies and sickened at the thud of a fist against a cheek. The feeling was the same to-day, the longing to explain somehow to the men that they *could* not fight.... Half-past seven. Perhaps there would not be an A.B.C.[5] so far down. It would be impossible to get a meal. Perhaps the girls would have some coffee. An A.B.C. appeared suddenly at her side,

---

1 A famous London street running from Trafalgar Square to Fleet Street. Several theatres line the Strand, and many famous writers and thinkers congregated there.

2 A fashionable area of London, west of Charing Cross.

3 London's Holywell Street was noted in the Victorian era for its book-sellers and publishing houses. It was particularly popular as a spot for purchasing pornography. For a good social history of the area, see Lynn Nead, *Victorian Babylon* (New Haven: Yale UP, 2005). See also Scott McCracken, *Masculinities, Modernist Fiction and the Urban Public Sphere* (Manchester: Manchester UP, 2007).

4 A major public square and tourist attraction in London near Charing Cross. Its name refers to the 1805 Battle of Trafalgar, which a number of statues in the square commemorate.

5 Aerated Bread Company tearooms were very popular casual restaurants.

its panes misty in the cold air. She went confidently in. It seemed nearly full of men. Never mind, City men; with a wisdom of their own which kept them going and did not affect anything, all alike and thinking the same thoughts; far away from anything she thought or knew. She walked confidently down the centre, her plaid-lined golf-cape thrown back; her small brown boat-shaped felt hat suddenly hot on her head in the warmth. The shop turned at a right angle showing a large open fire with a fireguard, and a cat sitting on the hearth-rug in front of it. She chose a chair at a small table in front of the fire. The velvet settees at the sides of the room were more comfortable. But it was for such a little while to-night, and it was not one of her own A.B.C.s. She felt as she sat down as if she were the guest of the City men, and ate her boiled egg and roll and butter and drank her small coffee in that spirit, gazing into the fire and thinking her own thoughts unresentful of the uncongenial scraps of talk that now and again penetrated her thoughts; the complacent laughter of the men amazed her; their amazing unconsciousness of the things that were written all over them.

The fire blazed into her face. She dropped her cape over the back of her chair and sat in the glow; the small pat of butter was not enough for the large roll. Pictures came out of the fire, the strange moment in her room, the smashing of the plaque, the lamplit den; Mr Orly's song, the strange, rich, difficult day and now her untouched self here, free, unseen, and strong, the strong world of London all round her, strong free untouched people, in a dark lit wilderness, happy and miserable in their own way, going about the streets looking at nothing, thinking about no special person or thing, as long as they were there, being in London.

Even the business people who went about intent, going to definite places, were in the secret of London and looked free. The expression of the collar and hair of many of them said they had homes. But they got away from them. No one who had never been alone in London was quite alive.... I'm free—I've got free—nothing can ever alter that, she thought, gazing wide-eyed into the fire, between fear and joy. The strange familiar pang gave the place a sort of consecration. A strength was piling up within her. She would go out unregretfully at closing time and up through wonderful unknown streets, not her own streets, till she found Holborn[1] and then up and round through the squares.

---

1 An area of London bordering the Bloomsbury neighbourhood, near the British Museum.

On the hall table lay a letter ... from Alma; under the shadow of the bronze soldier leaning on his gun. Miriam gathered it up swiftly. No one knew her here ... no past and no future ... coming in and out unknown, in the present secret wonder. Pausing for a moment near the smeary dimly-lit marble slab, the letter out of sight, she held this consciousness. There was no sound in the house ... its huge high thick walls held all the lodgers secure and apart, fixed in richly enclosed rooms in the heart of London; secure from all the world that was not London, flying through space, swinging along on a planet spread with continents—Londoners. Alma's handwriting, the same as it had been at school, only a little larger and firmer, broke into that. Of course Alma had answered the post card ... it had been an impulse, a cry of triumph after years of groping about. But it was like pulling a string. Silly. And now this had happened. But it was only a touch, only a finger laid on the secret hall table that no one had seen. The letter need not be answered. Out of sight it seemed to have gone away ... destroyed unopened it would be as if it had never come and everything would be as before.... Enough, more than enough without writing to Alma. An evening-paper boy was shouting raucously in the distance. The letter-box brought his voice into the hall as he passed the door. Miriam moved on up the many flights.

Upstairs, she found herself eagerly tearing open the letter.... "I've just heard from an old schoolfellow," she heard herself saying to the girls in Kennett Street. There was something exciting in the letter ... at the end "Alma Wilson (officially Mrs G. Wilson)" ... strange people in the room ... Alma amongst them; looking out from amongst dreadfulness. *Married.* She had gone in amongst the crowd already—for ever. How clever of her ... deceitful ... that little spark of Alma in her must have been deceitful ... sly, at some moment. Alma's eyes glanced at her with a new, more preoccupied and covered look ... she used to go sometimes to theatres with large parties of people with money and the usual dresses who never thought anything about anything ... perhaps that was part of the reason, perhaps Alma was more that than she had thought ... marrying in the sort of way she went to theatre-parties—clever. The letter was full of excitement ... Alma leaping up from her marriage and clutching at her ... not really married: dancing to some tune in some usual way like all those women and jumping up in a way that fizzled and could not be kept up....

"You dear old thing! ... fell out of the sky this morning ... to fill pages with 'you dear old thing!' ... see you at *once*! *Immediately*! ... come up to town and meet you some sequestered tea-shop ... our ancient heads together ... tell you all that has happened to me since those days ... next Thursday ... let you know how really really rejoiced I am ... break the very elderly fact that I am married ... but that makes no difference...." That would not be so bad—seeing Alma alone in a tea-shop in the West End; in a part of the new life, that would be all right; nothing need happen, nothing would be touched, "all I have had the temerity to do ..." what did that mean?

Unpinning the buckram-stiffened[1] black velvet band from her neck, she felt again with a rush of joy that her day was beginning and moved eagerly about amongst the strange angles and shadows of her room, the rich day all about her. Somebody had put up her little varnished oak bookshelf just in the right place, the lower shelf in a line with the little mantelpiece. When the gas bracket was swung out from the wall, the naked flame shone on the backs of the indiscriminately arranged books ... the calf-bound Shakespeare could be read now comfortably in the immense fresh dark night under the gas flame; the Pernes'[2] memorial edition of Tennyson[3].... She washed her face and hands in hard cold water at the little rickety washstand, yellow-grained, rich, beloved, drying them on the thin holey face towel hurriedly. Lying neatly folded amongst the confusion of oddments in a top drawer was her lace tie. Holding it out to its full length she spread it against her neck, crossed the ends at the back bringing them back round her neck to spread in a narrow flat plastron to her waist, kept in place by a brooch at the top and a pin fastened invisibly half-way down. Her face shone fresh and young above the creamy lace ... the tie was still fairly new and crisp ... when it had to be washed it would be limp ... but it would go on some time just for evenings transforming her harsh

---

1 Buckram is a stiff cotton used to stiffen clothes.
2 In *Backwater* (*Pilgrimage* vol. 2), Miriam works at a boarding school run by the three Perne sisters.
3 Alfred, Lord Tennyson (1809–92), England's Poet Laureate 1850–92. The "memorial edition" mentioned here would have been a deluxe edition of Tennyson's work issued in commemoration of his death in 1892. Tennyson, the longest-serving Poet Laureate, became closely associated with British ascendancy in the nineteenth century.

black John Noble[1] half-guinea costume into evening dress. For some moments she contemplated its pleasant continuous pattern and the way the rounded patterned ends fell just below the belt....

The top-floor bell would not ring. After some hesitation, Miriam rang the house bell. The door was opened by a woman in a silk petticoat and a dressing jacket. Miriam gazed dumbly into large clear blue eyes gazing at her from a large clean clear fresh face, feathered with little soft natural curls, cut out sharply against the dark passage.

"Are you for the top?" inquired the woman in a smooth serene sleepy voice.

"Yes," announced Miriam eagerly coming in and closing the door, her ears straining to catch the placid words spoken by the woman as she disappeared softly into a softly-lit room. She went tremulously up the dark stairs into a thick stale odour of rancid fried grease and on towards a light that glimmered from the topmost short flight of steep uncarpeted winding stairs. "They're in," said her thoughts with a quick warm leap. "Hallo," she asserted, ascending the stairs.

"Hallo," came in response a quick challenging voice ... a soft clear reed-like happy ring that Miriam felt to her knees while her happy feet stumbled on.

"Is that the Henderson?"

"It's me," said Miriam, emerging on a tiny landing and going through the open door of a low-ceiled lamplit room. "It's me, it's me," she repeated from the middle of the floor. An eager face was turned towards her from a thicket of soft dull wavy hair. She gazed. The small slippered feet planted firmly high up against the lintel,[2] the sweep of the red dressing-gown, the black patch of the Mudie book with its yellow label, the small ringed hand upon it, the outflung arm and hand, the little wreath of smoke about the end of the freshly lit cigarette, the cup of coffee on the little table under the lamp, the dim shapes about the room lit by the flickering blaze....

Miriam smiled into the smiling steel blue of the eyes turned

---

1 A line of off-the-rack women's clothing marketed as suitable for outdoors activities, general wear, and sports (i.e., not as evening wear). See
Amy de la Haye and Elizabeth Wilson, eds., *Defining Dress. Dress as
Object, Meaning, and Identity* (Manchester: Manchester UP, 1999), p. 44.
2 Doorway.

towards her, and waited smiling for the silver reed of tone to break again. "I'm so glad you've come. I wanted you. Sit down and shut the door, my child.... I don't mind which you do first, but—do—them—both," she tinkled, stretching luxuriously and bringing her feet to the ground with a swing.

Miriam closed the door. "Can I take off my things?"

"Of course, child ... take them all off; you know I admire you most draped in a towel."

"I've got such awful feet," said Miriam hugging the compliment as she dropped her things in a distant arm-chair.

"It's not your feet, it's your extraordinary shoes."

"M'm."

"How beautiful you look. You put on ties better than any one I know. I wish I could wear things draped round my neck."

Miriam sat down in the opposite wicker chair.

"Isn't it cold?—my feet are freezing; it's raining."

"Take off your shoes."

Miriam got off her shoes and propped them in the fender to dry.

"What is that book?"

"Eden Phillpotts's *Children of the Mist*,"[1] fluted the voice reverently. "Read it?"

"No," said Miriam expectantly.

The eager face turned to an eager profile with eyes brooding into the fire. "He's so wonderful," mused the voice and Miriam watched eagerly. Mag read books—for their own sake; and could judge them and compare them with other books by the same author ... but all this wonderful knowledge made her seem wistful; knowing all about books and plays and strangely wistful and regretful; the things that made her eyes blaze and made her talk reverently, or in indignant defence, always seemed sad in the end ... wistful hero worship ... raving about certain writers and actors as if she did not know they were people.

"He's so wonderful," went on the voice with its perpetual modulations, "he gets all the atmosphere of the west country—perfectly. You *live* there while you're reading him."

With a little chill sense of Mag in this wonderful room alone, living in the west country and herself coming in as an interruption, Miriam noted the name of the novelist in her mind ... there was something about it, she knew she would not forget it; soft

---

1   Eden Phillpotts's (1862-1960) novel *Children of the Mist* (1898) is one of many about England's Dartmoor region.

and numb with a slight clatter and hiss at the end, a rain-storm, the atmosphere of Devonshire[1] and the mill-wheel.

"Devonshire people are all consumptive,"[2] she said decisively.

"Are they?"

"Yes, it's the mild damp air. They have lovely complexions; like the Irish. There must be any amount of consumption in Ireland."

"I suppose there is."

Miriam sat silent and still watching Mag's movements as she sipped and puffed, so strangely easy and so strangely wistful in her wonderful rich Bloomsbury[3] life—and waiting for her next remark.

"You look very happy to-night, child; what have you been doing?"

"Nothing."

"You look as happy as a bird."

"Are birds happy?"

"Of *course* birds are happy."

"Well—they prey on each other—and they're often frightened."

"How wise we are."

Brisk steps sounded on the little stairs.

"Tell me what you have been doing."

"Oh, I don't know. Weird things have been happening.... Oh, weird things."

"Tell your aunt at once." Mag gathered herself together as the brisk footsteps came into the room. "Hoh," said a strong resonant voice, "it's the Henderson. I thought as much."

"Yes. Doesn't she look pretty?"

"Yes—she has a beautiful lace tie."

"I wish I could wear things like that round my neck, don't you, von Bohlen?"

"I *do*. She can stick *anything* round her neck—and look nice."

"Anything; a garter or a—a *kipper*...."[4]

"Don't be so cracked."

---

1 English country district, located in the south.
2 That is, tending towards tubercular sclerosis, a potentially fatal lung disease.
3 A London neighbourhood, noted for the many famous authors and thinkers who lived and congregated there, such as Virginia Woolf (1882-1941), Charles Darwin (1809-82), Charles Dickens (1812-70), John Maynard Keynes (1883-1946), Vanessa Bell (1879-1961), Vera Brittain (1893-1970), and J.M. Barrie (1860-1937).
4 A whole herring fish that has been gutted, split lengthwise, salted, and smoked; often eaten for breakfast.

"She says weird things have been happening to her. I say, I didn't make any coffee for you and the spirit lamp[1] wants filling."

"Damn you—Schweinhund."[2]

Miriam had been gazing at the strong square figure in the short round fur-lined cloak and sweeping velvet hat, the firm decisive movements, and imagining the delicate pointed high-heeled shoes. Presently those things would be off and the door closed on the three of them.

"There's some Bass."[3]

"I'm going to have some suppe.[4] Have some suppe, Henderson."

"Non, merci."[5]

"She's proud. Bring her some. What did you have for supper, child?"

"Oh, we had an enormous lunch. They'd had a dinner-party."

"What did you have for supper?"

"Oh, lots of things."

"Bring her some suppe. I'm not sure I won't have a basin myself."

"All right. I'll put some on." The brisk steps went off and a voice hummed in and out of the other rooms.

Watching Mag stirring the fire, giving a last pull at her cigarette end and pushing back the hair from her face ... silent and old and ravaged, and young and animated and powerful, Miriam blushed and beamed silently at her reiterated demands for an account of herself.

"I say, I saw an extraordinary woman downstairs."

Mag turned sharply and put down the poker.

"Yes?"

"In a petticoat."[6]

"Frederika Elizabeth! She's seen the Pierson!"

"Hoh! Has she?" The brisk footsteps approached and the door was closed. The dimly shining mysteries of the room moved about Miriam, the outside darkness flowing up to the windows

---

1   See p. 66, note 4.

2   German: filthy swine.

3   A popular brand of ale.

4   German: soup.

5   French: No, thank you.

6   An article of women's clothing designed to wear under a skirt or dress. It is an undergarment, not meant to be worn on its own. The woman in question here has essentially gone out in public in her underwear.

moved away as the tall dressing-gowned figure lowered the thin, drab, loosely rattling Venetian blinds; the light seemed to go up and distant objects became more visible; the crowded bookshelf, the dark littered table under it, the empty table pushed against the wall near the window—the bamboo bookshelf between the windows above a square mystery draped to the ground with a table cover—the little sofa behind Mag's chair, the little pictures, cattle gazing out across a bridge of snow, cattish complacent sweepy women—Albert ...? Moore?—the framed photographs of Dickens[1] and Irving,[2] the litter on the serge-draped mantelpiece in front of the mirror of the bamboo overmantel, silver candlesticks, photographs of German women and Canon Wilberforce[3] ... all the riches of comfortable life.

"You are late."

"Yes, I am fearfully late."

"Why are you late, Frederika Elizabeth von Bohlen?"

The powerful rounded square figure was in the leather armchair opposite the blaze, strongly moulded brown-knickered, black-stockinged legs comfortably crossed, stuck firmly out between the heavy soft folds of a grey flannel dressing gown. The shoes had gone, grey woollen bedroom slippers blurred all but the shapely small ankles. Mag was lighting another cigarette, von Bohlen was not doing needlework, the room settled suddenly to its best rich exciting blur.

"To-night I must smoke or die."

"*Must* you, my dear."

"Why."

"To-*nate*—a, ay must smoke—a, or *daye*."

"Es ist bestimmt, in Gottes Rath."[4]

"Tell us what you think of the Pierson, child."

"She was awfully nice. Is it your landlady?"

"Yes—isn't she nice? We think she's extraordinary—all things considered. You know we hadn't the least idea what she was, when we came here."

"What is she?"

---

1 Charles Dickens (1812-70), English author.
2 Henry Irving (1838-1905), English actor.
3 Albert Basil Orme Wilberforce (1841-1916), Anglican priest and author, Chaplain of the House of Commons 1896.
4 German: It is decided, according to God's will. This is the title of a popular hymn, set to music by a number of different composers, most famously Felix Mendelssohn in 1839.

"Well—er—you embarrass me, child, how shall we put it to her, Jan?"

"D'you mean to say she's improper?"[1]

"Yes—she's improper. We hadn't the faintest notion of it when we came."

"How extraordinary."

"It is extraordinary. We're living in an improper house—the whole street's improper, we're discovering."

"How absolutely awful."

"*Now* we know why Mother Cosway hinted, when we left her to come here, that we wanted to be free for devil's mirth."

"How did you find out?"

"Henriette told us; you see she works for the Pierson."

"What did she tell you?"

"Well—she told us."

"Six," laughed Mag, quoting towards Jan.

"Six," trumpeted Jan, "and if not six, seven."

They both laughed.

"In one evening," trumpeted Jan.

"I say, are you going to leave?" The thought of the improper street was terrible and horrible; but they might go right away to some other part of London. Mag answered instantly, but the interval had seemed long and Miriam was cold with anxiety.

"No; we don't see why we should."

Miriam gazed dumbly from one to the other, finding herself admiring and wondering more than ever at their independence and strength.

"You see the woman's so absolutely self-respecting."

"Much more so than we are!"

"Out of doors she's a model of decorum and good style."

"We're ashamed when we meet her."

"We are. We skip into the gutter."

"We babble and slink!"

"Indoors she's a perfect landlady. She's been awfully good to us."

"A perfect brick!"

"She doesn't drink; she's most exquisitely clean. There's nothing whatever to—to indicate the er—nature of her profession."

"Except that she sits at the window."

"But she does not tire her hair and look forth."

"Or fifth."

---

1 Euphemistic allusion to a prostitute.

"*Fool.*"

Miriam giggled.

"Really, Miriam, she *is* rather wonderful, you know. We like her."

"Henriette is devoted to her."

"And so apparently is her husband."

"Her *husband?*"

"Yes—she has a husband—he appears at rare intervals—and a little girl at boarding school. She goes to see her, but the child never comes here. She tells us quite frankly that she wants to keep her out of harm's way."

"How amazing!"

"Yes, she's extraordinary. She's Eurasian.[1] She was born in India."

"That accounts for a good deal. Eurasians are awful; they've got all the faults of both sides."

"East is East and West is West and never the two shall meet."[2]

"Well, we like her."

"So we have decided to ignore her little peccadillos."[3]

"I don't see that it's our business. Frankly I can't see that it has anything whatever to do with us. Do you?"

"Well, I don't know; I don't suppose it has really."

"What would you do in our place?"

"I don't know ... I don't believe I should have found out."

"I don't believe you would; but if you had?"

"I think I should have been awfully scared."

"You would have been afraid that the sixth——"

"Or the seventh——"

"Might have wandered upstairs."

"No; I mean the whole idea."

"Oh; the idea...."

"London, my dear Miriam, is full of ideas."

"I will go and get the suppe."

Jan rose; her bright head and grey shoulders went up above the lamplight, darkening to steady massive outlines, strongly moving as she padded and fluttered briskly out of the room.

The rich blur of the room, free of the troubling talk and the swift conversational movements of the two, lifted and was touched with a faint grey, a suggestion of dawn or twilight, as if coming

---

1 Of mixed parentage, with one English parent and one Indian parent.

2 A line from Rudyard Kipling's "Ballad of East and West." See p. 98, note 3.

3 A minor sin or offence.

from the hidden windows. Mag sat motionless in her chair, gazing into the fire.

"... Wise and happy infant, I want to ask your opinion."

Miriam roused herself and glanced steadily across. The outlines of things grew sharp. She could imagine the room in daylight and felt a faint sharp sinking; hungry.

"I'm going to state you a case. I think you have an extraordinarily sharp sense of right and wrong."

"Oh, *no*."

"You have an extraordinarily sharp sense of right and wrong. Imagine a woman. Can you imagine a woman?"

"Go on."

"Imagine a woman engaged to a man. Imagine her allowing—another man—to kiss her."

Miriam sat thinking. She imagined the two, the snatched caress, the other man alone and unconscious.

"Would you call that treachery to the other person?"

"It would depend upon which she liked best."

"That's just the difficulty."

"*Oh!* That's awful."

"Don't you think a kiss, just a kiss—might be—well—neither here nor there?"

"Well, if it's nothing, there's nothing in the whole thing. If there *is* anything—you can't talk about just kisses."

"Dreadful Miriam."

"Do you believe in blunted sensibilities?" How funny that Mag should have led up to that new phrase ... but this was a case.

"You mean——"

"Whether if a sensibility is blunted it can ever grow sharp again."

"No. I suppose that's it. How can it?"

"I don't know. I'm not sure. It's a perfectly awful idea, I think."

"It is awful—because we are all blunting our sensibilities all the time—are we not?"

"That's just it—whether we ought."

"Does one always know?"

"Don't you think so? There's a feeling. Yes I think one always knows."

"Suppe, children."

Miriam took her bowl with eager embarrassment ... the sugar-basin, the pudding basin and the slop bowl together on a tray, the quickly produced soup—the wonderful rich life the girls lived in their glowing rooms—each room with a different glow.... Jan's narrow green clean, room, with its suite and hair brushes and cosmetics and pictures of Christ, Mag's crowded shadowy little square, its litter and its many photographs, their eiderdowns[1] and baths and hot-water bottles; the kitchen alive with eyes and foreheads—musicians, artists, philosophers pasted on the walls ... why? Why? ... Jan with wonderful easy knowledge of the world's great people ... and strange curious intimate liking for them ... the sad separate effect of all those engraved faces ... the perfectly beautiful blur they made all together in patches on the walls ... the sitting-room, Mag, nearly all Mag, except the photographs on the mantelpiece ... the sight of the rooms from the top of the stairs ... her thoughts folded down; they were not going away; not; that was certain.

"I say, I can't go on for ever eating your soup."

"*Drink* it then for a change, my child."

"No, but really."

"This is special soup; there is a charge; one guinea[2] a basin."

"Use of room, two guineas."

"Intellectual conversation——"

"One-and-eleven-three."

Miriam flung out delighted admiring glances and laughed unrestrainedly. Mag's look saying "it does not take much to keep the child amused," took nothing from her mirthful joy. Their wit, or was it humour?—always brought the same happy shock ... they were so funny; there was a secret in it.

"It's awfully good soup."

"Desiccated——"

"A penny a packet."

"Thickened with pea flour——"

"Twopence a packet."

"Was she your favourite schoolfellow?"

Miriam's jarred mind worked eagerly. The girls thought this was a revival of some great school friendship ... they would not be in the least jealous; they were curious and interested, but they must understand ... they must realize that Alma was wonderful ... something to be proud of ... in the strange difficult scientific way; something they knew hardly anything about, Mag almost not at all, and Jan only in a general way in her neat wide education; but not in Alma's way of being rigid and reverent and personally

---

1 A comforter filled with duck down feathers.

2 See p. 79, note 6.

interested about, so that every other way of looking at things made her angry. But they must understand, they must in some quite certain way be quickly made to understand at the same time that she was outside ... an extra ... a curious bright distant resource, nothing whatever to do with the wonderful present ... the London life was sacred and secret, away from everything else in the world. It would disappear if one had ties outside ... anything besides the things of holidays and week-ends that they all three had, and brought back from outside to talk about. It would be easy and exciting to meet Alma if that were clear, and to come back and tell the girls about it.

"I don't think so."

They both looked up, stirring in their quick way, and waited.

Miriam moved her head uneasily. It was painful. They were using a sort of language ... that was the trouble ... your favourite flower ... your favourite colour ... it was just the sort of pain that came in trying to fill up confession albums. This bit of conversation would be at an end presently. Her anger would shut it up, and they would put it away without understanding, and Mag would go on to something else.

"No—I don't think she was. She was very small and pretty—petite. She had the most wonderful, limpid eyes."

Mag was sitting forward, with her elbows on her knees and her little clasped hands sticking out into the air. A comfortable tinkling chuckle shook her shoulders. Miriam tugged and wrenched.

"I don't think she cared for me, really ... she was an only child."

Mag's chuckle pealed up into a little festoon of clear laughter.

"She doesn't care for you because—she's—an—only—child," she shook out.

"One of the sheltered ones." Jan returned to her chiffon pleats. She was making conversation. She did not care how much or how little Alma mattered.

"She's sheltered now, anyhow—she's married."

"Oh—she's married...."

"She's married, is she?"

Polite tones ... they were not a bit surprised ... both faces looked calm, and abstracted. The room was dark and clear in the cold entanglement. It must be got over now, as if she had not mentioned Alma. She felt for her packet of cigarettes with an uneasy face, watching Mag's firm movements as she rearranged herself and her dressing-gown in her chair.

"How old is she?"

"About my age."

"Oh—about nine; that's early to begin the sheltered life."

"You can't begin the sheltered life too early; if you are going to begin it at all."

"Why begin it at all, Jan?"

"Well, my dear little Miriam, I think there is a good deal to be said for the sheltered life."

"Yes"—Mag settled more deeply into her chair, burrowing with her shoulders and crossing her knees with a fling—"and if you don't begin it jolly early it's too late to begin it at all...."

Then Mag meant to stay always as she was ... oh, good, good ... with several people interested in her ... what a curious worry her engagement must be ... irrelevant ... and with her ideas of loyalty. "Don't you think soh?" Irritating—why did she do it?—what was it?—not a provincialism—some kind of affectation as if she were on the stage. It sounded brisk and important—soh—as if her thoughts had gone on and she was making conversation with her lips. Why not let them, and drop it ... there was something waiting, always something waiting just outside the nag of conversation.

"I can't imagine anything more awful than what you call the sheltered life," said Miriam with a little pain in her forehead. Perhaps they would laugh and that would finish it and something would begin.

"For us, yes. Imagine either of us coming down to it in the morning; the regular breakfast table, the steaming coffee, the dashes of rishers ... dishers of rashes[1] I mean, the eggs...."

"You are alluding, I presume, to the beggs and acon."

"Precisely. We should die."

"Of boredom."

"Imagine not being able to turn up on Sunday morning in your knickers, with your hair down."

"I love Sundays. That first cigarette over the *Referee*[2]——"

"Is like nothing on earth."

"Or in heaven."

"Well, or in heaven."

---

1   Slices of bacon. This mix up with the letters could be regarded as parapraxis, or a "Freudian Slip," first described by psychologist Sigmund Freud (1856-1939) in *The Psychopathology of Everyday Life* (1901). Freud felt these types of minor errors in daily speech and practices occurred because of repressed thoughts and memories.

2   See p. 67, note 1.

"The first cigarette anyhow, with or without the *Referee*. It's just pure absolute bliss, that first bit of Sunday morning; complete well-being and happiness."

"While the sheltered people are flushed with breakfast-table talk——"

"Or awkward silences."

"The deep damned silence of disillusionment."

"And thinking about getting ready for church."

"The men smoke."

"Stealthily and sleepily in arm-chairs, like cats—ever seen a cat smoke?—like cats—with the wife or somebody they are tired of talking to, on the doormat—as it were—tentatively, I speak *tentatively* ... in a dead-alley—Dedale—Dedalus[1]—coming into the room any minute, in Sunday clothes——"

"To stand on the hearthrug."

"No, hanging about the room. If there's any hearthrug standing it's the men who do it, smoking blissfully alone, and trying to look weary and wise and important if any one comes in."

"Like Cabinet ministers?"

"Yes; when they are really—er——"

"Cabinets."

"Footstools; office stools; you never saw a sheltered woman venture on to the hearthrug, except for a second if she's short-sighted, to look at the clock." Miriam sprang to the hearthrug and waved her cigarette. "Con-fu-sion to the sheltered life!" The vast open of London swung, welcoming, before her eyes.

"Hoch! Hoch!"

"Banzai!"[2]

"We certainly have our compensations."

"Com-pen-*sa*-tions?"

---

1   This string of words reflects the practice of "free association," a technique devised by Sigmund Freud and used in psychoanalysis to unlock repressed memories. Dedalus is a Greek mythological figure, his name meaning "cunning worker." Richardson could also be alluding to the protagonist of James Joyce's *A Portrait of the Artist as a Young Man*, Stephen Dedalus. Although Joyce wrote well after this novel is set, *Portrait* was published in 1914-15, the same year as Richardson's *Pointed Roofs* (1915), the first volume of *Pilgrimage*. The two were often cited together as pioneers of the modern novel.

2   "Hoch" (German) is an "exclamation of loyal approval" deriving from "hoch lebe," or "long live." "Banzai" (Japanese) translates as "ten thousand years"; it is a conventional cheer or exclamation either for greeting the Emperor or going into battle (*OED*).

"Well—for all the things we have to give up."

"What things?"

"The things that belong to us. To our youth. Tennis, dancing—er, irresponsibility in general...."

"I've never once thought about any of those things; never once since I came to town," said Miriam grappling with little anxious pangs that assailed her suddenly; dimly seeing the light on garden trees, hearing distant shouts, the sound of rowlocks, the lapping of water against smoothing swinging sculls. But all that life meant people, daily association with sheltered women and complacent abominable men, there half the time and half the time away on their own affairs which gave them a sort of mean advantage, and money. There was nothing really to regret. It was different for Mag. She did not mind ordinary women. Did not know the difference; or men.

"Yes, but anyhow. If we were in the sheltered life we should either have done with that sort of thing and be married—or still keeping it up and anxious about not being married. Besides anyhow; think of the awful *people*."

"Intolerant child."

"Isn't she intolerant? What a good thing you met us."

"Yes of course; but I'm not intolerant. And look here. Heaps of those women envy us. They envy us our freedom. What we're having is wanderyahre;[1] the next best thing to wanderyahre."

"Women don't want wanderyahre."

"I do, Jan."

"So do I. I think the child's quite right there. Freedom is life. We may be slaves all day and guttersnipes all the rest of the time but, ach Gott,[2] we are free."

"What a perfectly extraordinary idea."

"I know. But I don't see how you can get away from it," mused Miriam, dreamily holding out against Jan's absorbed sewing and avoiding for a moment Mag's incredulously speculative eyes; "if it's true," she went on, the rich blur of the warm room becoming, as she sent out her voice evenly, thinking eagerly on, a cool clear even daylight, "that everything that can possibly happen does happen, then there must be, somewhere in the universe, every possible kind of variation of us and this room."

---

1 German: Wanderjahre, the journeyman years, the German tradition of travelling after completing an apprenticeship to improve one's skills.

2 German: oh God.

"D'you mean to say," gurgled Mag with a fling of her knick-ered leg and an argumentative movement of the hand that hung loosely dangling a cigarette over the fireside arm of the chair, "that there are millions of rooms exactly like this each with one thing different—say the stem of one narcissus broken instead of whole, for instance?"

"My dear Miriam, infinitude couldn't hold them."

"Infinitude can hold anything—of course I can see the impos-sibility of a single world holding all the possible variations of everything at once—but what I mean is that I can think it, and there must be something corresponding to it in life—anything that the mind can conceive is realized, somehow, all possibilities must come about, that's what I mean, I think."

"You mean you can see, as it were in space, millions of little rooms—a little different," choked Mag.

"Yes, I can—quite distinctly—solid—no end to them."

"I think it's a perfectly horrible idea," stated Jan complacently.

"It isn't—I love it and it's true ... you go on and on and on, filling space."

"Then space is solid."

"It is solid. People who talk of empty space don't think space is more solid than a wall ... yes ... more solid than a diamond—girls, I'm sure."

"Space is full of glorious stars...."

"Yes, I know, but that's such a tiny bit of it...."

"Millions and trillions of miles."

"Those are only words. Everything is words."

"Well, you *must* use words."

"You ought not to think in words. I mean—you can think in your brain, by imagining yourself going on and on through it, endless space."

"You can't grasp space with your mind."

"You don't GRASP it. You go through it."

"I see what you mean. To me it is a fearful idea. Like eternal punishment."

"There's no such thing as eternal punishment. The idea is too silly. It makes God a failure and a fool. It's a man's idea. The men who take the hearthrug. Sitting on a throne judging everybody and passing sentence, is a thing a man would do."

"But humanity is wicked."

"Then God is. You can't separate God and humanity, and that includes women who don't really believe any of those things."

"*But.* Look at the churches. Look at women and the parsons."

"Women like ritual and things and they like parsons, *some* parsons, because they are like women, penetrable to light, as Wilberforce said the other day, and understand women better than most men do."

"Miriam, are you a pantheist?"[1]

"The earth, the sea, and the sky——"

"The sun, the moon, and the stars——"

"Are not these, O soul——"

"That's the Higher Pantheism."

"Nearer is he than breathing, closer than hands and feet.[2] It doesn't matter what you call it."

"If you don't accept eternal punishment, there can't be eternal happiness."

"Oh, punishment, happiness; tweedledum, tweedledee."

"Well—look here, there's remorse. That's deathless. It must be. If you feel remorseful about anything, the feeling must last as long as you remember the thing."

"Remorse is real enough. I know what you mean. But it may be short-sightedness. Not seeing all round a thing. Is that Tomlinson?[3] Or it may be cleansing you. If it were *complete*, Mag, it would *kill* you outright. I can believe that. I can believe in annihilation. I am prepared for it. I can't think why it doesn't happen to me. That's just it."

"I should like to be annihilated."

"Shut up, von Bohlen; you wouldn't. But look here, Miriam child, do you mean to say you think that as long as there is something that keeps on and on, fighting its way on in spite of everything, one has, well, a right to exist?"

"Well, that may be the survival of the fittest, which doesn't mean the ethically fittest as Huxley had to admit.[4] We kill the eth-

---

1 Pantheism is the belief that everything in the universe is part of God, thus there is no God separate from the world and the self.

2 The lines Mag and Jan are quoting are from Alfred, Lord Tennyson's poem "The Higher Pantheism" (1869).

3 Possibly Charles Tomlinson (1808-97), an educator, scientist, and writer. Educated as a mechanical engineer, Tomlinson made original contributions to the study of surface tension of liquids before turning to literature, holding the Dante lectureship at University College London 1878-80.

4 The theory of the "survival of the fittest" derives from Charles Darwin's *On the Origin of Species* (1859), though the phrase was coined by British philosopher and biologist Herbert Spencer (1820-1930) while reading Darwin. The theory, which Darwin actually called "natural *(continued)*

ically fittest at present. We killed Christ. They go to heaven. All of us who survive, have things to learn down here in hell. Perhaps this is hell. There seems something, ahead."

"Ourselves. Rising on the ashes of our dead selves. Lord, it's midnight——"

The chill of the outside night, solitude and her cold empty room....

"I'm going to bed."

"So am I. We shall be in bed, Miriam, five minutes after you have gone."

Jan went off for the hot-water bottles.

"All right, I'm going——" Miriam bent for her shoes. The soles were dry, scorching; they scorched her feet as she forced on the shoes; one sole cracked across as she put her foot to the ground ... she braced the muscles of her face and said nothing. It must be forgotten before she left the room that they were nearly new and her only pair; two horrid ideas, nagging and keeping things away.

Outside in the air, daylight grew strong and clear in Miriam's mind. Patches of day came in a bright sheen from the moonlit puddles, distributed over the square. She crossed the road to the narrow pathway shadowed by the trees that ran round the long oblong enclosure. From this dark pathway the brightness of the wet moonlit roadway was brighter, and she could see façades that caught the moonlight. There was something trying to worry her, some little thing that did not matter at all, but that some part of her had put away to worry over and was now wanting to consider. Mag's affairs ... no, she had decided about that. It might be true about blunted sensibilities; but she had meant for some reason to let that other man kiss her, and people never ask advice until they have made up their minds what they are going to do, and Mag was Mag quite apart from anything that might happen. She would still be Mag if she were old ... or mad. That was a firm settled real thing, real and absolute in the daylight of the moonlit square. She wandered slowly on humming a tune; every inch of the way would be lovely. The figure of a man in an overcoat and

---

selection," is that the strongest of a species adapt to their environments and survive, whereas the weakest die out, and that is the basis for evolution. The Huxley referred to here is English biologist Thomas Henry Huxley (1825-95), who advocated for the theory of evolution. In 1893, he published *Evolution and Ethics*, which deals with the moral development of humankind.

a bowler hat loomed towards her on the narrow pathway and stopped. The man raised his hat, and his face showed smiling, with the moonlight on it. Miriam had a moment's fear; but the man's attitude was deprecating and there was her song; it was partly her own fault. But why, why ... fierce anger at the recurrence of this kind of occurrence seized her. She wanted him out of the way and wanted him to know how angry she was at the interruption.

"Well," she snapped angrily, coming to a standstill in the moonlit gap.

"Oh," said the man a little breathlessly in a lame broken tone, "I thought you were going this way."

"So I am," retorted Miriam in a loud angry shaking tone, "obviously."

The man stepped quickly into the gutter and walked quickly away across the road. St Pancras church chimed the quarter.

Miriam marched angrily forward with shaking limbs that steadied themselves very quickly ... the night had become suddenly cold; bitter and penetrating; a north-east wind, of course. It was frightfully cold, after the warm room; the square was bleak and endless; the many façades were too far off to keep the wind away; the pavement was very cold under her right foot; that was it; the broken sole was the worry that had been trying to come up; she could walk with it; it would not matter if the weather kept dry ... an upright gait, hurrying quickly away across the moonlit sheen; just the one she had summoned up anger and courage to challenge, was not so bad as the others ... they were not so bad; that was not it; it was the way they got in the way ... figures of men, dark, in dark clothes, presenting themselves, calling attention to themselves and the way they saw things, mean and suggestive, always just when things were loveliest. Couldn't the man see the look of the square and the moonlight? ... that afternoon at Hyde Park Corner ... just when everything flashed out after the rain ... the sudden words close to her ear ... my beauty ... my sweet ... you sweet girl ... the puffy pale old face, the puffs under the, sharp brown eyes. A strange ... *conviction* in the trembling old voice ... it was deliberate; a sort of statement; done on purpose, something chosen that would please most. It was like the conviction and statement there had been in Bob Greville's voice. Old men seemed to have some sort of understanding of things. If only they would talk about other things with the same conviction as there was in their tone when they said those personal things. But the things they said were worldly—generalizations, like the things one read in books that tired you out with trying to find the answer, and made books so awful ... things that might look true about everybody at some time or other, and were not really true about anybody—when you knew them. But people liked those things and thought them clever and smiled about them. All the things the old men said about life and themselves and other people, about everything but oneself, were sad; disappointed and sad with a glint of far-off youth in their faces as they said them ... something moving in the distance behind the blue of their eyes.... "Make the best of your youth, my dear, before it flies."[1] If it all ended in sadness and envy of youth, life was simply a silly trick. *Life* could not be a silly trick. Life cannot be a silly trick. That is the simple truth ... a certainty. Whatever happens, whatever things look like, life is not a trick.

Miriam began singing again when she felt herself in her own street, clear and empty in the moonlight. The north wind blew down it unobstructed and she was shivering and singing ... "spring is *co*-ming a-and the *swa*-llows—have come *back* to te-ell me *so*."[2] Spring could not be far off. At this moment in the dark twilight behind the thick north wind, the squares were green.

Her song, restrained on the doorstep and while she felt her already well-known way in almost insupportable happiness through the unlit hall and through the moonlight up the seventy-five stairs, broke out again when her room was reached and her door shut; the two other doors had stood open showing empty moonlit spaces. She was still alone and unheard on the top floor. Her room was almost warm after the outside cold. The row of attic and fourth-floor windows visible from her open lattice were in darkness, or burnished blue with moonlight. Warm blue moonlight gleamed along the leads sloping down to her ink-black parapet. The room was white and blue lit, with a sweet morning of moonlight. She had a momentary impulse towards prayer, and glanced at the bed. To get so far and cast herself on her knees and hide her face in her hands against the counterpane, the bones behind the softness of her hands meeting the funny familiar round shape of her face, the dusty smell of the counterpane coming up, her face praying to her hands, her hands praying to

---

1   This line articulates the philosophy of *carpe diem* (Latin: seize the day), which urges taking action in the present, particularly while one is young.

2   From the popular song "The Swallows," by British composer Frederick H. Cowen (1852-1935).

her face, both throbbing separately with their secret, would drive something away. Something that was so close in everything in the room, so pouring in at the window that she could scarcely move from where she stood. She flung herself more deeply into her song and passed through the fresh buoyant singing air to light the gas. The room turned to its bright evening brown. *Prayer.* Being so weighed down and free with happiness was the time ... sacrifice ... the evening *sacrifice* of praise and prayer. That is what that means. To toss all the joys and happiness away and know that you are happy and free without anything. That you cannot escape being happy and free. It always comes.

Why am I so happy and free? she wondered, with tears in her eyes. Why? Why do lovely things and people go on happening? To *own* that something in you had no right. But not crouching on your knees ... standing and singing till everything split with your joy and let you through into the white white brightness.

To *see* the earth whirling slowly round, coloured, its waters catching the light. She stood in the middle of the floor hurriedly discarding her clothes. They were old and worn, friendly and alive with the fresh strength of her body. Other clothes would be got somehow; just by going on and working ... there's so much—eternally. It's stupendous. I've no right to be in it; but I'm in. Someone means me to be in. *I* can't help it. Fancy people being alive. You would think every one would go mad. She found herself in bed, sitting up in her flannellette dressing jacket. The stagnant air beneath the sharp downward slope of the ceiling was warmed by the gas. The gaslight glared beautifully over her shoulder down on to the page....

All that has been said and known in the world is in *language*, in words; all we know of Christ is in Jewish words;[1] all the dogmas of religion are words; the meanings of words change with people's thoughts. Then no one *knows* anything for certain. Everything depends upon the way a thing is put, and that is a question of some particular civilization. Culture comes through literature, which is a half-truth. People who are not cultured are isolated in barbaric darkness. The Greeks were cultured; but they are barbarians ... why? Whether you agree or not, language is the

---

1 Jesus Christ was Jewish, and many scholars maintain that the original language of the New Testament, the part of the Bible that recounts the story of Jesus, was Hebrew.

only way of expressing anything and it dims everything. So the Bible is not true; it is a culture. Religion is wrong in making word-dogmas out of it. Christ was something. But Christianity which calls Him divine and so on, is false. It clings to words which get more and more wrong ... then there's nothing to be afraid of and nothing to be quite sure of rejoicing about. The Christians are irritating and frightened. The man with side-whiskers understands something. But——

CHAPTER V

Then all these years they might have been going sometimes to those lectures. Pater talking about them—telling about old Rayleigh[1] and old Kelvin[2] as if they were his intimates—flinging out remarks as if he wanted to talk and his audience were incapable of appreciation ... light, heat, electricity, sound-waves; and *never* saying that members could take friends or that there were special lectures for children ... Sir Robert Ball[3] ... "a fascinating Irish fellow with the gift of the gab who made a volcano an amusing reality," Krakatoa[4] ... that year of wonderful sunsets and afterglows ... the air half round the world, full of fine dust ... it seemed cruel ... deprivation ... all those years; all that wonderful knowledge, just at hand. And, now it was coming, the Royal Institution[5] ... this evening. She must find out whether one had to dress and exactly how one got in. Albemarle Street[6].... It all went on in *Albemarle* Street.

"We might meet," said Mr Hancock, busily washing his hands and lifting them in the air to shake back his coat sleeves. Miriam listened from her corner behind the instrument cabinet, stupid with incredulity; he *could* not be speaking of the lecture ... he must be ... he had meant all the time that he was going to be with her at the lecture.

"... in the library, at half past eight."

"Oh, yes," she replied casually.

---

1 Lord Rayleigh, or John William Strutt, third Baron Rayleigh (1842-1919), British physicist. He won the Nobel Prize in Physics (1904) for his discovery of the element argon.

2 Lord Kelvin, or William Thomson, 1st Baron Kelvin (1824-1907), British physicist and engineer, most notable for his work on thermodynamics. The kelvin, a unit of temperature measurement, is named after him.

3 Sir Robert Stawell Ball (1840-1913), Irish astronomer and mathematician.

4 A volcano in Indonesia that massively erupted in 1883, the effects of which were felt around the world.

5 The Royal Institution of Great Britain, a highly influential scientific organization founded in 1799, which has, through its history, hosted public lectures by leading scientists.

6 The central London street where the Royal Institution is located, just off Piccadilly.

To sit hearing the very best in the intellectual life of London, the very best science there was; the inner circle suddenly open ... the curious quiet happy laughter that went through the world with the idea of the breaking up of air and water and rays of light; the strange *love* that came suddenly to them all in the object-lesson classes at Banbury Park.[1] That was to begin again ... but now not only books, not the strange heavenly difficult success of showing the children the things that had been found out; but the latest newest things from the men themselves—there would be an audience, and a happy man with a lit face talking about things he had just found out. Even if one did not understand there would be that. Fancy Mr Hancock being a member and always going and not talking about it ... at lunch. He must know an enormous number of things besides the wonders of dentistry and pottery and Japanese art.

It was education ... a liberal education. It made up for only being able to say one was secretary to a dentist at a pound a week ... it sounded strange at the end of twelve years of education and five months in Germany and two teaching posts—to people who could not see how wonderful it was from the inside; and the strange meaning and rightness there was; there had been a meaning in Mr Hancock from the beginning, a sort of meaning in her privilege of associating with fine rare people, so different from herself and yet coming one after another, like questions into her life, and staying until she understood ... somebody struggled all night with the angel ... I will not let thee go until thou bless me[2] ... and there was some meaning—of course, meanings everywhere ... perhaps a person inside a life could always feel meanings ... or perhaps only those who had moved from one experience to another could get that curious feeling of a real self that stayed the same through thing after thing.

"This is the library," said Mr Hancock, leading Miriam along from the landing at the top of the wide red-carpeted staircase. It seemed a vast room—rooms leading one out of the other, lit with soft red lights and giving a general effect of redness, dull crimson velvet in a dull red glow and people, standing in groups and walking about—a quite new kind of people. Miriam glanced at

---

1 Beginning with *Lessons on Objects* (1830), Elizabeth Mayo (1793-1865) introduced the very popular method of teaching students through direct encounters with material objects rather than abstract approaches.
2 Miriam is recalling the biblical episode in which Jacob wrestles with an angel (Gen. 35:1-7, Hos. 12).

her companion. He looked in place; he was in his right place; these were his people; people with gentle enlightened faces and keen enlightened faces. They were all alike in some way. If the room caught fire there would be no panic. They were gentle, shyly gentle or pompously gentle, but all the same and in agreement because they all knew everything, the real important difficult things. Some of them were discussing and disagreeing; many of the women's faces had questions and disagreements on them, and they were nearly all worn with thought; but they would disagree in a way that was not quarrelsome, because every one in the room was sure of the importance of the things they were discussing ... they were all a part of science ... "Science is always right and the same, religion cannot touch it or be reconciled with it, theories may modify or cancel each other, but the methods of science are one and unvarying. To question that fundamental truth is irreligious"[1] ... these people were that in the type of their minds—one and unvarying; always looking out at something with gentle intelligence or keen intelligence ... this was Alma's world ... it would be something to talk to Alma about.

There was something they were not. They were not ... jolly. They could not be. They would never stop "looking." Culture and refinement; with something about it that made them quite different from the worldly people, a touch of rawness, raw school harshness about them that was unconscious of itself and could not come to life. Their shoulders and the back of the heads could never come to life. It gave them a kind of deadness that was quite unlike the deadness of the worldly people, not nearly so dreadful—rather funny and likeable. One could imagine them all washing, very carefully, in an abstracted way, still looking and thinking, and always with the advancement of science on their minds; never really aware of anything behind or around them because of the wonders of science. Seeing these people changed science a little. They were almost something tremendous; but not quite.

"That's old Huggins,"[2] murmured Mr Hancock, giving Miriam's arm a gentle nudge as a white-haired old man passed

---

1 The quotation is not exact, but it paraphrases closely Immanuel Kant (1724-1804) in the "Preface" to the second edition of his *Critique of Pure Reason* (1797).
2 Sir William Huggins (1824-1910), English astronomer noted for his work in spectroscopy. He was the first to use spectrum analysis to determine the nature and properties of astronomical bodies, beginning in the mid-1860s.

close by them with an old woman at his side, with short white hair, exactly like him. "The man who invented spectrum analysis[1]—and that's his wife; they're both great fishermen." Miriam gazed. *There*, was the splendid thing.... In her mind blazed the coloured bars of the spectrum. In the room was the light of the beauty, the startling *life* these two old people shed from every part of their persons. The room blazed in the light they shed. She stood staring, moving to watch their gentle living movements. They moved as though the air through which they moved was a living medium—as though everything were alive all round them—in a sort of hushed vitality. They were young. She felt she had never seen any one so young. She longed to confront them just once, to stand for a moment the tide in which they lived.

"*Ah*, Meesturra Hancock—you *are* a faceful[2] votary."

That's German, thought Miriam, as the flattering, deep, caressing gutturals rebounded dreadfully from her startled consciousness. What a determined intrusion. How did he come to know such a person? Glancing she met a pair of swiftly calculating eyes fixed full on her face. There was fuzzy black hair lifted back from an anxious, yellowish, preoccupied little face. Under the face came the high collar-band of a tightly-fitting, dark claret-coloured[3] ribbed silk bodice, fastened from the neck to the end of the pointed peak by a row of small round German buttons, closely decorated with a gilded pattern. Mr Hancock was smiling an indulgent, deprecating smile. He made an introduction and Miriam felt her hand tightly clasped and held by a small compelling hand, while she sought for an answer to a challenge as to her interest in science. "I don't really know anything about it," she said vaguely, strongly urged to display her knowledge of German. The eyes were removed from her face and the little lady, boldly planted and gazing about her, made announcements to Mr Hancock—about the fascinating subject of the lecture and her hopes of a large and appreciative audience.

What did she want? She could not possibly fail to see that Mr Hancock was telling her that he could see through her social insincerities. It was dreadful to find that even here there were social insincerities. She was like a busy ambassador for things that belonged somewhere else, and that he was laughing at in an

---

1 Spectrum analysis was actually discovered by German scientists Robert Bunsen (1811-99) and Gustav Kirchhoff (1824-87) around 1859.

2 "Faithful" pronounced in a German accent.

3 The colour of red wine.

indulgent, deprecating way that must make her blaze with an anger that she did not show. Looking at her, as her eyes and mouth made and fired their busy sentences, Miriam suddenly felt that it would be easy to deal with her, take her into a corner and talk about German things, food and love affairs and poetry and music. But she would always be breaking away to make a determined intrusion on somebody she knew. She could not really know any English person. What was she doing, bearing herself so easily in the inner circle of English science? Treating people as if she knew all about them and they were all alike. How surprised she must often be, and puzzled.

"That was Miss Teresa Szigmondy," said Mr Hancock, reproducing his amused smile as they took their seats in the dark theatre.

"Is she German?"

"Well ... I think, as a matter of fact, she's part Austro-Hungarian and part—well, *Hebrew*." A Jewess ... Miriam left her surroundings, pondering over a sudden little thread of memory. An eager, very bright-eyed, curiously dimpling school-girl face peering into hers, and a whispering voice—"D'you know why we don't go down to prayers? 'Cos we're *Jews*"—they had always been late; fresh-faced and shiny-haired and untidy and late, and clever in a strange brisk way, and talkative and easy and popular with the teachers.... Their guttural voices ringing out about the stairs and passages, deep and loud and stronger than any of the voices of the other girls. The Hyamson girls—they had been foreigners, like the Siggs and the de Bevers, but different ... what was the difference in a Jew? Mr Hancock seemed to think it was a sort of disgraceful joke ... what was it? Max Sonnenheim[1] had been a Jew, of course, the same voice. Banbury Park "full of Jews" ... the Brooms said that in patient contemptuous voices. But what *was* it? What did everybody mean about them?

"Is she scientific?"

"She seems to be interested in science," smiled Mr Hancock.

"How funny of her to ask me to go to tea with her, just because you told her I knew German."

"Well, you go; if you're interested in seeing notabilities, you'll meet all kinds of wonderful people at her house. She knows everybody. She's the niece of a great Hungarian poet. I believe he's to be seen there sometimes. They're all coming in now." Mr

---

1 A man Miriam meets at a party in *Backwater* (*Pilgrimage* vol. 2).

Hancock named the great names of science one by one as the shyly gentle and the pompously gentle little old men ambled and marched into the well of the theatre and took their seats in rows at either end of the central green table.

"*There*'s a pretty lady," said Mr Hancock, conversationally, just as the light was lowered. Miriam glanced across the half-circle of faintly shining faces and saw an effect, a smoothly coiffured head and smooth neck and shoulders draped by a low deep circular flounce of lace rising from the gloom of a dark dress, sweep in through a side door, bending and swaying—"or a pretty dress at any rate"—and sat through the first minutes of the lecture, recalling the bearing and manner of the figure, with sad fierce bitterness. Mr Hancock admired "feminine" women ... or at any rate he was bored by her own heavy silence, and driven into random speech by the sudden dip and sweep of the lace appearing in the light of the doorway. He was surprised, himself, by his sudden speech and half corrected it ... "or a pretty dress." ... But anyhow he, even he, was one of those men who do not know that an effect like that was just an effect, a deliberate "charming" feminine effect. But if he did not know that, did not know that it was a trick and the whole advertising manner, the delicate, plunging fall of the feet down the steps—"I am late; look how nicely and quietly I am doing it; look at me being late and apologetic and interested"—out of place in the circumstances, then what was he doing here at all? Did he *want* science, or would he really rather be in a drawing-room with "pretty ladies" advertising effects and being "arch" in a polite, dignified, lady-like manner? How dingy and dull and unromantic and unfeminine he must find her. She sat in a lively misery, following the whirling circle of thoughts round and round, stabbed by their dull thorns, and trying to drag her pain-darkened mind to meet the claim of the platform, where, in a square of clear light, a little figure stood talking eagerly and quietly in careful slow English. Presently the voice of the platform won her—clear and with its curious, even, unaccented rat-tat-tat flowing and modulated with pure passion, the thrill of truth and revelation running alive and life-giving through every word. That, at least, she was sharing with her companion ... "development-in-thee-method-of-intaircepting-thee-light." "Daguerre"[1] ... a little

---

1   Louis Daguerre (1787-1851), French artist who invented the "daguerrotype," one of the earliest photographic processes, around 1839. Though the process died out around the 1860s, Daguerre is considered one of the fathers of modern photography.

Frenchman, stopping the sunlight, breaking it up, making it paint faces in filmy black and white on a glass.... There would only be a few women like the one with the frill in an audience like this ... "women will talk shamelessly at a concert or an opera, and chatter on a mountain top in the presence of a magnificent panorama; their paganism is incurable." Then men mustn't stare at them, and treat them as works of art. It was entirely the fault of men ... perfectly reasonable that the women who got that sort of admiration from men should assert themselves in the presence of other works of art. The thing men called the noblest work of God must be bigger than the work by a man. Men plumed themselves and talked in a clever expert way about women and never thought of their own share in the way those women went on ... unfair, unfair; men were stupid complacent idiots. But they were wonderful with their brains. The life and air and fresh breath coming up from the platform amongst the miseries and uncertainties lurking in the audience, was a man ... waves of light which would rush through the film at an enormous speed and get away into space without leaving any impression, were stopped by some special kind of film and went surging up and down in confinement—making strata ... "supairposeetion of strata" ... no Englishman could move his hands with that smoothness, making you see. "Violet subchloride of silver."[1] That would interest Mr Hancock's chemistry. She glanced at the figure sitting very still, with bent head, at her side. He was asleep. Her thoughts recoiled from the platform and bent inwards, circling on their miseries. That was the end, for him, of coming to a lecture, with her. If she had been the frilled lady, sitting forward with her forward-falling frill, patronizing the lecture and "exhibiting" her interest, he would not have gone to sleep.

---

1   Silver iodide and silver bromide were the light-sensitive material on a daguerrotype film plate, which allowed for an image to form when exposed to light through the camera lens. Daguerrotype photography was very slow, but by the 1890s photographic technology began to rapidly improve, leading to the development of the cinématographe in 1895 by the French Lumière brothers. Richardson had a great interest in film and published a number of articles in the film journal *Close Up* between 1927 and 1933.

When the colour photographs came,[1] Miriam was too happy for thought. Pictures of stained glass, hard crude clear brilliant opaque flat colour, stood in miraculous squares on the screen, and pieces of gardens, grass and flowers and trees, shining with a shadeless blinding brilliance.

She made vague sounds. "It's a wonderful achievement," said Mr Hancock, smiling with grave delighted approval towards the screen. Miriam felt that he understood, as her ignorance could not do, exactly what it all meant scientifically; but there was something else in the things as they stood, blinding, there, that he did not see. It was something that she had seen somewhere, often.

"They'll never touch pictures."[2]

"Oh, no—there's no atmosphere; but there's something else; they're exactly like something else...."

Mr Hancock laughed, a little final crushing laugh, and turned away sceptical of further enlightenment.

Miriam sat silent, busily searching for something to express the effect she felt. But she could not tell him what she felt. There was something in this intense hard rich colour like something one sometimes *saw* when it wasn't there, a sudden brightening and brightening of all colours till you felt something must break if they grew any brighter—or in the dark, or in one's mind, suddenly, at any time, unearthly brilliance. He would laugh and think one a little insane; but it was the real certain thing; the one real certain happy thing. And he would not have patience to hear her try to explain; and by that he robbed her of the power of trying to explain. He was not interested in what she thought. Not interested. His own thoughts were statements, things that had been agreed upon and disputed and that people bandied about, competing with each other to put them cleverly. They were not *things*. It was only by pretending to be interested in these statements and taking sides about them that she could have conversation with him. He liked women who thought in these statements. They always succeeded with men. They had a reputation for wit. Did they really think and take an interest in the things they said,

---

1 The first colour photograph was taken by Scottish physicist James Clerk Maxwell (1831-79), and presented in a lecture at the Royal Institution in 1861. Colour photography processes improved dramatically in the 1890s, leading to the development of the first commercial colour film in 1907, again by the Lumière brothers.

2 Hancock is referring to paintings, not photographs.

or was it a trick, like "clothes" and "manners"—or was it that the women brought up with brothers or living with husbands, got into that way of thinking and speaking? Perhaps there was something in it. Something worth cultivating; a fine talent. But it would mean hiding so much, letting so much go; all the real things. The things men never seemed to know about at all. Yet he loved beautiful things; and worried about religion and had found comfort in *Literature and Dogma*,[1] and wanted her to find comfort in it, assuming her difficulties were the same as his own; and knowing the dreadfulness of them. The brilliant unearthly pictures remained in her mind, supporting her through the trial of her consciousness of the stuffiness of her one long-worn dress. Dresses should be fragrant in the evening. The Newlands evening dress was too old-fashioned. Things had changed so utterly since last year. There was no money to have it altered. But this was awful. Never again could she go out in the evening, unless alone or with the girls. That would be best, and happiest, really.

---

1   An 1873 essay by English poet and critic Matthew Arnold (1822-88).

CHAPTER VI

Miriam sat on a damp wooden seat at the station. Shivering with exhaustion, she looked across at the early morning distance, misty black and faint misty green.... Something had happened to it. It was not beautiful; or anything. It was not anything.... That was the punishment.... The landscape was dead. All that had come to an end. Her nimble lifeless mind noted the fact. There was dismay in it. Staring at the landscape she felt the lifelessness of her face; as if something had brushed across it and swept the life away, leaving her only sight. She could never feel any more.

Behind her fixed eyes, something new seemed moving forward with a strange indifference. Suddenly the landscape unrolled. The rim of the horizon was no longer the edge of the world. She lost sight of it in the rolling out of the landscape in her mind, out and out, in a light easy stretch, showing towns and open country and towns again, seas and continents on and on; empty and still. *Nothing.* Everywhere in the world, nothing. She drifted back to herself and clung, bracing herself. She was somebody. If she were somebody who was going to do something ... not roll trolleys along a platform. The train swept busily into the landscape; the black engine, the brown, white-panelled carriages, warm and alive in the empty landscape. Her strained nerves relaxed. In a moment she would be inside it, being carried back into her own world. She felt eagerly forward towards it. Heartsease[1] was there. She would be able to breathe again. But not in the same way; unless she could forget. There were other eyes looking at it. They were inside her; not caring for the things she had cared for, dragging her away from them.

They are not my sort of people. Alma does not care for me, personally. Little cries and excitement and affection. She wants to; but she does not care for any one, personally. Neither of them do. They live in a world ... "Michael Angelo"[2] and "Steven-

---

1   A wild pansy used as a folk remedy for respiratory problems.
2   Michelangelo Buonarroti (1475-1564), Italian Renaissance artist best known for his statue "David" and the frescoes in the Vatican's Sistine Chapel.

son"[1] and "Hardy"[2] and "Dürer"[3] and that other man ... Alma ... popping and sweeping gracefully about with little cries and clever sayings and laughter, trying to be real; in a bright outside way, showing all the inside things because she kept crushing them down. It was so tiring that one could not like being with her. She seemed to be carrying something off all the time; and to be as if she were afraid if the talk stopped for a moment, it would be revealed.

In the tea-shop with Alma alone it had been different; all the old school-days coming back as she sat there. Her eager story. It was impossible to do anything but hold her hands and admire her bravery and say you did not care. But it was not quite real; it was too excited and it was wrong, certainly wrong, to go down not really caring. I need not go down again.

Cold and torpid she got up and stepped into an empty carriage. Both windows were shut and the dry stuffy air seemed almost warm after her exposure. She let one down a little; sheltered from the damp the little stream of outside air was welcome and refreshing. She breathed deeply, safe, shut in and moving on. With an unnecessarily vigorous swing of her arms, she hoisted her pilgrim basket[4] on to the rack. Of *course*, she murmured smiling, of *course* I shall go down again ... ra*ther*.

That extraordinary ending of fear of the great man at the station. Alma and the little fair square man not much taller than herself, looking like a grocer's assistant with a curious, kind, confidential ... unprejudiced eye ... they had come, both of them, out of their house to the station to meet her ... "this is Hypo"[5] and

---

1 Robert Louis Stevenson (1850-94), Scottish author. He was very famous in his time, and his works remain popular, most notably *Treasure Island* (1883) and *The Strange Case of Dr Jekyll and Mr Hyde* (1886).
2 Thomas Hardy (1840-1928), English novelist and poet of the realist tradition. Much of his work is about struggle and tragedy. His best known novels include *Tess of the D'Urbervilles* (1891) and *Jude the Obscure* (1896).
3 Albrecht Dürer (1471-1528), German Renaissance artist, noted for his printmaking and his classical painting style. He was regarded during the Romantic period as a German national hero.
4 An open-topped wicker basket with a rigid handle.
5 The Hypo Wilson character is based on English author H.G. Wells (1866-1946), with whom Richardson had an affair.

the quiet shy walk to the house, he asking questions by saying them—statements. You caught the elusive three-fifteen. This is your bag. We can carry it off without waiting for the ... British porter. You've done your journey brilliantly. We haven't far to walk.

The strange shock of the bedroom, the strange new thing springing out from it ... the clear soft bright tones, the bright white light streaming through the clear muslin, the freshness of the walls ... the flattened dumpy shapes of dark green bedroom crockery gleaming in a corner; the little green bowl standing in the middle of the white spread of the dressing-table cover ... wild violets with green leaves and tendrils put there by somebody, with each leaf and blossom standing separate ... touching your heart; joy, looking from the speaking pale mauve little flowers to the curved rim of the green bowl and away to the green crockery in the corner; again and again the fresh shock of the violets ... the little cold change in the room after the books; strange fresh bindings and fascinating odd shapes and sizes, gave out their names ... *The White Boat—Praxiter—King Chance—Mrs Prendergast's Palings*[1] ... the promise of them in their tilted wooden case by the bedside table from every part of the room, their unchanged names, the chill of the strange sentences inside like a sort of code written for people who understood, written at something, clever raised voices in a cold world. In *Mrs Prendergast's Palings* there were cockney[2] conversations spelt as they were spoken. None of the books were about ordinary people ... three men, seamen, alone, getting swamped in a boat in shallow water in sight of land ... a man, and a girl he had no right to be with, wandering on the sands, the cold wash and sob of the sea; her sudden cold salt tears; the warmth of her shuddering body. *Praxiter* beginning without telling you anything, about the thoughts of an irritating contemptuous superior man, talking at the expense of everybody. Nothing in any of them about anything one knew or felt; casting you off ... giving a chill ache to the room. To sit ... alone, reading in the white light, amongst the fresh colours—but not these books. To go downstairs was a sacrifice: coming back, there would be the lighting of the copper candlestick, twisting beauti-

---

1 Apparently fictitious titles.
2 An accent particular to working-class Londoners. Richardson occasionally writes words phonetically to reflect accents.

fully up from its stout stem. What made it different from ordinary candlesticks? *What?* It was like ... a gesture.

"You knew Susan at school." The brown, tweed-covered arm of the little square figure handed a tea-cup. The high, huskily hooting voice ... what was the overwhelming impression? A common voice, with a cockney twang. Overwhelming. "What was Susan like at school?" The voice was saying two things; that was it; doing something deliberately; it was shy and determined, and deliberate and expectant. Miriam glanced incredulously, summoning all her forces against her sense of strange direct attack, pushing through and out to some unknown place, dreading her first words, not taking in a further remark of the live voice. She could get up and go away for ever; or speak, and whatever she spoke would keep her there for ever. Alma, sitting behind the tea-tray in a green Alma dress with small muslin cuffs and collars, had betrayed her into this. Alma had been got by this and had brought her to the test of it. The brown walls, brown paper all over, like parcel paper, and Japanese prints; nothing else, high-backed curious-shaped wooden chairs all with gestures, like the candlestick, and the voice that was in the same difficult, different world as the books upstairs.... Alma had betrayed her, talking as if they were like other people and not saying anything about this strange cold difference. Alma had come to it and was playing some part she had taken up ... there was some wrong hurried rush somewhere within the beautiful room. Stop, she wanted to say, you're all wrong. You've dropped something you don't know anything about, deliberately. Alma ought to have told you. Hasn't she told you?

"Alma hasn't changed," she said, desperately questioning the smooth soft movements of the smooth soft hands, the quiet controlled pose of the head. Alma had the same birdlike wide blink and flash of her limpid brown eyes, the same tight crinkle and snicker when she laughed, the same way of saying nothing, or only the clever superficially true things men said. Alma had agreed with this man and had told him nothing, or only things in the clever way he would admire.

He made little sounds into his handkerchief. He was nonplussed at a dull answer. It would be necessary to be brilliant and amusing to hold his attention—in fact to tell lies. To get on here, one would have to say clever things in a high bright voice.

The little man began making statements about Alma. Sitting

back in his high-backed chair, with his head bent and his fine hands clasping his large handkerchief, he made little short statements, each improving on the one before it and coming out of it, and little subdued snortings at the back of his nose in the pauses between his sentences as if he were afraid of being answered or interrupted before he developed the next thing. Alma accompanied his discourse with increasing snickerings. Miriam, after eagerly watching the curious mouthing half hidden by the drooping straggle of moustache and the strange, concentrated gleam of the grey-blue eyes staring into space, laughed outright. But how could he speak so of her? He met the laughter with a minatory[1] outstretched forefinger, and raised his voice to ·a soft squeal ending, as he launched with a little throw of the hand his final jest, in a rotund crackle of high hysterical open-mouthed laughter. The door opened and two tall people were shown in; a woman with a narrow figure and a long, dark-curtained, sallow, horse-like face, dressed in a black-striped cream serge coat and skirt, and a fair florid troubled fickle smiling man in a Norfolk tweed[2] and pale blue tie. "Hullo," said the little man propelling himself out of his chair with a neat swift gesture, and standing small and square in the room making cordial sounds and moving his arms about as if to introduce and seat his guests without words and formalities. Alma's thin excited hubbub and the clearly enunciated, obviously prepared facetiousnesses of the newcomers—his large and tenor and florid ... a less clever man than Mr Wilson ... and hers bass and crisp and contemptuous ... nothing was hidden from her; she would *like* the queer odd people who went about at Tansley Street—was broken into by the entry of three small young men, all three dark and a little grubby and shabby looking. The foremost stood with vivid, eager eyes, wide open, as if he had been suddenly checked in the midst of imparting an important piece of news. Alma came forward to where they stood herded and silent just inside the door, and made little faint encouraging maternal sounds at them as she shook hands.

As she did this, Miriam figured them in a flash coming down the road to the house; their young men's talk and arguments, their certainty of rightness and completeness, their sudden embarrassment and secret anger with their precipitate rescuer.

---

1   To express threat, usually finger-wagging.
2   A rough wool typically used to make suits, jackets, and skirts, among other articles. Norfolk jackets are associated with upper-class gentlemen, who liked to wear them for activities such as hunting and golfing.

Mr Wilson was on his feet again, not looking at them nor breaking up the circle already made, but again making his sociable sounds and circular movements with his arms as if to introduce and distribute them about the room. The husband and wife kept on a dialogue in strained social voices as if they were bent on showing that their performance was not dependent on an audience. Miriam averted her eyes from them, overcome by painful visions of the two at breakfast, or going home after social occasions. The three young men retreated to the window alcove behind the tea-table, one of them becoming Miriam's neighbour as she sat in the corner near the piano, whither she had fled from the centre of the room when the husband and wife came in.

It was the young man with the important piece of news. He sat bent forward, holding his cup and plate with outstretched arms. His headlong expression remained unchanged. Wisps of black hair stood eagerly out from his head, and a heavy thatch fell nearly to his eyebrows. "Did anybody see anything of Mrs Binks at the station?" asked Alma from her table. "Oh, my dear," she squealed gently as the maid ushered in a little lady in a straight dress of red flannel, frilled with black chiffon at the neck and wrists, "we were all afraid you weren't coming." "Don't anybody move"—the deep reedy voice reverberated amongst the standing figures; the firm compact undulating figure came across the room to Alma. Its light-footed swiftness and easy certainty filled Miriam with envy. The envy evaporated during the embracing of Alma and the general handshaking. The low strong reedy voice went on saying things out into the silence of the room in a steady complete way. There was something behind it all that did not show, or showed in the brilliant ease, something that Miriam did not envy. She tried to discover what it was as the room settled, leaving Mrs Binkley on a low chair near to Alma, taking tea and going on with her monologue, each of her pauses punctuated by soft appreciative sounds from Alma and little sounds from Mr Wilson. She was popular with them. Mr Wilson sat surveying her. Did they know how hard she was working? Perhaps they did, and admired or even envied it. But what was it for? Surely she must feel the opposition in the room? Alma and Mr Wilson approved and encouraged her exhibition. She was in their curious league for keeping going high-voiced clever sayings. So had the husband appeared to be, at first. Now he sat silent with a kind polite expression about his head and figure. But his mouth was uneasy, he was afraid of something or somebody and was staring at Mrs Binkley. The wife sat in a gloomy abstraction smoking a large cigarette ... she was something like Mrs Kronen, in her way; only instead of belonging to South Africa she had been a hard-featured English schoolgirl; she was still a hard-featured English schoolgirl, with the oldest eyes Miriam had ever seen.

"Why not write an article about a lamp-post?" said one of the young men suddenly, in a gruff voice, in answer to a gradually growing murmur of communications from one of his companions. Miriam breathed easier air. The shameful irritating tension was over. It was as if fresh wonderful life-giving things that were hovering in the room, driven back into corners, pressing up and away against the angles of the ceiling and about the window-door behind the young men and against the far-away door of the room, came back, flooding all the spaces of the room. Mr Wilson moved in his chair, using his handkerchief towards the young men with an eye on the speaker. "Or a whole book," murmured the young man farthest from Miriam, in an eager cockney voice. The two young men were speaking towards Mr Wilson, obviously trying to draw him in bringing along one of his topics; something that had been discussed here before. There would be talk, men's talk, argument and showing off; but there would be something alive in the room. In the conflict there would be ideas, wrong ideas, men taking sides, both right and both wrong; men showing off; but wanting with all their wrongness to get at something. Perhaps somebody would say something. She regretted her shy refusal of a cigarette from Mr Wilson's large full box. It stood open now by the side of the tea-tray. He would not offer it again. Cigarettes and talk.... What would Mr Hancock think? "People do not meet together for conversation, nowadays." ... There was going to be conversation, literary conversation, and she was going to hear it ... be in it. Clever literary people trying to say things well; of course they were all literary; they were all the same set, knowing each other, all calling Mr Wilson "Hypo"; talk about books was the usual Saturday afternoon thing here; and she was in it and would be able to be in it again, any week. It was miraculous. All these people were special people, emancipated people. Probably they all wrote, except the women. There were too many women. Somehow or other she must get a cigarette. Life, suddenly full of new things made her bold. Presently, when the conversation was general she would beg one of the young man at her side. Mr Wilson would not turn to her again. She had failed twice already in relation to him; but after her lame refusal of a cigarette, which he had accepted instantly and sat down with, he had glanced sharply at her in a curious personal way, noticing the little flat square of white collarette[1]—the knot of violets upon it, the long-sleeved black nun's-veiling blouse, the long skirt of her old silkette[2] evening dress. These items had made her sick with anxiety in their separate poverty as she put them on for the visit; but his eyes seemed to draw them all together. Perhaps there in the dark corner they made a sort of whole. She rejoiced gratefully in the memory of Mag's factory girl, in her own idea of having the sleeves gauged[3] at the wrists in defiance of fashion, to make frills extending so as partly to cover her large hands; over the suddenly realized possibility of wearing the silkette skirt as a day skirt. She must remain in the corner, not moving, all the afternoon. If she moved in the room the bright light would show the scrappiness of her clothes. In the evening it would be all right. She sat back in her corner, happy, and forgetful. She had not had so much tea as she wanted. She had refused the cigarette against her will. Now she was alive. These weak things would not happen again, and the next time she would bring her own cigarettes. To take out a cigarette and light it here, at home amongst her own people. These were her people. There was something here in the exciting air that she did not understand; something that was going to tax her more than she had ever been taxed before. She had found her way to it through her wanderings; it had come; it was her due. It corresponded to something in herself, shapeless and inexpressible; but there. She knew it by herself, sitting in her corner; her own people would know it, if they could see her here; but no one here would find it out. Every one here was doing something; or the wife of somebody who did something. They were like a sort of secret society ... all agreed about something ... about what? *What* was it Mr Wilson was so sure about? They would despise everybody who was living an ordinary life, or earning a living in anything but something to do with books. Seeing her here, they would take for granted that she, too, was somebody ... and she was, somehow, within herself somewhere; although she had made herself into a dentist's secretary. She was better qualified to be here and to understand the strange secret here, in the end, than any one else she knew. But it was a false position, unless they all knew what she was. If she could say clever things they

---

1 An accessory for women, usually a type of necklace made from fabric.

2 "A fabric made of silk and cotton, chiefly used for lining dresses" (*OED*).

3 Slightly tightened.

would like her; but she would be like Alma and Mrs Binkley; pretending; and without any man to point to as giving her the right to be about here. It was a false position. It was as if she were here as a candidate to become an Alma or a Mrs Binkley; imitating the clever sayings of men, or flattering them.

"*Do* it, Gowry," said Mr Wilson ... "a book" ... he made his little sound behind his nose as he felt for the phrases that were to come after his next words ... "a—er—book; about a lamp-post. You see," he held up his minatory finger to keep off an onslaught, and quench an eager monologue that began pouring from Miriam's nearest neighbour, and went on in his high weak husky voice. The young men were quiet. For a few moments the red lady and Alma made bright conversation as if nothing were happening; but with a curious hard emptiness in their voices, like people rehearsing and secretly angry with each other. Then they were silent, sitting posed and attentive, with uneasy intelligent smiling faces; their costumes and carefully arranged hair useless on their hands. Mrs Binkley did not suffer so much as Alma; her corsetless eager crouch gave her the appearance of intentness, her hair waved naturally, had tendrils and could be left to look after itself; her fresh easy strength was ready for the next opportunity. It was only something behind her face that belied her happy pose. Alma was waiting in some curious fixed singleness of tension; her responses hovered fixed about her mouth, waiting for expression, she sat fixed in a frozen suspension of deliberate amiability and approval, approval of a certain chosen set of things; approval which excluded everything else with derision ... it was Alma's old derision, fixed and arranged in some way by Mr Wilson.

"There will be books—with all that cut out—him and her—all that sort of thing. The books of the future will be clear of all that," he was saying.

Miriam sat so enclosed in her unarmed struggle with this new definition of a book, that the entry of the newcomers left her unembarrassed. Two rotund ruddy men in mud-spotted tweeds, both fair, one with a crest like a cockatoo standing straight up from his forehead above a smooth pink face, the other older than anybody in the room, with a shaggy head and a small pointed beard. They came in talking aloud, and stumped about the room, making their greetings. Miriam bowed twice and twice received a sturdy handclasp and the kindly gleam of blue eyes, one pair large, mild, and owl-like behind glasses; the other fierce and glinting, a shaft of whimsical blue light. The second pair of eyes surely would not agree with what Mr Wilson had been saying. But their coming in had broken a charm; the overwhelming charm of the way he put things; so that even while you hated what he was saying, and his way of stating things as if they were the final gospel and no one else in the world knew anything at all, you wanted him to go on; only to go on and to keep on going on. It was wrong somehow; he was all wrong; "though I speak with the tongues of men and of angels";[1] it was wrong and somehow wicked; but it caught you, it had caught Alma and all these people; and in a sense he despised them all, and was talking to something else; the thing he knew; the secret that made him so strong, even with his weak voice and weak mouth; strong and fascinating. It was wrong to be here; it would be wrong to come again; but there was nothing like it anywhere else; no other such group of things; and thought and knowledge of things. More must be heard. It would be impossible not to risk everything to hear more.

Alma ordered fresh tea; Mr Wilson and the husband and the two new men were standing about. The elder man was describing, in a large shouting voice, a new mantelpiece—a Tudor mantelpiece. What was a Tudor mantelpiece?[2] ... to buy a *house* to put round it. What a clever idea.... Little Mr Wilson seemed to be listening; he squealed amendments of the jests between the big man's boomings ... buy a *town* to put round it.... What a lovely idea ... buy a NATION to put round it ... there was a burst of guffaws. Mr Wilson's face was crimson; his eyes appeared to be full of tears. The big man went on. Mrs Binkley kept uttering deep reedy caressing laughs. Two of the young men were leaning forward talking eagerly with bent heads. Miriam's neighbour sat upright with his hands on his knees, his eyes glaring as if ... as if he were just going to jump out of his skin. Hidden by the increased stir made by the re-entry of the maid, and encouraged by the extraordinary clamour of hilarious voices, Miriam ventured to ask him if he would perform an act of charity by allow-

---

1   Paul's first letter to the Corinthians, in which he urges faith, hope, and
    charity (or love): "Though I speak with the tongues of men and of
    angels, and have not charity, I am become as sounding brass, or a tink-
    ling cymbal" (I Cor. 13:1, King James Version).
2   A fireplace design developed during the Tudor era (1485-1603). Typical
    Tudor mantels were modest, not especially decorative, with a pointed
    arch in the middle, and usually made from either marble or limestone.

ing her to rob him of one of his cigarettes. She liked her unrecognizable voice. It was pitched deep, but strong; a little like Mrs Binkley's. The young man started and turned eagerly towards her, stammering and muttering and fumbling about his person. "I swear," he brought out, "I could cut my throat ... my *God* ... oh, here we are." Seizing the open box from the tea-table he swung round with his crossed legs extended across her corner so that she was cut off from the rest of the room, and held the box eagerly towards her. They both took cigarettes and he lit them with matches obtained from his neighbour. "Thank you," said Miriam blissfully drawing "that has saved my life." Precipitately restoring the matches he swung round again leaning forward with his elbow on his knee, blocking out Miriam's view. Before it was blocked, she had caught the eye, of Mr Wilson who was standing facing her in the little group of men about the tea-table and still interpolating their hubbub with husky squeals of jocularity, quietly observing the drama in her corner. For the moment she did not wish to listen; Alma's appreciative squeals were getting strained and the big man was a bore. Seen sitting in profile taking his tea, he reminded her of Mr Staple-Craven;[1] her eye caught and recoiled from weak patches, touches of frowsy softness here and there about the shaggy head. Cut off from the room, safe in the extraordinary preoccupation of the young man whose eager brooding was moving now towards some tremendous communication—she had undisturbed knowledge of what she had done. Speech and action had launched her, for good or ill, into the strange tide running in this house. Its cold waters beat against her breast. She was no longer quite herself. There was something in it that quickened all her faculties, challenged all the strength she possessed. By speech and action she had accepted something she neither liked, nor approved nor understood; refusal would have left its secret unplumbed, standing aside in her life, tormenting it. The sense of the secret intoxicated her ... perhaps I am selling my soul to the devil. But she was glad that Mr Wilson had witnessed her launching.

"You are magnificent," gasped the young man glaring at the wall. "I mean you are simply magnificent." He flashed unconscious eyes at her—*he* had no consciousness of the cold tide with its curious touch of evil; it was hand in hand with him and his simplicity that she had stepped down into the water—and hurried on. "An angel of dreams. Dreams ... you know—I say,"

---

1 A character in *Backwater* (*Pilgrimage* vol. 3).

he spluttered incoherently, "I *must* tell you." His working, preoccupied face turned to face hers with a jerk that brought part of
the heavy sheaf of hair across one of his eyes. "I've been doing the
best work this week I ever did in my life!" Red flooded the whole
of his face and the far-away glare of his one visible eye became a
blaze of light, near, and smiling a guilty delighted smile. He was
demanding *her* approval, *her* sympathy, just on the strength of her
being there. It was a moment of consenting to Alma that had
brought this. However it had come, she would have been unable
to withstand it. He wanted approval and sympathy; someone here
had some time or other shut him up; perhaps he was considered
second-rate, perhaps he was second-rate; but he was innocent as
no one else in the room was innocent. "*Oh*, I *am* glad," she
replied swiftly. Putting his cigarette on the edge of the piano he
seized one of her hands and crushed it between his own. His face
perspired and there were tears in his eye. "*Do* tell me about it,"
she said with bold uneasy eagerness, hoping he would drop her
hand when he spoke. "It's a play," he shouted in a low whisper, a
spray of saliva springing through his lips, "a play—it's the finest
stuff I ever rout." Were all these people either cockney or with that
very bland Anglican cultured way of speaking—like the husband
and the man with the Tudor mantelpiece?

"I can of course admit that the growth of corn was, at first,
accidental and unconscious, and that even after the succession of
processes began to be grasped and the soil methodically cultivated, the success of the crop was supposed to depend upon the
propitiation of a *god*. I can see that the discovery of the possibility of growing *food* would enormously alter the savage's conception of God, by introducing a new set of attributes into his *consciousness* of him; but in defining the God of the Christians as a
corn deity[1] you and Allen are putting the cart before the horse."
That was it, that was it—that was right somehow; there was
something in this big red-faced man that was not *in* Mr Wilson;
but why did his talk sound so lame and dull, even while he was
saving God—and Mr Wilson's, while he made God from the
beginning a nothing created by the fears and needs of man, so
thrilling and convincing, so painting the world anew? He was

---

1   Richardson is writing during the height of new insights into the origins
    of world religions, linking Christianity to ancient vegetation cults. Cf.
    James G. Frazer's (1854-1941) *The Golden Bough* (1890) and Jesse L.
    Weston's (1850-1928) *From Ritual to Romance* (1920).

wrong about everything and yet while he talked everything changed in spite of yourself.

The earlier part of the afternoon looked a bright happy world behind the desolation of this conflict; the husband and wife and the young men and Mrs Binkley and the bright afternoon light, dear far-off friends ... withstanding, in their absence, the chilly light of Mr Wilson's talk. Who was Mr Wilson? But he was so certain that men had created God ... life in that thought was a nightmare. Nothing that could happen could make it anything but a nightmare henceforth ... it did not matter what happened, and yet he seemed pleased, amused about everything and eager to go on and "do" things and get things done.... His belief about life was worse than agnosticism.[1] There was no doubt in it. "Mr G."[2] was an invention of man. There was nothing but man; man, coming from the ape, some men a little cleverer than others, men had discovered science, science was the only enlightenment, science would put everything right; scientific imagination, scientific invention. Man.[3] Women were there, cleverly devised by nature to ensnare man for a moment and produce more men to bring scientific order out of primeval chaos; chaos was decreasing, order increasing; there was nothing worth considering before the coming of science; the business of the writer was imagination, not romantic imagination, but realism, fine realism, the truth about "the savage," about all the past and present, the avoidance of cliché ... what was cliché? ...

"Well, my dear man, you've got the Duke of Argyll[4] to keep you company," sighed Mr Wilson with a smothered giggle, getting to his feet.

Miriam went from the sitting-room she had entered in another age with the bedroom violets pinned against her collarette, stripped and cold and hungry into the cold of the brightly-lit little dining-room. The gay cold dishes, the bright jellies and fruits, the brown nuts, the pretty Italian wine in thin white long-necked

---

1 See p. 367, note 2.

2 That is, God.

3 The ideas represented here correspond directly with those of H.G. Wells, as articulated in his fiction and non-fiction.

4 Originally only a Scottish title, the 8th Duke of Argyll, George Campbell (1823-1900), was admitted to the Peerage of the United Kingdom in 1892. Campbell served in many political posts, including Secretary of State for India. He was a notably conservative thinker.

decanters ... Chianti[1]... Chianti ... they all seemed familiar with the wine and the word; perhaps it was a familiar wine at the Wilson supper-parties; they spoke of it, sitting at the little feast amongst the sternness of nothing but small drawings and engravings on walls that shone some clear light tone against the few pieces of unfamiliar grey-brown furniture, like people clustering round a fire. But it was a feast of death; terrible because of their not knowing that it was a feast of death. The wife of the cockatoo had come in early enough to hear nearly the whole of the conversation, and had sat listening to it with a quiet fresh talkative face under her fresh dark hair; the large deep furrow between her eyebrows was nothing to do with anything here, it was permanent, belonging to her life. She had brought her life in with her and kept it there, the freshness and the furrow; she seemed now, at supper, to be out for the evening, to enjoy herself—at the Wilsons' ... coming to the Wilsons' ... for a jolly evening, just as anybody would go anywhere for a jolly evening. She did not know what was there, what it all meant. Perhaps because of the two little boys. She, with two little unseen boys and the big house so near, big and full of her and noise and things, and her freshness and the furrow of her thought about it, prevented anything from going on; the dreadful thing had to be dropped where it was, leaving the big man who had fought to pretend to be interested and amused, leaving Mr Wilson with the last word, and his quiet smothered giggle.

Alma tried to answer Mrs Pinner's loud fresh talking in the way things had been answered earlier in the afternoon, before the departure of all the other people. Everything she said was an attempt to beat things up. Every time she spoke, Miriam was conscious of something in the room that would be there with them all if only Alma would leave off being funny; something there was in life that Alma had never yet known, something that belonged to an atmosphere she would call "dull." Mr Wilson knew that something ... had it in him somewhere, but feared it and kept it out by trying to be bigger, by trying to be the biggest thing there was. Alma went on and on, sometimes uncomfortably failing, her thin voice sounding out like a corkscrew in a cork without any bottle behind it, now and again provoking a response which made things worse because it brought to the table the shamed sense of trying to keep something going.... The clever excitements would

---

1 An Italian wine from Tuscany.

not come back. Mrs Binkley would have helped her.... Miriam sat helpless and miserable between her admiration of Alma's efforts and her longing for the thing Alma kept out. Her discomfiture at Alma's resentment of her dullness and Alma's longing for Mrs Binkley, was made endurable by her anger over Alma's obstructiveness. Mr Pinner and the big man were busily feeding. Mrs Pinner laughed and now and again tried to imitate Alma; as if she had learned how it was done by many visits to the Wilsons', and then forgot and talked in her own way, forgetting to try to say good things. Alma grew smaller as supper went on, and Mr and Mrs Pinner larger and larger. Together they were too strong for their sense of some other life and some other way of looking at things, to give the Wilson way a clear field. Mr Wilson began monologues at favourable intervals, but they tailed off for lack of nourishing response. Miriam listened eagerly and suspiciously; lost in admiration and a silent, mentally wordless opposition. She felt the big man was on her side and that the Pinners would be, if they could understand. They only saw the jokes ... the—the—higher facetiousness ... good phrase, that was the Chianti. And they were getting used to that; perhaps they were secretly a little tired of it.

After supper, Mr Pinner sang very neatly in a small clear tenor voice an English translation of *Es war ein König im Thule.*[1] Miriam longed for the German words; Mr Pinner cancelled even the small remainder of the German sentiment by his pronunciation of the English rendering; "There was a king of old *tame*" he declared, and so on throughout the song. Alma followed with a morsel of Chopin.[2] The performance drove Miriam into a rage. Mr Pinner had murdered his German ballad innocently, his little Oxford voice and his false vowels did not conceal the pleasure he took in singing his unimagined little song. Alma played her piece at her audience, every line of her face and body proclaiming it fine music, the right sort of music, and depreciating all the com-

---

1   German: There was a king in Thule. A 1774 poem by Johann Wolfgang von Goethe (1749-1832) that was set to music by Hungarian composer Franz Liszt (1811-86) in 1842 and in a second version in 1856. Thule is the name given to an indeterminate far northern locale possibly Norway, Greenland, or Iceland in classical European literature and maps.

2   Frederic Francois (Polish: Fredyryk Frantiszek) Chopin (1810-49), Polish Romantic composer.

positions that were not "music." It was clear that her taste had become cultivated, that she *knew* now, that the scales had fallen from her eyes[1] as they had fallen from Miriam's eyes in Germany; but the result sent Miriam back with a rush to cheap music, sentimental "obvious" music, shapely waltzes, the demoralizing chromatics[2] of Gounod,[3] the demoralizing descriptive passion pieces of Chaminade,[4] those things by Liszt, whom somebody had called a charlatan, who wrote to make your blood leap and your feet dance and made your blood leap and your feet dance ... why not? ...

Her mind went on amazed at the rushing together of her ideas on music, at the amount of certainty she had accumulated. Any of these things she declared to herself played, really *played*, would be better than Alma's Chopin. The Wilsons had discovered "good" music, as so many English people had, but they were all wrong about music; nearly all English people were. Only in England would either the song or the solo have been possible. The song was innocent, the solo was an insult. The player's air of superiority to other music was insufferable; her way of playing out bar by bar of the rain on the roof as if she were giving a lesson, was a piece of intellectual snobbery. Chopin she had never met, never felt or glimpsed. Chopin was a shape, an endless delicate stern rhythm as stern as anything in music; all he was, came through that, could come only through it, and she played tricks with the shape, falsified all the values, outdid the worst trickery of the music she was deprecating. At the end of the performance, which was applauded with a subdued reverence, Miriam eased her agony by humming the opening phrase of the motive[5] again and again in her brain, and very nearly aloud, it was such a perfect rhythmic drop. For long she was haunted and tortured by

---

1 Acts 9:18 in the Bible tells of Saul's conversion to Christianity (thereafter he is Paul): "And immediately there fell from his eyes as it had been scales: and he could see again. He got up and was baptized" (King James Version).

2 The chromatic scale divides octaves into semi-tones, rather than full tones, meaning one gets a larger array of notes to work with, but it can be less harmonic.

3 Charles-François Gounod (1818-93), French composer.

4 Cécile Louise Stéphanie Chaminade (1857-1944), French composer. She was popular in England in the 1890s, and notable for being one of few female composers.

5 A musical term, usually "motif" or "leitmotif," referring to a work's repeated, unifying theme.

Alma's horrible holding back of the third note for emphasis where there was no emphasis ... it was like ... finding a *wart* at the dropping end of a fine tendril, she was telling herself furiously, while she fended off Alma's cajoling efforts to make her join in a game of cards. She felt too angry and too suffering—what *was* this wrong thing about music in all English people?—even if she had not been too shy to exhibit her large hands and her stupidity at cards. So they were going to play cards, actually cards. The room felt cold to her in her long-suppressed anger and misery. She began to wish the Pinners would go. Sitting by the fire, shivering and torpid, she listened to Mrs Pinner's outcries and the elaboration, between the rounds, of jests that she felt were weekly jests. Sitting there dully listening she began to have a sort of insight into the way these jests were made. It was a thing that could be cultivated. Her tired brain experimented. Certain things she heard she knew she would remember; she felt she would repeat them—with an air of originality. They would seem very brilliant in any of her circles—though the girls did that sort of thing rather well; but in a less "refined" way; that was true! This was the sort of thing the girls did; only their way was not half so clever ... if she did, every one would wonder what was the matter with her; and she would not be able to keep it up, without a great deal of practice; and it would keep out something else ... but perhaps for some people there was something in it; it was their way. It had always been Alma's way, a little. Only now she did it better. Perhaps ... it was like Chopin's shape.... They do not know how angry I have been ... they are quite amiable. I am simply horrid ... wanting Alma to know I know she's wrong, quite as much as caring for Chopin; perhaps more ... no; if *anybody* had *played*, I should be happy; perfectly happy ... what does that mean ... because real musicians are not at all nice people ... "a queer soft lot."[1] But why are the English so awful about music? They are poets. Why are they not musicians? I hope I shall never hear Alma play Beethoven. As long as she plays Chopin like that, I shall never like her.... Perhaps English people ought never to play, only to listen to music. They are not innocent enough to play. They cannot forget themselves.

At ten o'clock they trooped into the kitchen. Miriam, half asleep and starving for food, eagerly ate large biscuits, too hungry

---

1 In *Backwater* (*Pilgrimage* vol. 2), Miriam also recalls someone saying this about musicians, though she never identifies the source of the remembered quote.

to care much for Alma's continued resentment of her failure to join the card party and her unconcealed contempt of her sudden return to animation at the prospect of nourishment. She had never felt so hungry.

Going at last to her room she found its gleaming freshness warm and firelit. Warm fresh deeps of softly coloured room, that were complete before she came in with her candle. She stood a moment imagining the emptiness. The April night air was streaming gently in from meadows. Going across to the windows, she hesitated near the flowered curtain. It stirred gently; but not in that way as if moved by ghostly fingers. The meadows here were different. They might grow the same again. But woods and meadows were always there, away from London. One could go to them. They were going on all the time. All the time in London, spring and summer and autumn were passing unseen. But this was not the time. They were *different* here. She pulled a deep wicker chair close up to the exciting white ash-sprinkled hearth. The evening she had left in the flames downstairs was going on up here. To-morrow, to-day, in a few hours she would be sitting with them again, facing flames; no one else there. She sat with her eyes on the flames. A clock struck two.... I've got to them at last, the people I ought to be with. The books in the corner showed their bindings and opened their pages here and there. They made a little sick patch on her heart. The Wilsons approved of them. Other people approved of things. Nothing had been done yet that anybody could approve of ... the *some*thing village of Grandpré[1]... und dann sagte darauf, die gute vernünftige Hausfrau[2].... It all floated in the air. They would see it if somebody showed it. They would be angry and amused if anybody tried to show it. It was wrong in some way to try and show the things you were looking at. Keep quiet about them. Then somebody else expressed them; and those other people turned to you, and demanded your admiration—and wondered why you were furious. It's too long to wait, until the things come up of themselves. You *must* attend to them....

How the fragrance of the cigarette stood out upon the fresh warm air ... that was perique,[3] that curious strong flavour. They

---

1 "the beautiful village of Grandpré," from American Henry Wadsworth Longfellow's (1807-82) epic poem *Evangeline, A Tale of Acadie* (1847).

2 German: and thereupon the good sensible housewife said ...

3 A type of tobacco with a strong aroma, cultivated by Acadians in Louisiana.

were very strong, he had said so; but downstairs, talking like that, they had had no particular flavour, just cigarettes, bringing the cigarette mood ... no wonder he had been surprised, really surprised, at her smoking so many ... but then he had been surprised at her eating a hard apple at midnight ... the sitting-room had suddenly looked familiar, going into it alone while they were seeing out the Pinners and the big man. Strange unknown voices that perhaps she would not hear again, going out into the night ... their voices jesting the last jests as the guests went down the garden, sounding in the hall, familiar and homely, well known to her, presently coming back into the sitting-room; the fire burning brightly like any other fire, the exciting deep pinkness of the shaded lamplight like nothing else in the world. Alma knew it, rushing in ... whirling about with Alma in that room with that afternoon left in it; the sounds of bolting and locking coming in from the hall.

... "You looked extraordinarily pretty...."

"You have come through it all remarkably well" ... remarkable had a k in it in English, and German, merkwürdig, and perhaps in Scandinavian languages; but not in other languages; it was one of the things that separated England from the south ... remarkable ... hard and chilly.

"You know you're awfully good stuff. You've had an extraordinary variety of experience; you've got your freedom; you ought to write."

"That is what a palmist[1] told me at Newlands. It was at a big afternoon 'at home'; there was a palmist in a little dark room sitting near a lamp; she looked at nothing but your hands; she kept saying 'Whatever you do, write. If you haven't written yet, write, if you don't succeed go on writing.'"

"Just so, have you written?"

"Ah, but she also told me my self-confidence had been broken; that I used to be self-confident and was so no longer. It's true."

"Have you written anything?"

"I once sent in a thing to *Home Notes*.[2] They sent it back but asked me to write something else and suggested a few things."

"If they had taken your stuff you would have gone on and learnt to turn out stuff bad enough for *Home Notes*, and gone on doing it for the rest of your life."

---

1 That is, a palm reader or fortune teller.

2 A women's monthly magazine (1894-1957).

"But then an artist, a woman who had a studio in Bond Street and knew Leighton,[1] saw some things I had tried to paint and said I ought to make any sacrifice to learn painting, and a musician said the same about music."

"You could work in writing quite well with your present work."

... "Pieces of short prose; anything; a description of an old woman sitting in an omnibus ... anything. There's plenty of room for good work. There's the *Academy*,[2] always ready to consider well-written pieces of short prose. Write something and send it to me."

Nearing London, shivering and exhausted, she recalled Sunday morning and the strangeness of it being just as it had promised to be. Happy waking with a clear refreshed brain in a tired drowsy body, like the feeling after a dance; making the next morning part of the dance, your mind full of pictures and thoughts, and the evening coming up again and again, one great clear picture in the foreground of your mind. The *evening* in the room as you sat propped on your pillows, drinking the clear pale, curiously refreshing tea left by the maid on a little wooden tray by your bedside; its fragrance drew you to sip at once, without adding milk and sugar. It was delicious; it steamed aromatically up your nostrils and went straight to your brain; potent without being bitter. Perhaps it was "China"[3] tea; it must be. The two biscuits on the little plate disappeared rapidly, and she poured in milk and added much sugar to her remaining tea to appease her hunger. The evening strayed during her deliberately perfunctory toilet; she wanted only to be down. It began again unbroken with the first cigarette after breakfast, when a nimble remark, thrown out from the excited gravity of her happiness, made Mr Wilson laugh. She was learning how to do it. It stayed on through the day, adding the day to itself in a chain, a morning of talk, a visit to Mr Wilson's study—the curious glimpses of pinewood from the windows; pinewood looking strange and far away—there were people in Weybridge[4] to whom those woods were real woods,

---

1 This could refer to one of two unrelated English painters: Edmund Leighton (1852-1922) or Frederic Leighton, first Baron Leighton (1830-96).

2 A literary journal (1869-1916). A number of notable authors published prose and book reviews in the journal. It appears as *The Sacred Grove* in H.G. Wells's novel *Tono-Bungay* (1909), represented as significant to British intellectual culture.

3 That is, tea from China rather than India, where most English tea came from at the time.

4 A town in Surrey, in southeast England.

where they walked and perhaps had the thoughts that woods bring; here they were like woods in a picture book; not real, just a curious painted background for Mr Wilson's talk ... all those books, in fifty years' time, burnt up by the air; he did not seem to think it an awful idea ... you can do anything with English ... and then the names of authors who had done some of these things with English ... making it sing and dance and march, making it like granite or like film and foam. Other languages were more simple and single in texture; less flexible.... Gazing out at the exciting silent pines—so dark and still, waiting, not knowing about the wonders of English—Miriam recalled her impressions of the authors she knew. It was true that those were their effects and the great differences between them. How did he come to know all about it, and to put it into words? Did the authors know when they did it? She passionately hoped not. If they did, it was a trick and spoilt books. Rows and rows of "fine" books; nothing but men sitting in studies doing something cleverly, being very important, "men of letters"; and looking out for approbation. If writing meant that, it was not worth doing. English a great flexible language; more than any other in the world. But German was the same? Only the inflections filled the sentences up with bits. English was flexible and beautiful. Funny. Foreigners did not think so. Many English people thought foreign literature the best. Perhaps Mr Wilson did not know much foreign literature. But he wanted to; or he would not have those translations of Ibsen[1] and Björnsen.[2] German poetry marched and sang and did all sorts of things. Anyhow it was wonderful about English—but if books were written like that, sitting down and doing it cleverly and knowing just what you were doing, and just how somebody else had done it, there was something wrong, some mannish cleverness that was only half right. To write books, knowing all about style, would be to become like a man. Women who wrote books and learned these things would be absurd and would make men absurd. There was something wrong. It was in all those books upstairs. "Good stuff" was wrong, a clever trick, not worth doing. And yet everybody seemed to want to write.

The rest of the day—secret and wonderful. Sitting about, taken for one of the Wilson kind of people, someone who was

---

1 Henrik Ibsen (1828-1906), very influential modernist playwright.

2 Bjørnstjerne Bjørnson (1832-1910), Norwegian author, playwright, and 1903 Nobel Prize winner for Literature.

writing or going to write, by the two Scotch professors; sitting about listening to their quiet easy eager unconcerned talk, seeing them "all round" as Mr Wilson saw them, the limits of professorship and teaching, the silly net and trick of examinations, their simplicity and their helplessness; playing the lovely accompaniment, like quiet waves, of Schubert's *Ave Maria*,[1] the sudden, jolly, sentimental voice of Professor Ewings, his nice attentions ... if it had been Wimpole Street, or anywhere in society, he would not have seen me....

It would be wrong to try to write just because Mr Wilson had said one ought.... The reasons he had given for writing were the wrong ones ... but it would be impossible to go down again without doing some writing.... Impossible not to go down again.... They knew one was "different"; and liked it and thought it a good thing; a sort of distinction. No one had thought that before. It made them a home and a refuge. The only refuge there was, except being by oneself ... only their kind of difference was not the same. They thought nearly every one "futile" and "dull"—every one who did not see things in their way was that. Presently they would find that one was not different in the same way. He had spoken of people who grow "dull" as you get to know them. Awful ... perhaps already, he meant——

"It's all very well ... people read Matthew Arnold's[2] simple profundities; er—simple profundities, and learn his little trick; and go *about*—hcna, hcna—arm in arm with this swell ... hcna ... *puffing* with illumination. All about *nothing*. It's all, my dear Miss Henderson, about absolutely nothing."

The train stopped. Better not to go down again. There was something all wrong in it. Wrong about everything. The Pinners and the big man were right ... but there was something dreadful in them, the something that is in all simple right sort of people, who just go on, never thinking about anything. Were they good and right? It did not enter their heads to think that they were wrong in associating with him.... Here in London it seemed wrong ... she hurried wearily with aching head up the long platform. The Wimpole Street people would certainly think it wrong; if they knew about the marriage. They knew he was a coming

---

1 That is, Franz Schubert's (1797-1828) setting of the Catholic prayer "Ave Maria" ("Hail Mary") to music.

2 See p. 151, note 1.

great man; the great new "critic"; a new kind of critic ... they knew everybody was beginning to talk about him. But if they knew they would not approve. They would never understand his way of seeing things. Impossible to convey anything to them of what the visit had been.

The hall clock said half-past nine. The hall and the large rooms had shrunk. Everything looked shabby and homely. The house was perfectly quiet. Passing quietly and quickly into her room, she found the table empty. The door into the den was shut and no sound came from behind it. No one but James had seen her. The holiday was still there. Perhaps there would be time to take hold in a new way before any one discovered her and made demands. Perhaps they were all three wanting her at this moment. But the house was so still, there was nothing urgent. Perhaps she would never feel nervous at Wimpole Street again. It was really all so easy. There was nothing she could not manage, if only she could get a fair start and get everything in order and up to date. Her mind tried to encircle the book-keeping. There must be a plan for it all; so much work on the accounts, to keep the whole ledger-full sent out to date, so much on the address books, and so much on the monthly cash books—a little of all these things every day in addition to the day's work, whatever happened; that would do it. Then there would be no muddle and nothing to worry about and perhaps time to write. They must be told that she would use any spare time there was on other things.... They would be quite ready for that, provided the books were always up to date and the surgeries always in order. That is what a Wilson would have done from the first.

"Mr Grove[1] to see you, miss."

"Mr *Grove*?"

"Yes miss; a dark gentleman."

Miriam rose from her chair. James had gone, after a moment of sympathetic waiting, back down the basement stairs to her dinner. Miriam felt herself very tall and slender—set apart and surrounded; healed of all fighting and effort. She went quickly through the hall, thinking of nothing; herself, walking down Harriett's garden path. At the door of the waiting-room she hesitated. Mr Grove was the other side of the door, waiting for her to come in. She opened the door with a flourish, and advanced with stiffly

---

1 See p. 74, note 3.

outstretched hand. Before she said "Teeth?" in a cheerful, breezy, professional tone that exploded into the past and scattered it, she saw the pained anxiousness of his face and the flush that had risen under his dark skin.

"No," he said, recoiling swiftly from his limp handshake and sitting abruptly down on the chair from which he had risen. Miriam watched him go helplessly on to say in stiff resentfulness what he had come to say, while she stood apologetically at his chair side.

"I meant to write to you—two or three times."

"Oh why didn't you?" she responded emphatically.... Why can't I be quiet and hear what he has to say? He must have wanted to see me dreadfully to come here like this.

His eyes were fixed blindly upon the far-off window.

"Yes. I wanted to very much. How do you like your life here?" He was flushing again. His skin still had that shiny film over it, so unlike the clear snaky brilliance of the eyes. They were dreadful, and all the rest flappy and floppy and somehow feverish.

"Oh—I like it immensely."

"That is a very good thing."

"Do you like your life?"

He drew in his lower lip on an indrawn breath and held it with his teeth. His eyes were thinking busily under a slight frown.

"That is one of the things I wished to discuss with you."

"Oh *do* discuss it with me," cried Miriam.

"I am very glad you are getting on here so well," he murmured thoughtfully, gazing through the window, to and fro as if scanning the opposite house-fronts.

"Oh, I like it immensely," said Miriam after a silence. Her head was beginning to ache. He sat quite still, scanning to and fro, his lip recaptured under his teeth.

"They are such nice people. I like it for so many things."

He looked absently round at her.

"M-yes. On several occasions I thought of writing to you."

"Yes," said Miriam sitting down opposite to him.

He shifted a little in his chair, to keep his way clear to the window.

For a few moments they sat silent; then he suddenly took out his watch and stood up.

Miriam rose. "Have you seen the Ducaynes lately?" she asked hurriedly, moving nervously towards the door. Murmuring an indistinct response he led the way to the door and held it open for her.

James was coming forward with a patient. They stood aside for the patient to pass in, James waiting to escort Mr Grove to the front door. They shook hands limply and silently. Miriam stood watching his narrow, loosely knit clerical back as he plunged along through the hall and out. She turned as James turned from the door.... What it must have cost him to break in here and ask for me ... how silly and how rude I was.... I *can't* believe he's been; it's like a dream. He's seen me in the new life, changed ... and I'm not really changed.

CHAPTER VII

Why must I always think of her in this place?[1] ... It is always worst just along here.... Why do I always forget there's this piece ... always be hurrying along seeing nothing and then, suddenly, Teetgen's Teas[2] and this row of shops? I can't bear it. I don't know what it is. It's always the same. I always feel the same. It is sending me mad. One day it will be worse. If it gets any worse I shall be mad. Just here. Certainly. Something is wearing out of me. I am meant to go mad. If not, I should not always be coming along this piece without knowing it, whichever street I take. Other people would know the streets apart. I don't know where this bit is or how I get to it. I come every day because I am meant to go mad here. Something that knows brings me here and is making me go mad because I am myself and nothing changes me.

---

1 Miriam is reminded of her mother, who dies at the end of *Honeycomb* (*Pilgrimage* vol. 3). Though the death is obscured in the text, readers of the whole *Pilgrimage* series can piece the surrounding events together through Miriam's memories, which become increasingly clear and more explicit. In *The Tunnel*, she is clearly still feeling trauma, as all references to her mother are vague and troubled.

2 A famous London tea company established in 1834.

CHAPTER VIII

The morning went on. It seemed as though there was to be no opportunity of telling Mr Hancock until lunch had changed the feeling of the day. He knew there was something. Turning to select an instrument from a drawer she was at work upon, he had caught sight of her mirth and smiled his amusement and anticipation into the drawer before turning gravely back to the chair. Perhaps that was enough, the best, like a moment of amusement you share with a stranger and never forget. Perhaps by the time she was able to tell him, he would be disappointed. No. It was too perfect. Just the sort of thing that amused him.

He had one long sitting after another, the time given to one patient overlapping the appointment with the next, so that her clearings and cleansings were done with a patient in the chair, noiselessly and slowly, keeping her in the room, making to-day seem like a continuation of yesterday afternoon. Yesterday shed its radiance. The shared mirth made a glowing background to her toil. The duties accumulating downstairs made her continued presence in the surgery a sort of truancy. She felt more strongly than ever the sense of her usefulness to him. She had never so far helped him so deftly and easily, being everywhere and nowhere, foreseeing his needs without impeding his movements, doing everything without reminding the patient that there was a third person in the room. She followed sympathetically the long slow process of excavation and root treatment, the delicate shaping and undercutting of the walls of cavities, the adjustment and retention of the many appliances for the exclusion of moisture, the insertions of the amalgams and pastes whose pounding and mixing made a recurrent crisis in her morning. She wished again and again that the dentally ignorant, dentally ironic world could see the operator at his best; in his moments of quiet intense concentration on giving his best to his patients.

The patients suffering the four long sittings were all of the best group, leisurely and untroubled as to the mounting up of guineas, and three of them intelligently appreciative of what was being done. *They* knew all about the "status" of modern dentistry and the importance of teeth. They were all clear serene tranquil cheerful people who probably hardly ever went to a doctor. They would rate oculists and dentists on a level with doctors, and two of them at least would rate Mr Hancock on a level with anybody.... To-morrow would be quite different, a rush of gas cases, that man who was sick if an instrument touched the back of his tongue; Mrs Wolff, disputing fees, the deaf-mute, the grubby little man on a newspaper ... he ought to have no patients but these intelligent ones and really nervous and delicate people and children.

"I sometimes wish I'd stuck to medicine."

"Why?"

"Well—I don't know. You know they get a good deal more all round out of their profession than a dentist does. It absorbs them more.... I don't say it ought not to be the same with dentistry. But it isn't. I don't know a dentist who wants to go on talking shop until the small hours. I'm quite sure I don't. Now look at Randle. He was dining here last night. So was Bentley. We separated at about midnight; and Randle told me this morning that he and Bentley walked up and down Harley Street telling each other stories, until two o'clock."

"That simply means they talk about their patients."

"Well—yes. They discuss their cases from every point of view. They get more human interest out of their work."

"Of course everybody knows that medical students and doctors are famous for stories. But it doesn't really mean they know anything about *people*. I don't believe they do. I think the dentist has quite as much opportunity of studying human nature. Going through dentistry is like dying. You must know almost everything about a patient who has had much done, or even a little——"

"The fact of the matter is their profession is a hobby to them as well as a profession. That's the truth of the matter. Now I think a man who can make a hobby of his profession is a very fortunate man."

How surprised the four friendly wealthy patients, especially the white-haired old aristocrat who was always pressing invitations upon him, would have been, ignoring or treating her with the kindly consideration due to people of her station, if they could have seen inside his house yesterday and beheld her ensconced in the most comfortable chair in his drawing-room ... talking to Miss Szigmondy.

Each time she came downstairs, she sat urgently down to the most pressing of her clerical duties and presently found her mind ranging amongst thoughts whose beginnings she could not remember. She felt equal to anything. Every prospect was open to her. Simple solutions to problems that commonly went unanswered round and round in her head, presented themselves in flashes. At intervals she worked with a swiftness and ease that astonished her, making no mistakes, devising small changes and adjustments that would make for the smoother working of the practice, dashing off notes to friends in easy expressive phrases that came without thought.

Rushing up towards lunch-time in answer to the bell, she found Mr Hancock alone. He turned from the washstand and stood carefully drying his hands. "Are they showing up?" he murmured and seeing her, smiled his sense of her eagerness to communicate and approached a few steps, waiting and smiling with the whole of his face exactly as he would smile when the communication was made. There was really no need to tell. Miriam glanced back for an incoming patient. "Miss Szig*mon*dy," she began in a voice deep with laughter.

He laughed at once, with a little backward throw of his head, just as the patient came in. Miriam glided swiftly into her corner.

At tea-time she found herself happily exhausted, sitting alone in the den waiting for the sound of footsteps. For the first time the gas-stove was unlit. The rows of asbestos balls stood white and bare.[1] But a flood of sunlight came through the western panes of the newly washed skylight. The little low tea-table, with its fresh uncrumpled low-hanging white cover and compact cluster of delicate china, stood in full sunshine amidst the comfortable winter shabbiness. The decorative confusion on the walls shone richly out of the new bright light. It needed only to have all the skylights open, the blue of the sky visible, the thin spring air coming in, the fire alight making a summery glow, to be perfect; like spring tea-time in a newly visited house. The Wilsons' sitting-room would be in an open blaze of shallow spring sunshine. She saw it going on day by day towards the rich light of summer ... jealously. One ought to be there every day. So much life would have passed through the room. Every day last week had been full of it, everything changed by it, and now, since yesterday, it seemed months ago. It seemed too late to begin going down again. One thing blots out another. You cannot have more than

---

1 Asbestos balls were used in gas stoves to conserve fuel, as they burned more efficiently than coal and left less of a mess.

one thing intensely. Quite soon it would be as if she had never been down; except in moments now and again, when something recalled the challenge of their point of view. They would not want her to go down again, unless she had begun to be different. Until yesterday she might have begun. But yesterday afternoon they had been forgotten so completely, and waking up from yesterday she no longer wanted to begin their way of being different. But other people had already begun to identify her with them. That came of talking. If she had said nothing, nothing would have been changed; either at Wimpole Street or with the girls. Did they really like reading *The Evolution of the Idea of God*,[1] or were they only pretending? Sewing all the time, busily, like wives, instead of smoking and listening and thinking.

Which was the stronger? The interest of getting the whole picture there, and struggling with Mr Wilson's deductions, or the interest of getting the girls to grasp and admire his conclusions even while she herself refused them? ...

"Why can't I keep quiet about, the things that happen? It's all me, my conceit and my way of rushing into things." ... But other people were the same in a way. Only there was something real in their way. They believed in the things they rushed into. "Miss Henderson knows the great critic, intimately." He had thought that would impress Miss Szigmondy. It did. For a moment she had stopped talking and looked surprised. There was time to disclaim, to tell them they were being impressed in the wrong way; to tell them something, to explain in some way. The moment had passed, full of terrible far-off trouble, "decisive."

There is always a fraction of a second when you know what you are doing. Miss Szigmondy would have gone on talking about bicycling, until Mr Hancock came back. There was no need to say suddenly, without thinking about it, "I am dying to learn."[2] *Really* that sudden remark was the result of having failed to speak when they were all talking about Mr Wilson. If, then, one

---

1   Published in 1897 by Grant Allen (1848-99), who was a supporter of evolutionary theory and well known for his science fiction works.

2   Bicycles were developed in the nineteenth century and became very popular in the 1890s, when their design came to look much like today's bicycles. The proliferation of bicycles gave women in particular much more freedom of mobility. Feminist Susan B. Anthony called the bicycle a "freedom machine."

had suddenly said "I am dying to learn bicycling," or *anything*, they would have known something of the truth about Mr Wilson. It was the worrying thought of him, still there, that made one say, without thinking, "I am dying to learn." It was too late. It linked up with the silence about Mr Wilson and left one being a person who knew and altogether approved of Mr Wilson and wanted to learn bicycling. Altogether wrong. "You know—I don't approve of Mr Wilson; and you might not if you heard him talk, and ... his marriage ... you know...."

... If I had done that, I should have been easy and strong and should have "made conversation" when she began talking about bicycling. I was like the man who proposed to the girl at the dance because he could not think of anything to say to her. He could not think of anything to say, because he had something on his mind....

And Miss Szigmondy would not have called this morning.

"*No* one can pgonounce my name. You had better call me Thégèse,[1] my dear girl. Yes, do; I want you to." She had said that with a worried face, a sudden manner of unsmiling intimacy. She certainly had some plan. Standing there, with her broken-hearted voice and her anxious face, she seemed to be separate from the room, even from her own clothes. Yet something within her was moving so quickly that it made one breathless. She was so intent that she was unconscious of the appealing little figure she made, huddled in her English clothes. She stood dressed and determined and prosperous, her smart little toque[2] held closely against her dark hair and sallow face with the kind of chenille-spotted veil that was a rampart against *everything* in the world, for an Englishwoman. But it did not touch her or do anything for her. It gave an effect of prison bars behind which she was hanging her head and weeping and appealing. One could have laughed and gathered her up. Why was she forlorn? Why did she imagine that one was also forlorn? The sight of her made all the forlornness one had ever seen or read about seem peopled with knowledge and sympathy and warm thoughts that flew crowding along one's brain as close and bright as the texture of everybody's everyday. But the eyes were anxious and preoccupied, blinking now and then in her long unswerving appealing gaze, shutting swiftly for

---

1 Richardson's attempt to capture a Hungarian accent.
2 Knit woolen cap.

lightning calculations between her rapid appealing statements. What was she trying to do?

She tried to stand in front of everything, to put everything aside as if it were part of something she knew. Laughing over it with Mr Hancock would not dispose of that. After the fun of telling him, she would still be there, with the two bicycle lessons that were going begging. He knew already that Miss Szigmondy had called, and would assume that she had suggested things and that one was not going to do them. If one told him about the lessons he would say that is very kind and would mean it. He was always fine in thinking a "kind" action kind ... but she does not come because she wants me. She does not want anybody. She does not know the difference between one person and another.... He knows only her social manner. She has never been alone with him and come close and shown him her determination and her sorrow ... sorrow ... sorrow....

He could never see that it was impossible, without forcibly crushing her, to get out of doing some part of what she desired....

If one were drawn in and did things, let oneself want to do things for any one else, there would be a change in the atmosphere at Wimpole Street. That never occurred to him. But he would feel it if it happened. If there were someone near who made distractions, there would be a difference, something that was not given to him. He was so unaware of this. He was absolutely ignorant of what it was that kept things going as they were.

.

CHAPTER IX

The cycling school was out of sight and done with, and Miriam hurried down the Chalk Farm Road.[1] If only she could see an omnibus and be in it, going anywhere down away from the north. Miss Szigmondy had brought shame and misery upon her, in Chalk Farm. There was nothing there to keep off the pain. Once back, she would never think of Chalk Farm again. How could any one think it was a place, like other places? It was torture even to be in it, going through it.... Of course the man had thought I should take on a course of lessons and pay for them. I have to learn everything meanly and shamefully. He thinks I'm getting all I can for nothing. The people in the bus will see me pay my fare and I shall be all right again, going down there. What an *awful* road, going on and on with nothing in it. I am shamed and help-less; *helpless*. It's no use to try and do anything. It always exposes me and brings this maddening shame and, pain. It's over again this time, and I shall soon forget it altogether. I might just as well begin to stop thinking about it now. It's this part of London. It's like Banbury Park. The people are absolutely awful. They take cycling lessons quite coolly. They are not afraid of anybody. To them this part is the best bit of north London. They are that sort of people. They are all alike. All of them would dislike me. I should die of being with them.

Why is it that no one seems to know what north London is? They say it is healthy and open. Perhaps I shall meet someone who feels like I do about it, and would get ill and die there. It is not imagination. It is a real feeling that comes upon me....

The north London omnibus reached the tide of the Euston Road and pulled up at Portland Road station. Miriam got out, weak and ill. The first breath of the central air revived her. Stand-ing there, the omnibus looked like any other omnibus. She crossed the road, averting her eyes from the north-going roads on either side of the church, and got into the inmost corner of another bus. She wanted to ride about, getting from bus to bus, inside London until her misery had passed. Opposite her was a stout woman in a rusty bonnet and shawl and dust-defaced black skirt, looking about with eyes that did not see what they looked at, all the London consciousness in her. Miriam sat gazing at her. The woman's eyes crossed her and passed unperturbed....

---

1   An area of north London. Many cycling schools opened around London in the 1890s, though there is no specific reference to one at Chalk Farm.

The lane of little shops flowed away, their huddled detail crushing together, wide shop windows glittered steadily by and narrowed away. When the bus stopped at Gower Street,[1] the tower of St Pancras church came into sight soaring majestically up, screened by trees.

The trees in Endsleigh Gardens came along, gently waving their budding branches in bright sunshine. The colour of the gardens was so intense that the sun must just be going to set behind Euston station. The large houses moved steadily behind the gardens, in blocks, bright white, with large quiet streets opening their vistas in between the blocks, leading to green freshness and then safely on down into Soho.[2] The long square came to an end. The shrub-trimmed base of St Pancras church came heavily nearer and stopped. As Miriam got out of the bus, she watched its great body rise in clear sharp outline against the blue. Its clock was booming the hour out across the gardens through the houses and down into the squares. On this side its sound was broken up by the narrow roar of the Euston Road and the clamour coming right and left from the two great stations.[3]

Her feet tramped happily across the square of polished roadway patterned with shadows, and along the quiet clean sunlit pavement behind the gardens. It was always bright and clean and quiet and happy there, like the pavement of a road behind a seafront. The sound of a mail van, rattling heavily along Woburn Place, changed to a soft rumble as she turned in between the great houses of Tansley Street and walked along its silent corridor of afternoon light. Sparrows were cheeping in the stillness. To be able to go down the quiet street and on into the squares—on a bicycle.... I must learn somehow to get my balance. To go along, like in that moment when he took his hands off the handle-bars, in knickers and a short skirt[4] and all the summer to come.... Everything shone with a greater intensity. Friends and thought and work were nothing compared to being able to ride alone, balanced, going along through the air.

---

1   Miriam is back in Bloomsbury now, in central London.

2   A neighbourhood in London known for its Bohemian flair and improper character. Soho is commonly associated with prostitutes, thieves, and popular entertainments such as music halls.

3   That is, Euston Station and St. Pancras Station, two large rail terminals in London.

4   In addition to increased mobility, bicycling influenced women's dress, eventually allowing them to shed their large, cumbersome skirts for shorter ones, and eventually pants.

On the hall table was a post card. "Come round on Sunday if you're in town—Irländisches Ragout,[1] Mag." Her heart stirred; that settled it—the girls wanted her; Mag wanted her. She took Alma's crumpled letter from her pocket and glanced through it once more ... "such a dull Sunday and all your fault. Why did you not come? Come on Saturday *any* time, or Sunday morning if you can't manage the week-end." What a good thing she had not written promising to go. She would be in London, safe in Kenneth Street for Sunday. Mag was quite right; going away unsettled you for the week and you did not *get* Sunday. She looked at her watch, five-thirty; in half an hour the girls would probably be at Slater's;[2] the London week-end could begin this minute; all the people who half-expected her, the Brooms, the Pernes, Sarah and Harriett, the Wilsons, would be in their homes far away; she safe in Bloomsbury, in the big house, the big kind streets, Kenneth Street; places they none of them knew; safe for the whole length of the week-end. Saturday had looked so obstructed, with the cycling lesson, and the visit to Miss Szigmondy, and the many alternatives for the rest of the time.... "Oh, I've got about *fifty* engagements for Saturday," and now Saturday was clear and she felt equal to anything for the week-end. What a discovery, standing hidden there in the London house, to drop everything and go down, with all the discarded engagements, all the solicitous protecting friends put aside; easy and alone through the glimmering green squares to the end of the Strand and find Slater's.... I'll never stir out of London again. The girls are right. It isn't worth it.

She saw the girls seated at a table at the far end of the big restaurant, and shyly advanced.

"Hulloh child!"

"What you having?" she asked, sitting down opposite to them. The empty white table-cloth shone under a brilliant incandescent light; far away down the vista the door opened on the daylit street.

"Isn't it a glorious spring evening?" Spring? It was, of course. Every one had been saying the spring would never come, but to-day it was very warm. Spring was here, of course. Perspiring in a dusty cycling school and sitting in a hot restaurant was not spring. Spring was somewhere far away. Going to stay and talk in people's houses did not bring spring—landscapes belonging to

1 German: Irish stew.
2 A popular restaurant and tea room in Piccadilly.

people were *painted*; you must be alone ... or perhaps at the Brooms'. Perhaps next week-end at the Brooms' would be in time for the spring; in their back garden, the watered green lawn and the sweetbrier, and the distant trees in the large garden beyond the fence. In London it was better not to think about the times of year.

But Mag seemed to find spring in London. Her face was all glowing with the sense of it.

"What you having?"

"Have you observed with what a remarkable brilliance the tender green shines out against the soot-black branches?" Yes, that was wonderful, but what was the joke?

"Every spring I have spent in Lonndonn, I have heard that remark at least fifty times."

Miriam laughed politely. "Jan, *what* have you ordered?"

"We've ordered beef, my child, cold beefs and salads."

"Do you think I should like salad?"

"If you *had* a brother would he like salad?"

"Do they put dressing on it? If I could have just plain lettuce."

"Ask for it, my child, ask and it shall be given unto thee."

A waitress brought the beef and salad, two glasses with an inch of whisky in each, and a large siphon.

Miriam ordered beef and potatoes.

"I suppose the steak and onion days are over."

"I shan't have another steak and onions, please God, until next November."

Miriam laughed delightedly.

"Why haven't you gone away for the week-end, child?"

"I told you she wouldn't."

"I don't know. I wanted to come down here."

"Is that a compliment to us?"

"I say, I've had a bicycle lesson."

Both faces came up eagerly.

"You remember; that extraordinary woman I met at the Royal Institution."

The faces looked at each other.

"Oh, you know; I *told* you about it—the two lessons she didn't want."

"Go on, my child; we remember; go on."

Miriam sat eating her beef.

"Go on, Miriam. You've really had a lesson. I'm delighted, my child. Tell us all about it."

"D'you remember the extraordinary moment when you felt

the machine going along; even with the man holding the handle-bars?"

"You wait until there's nobody to hold the handle-bars."

"Have you been out alone yet?"

The two faces looked at each other.

"Shall we tell her?"

"You *must* tell me; es ist bestimmt in Gottes Rath."[1]

They leaned across the table and spoke low, one after the other. "We went out—last night—after dark—and rode—round Russell Square[2]—twice—in our knickers——"

"*No!* Did you really? How simply heavenly."

"It *was*. We came home nearly crying with rage at not being able to go about, permanently, in nothing but knickers. It would make life an *absolutely* different thing."

"The freedom of movement."

"Exactly. You feel like a sprite you are so light."

"And like a poet though you don't know it."

"You feel like a sprite you are so light, and you feel so strong and capable and so broadshouldered you could knock down a policeman. Jan and I knocked down several last night."

"Yes; and it is not only that; think of never having to brush your skirt."

"I know. It would be bliss."

"I spend half my life brushing my skirt. If I miss a day I notice it—if I miss two days, the office notices it. If I miss three days the public notices it."

"La vie est dure; pour les femmes."[3]

"You don't want to be a man, Jan."

"Oh, I do, sometimes. They have the best of everything all round."

"*I* don't. I wouldn't be a man for anything. I wouldn't have a man's—*consciousness*, for anything."

"Why not, asthore?"[4]

"They're too absolutely pig-headed and silly...."

"*Isn't* she intolerant?"

---

1 German: It is decided, according to God's will. See p. 127, note 4.

2 Russell Square is a large garden square in the centre of the Bloomsbury neighbourhood of London; it was, at the time, a hotbed of intellectual and artistic talent.

3 French: Life is hard for women.

4 Irish-Gaelic: treasure.

Miriam sat flaring. That was not the right answer. There was something; and they must know it; but they would not admit it.

"Then you can both really ride?"

"We do nothing else; we've given up walking; we no longer walk up and down stairs; we ride."

Miriam laughed her delight. "I can quite understand; it alters everything. I realized that this afternoon at the school. To be able to bicycle would make life utterly different; on a bicycle you feel a different person; nothing can come near you, you forget who you are. Aren't you glad you are alive to-day, when all these things are happening?"

"What things, little one?"

"Well, cycling and things. You know, girls, when I'm thirty I'm going to cut my hair short and wear divided skirts."

Both faces came up.

"Why on earth?"

"I can't face doing my hair and brushing skirts and keeping more or less in the fashion, that means about two years behind because I never realize fashions till they're just going, even if I could afford to—all my life."

"Then why not do it now?"

"Because all my friends and relatives would object. It would worry them too—they would feel quite sure then I should never marry—and they still entertain hopes, secretly."

"Don't you want to marry—ever; ever?"

"Well—it would mean giving up this life."

"Yes, I know. I agree there. That can't be faced."

"I should think *not*. Aren't you going to have any pudding?"[1]

"But why thirty? Why not thirty-one?"

"Because nobody cares what you do when you're thirty; they've all given up hope by that time. Aren't you two going to have any pudding?"

"No. But that is no reason why you should not."

"What a good idea—to have just one dish and coffee."

"That's what we think; and it's cheap."

"Well, I couldn't have had any dinner at all, only I'm cadging dinner with you to-morrow."

"What would you have done?"

"An egg, at an A.B.C."

"How fond you are of A.B.C.s."

---

1 English term for dessert.

"I love them."

"What is it that you love about them?"

"Chiefly, I think, their dowdiness. The food is honest; not showy, and they are so blissfully dowdy."

Both girls laughed.

"It's no good. I have come to the conclusion I like dowdiness. I'm not smart. You are."

"This is the first we have heard of it."

"Well, you know you are. You keep in the fashion. It may be quite right, perhaps you are more sociable than I am."

"One is so conspicuous if one is not dressed more or less like other people."

"That's what I hate; dressing like other people. If I could afford it I should be stylish—not smart. Perfect coats and skirts, and a few good evening dresses. But you must be awfully well off for that. If I can't be stylish I'd rather be dowdy, and in a way I like dowdiness even better than stylishness."

The girls laughed.

"But aren't clothes awful, anyhow? I've spent four and eleven on my knickers and I can't possibly get a skirt till next year, if then, or afford to hire a machine."

"Why don't you ask them to raise your salary?"

"After four months? Besides, any fool could do the work."

"If I were you I should tell them. I should say 'Gentlemen—I wish for a skirt and a bicycle.'"

"Mag, don't be so silly."

"I *can't* see it. *They* would benefit by your improved health and spirits. Jan and I are new women since we have learned riding. *I* am thinking of telling the governor I must have a rise to meet the increased demands of my appetite. Our housekeeping expenses, I should say, are doubled. What *will* you? Que faire?"[1]

"You see the work I'm doing is not worth more than a pound a week—my languages are no good there. I suppose I ought to learn typing and shorthand; but where could I find the money for the training?"

"Will you teach her shorthand, if I teach her typing?"

"Certainly, if the child wants to learn. I don't advise her."

"Why not, Jan? *You* did. How long would it take me in evenings?"

---

1 French: What to do?

"A year at least, to be marketable. It's a vile thing to learn, unless you are thoroughly stupid."

"That's true. Jan was a perfect fool. The more intelligent you are, the longer you take."

"You see it isn't a language. It is an arbitrary system of signs."

"With your intelligence you'd probably grow grey at the school. Wouldn't she, Jan?"

"Probably."

"Besides, I can't imagine Mistress Miriam in an office."

"Nobody would have me. I'm not business-like enough. I am learning book-keeping at their expense. And don't forget they give me lunch and tea. I say, we are going to read *The Evolution of the Idea of God*[1] to-night?"

"Yes. Let's get back and get our clothes off. If I don't have a cigarette within half an hour, I shall die."

"Oh, so shall I. I had forgotten the existence of cigarettes."

Out in the street, Miriam felt embarrassed. The sunset glow broke through wherever there was a gap towards the north-west, and flooded a strip of the street and struck a building. The presence of the girls added a sharpness to its beauty, especially the presence of Mag, who felt the spring even in London. But both of them seemed entirely oblivious. They marched along at a great rate, very upright and swift—like grenadiers—why grenadiers?[2] Like grenadiers, making her hurry in a way that increased the discomfort of her hard cheap down-at-heel shoes. Their high-heeled shoes were in perfect condition and they went on and on, laughing and jesting as if there were no spring evening all round them. She wanted to stroll, and stop at every turn of the road. She grew to dislike them both long before Kenneth Street was reached, their brisk gait as they walked together in step, leaving her to manœuvre the passing of pedestrians on the narrow pavements of the side streets, the self-confident set of their this-season's clothes, "line"[3] clothes, like every one else was wearing, every one this side of the West End; Oxford Street clothes ... and to long to be wandering home alone through the leafy squares. Were people who lived together always like this, always brisk and joking and

---

1 Published in 1897 by Grant Allen (1848-99). See p. 181, note 1.

2 Soldiers who usually led full frontal assaults the largest and strongest soldiers.

3 That is, designer clothes.

keeping it up? They got on so well together ... and she got on so well, too, with them. "No one ever feels a third," Mag had said. I am tired, too tired. They are stronger than I am. I feel dead; and they are perfectly fresh.

"D'you know I believe I feel too played out to read," she said at their door.

"Then come in and smoke," said Mag taking her arm. "The night is yet young."

CHAPTER X

Miriam swung her legs from the table and brought her tilted chair to the ground. The leads[1] sloped down as she got to her feet and the strip of sky disappeared. The sunlight made a broad strip of gold along the parapet and a dazzling plaque upon the slope of the leads. She lounged into the shadowy middle of the room and stood feeling tall and steady and easy and agile in the freedom of knickers. The clothes lying on the bed were transformed. "I say," she murmured, her cigarette end wobbling encouragingly from the corner of her lips as she spoke, "they're not bad." She strolled about the room glancing at them from different points of view. They really made quite a good whole. It was the lilac that made them a good whole, the fresh heavy blunt cones of pure colour. In the distance, the bunched ribbon looked almost all green. She drew the hat nearer to the light, and the ribbon became mauve with green shadows and green with mauve shadows as it moved. The girl had been right about bunching the ribbon a little way up the sugar-loaf[2] and over the wide brim. It broke the papery stiffness of the lilac and the harshness of the black straw. The straw looked very harsh and black in the clearer light. Out of doors it would look almost as if it had been done with that awful shiny hat polish. If the straw had been dull and silky and some shaded tone of mauve and green, it would have been one of those hats that give you a sort of madness, taking your eyes in and in, with the effect of a misty distant woodland brought near and moving, depths of interwoven colour under your eyes. But it would not have gone with the black-and-white check. The black part of the hat was right for the tiny check. That is the idea of some smart woman.... I did not think of it in the shop, but I got it right somehow, I can see now. It's right. Those might be someone else's things.... The sight of the black suède gloves and the lace-edged handkerchief and the powder-box laid out on the chest of drawers made her eager to begin. This was dressing. The way to feel you were dressing was to put everything out first, and then come back as another person and make a grand toilet.[3] It makes you feel free and leisurely. There had been the long strange morning. In half an hour the adventure would begin and go on

---

1 Sheets or strips of lead used to cover a roof.
2 The rounded crown of the hat.
3 Making a toilet was an expression for getting dressed then fixing one's hair, skin, and makeup.

and be over. The room would not be in it. Something nice, or horrible, would come back. But the room would not be changed.

She found the dark green Atlas bus[1] standing ready by the kerb and waited until it was just about to start, looking impatiently up and down the long vistas of the empty Sunday street, and then jumped hurriedly in with the polite half-irritated resignation of the man about town who finds himself stranded in a god-forsaken part of London, and steered herself carefully, against the swaying of the vehicle, along between the rows of seated forms, keeping her eyes carefully averted and fixed upon distant splendours. Securing an empty corner she sat down provisionally, on the edge of the seat, occupying the least possible space, clear of her neighbour, her eyes, turned inwards on splendours, still raking the street, her person ready to leap up at the sight of a crawling hansom[2]—telling herself in a drawl that she felt must somehow be audible to an observant listener, how damnable it was that there were not hansoms in these remarkable backwoods—so damned inconvenient when your own barrow[3] is laid up at Windover's. But a hansom might possibly appear.... She turned to the little corner window at her side and gazed with fierce abstraction down the oncoming street. Presently she would really be in a hansom. Miss Szigmondy had mentioned hansoms ... supposing she should have to pay her share? Her heart beat rapidly and her face flushed as she thought of the fourpence in her purse. She would not be able even to offer. But if Miss Szigmondy were alone she would take cabs. There would be no need to mention it. The ambling trit-trot of the vehicle gradually prevailed over the mood in which she had dressed. She was becoming aware of her companions. Presently she would be taking them all in and getting into a world that had nothing to do with her afternoon. Turning aside so that her face could not be seen and her own vision might be restricted to the roadway rolling slowly upon her through the little end window, she dreamed of contriving somehow or other to save money for hansoms. Hansoms were a necessary part of the worldly life. Floating about in a hansom in the West End, in the season, was like nothing else in the world. It changed you, your feelings, manner, bearing, everything. It

---

1 A bus to Atlas Road, in north London.
2 Hansom cabs were small, private horse-drawn carriages widely used in Victorian London.
3 Carriage.

made you part of a wonderful exclusive difficult triumphant life, a streak of it, going in and out. It cut you off from all personal difficulties, made you drop your personality and lifted you right out into the freedom of a throng of happy people, a great sunlit tide, singing, all the same laughing song, wave after wave, advancing, in open sunlight. It took you on to a great stage, lit and decked, where you were lost, everything was lost and forgotten in the masque.[1] Nothing personal could matter so long as you were there and kept there, day and night. Every one was invisible and visionless, united in the spectacle, gilding and hiding the underworld in a brilliant embroidery ... continuously.

As they rumbled up Baker Street,[2] she wondered impatiently why Miss Szigmondy had not appointed a meeting place in the West End. Baker Street began all right; one felt safe going up Orchard Street,[3] past the beautiful china shop and the Romish richness of Burns and Oates,[4] seeing the sequestered worldliness of Granville Place and rolling through Portman Square[5] with its enormous grey houses masking hidden wealth; but after that it became a dismal corridor retreating towards the full chill of the north. If they had met in Piccadilly, they could have driven straight down through heaven into Chelsea.[6] Perhaps it would not be heaven with Miss Szigmondy. She would not know the difference in the feeling of the different parts of London. She would drive along like a foreigner—or a member of a provincial antiquarian society,[7] "intelligently" noticing things, knowing about the buildings and the statues. Londoners were always twitted with not knowing about London ... the reason why they jested about it, half proudly, their consciousness of being Londoners, living in London, was going about happy, the minute they were outside their houses, looking at nothing and feeling everything,

---

1 A dramatic performance involving music and dance, in which performers frequently wear masks.

2 A London street in the Marylebone district, running between Hyde Park and Regent's Park, home of Sherlock Holmes, Sir Arthur Conan Doyle's (1859-1930) fictional detective.

3 A London street just off Baker Street, near the Hyde Park end.

4 A Roman Catholic publishing house.

5 A public square in London, with a number of famous large houses on its edges.

6 An area of central London, noted in the nineteenth century for its community of bohemian artists.

7 An organization of people from outside London who study (as amateurs) its history and antiquities.

like people wandering happily from room to room in a well-known house at some time when everybody's attention was turned away by a festival or a catastrophe.... London was like a prairie. In a hansom it would be heaven, with anybody. A hansom saved you from your companion more than any other vehicle. You were as much outside it in London as you were inside with your companion, if you were anywhere south of Marylebone ... the way the open hood framed the vista....

There was a hansom waiting outside Miss Szigmondy's garden gate. The afternoon would begin at once with a swift drive back into the world. Miss Szigmondy met her in the dark hall, with an outbreak of bright guttural talk, talking as she collected her things, breaking in with shouted instructions to an invisible servant. Her voice sounded very foreign in the excited upper notes, but it rang, a thin wiry ring, not shrieking and breaking like the voices of excited Englishwomen. Perhaps that was "voice production."

In the cab she sat sorting her cards, reading out names. Miriam thrilled as she heard them. Miss Szigmondy's attention was no longer on her. Her mind slipped easily back; the intervening time fell away. She was going with her sisters along past the Burlington Arcade, she saw the pillar box, the old man selling papers, the old woman with the crooked black sailor hat and the fringed shawl, sitting on a box behind her huge basket of tulips and daffodils ... the great grimed stone pillars, the court-yard beyond them blazing with sunshine, the wide stone steps at the far end of the court-yard leading up into cool shadow, the turnstile and great hall, an archway, and the sudden fresh blaze of colours....

But the hansom had turned into the main road and was going *north*. They were going even further north than Miss Szigmondy's ... up a straight empty Sunday suburban road between rows of suburban houses with gardens that tried to look pretty ... an open silly prettiness like suburban ladies coming up to town for matinées ... if there were artists living up here, it would not be worth while to go and see them....

As the afternoon wore on it dawned upon Miriam that if Miss Szigmondy were to be at the poet's house in evening dress by half past six, they had seen nearly all they were going to see. There could be no thought of Chelsea. But she answered with a swift negative when Miss Szigmondy inquired, as they were shown into their hansom outside their eighth large Hampstead[1] house, whether she were tired. Her unsatisfied consciousness ran ahead, waiting; just beyond, round the next corner, was something that would relieve the oppression. "I just want to run in and see that poor boy Gilbert Haze." Then it was over, and she must go on enduring whilst Miss Szigmondy paid a call; unable to get free because she was being paid for and could not afford to go back alone. They drove for some distance, the large houses disappeared, they were in amongst little drab roadways like those round about Mornington Road. Perhaps if she improvised an engagement, she could find her way to Regent's Park and get back. But they had come so far. They must be on the outskirts of N.W., perhaps even in N.[2] They pulled up before a small drab villa. The sun had gone behind the clouds, the short street was desolate. No touch of life or colour anywhere, hardly a sign of spring in the small parched shrub-filled front gardens, uniformly enclosed by dusty railings. She dreaded her wait alone in the cab with her finery and her empty afternoon, while Miss Szigmondy visited her sick friend.

"Come along," said Miss Szigmondy from the little garden path; "poor creature, you *do* look tired." Miriam got angrily out of the cab. Whose fault was it that she was tired? Why did Miss Szigmondy go to these things? She had not cared, and was not disappointed at not caring. She was just the same as when she had started out.

"I will wait in the garden," she said hurriedly as the door opened on the house of sickness. A short young man with untidy dark hair and a shabby suit stood in the doorway. His brilliant dark eyes smiled sharply at Miss Szigmondy and shot beyond her towards Miriam as he stood aside holding the door wide. "Come along," shouted Miss Szigmondy, disappearing. Miriam came reluctantly forward and got herself through the door, reaping the second curious sharp smile as she passed. The young man had an extraordinary face, cheerful and grimy, like a street

---

1   An area of north London. The site of a fashionable spa in the 1700s, Hampstead was gradually superseded by other spas, becoming by the late 1800s a wealthy neighbourhood linked to literary and artistic pursuits.

2   Regions of London are designated by letters indicating their orientation to central London in terms of the cardinal directions: North, South, East, West. "N.W.": North-West.

arab;[1] he was rather like a street arab. Miss Szigmondy was talking loudly from a little room to the right of the door. Miriam's embarrassment in the impossibility of explaining her own superfluous presence was not relieved when she entered the room. The young man was clearly not prepared. It was a most unwarrantable intrusion. She stood at a loss behind Miss Szigmondy who was planted, still eagerly talking, on the small clear space of bare boards—cracked and dusty, like a warehouse—in the middle of the room, and tried not to see anything in particular; but her eyes already had the sense that there was nothing to sit upon, no corner to retire into, nothing but an extraordinary confusion of shabby dust-covered things laid bare by the sunlight that poured through the uncurtained window. Her eyes took refuge in the face of the young man confronting Miss Szigmondy making replies to her volley of questions. He had no front teeth, nothing but blackened stumps; dreadful, one ought not to look, unless he were going to be helped. Perhaps Miss Szigmondy was going to help him. But he did not look ill. His bright glancing eyes shot about as if looking at something that was not there, and he answered Miss Szigmondy's sallies with a sort of cheerful convulsion of his whole frame. He seemed to be "on wires";[2] but not weak; strong and cheerful; happy; a kind of cheerfulness and happiness she had never met before. It was quiet. It came from him soundlessly, making within his pleasant voice a gay noise that conquered the strange embarrassing room. Presently, in answer to a demand from Miss Szigmondy he opened folding doors and ushered them into an adjoining room.

Miriam stood holding the little group in her hands, longing for words. She could only smile and smile. The young man stood by looking at it and smiling, too, giving his attention to Miss Szigmondy's questions about some larger white things standing in the bare room. When he moved away towards these and she could leave off wondering whether it would do to say "And is this really going to the Academy[3] next week?" instead of again repeating "How beautiful," and her eye could run undisturbed over and over the outlines of the two horses, impressions crowded upon her. The thing moved and changed as she looked at it; it seemed

---

1 Nineteenth-century term for "a homeless child or young person living on the streets" (*OED*).

2 Nervous, tense.

3 The Royal Academy of Arts. See p. 62, note 4.

as if it must break away, burst out of her hands into the surrounding atmosphere. Everything about took on a happy familiarity, as if she had long been in the bright bare plaster-filled little room. From the edges of the small white group a radiance spread, freshening the air, flowing out into the happy world, flowing back over the afternoon, bringing parts of it to stand out like great fresh bright Academy pictures. The great studios opening out within the large garden-draped Hampstead houses, rich and bright with colour in a golden light, their fur rugs and tea services on silver trays, and velvet-coated men, the wives with trailing dresses and the people standing about, at once conspicuous and lost, were like Academy pictures. It was all real now, the pictures on the great easels, scraps of the Academy blaze; the studio with the bright light, and marble, and bright clear tiger-skins on the floor, the big clean fresh tiger almost filling the canvas ... the dark studio with antique furniture and pictures of people standing about in historical clothes....

"Goodness gracious, *isn't* she a swell!"

"Are they all right?"

"Are you a millionaire my dear? Have they raised your salary?"

"Do you really like them?"

"Yes. I've never seen you look so nice. You ought always to go about in a large black hat trimmed with lilac."

"Didn't one of the artists want to paint your portrait?"

"They all did. I've promised at least twenty sittings."

"Come nearer to the lamp, fair child, that I may be even more dazzled by thy splendour."

"I'm awfully glad you like them—they'll have to go on for ever."

"Where on earth did you find the money, child?"

"Borrowed it from Harry. It was her idea. You see I shall get four pounds[1] for my four weeks' holiday; and if I go to stay with them it won't cost me anything; so she advanced me two pounds."

"And you got all this for two pounds?"

"Practically; the hat was ten and six and the other things twenty-seven and six, and the gloves half a crown."[2]

---

1 Roughly £270 in today's currency.

2 Ten shillings sixpence, worth about £35 in today's currency, twenty-seven shillings sixpence, worth about £92 in today's currency, and half a crown, worth about £8.50.

"Where did you get them?"

"Edgware Road."[1]

"And just put them on?"

"It is really remarkable. Do you realize how lucky you are in being a stock size?"

"I suppose I am. But you know the awful thing about it is that they will never come in for Wimpole Street."

"Why on earth not? What could be more ladylike, more simple, more altogether suitable?"

"You see I have to wear black there."

"What an extraordinary idea. *Why?*"

"Well they asked me to. I don't know. I believe it's the fault of my predecessor. They told me she *rustled* and wore all kinds of dresses——"

"I see—a series of explosions."

"On silk foundations."

"But why should they assume that you would do the same?"

"I don't know. It's an awful nuisance. You can't get black blouses that will wash; it will be awful in the summer; besides, it's so unbecoming."

"There I can't agree. It would be for me. It makes me look dingy; but it suits you, throws up your rose-leaf complexion and your golden hair. But I call it jolly hard lines I'd like to see the governor dictating to me what I should wear."

"It's so expensive if one can't wear out one's best things."

"It's intolerable. Why do you stand it?"

"What can I do?"

"Tell them you must either wear *scarlet* at the office or have a higher *screw*."[2]

"It isn't an office, you see. I have to be so much in the surgeries and interviewing people in the waiting-room, you know."

"Yes—from dukes to dustmen. But would either the dukes or the dustmen disapprove of scarlet?"

"One has to be a discreet nobody. It's the professional world; you don't understand; you are equals, you two, superiors, pampered countesses in your offices."

"Well I think it's a beastly shame. I should brandish a pair of forceps at Mr Hancock and say 'Scarlet—or I leave.'"

"Where should I go? I have no qualifications."

"You wouldn't leave. They would say, 'Miss Henderson, wear

---

1 A major road in the west of London.

2 Slang for salary.

purple and yellow, only stay.' I think it's a reflection on her taste, don't you, Jan?"

"Certainly it is. It is fiendish. But employers *are* fiends—to women."

"I haven't found that soh."

"Ah, you keep yours in order, you rule them with a rod of iron."

"I do. I believe in it."

"I envy you your late hours in the morning."

"Ah-ha—she's had a row about that."

"*Have* you, Mag?"

"Not a row; simply a discussion."

"What happened?"

"Simply this. The governor begged me—almost in tears—to come down earlier—for the sake of the discipline of the office."

"What did you say?"

"I said Herr *Epstein*; what can I do? How do you suppose I can get up, have breakfast and be down here before eleven?"

"What did he say?"

"He protested and implored and offered to pay cabs for me."

"Good Lord, Mag, you are extraordinary."

"I am not extraordinary and it is no concern of the Deity's. I fail to see why I should get to the office earlier than I do. I don't get my letters before half-past eleven. I am fresh and gay and rested, I get through my work before closing-time. I work like anything whilst I am there."

"And you still go down at eleven?"

"I still go down at eleven."

"I *do* envy you. You see my people always want me most the first thing in the morning. It's awful, if one has been up very late."

"And what is our life worth, without late hours? The evening is the only life we have."

"Exactly. And they are the same really. They do their work to be free of it and live."

"Precisely; but they are waited on. They have their houses and baths and servants and meals and comforts. We get up in cold rooms untended and tired. *They* ought to be first at the office and wait upon us."

"She is a queen in her office; waited upon hand and foot."

"Well—why not? I do them the honour of bringing my bright petunia-clad feminine presence into their dingy warehouse; I expect some acknowledgment of the honour."

"You don't allow them either to spit or swear."

"I do not; and they appreciate it."

"Mine are beasts. I defy any one to do anything with them. I *loathe* the city man."

Miriam sighed. In neither of these offices, she felt sure, could she hold her own—and yet, compared to her own long day, what freedom the girls had—ten to five and eleven to six and any clothes they found it convenient to wear. But city men ... no restrictions were too high a price to pay for the privileges of her environment; the association with gentlemen, her quiet room, the house, the perpetual interest of the patients, the curious exciting streaks of social life, linking up with the past and carrying it forward on a more generous level. The girls had broken with the past and were fighting in the world. She was somehow between two worlds, neither quite sheltered, nor quite free ... not free as long as she wanted, in spite of her reason, to stay on at Wimpole Street and please the people there. Why did she want to stay? What future would it bring? Less than ever was there any chance of saving for old age. She could not for ever go on being secretary to a dentist.... She drove these thoughts away; they were only one side of the matter; there were other things; things she could not make clear to the girls; nor to any one who could not see and feel the whole thing from inside, as she saw and felt it. And even if it were not so, if the environment of her poorly paid activities had been trying and unsympathetic, at least it gave seclusion, her own room to work in, her free garret and her evening and week-end freedom.[1] But what was she going to do with it?

"Tell us about the *show*, Miriam. Cease to gaze at Jan's relations; sit down, light a cigarette."

"These German women fascinate me," said Miriam swinging round from the mantelshelf; "they are so like Jan and so utterly different."

"Yes; Jan is Jan and they are Minna and Erica."

Taking a cigarette from Mag's case, Miriam lit it at the lamp. Before her eyes the summer unrolled—concerts with Miss Szigmondy, going in the cooling day in her new clothes, with a thin blouse, from daylight into electric light and music, taking off the

---

1 Virginia Woolf's (1882-1941) essay *A Room of One's Own* (1929) expresses a similar idea, that a woman must have her own space and financial independence in order to write. Though Woolf's essay is the most famous articulation of this idea, Richardson has here anticipated her by ten years.

zouave[1] inside and feeling cool at once, the electric light mixing with the daylight,[2] the cool darkness to walk home in alone, full of music that would last on into the next day; Miss Szigmondy's musical at-homes,[3] evenings at Wimpole Street, week-ends in the flowery suburbs, windows and doors open, cool rooms, gardens in the morning and evening, week-ends in the country, each journey like the beginning of the summer holiday, week-ends in town, Sunday afternoons at Mr Hancock's and Miss Szigmondy's—all taking her away from Kenneth Street. All these things yielded their best reality in this room. Glowing brightly in the distance they made this room like the centre of a song. But a week-end taken up was a week-end missed at Kenneth Street. It meant missing Slater's on Saturday night, the week-end stretching out ahead immensely long, the long evening with the girls, its lateness protected by the coming Sunday, waking lazily fresh and happy and easy-minded on Sunday morning, late breakfast, the cigarette in the sunlit window space, its wooden sides echoing with the clamour of St Pancras bells, the three voices in the little rooms, irländisches ragout, the hours of smoking and talking out and out on to strange promontories where everything was real all the time, the faint gradual coming of the twilight, the evening untouched by the presence of Monday, no hurry ahead, no social performances, no leave-taking, no railway journey.

"Yes; Jan is Londonized; she looks German; her voice suggests the whole of Germany; these girls are Germany untouched, strong, cheerful, musical, tree-filled Germany, without any doubts. They've got Jan's sense of humour without her cynicism."

"Is that so, Jan?"

"Yes, I think perhaps it is. They are sweet simple children." Yes, sweet—but maddening too. German women were so sure and unsuspicious and practical about life. Jan had some of that left. But she was English too, more transparent and thoughtful.

"The show! The show!"

She told them the story of the afternoon in a glowing précis,[4] calling up the splendours upon which she felt their imaginations

---

1 A short, open-fronted jacket, originally part of the uniform of the French Zouave units of soldiers serving in North Africa 1831-1962.
2 Electric lighting was only just entering people's homes at this time.
3 That is, times when the house was open to receiving guests, in this case specifically for musical entertainment.
4 French: brief summary.

at work, describing it as they saw it and as, with them, in retrospect, she saw it herself. Her descriptions drew Mag's face towards her, glowing, rapt and reverent. Jan sat sewing with in-turned eyes and half open, half smiling appreciative face. They both fastened upon the great gold-framed pictures, asking for details. Presently they were making plans to visit the Academy, and foretelling her joy in seeing them again and identifying them. She had not thought of that; certainly, it would be delightful; and perhaps seeing the pictures in freedom and alone she might find them wonderful.

"Why do you say their wives were all like cats?"

"They were." She called up the unhatted figures moving about among the guests in trailing gowns—keeping something up, pretending to be interested, being cattishly nice to the visitors, and thinking about other things all the time.... I can't *stand* them, oh, I *can't* stand them.... But the girls would not have seen them in that way; they would have been interested in them and their dresses, they would have admired the prettiness of some of them and found several of them "charming" ... if Mag were an artist's wife she would behave in the way those women behaved....

"Were they all *alike*?" That was half sarcastic....

"Absolutely. They were all *cats*, simply."

"Isn't she *extraordinary*?"

"It's the cats who are extraordinary. Why do they do it, girls! *Why* do they do it?" She flushed, feeling insincere. At this moment she felt that she knew that Mag, in social life, would conform and be a cat. She had never thought of her in social life; here, in poverty and freedom, she was herself.

"Do *phwatt*, me dear?"

"Oh, let them go. It makes me tired, even to think of them. The thought of the sound of their voices absolutely wears me out."

"I'm not laaazy—I'm tie-erd—I was *born* tie-erd."

"I say, girls, I want to ask you something."

"Well?"

"Why don't you two write?"

"*Write?*"

"Write what?"

"Us?"

"Just as we are, without one"——

"Flea—I know. No. *Don't* be silly. I'm perfectly serious. I mean it. Why don't you write things—both of you. I thought of it this morning."

Both girls sat thoughtful. It was evident that the idea was not altogether unfamiliar to them.

"Someone kept telling me the other day I ought to write and it suddenly struck me that if any one ought it's you two. Why don't you, Mag?"

"Why should I? Have I not already enough on my fair young shoulders?"

"*Jan*, why don't *you*?"

"I, my dear? For a most excellent reason."

"What reason?" demanded Miriam in a shaking voice. Her heart was beating; she felt that a personal decision was going to be affected by Jan's reason, if she could be got to express it. Jan did not reply instantly, and she found herself hoping that nothing more would be said about writing, that she might be free to go on cherishing the idea, alone and unbiased.

"I do not write," said Jan slowly, "because I am perfectly convinced that anything I might write would be mediocre."

Miriam's heart sank. If Jan, with all her German knowledge and her wit and experience of two countries, felt this, it was probably much truer of herself. To think about it, to dwell upon the things Mr Wilson had said, was simply vanity. He had said *any one* could learn to write. But he was clever and ready to believe her clever in the same way, and ready to take ideas from him. It was true she had material, "stuff," as he called it, but she would not have known it, if she had not been told. She could see it now, as he saw it, but if she wrote at his suggestion, a borrowed sugges-· tion, there would be something false in it, clever and false.

"Yes—I think Jan's right," said Mag cheerfully. "That is an excellent reason, and the true one."

It was true. But how could they speak so lightly and cheerfully about writing? ... the thing one had always wanted to do, that every one probably secretly wanted to do, and the girls could give up the idea without a sigh. They were right. It would be wrong to write mediocre stuff. Why was she feeling so miserable? Of course, because neither of them had suggested that she should write. They knew her better than Mr Wilson and it never occurred to them that she should write. That settled it. But something moved despairingly in the void.

"Do you think it would be *wrong* to write mediocre stuff?" she asked huskily.

"It would be worse than *wrong*, child—it would be foolish; it wouldn't sell."

CHAPTER XI

Everything was ready for the two o'clock patient. There was no excuse for lingering any longer. Half past one. Why did they not come up? On her way to the door she opened the corner cupboard and stood near the open door hungry, listening for footsteps on the basement stairs, dusting and ranging the neat rows of bottles. At the end of five minutes she went guiltily down. If he had finished his lunch, they would wonder why she had lingered so long. If she had hurried down as soon as she could, no one would have known that she hoped to have lunch alone. Now, because she had waited deliberately someone would read her guilt. She wished she were one of those people who never tried to avoid anything. The lunch-room door opened and closed as she reached the basement stairs. James's cheerful footsteps clacked along—neat high-heeled shoes—towards the kitchen. She had taken something in. They were still at lunch, unconsciously, just in the same way. No. She was glad she was not one of those people who just went on—not avoiding things....

Mr Hancock was only just beginning his second course. He must have lingered in the workshop.... He was helping himself to condiments; Mr Orly proffered the wooden peppermill; "Oh—thank you"; he screwed it with an air of embarrassed appreciativeness. There was a curious fresh lively air of embarrassment in the room, making a stirring warmth in its cellar-like coolness. Miriam slipped quietly into her place, hoping she was not an interloper. At any rate every one was too much engrossed to ponder over her lateness. Mr Orly was sitting with his elbows on the table and his serviette crumpled in his hands, ready to rise from the table, beaming mildness and waiting. Mrs Orly sat waiting and smiling with her elbows on the table.

"Ah," said Mr Orly gently as Miriam sat down, "here comes the clerical staff."

Miriam beamed and began her soup. It was James waiting to-day too, with her singing manner; a happy day.

Mrs Orly asked a question in her happiest voice. They were fixing a date.... They were going ... to a *theatre* ... together. Her astonished mind tried to make them coalesce ... she saw them sitting in a row, two different worlds confronted by one spectacle ... there was not a scrap of any kind of performance that would strike them both in the same way.

"Got anything on on Friday, Miss Henderson?"

The sudden question startled her. Had it been asked twice? She answered, stammering, in amazed consciousness of what was to follow and accepted the invitation in a flood of embarrassment. Her delight and horror and astonishment seemed to flow all over the table. Desperately she tried to gather in all her emotions behind an easy appreciative smile. She felt astonishment and dismay coming out of her hair, swelling her hands, making her clumsy with her knife and fork. Far away, beyond her grasp was the sense she felt she ought to have, the sense of belonging; socially. It was being offered. But something or someone was fighting it. Always, everywhere someone or something was fighting it.

Mr Orly had given a ghostly little chuckle. "Like dining at restaurants?" he asked kindly and swiftly.

"I don't think I ever have."

"Then we shall have the pleasure of initiating you. Like caviare?"[1]

"I don't even know what it is," said Miriam trying to bring gladness into her voice.

"Oh—this is great. Caviare to the million, eh?—oh, I ought not to have put it like that, things one would rather have said otherwise—no offence intended—none taken, I hope—don't yeh know really?—Sturgeon's roe, y' know."

"Oh, I know I don't like *roe*," said Miriam gravely.

"Chalk it up. Miss Henderson doesn't like roe."

Miriam flushed. Pressing back through her anger to what had preceded, she found inspiration.

"My education has been neglected."

"Quite so, but now's your chance. Seize your opportunity; carpe diem.[2] See?"

"I thought it was caviare, not carp," said Mr Hancock quietly.

Was it a rescue, or a sacrifice to the embarrassing occasion? She had never heard him jest with the Orlys. Mrs Orly chuckled gleefully, flashing out the smile that Miriam loved. It took every line from her care-fashioned face and lit it with a most extraordinary radiance. She had smiled like that as a girl, in response to the jests of her many brothers ... her eyes were sweet; there was a perfect sweetness in her somewhere.

"Bravo, Hancock, that's a good one.... Ye gods and fishes large

---

1 Sturgeon roe (eggs), pressed and salted, and served as a delicacy.
2 Latin: seize the day.

and small,[1] listen to *that*," he murmured half turning towards the door.

The clattering of boots on the stone stairs was followed by the rattling of the loose door knob and the splitting open of the door. Mr Leyton shot into the room, searching the party with a swift glance and taking his place in the circle in a state of headlong silent volubility. By the way he attacked his lunch it was clear he had a patient waiting, or imminent. It occurred to Miriam to wonder why he did not always arrange his appointments round about lunch-time ... but any such manœuvre would be discovered and things would be worse than ever. Mr Orly watched quietly while he refused Mrs Orly's offer to ring for soup, devouring bread and butter until she should have carved for him—and then extended his invitation to his son.

"Oh, is this the annual?" asked Mr Leyton gruffly. "What's the show?"

"My dear, will you be so good as to inform Mr Leyton of——"

"Don't be silly, Ro," said Mrs Orly trying to laugh, "we're going to *Hamlet*,[2] Ley."

"We have the honour of begging Mr Leyton's company on the occasion of our visit, dinner included, to——"

"What's the date?" rapped Mr Leyton with his tumbler to his lips.

"The date, ascertained as suited to all present with the exception of your lordship—oh my God, Ley," sighed Mr Orly, hiding his face in his serviette, his huge shoulders shaking.

"What have I done now?" asked Mr Leyton, gasping after his long drink.

"Don't be so silly, Ley. You haven't answd fathez queshun."

"How can I answer till I'm told the *date*?"

"Don't be silly, you can come any evening."

"*Friday*," whispered Miriam.

"*What?*" said Mr Orly softly, emerging from his serviette, "a traitor in the camp?"

---

1 This exclamation was quite popular in the last half of the nineteenth century, though it quickly lost currency in the twentieth. It "appears for the first time in John Hamilton Reynolds's 1822 satire *The Press, or Literary Chit-Chat*, where it constitutes an appropriately ridiculous invocation for what Reynolds earlier calls his 'satiric muse.'" (Nicholas D. Nace, "Ye Gods and Little Fishes," *Notes and Queries* [2010] 57(2): 246-48).

2 A tragic play by William Shakespeare (1564-1616).

"Friday is it? Well, then it's pretty certain I *can't* come."

"Don't be silly, Ley—you haven't any engagements."

"*Haven't I?* There's a sing-song at headquarters Friday."

"Enough, my dear, enough, press him no more," said Mr Orly rising. "Far be it from us to compete. Going to sing, Ley, or to song, eh? Never mind, boy, sorry you can't come," he added, sighing gustily as he left the room.

"You'll be able to come, Ley, won't you?" whispered Mrs Orly, impatiently lingering.

"If you'd only let me know the date beforehand instead of springing it on me."

"Don't be si'y, Ley, it vexes father so. You needn't go to the si'y sing-song."

"I don't see how I can get out of it. It's rather a big function; as an officer I ought to be there."

"Oh never mind; you'd better come."

Mr Orly called from the stairs.

"All right darling," she said, in anxious cheerful level tones, hurrying to the door. "You *must* come, Ley, you can manage, somehow."

Miriam sat feeling wretchedly about in her mind. Mr Leyton was busily finishing his lunch. In a moment Mr Hancock would reassert himself by some irrelevant insincerity. She found courage to plunge into speech, on the subject of her two lessons at the school. Her story strove strangely against the echoes and fell, impeded. It was an attempt to create a quiet diversion.... It should have been done violently ... how many times had she seen it done, the speaker violently pushing off what had gone before and protruding his diversion, in brisk animated deliberately detached tones. But it was never really any good. There was always a break and a wound, something left unhealed, something standing unlearned ... something that can only grow clear in silence....

"You'll never learn cycling like *that*," said Mr Leyton with the superior chuckle of the owner of a secret, as he snatched up a biscuit and made off. She clung fearfully to his cheerful harassed departing form. There was nothing left now in the room but the echoes. Mr Hancock sat munching his biscuit and cheese with a look of determined steely preoccupation in his eyes that were not raised above the level of the spread of disarray along the table; but she could hear the busy circulation of his thoughts. If now she could endure for a moment. But her mind flung hither and thither, seeking with a loathed servility some alien neutral topic.

She knew anything she might say with the consciousness of his thoughts in her mind would be resented and slain. To get up and go quietly away with some murmured remark about her work, would be to leave him with his judgment upon him. What he wanted was to give her an instruction about something in a detached professional voice and get rid of her, believing that she had gone unknowing, and remaining in his circle of reasonable thoughts. She hit out with all her force, coming against the buttress of silent angry forehead with random speech.

"I can't believe that it's less than two months to the longest day."

"Time flies," responded Mr Hancock grimly. She recoiled exhausted by her effort and quailed under the pang in the midday gaslit room of realization of the meaning of her words. Her eye swept over the grey-clad form and the blunted features, seeking some power that would stay the inexorable consumption of the bright passing days.

"'Tempus fugit,' I suppose one ought to say," he said with a little laugh, getting up.

"Oui," said Miriam angrily, "le temps s'envole; die Zeit vergeht, in other words."[1]

---

1   "Time flies," here repeated in Latin, French, and German. In a final bid to gain the upper hand, Miriam shows off her languages.

CHAPTER XII

Running upstairs to Mr Hancock's room a quarter of an hour before his arrival in the morning, Miriam found herself wishing that she lived altogether at Wimpole Street. They were all so kind. Life would be simplified if she could throw in her lot with them. Coming in to breakfast after the lesson had been a sort of home-coming. There were pleasant noises about the house; the family shouted carelessly to each other on the stairs, the schoolboy slid down the banisters; the usual subdued manner of the servants was modified by an air of being a possession of the house and liking it. They rushed quietly and happily about. The very aroma of the coffee seemed tranquilly to feed one. At breakfast every one was cheerful and kind. It was home. They were so sympathetic and amused over the adventure. The meeting in the freshness of the morning made everything easier to handle. It gave the morning a beginning and shed its brightness over the professional hush that fell upon the house at nine o'clock. It would make lunch-time more easy; and, at the end of the day, if asked, she would join the family party again.

While Mr Hancock was looking through his letters, she elaborately suppressed a yawn.

"How did you get on?" he asked, with prompt amusement, his eyes on a letter.

"Well, I couldn't get off; that was just it," murmured Miriam quietly, enjoying her jest; how strong she felt after her good breakfast....

He turned an amused inquiring face, and they both laughed.

Everything in the room was ready for the day's work. She polished the already bright set of forceps, with a luxurious sense of leisure.

"It was perfectly awful. When we got to the Inner Circle, Mr Leyton simply put me on the bicycle and sent me off. *He* rode round the other way and I had to go on and on. He scorched about and kept passing me."

Mr Hancock waited, smiling, for the more that stood in her struggling excited voice.

"There were people going round on horseback and a few other people on bicycles."

"I expect they all gave you a pretty wide berth."

"They *did*; except one awful man, an old gentleman sailing along looking at nothing."

"What happened?" laughed Mr Hancock delightedly.

"It was awful, I was most fearfully rude—I shouted '*Get* out of the way' and *I* was on the wrong side of the road; but miles off, only I *knew* I couldn't get back. I had forgotten how to steer."

"What did he do?"

"He swept round me looking very frightened and disturbed."

"Hadn't you a bell?"

"Yes, but it meant sliding my hand along. I daren't do that; nobody seemed to want it, they all glided about; they were really awfully nice. I *had* to go on, because I couldn't get off. I can wobble along, but I can't mount or dismount. I was never so frightened in my life."

"I'm afraid you've had a very drastic time."

"I fell off in the end, I was so dead beat."

"But this is altogether too drastic. Where was Leyton?"

"Rushing round and round, meeting me and then overtaking me, startling me out of my wits by ringing behind for me to get to the side. Nobody else did that. It was awfully kind. I went tacking about from side to side."

"I'm afraid you've had a very drastic time. I think you'd better come up this evening and learn getting on and off on the lawn; that's the way to do it."

"Oh," said Miriam gratefully; "but I have no machine. Mrs Orly lent me hers."

"I dare say we can hire a machine."

CHAPTER XIII

Miriam found it difficult to believe that the girl was a dental secretary. She swept about among Miss Szigmondy's guests in a long Liberty[1] dress, her hands holding her long scarf about her person as if she were waiting for a clear space to leap or run, staying nowhere, talking here and there with the assurance of a successful society woman, laughing and jesting, swiftly talking down the group she was with and passing on, with a shouted remark about herself, as she had done in the library on the night of Lord Kelvin's lecture.... "I'm tired of being good; I'm going to try being naughty for a change." Mr Hancock had stood planted before her, in laughing admiration, waiting for the next thing that she might say. How could he, of all men in the world, be taken out of himself by an effective trick? He had laughed more spontaneously than Miriam had ever seen him do. What *was* this effective thing? An appearance of animation. That, it seemed, could make any man, even Mr Hancock, if it were free from any suggestion of loudness or vulgarity, stand gaping and disarmed. Why had he volunteered the information that she was eighteen, and secretary to his friend in Harley Street? "You don't seem very *keen*"; that was her voice from the other end of the room; using the new smart word with a delicate emphasis, pretending interest in something, meaning nothing at all. She was a middle-aged woman, she would never be older than she was now. She saw nothing and no one, nor ever would. In all her life she would never be arrested by anything. Nice kind people would call her "a charming girl." ... "Charming girls" were taught to behave effectively, and lived in a brilliant death, dealing death all round them. Nothing could live in their presence. No natural beauty, no spectacle of art, no thought, no music. They were uneasy in the presence of these things, because their presence meant cessation of "charming" behaviour—except at such moments as they could use the occasion to decorate themselves. *They had no souls.* Yet, in social life, nothing seemed to possess any power but their surface animation.

There was real power in that other woman. Her strong young comeliness was good, known to be good. It was strange that a student of music should be known for her work among the poor. The serene large outlines of her form gave out light in the room; and the light on her white brow, unconscious above her deliber-

---

1 A popular London department store founded in 1875.

ately kind face, was the loveliest thing to be seen; the deliberately kind face spoiled it, and would presently change it; unless some great vision came to her, it would grow furrowed over "the housing problem" and the face would dry up, its white life cut off at a source; at present she was at the source; one could tell her anything. Mr Hancock recognized her goodness, spoke of her with admiration and respect. What was she doing here, among all these worldly musicians? *She* would never be a musician, never a first-class musician. Then she had ambition. She was poor. Someone was helping her ... Miss Szigmondy! Why? She must know she would never make a musician. Miriam cowered in her corner. The good woman was actually going to sing before all these celebrities. What a fine great free voice.... "*When* shall we meet—*refined* and free, amongst the moorland *brack-en* ..."[1] if Mr Hancock could have heard her sing that, surely his heart must have gone out to her? She knew, to her inmost being, what that meant. She *longed* for cleansing fires, even she with her radiant forehead; her soul flew out along the sustained notes towards its vision, her dark eyes were set upon it as she sang, the clear tones of her voice called to the companion of her soul for the best that was in him. She was the soul of truth, counting no cost. She would attain her vision, though the earthly companion she longed for might pass her by. The pure beauty of the moorland would remain for her, would set itself along the shores of her life for ever....

But she could not sing. It was the worst kind of English singing, all volume and emphasis and pressure. Was there that in her goodness too ... deliberate kindness to everybody? Was it a method—just a social method? She was one of those people about whom it would be said that she never spoke ill of any one. But was not indiscriminate deliberate conscious goodness to everybody an insult to humanity? People who were like that never knew the difference between one person and another. "Philan-thropic" people were never sympathetic. They pitied. Pity was not sympathy. It was a denial of something. It assumed that life was pitiful. Yet her clear eyes would see through anything, any evil thing to the human being behind. But she knew it, and practised it like a doctor. She had never been amazed by the fact that there were any human beings at all ... and with all her goodness she had plans and ambitions. She wanted to be a singer—and she was

---

1 A line from the Scottish poet James Hogg's (1770-1835) song "The Mermaid."

thinking about somebody. Men were dazzled by the worldly little secretary, and they reverenced the singer and her kind. Irreligious men would respect religion for her sake—and would wish, thinking of her, to live in a particular kind of way; but she would never lead a man to religion, because she had no thoughts and no ideas.

The surprise of finding these two women here, and the pain of observing them, was a just reward for having come to Miss Szigmondy's At Home[1] without a real impulse—just to see the musicians and to be in the same room with them. All that remained was to write to someone about them by name. There was nothing to do but mention their names. There was no wonder about them. They were all *fat*. Not one of them was an artist and they all hated each other. It was like a ballad concert. They all sang in the English way. They were not in the least like the instrumentalists; or St James's Hall Saturday afternoon audiences,[2] not that kind of "queer soft lot"; not shadowy grey or dead white or with that curious transparent look; they all looked ruddy or pink, and sleek; they had the same sort of kindly common sense as Harriett's Lord and Lady Bollingdon ... perhaps to keep a voice going it was necessary to be fat.

---

1   Open house: times at which a house was considered open to visitors. When a lady was "at home," her friends and acquaintances could freely drop by for entertainment, conversation, and refreshment.

2   A London concert hall (established 1858) that did chamber concerts on Saturday afternoons called "Saturday Pops," meant to bring classical music to a larger public through cheap ticket prices.

CHAPTER XIV

"It was simply heavenly going off—all standing in the hall in evening dress, while the servants blew for hansoms. I wore my bridesmaid's dress with a piece of tulle arranged round the top of the bodice. It was wrong at the back so I had to sit very carefully the whole evening to prevent it going up like a muffler, but never mind; it was heavenly, I tell you. We bowled off down through the West End in three hansoms, one behind the other, in the dark. You know the gleam and shine inside a hansom sprinting along a dark empty street where the lamps are few and dim (see *The Organist's Daughter*):[1] and then came the bright streets all alight and full of dinner and theatre people in evening dress, in hansoms, and you kept getting wedged in between other hansoms with people talking and laughing all round you; and it took about ten minutes to get from the end of Regent Street across to the other side of Piccadilly, where we dined in wicked Rupert Street. Just as the caviare was brought in, we heard that the Prince of Wales had won the Derby.[2] Shakespeare is extraordinary. I had no idea *Hamlet* was so full of quotations."

Miriam flushed as the last words ran automatically from her pen. The sense of the richly moving picture that had filled her all the morning, and now kept her sitting happily under the hot roof at her small dusty table in the full breadth of Saturday afternoon, would be gone if she left that sentence. She felt a curious painful shock at the tips of her fingers as she re-read it; a current, singing within her, was driven back by it.... Mrs Orly's face had been all alive and alight when she had leant forward across Mr Hancock and said the words that had seemed so meaningless and irritating. Perhaps she too had felt something she wanted to express and had lost it at that moment. Certainly both she and Mr Orly would feel the beauty of Shakespeare. But the words had shattered the spell of Shakespeare, and writing them down like that was spoiling the description of the evening, though Harriett would not think so.

But anyhow the letter would not do for Harriett—even if words could be found to express "Shakespeare." That would not

---

1 Perhaps the novel *La Fille de l'organiste* (1882) by Gabrielle d'Éthampes, pseudonym of Gabrielle Praud de la Nicollière (c. 1820-c. 1905). D'Éthampes was a popular and prolific novelist, yet little is known about her. Thanks to Michel Pharand for suggesting this possibility.

2 In 1896, Persimmon, Edward VIII, the Prince of Wales's horse, won the Epsom Derby, one of Britain's classic horse races.

interest Harriett. She would think the effort funny and Miri-amish, but it would not mean anything to her. She had been to Shakespeare because she adored Ellen Terry[1] and put up with Irving for her sake.... People in London seemed to think that Irving was just as great as Ellen Terry.... Perhaps now Irving would seem different. Perhaps Irving was great.... I will go and hear Irving in Shakespeare ... no money and no theatres except with other people.... The rest of the letter would simply hurt Harriett, because it would seem like a reflection on theatres with her. Theatres with her had had a magic that last night could not touch ... sitting in the front row of the pit, safely in after the long wait, the walls of the theatre going up, softly lit buff and gold, fluted and decorated and bulging with red-curtained boxes, the clear view across the empty stalls of the dim height of fringed curtain hanging in long straight folds, the certainty that Harriett shared the sense of the theatre, that for her, too, when the orchestra began, the great motionless curtain shut them in in a life where everything else in the world faded away and was forgotten, the sight of the perfection of happiness on Harriett's little buff-shad-owed face, the sudden running ripple, from side to side, of the igniting footlights[2] ... the smoothly clicking rustle of the with-drawing curtain ... the magic square of the lit scene ... the daily growth of the charm of these things during that week when they had gone to a theatre every night, so that on looking back, the being in the theatre with the certainty of the moving changing scenes ahead was clearer than either of the plays they had seen.... She sat staring through the open lattice.... The sound of the violin from the house down the street, that had been a half-heard obbli-gato[3] to her vision of last night, came in drearily, filling the space whence the vision had departed, with uneasy questions. She turned to her letter to recapture the impulse with which she had sat down.... If she turned it into a letter to Eve, all the description of the evening would have to be changed; Eve knew all about grandeurs, with the Greens's large country house and their shooting-boxes[4] and visits to London hotels; the bright glories

---

1 Dame Ellen Terry (1847-1928), the era's most popular Shakespearean stage actress in England; for Sir Henry Irving, see p. 127, note 2.
2 Theatres still used gas lighting.
3 In a musical piece, a line that is essential to the composition.
4 A small country house for use as temporary residence while one is out shooting (i.e., hunting), pastime of wealthy English people who employed "beaters" to flush pheasants and other game birds from the brush so they could be shot while in flight.

must go—overwhelming and unexpressed. Why did that make one so sad? Was it because it suggested that one cared more for the gay circumstances than for the thing seen? What was it they had seen? Why had they gone? What *was* Shakespeare? Her vision returned to her, as she brooded on this fresh problem. The whole scene of the theatre was round her once more; she was sitting in the half darkness gazing at the stage. What had it been for her? What was it that came from the stage? Something—*real* ... to say that drove it away. She looked again and it clustered once more, alive. The gay flood of the streets, the social excitements and embarrassments of the evening were a conflagration; circling about the clear bright kernel of moving lights and figures on the stage. She gazed at the bright stage. Moments came sharply up, grouped figures, spoken words. She held them, her contemplation aglow with the certainty that something was there that set her alight with love, making her whole in the midst of her uncertainty and ignorance. Words and phrases came, a sentence here and there that had suddenly shaped and deepened a scene. Perhaps it was only in seeing Shakespeare acted that one could appreciate him? But it was *not* the acting. No one could act. They all just missed it. It was all very well for Mag to laugh. They *did* just miss it.... "Why, my child? In what way?" "They act at the audience, they take their cues too quickly, and have their emotions too abruptly; and from outside not inside." "But if they felt at all, all the time, they would go mad or die." "No, they would not. But even if they did not feel it, if they looked, it would be enough. They don't *look* at the thing they are doing." It was not the acting. Nor the play. The characters of the story were always tiresome. The ideas, the wonderful quotations, if you looked closely at them, were every one's ideas; things that everybody knew. To read Shakespeare carefully all through, would only be to find all the general things somewhere or other. But that did not matter. Being ignorant of him and of history did not matter, as long as you heard him. Poetry! The poetry of Shakespeare ...? Primers of literature told one that. It did not explain the charm. Just the sound. Music. Like Beethoven. Bad acting cannot spoil Shakespeare. Bad playing cannot destroy Beethoven. It was the *sound* of Shakespeare that made the scenes real—that made *Winter's Tale*,[1] so long ago and so bewildering, remain in beauty.... "Dear Eve, Shakespeare is a sound ..." She tore up the letter. The next time she wrote to Eve, she must remember to say

---

1   1623 romance play by William Shakespeare (1564-1616).

that. The garret was stifling. Away from the brilliant window, the room was just as hot; the close thick smell of dust sickened her. She came back to the table, sitting as near as possible to the open. The afternoon had been wasted trying to express her evening, and nothing had been expressed. The thought of last night was painful now. She had spoiled it in some way. Her heart beat heavily in the stifling room. Her head ached and her eyes were tired. She was too tired to walk; and there was no money; barely enough for next week's A.B.C. suppers. There was no comfort. It was May ... in a stuffy dusty room. May. Her face quivered and her head sank upon the hot table.

CHAPTER XV

Nearly all the roses were half-opened buds; firm and stiff. Larger ones put in here and there gave the effect of mass. Closest contemplation enhanced the beauty of the whole. Each rose was perfect. The radiant mass was lovely throughout. The body of the basket curved firmly away to its slender hidden base; the smooth sweep of the rim and the delicate high arch of the handle held the roses perfectly framed. It was a perfect gift.... It had been quite enough to have the opportunity of doing little things for Mrs Berwick ... the surprise of the roses. The *surprise* of them. Roses, roses, roses ... all the morning they had stood, making the morning's work happy; visible all over the room. Every one in the house had had the beautiful shock of them. And they were still as they had been when they had been gathered in the dew. If they were in water, by the end of the afternoon the buds would revive and expand ... even after the hours in the Lyceum.[1] If they were thrown now into the waste-paper basket it would not matter. They would go on being perfect—to the end of life. "And as long; as my heart is bea-ting; as long; as my eyes; have; tears."[2]

Winthrop came up punctually at one o'clock, as he had promised. "It would save you comin' down if I was to ph-come up." It would go on then. He had thought about it and meant to do it. She opened the cash box quickly and deftly in her gratitude and handed him his four sovereigns and the money for the second mechanic and the apprentices. He waited gently while she counted it out. Next Saturday she would have it ready for him. "Thank you Miss——; ph—ph *good* afternoon," he said cheerfully. "Good afternoon Mr Winthrop," she responded busily, with all her heart, and listened as he clattered away downstairs. A load was lifted from Saturday mornings, for good. No more going down to run the gauntlet of the row of eyes and get herself along the bench, depositing the various sums. Nothing in future but the letters, the overhauling of Mr Hancock's empty surgery, the easy lunch with Mr Leyton, and the week-end. She entered the sums

---

1 London's Lyceum Theatre (established 1834) is notable for its classical façade. In the late nineteenth century, the Lyceum staged a number of long-running Shakespeare plays, starring popular actors Henry Irving and Ellen Terry (see p. 127, note 2 and p. 217, note 1).

2 From "Those Wedding Bells Shall Not Ring Out," an 1896 song composed by Monroe H. Rosenfeld (1861-1918) and Edward Jonghmans (dates unknown).

in the petty-cash book. There was that. They would always be that, week after week. But to-day the worrying challenge of it disappeared in the joy of the last entry. "Self," she wrote, the light across the outspread prospect of her life steadying and deepening as she wrote, "one pound, five." The five, written down, sent a thrill from the contemplated page. Taking the customary sovereign from the cash-box she placed it carefully in the middle pocket of her purse and closed the clip. The five shillings she distributed about the side-pockets; half a crown, a shilling, two sixpenny bits and six coppers. The purse was full of money. By September she would have about four pounds five in hand, and two pounds ten of her month's holiday money still unspent; six pounds fifteen; she could go to a matinée every week and still have about half the four pounds five; about four pounds fifteen altogether; enough to hire a bicycle for the month and buy some summer blouses for the holiday.... She pocketed the heavy purse. Why was there always a feeling of guilt about a salary? It was the same every week. The life at Wimpole Street was so full and so interesting; she was learning so much and seeing so much. Salary was out of place—a payment for leading a glorious life, half of which was entirely her own. The extra five shillings was a present from the Orlys and Mr Hancock. She could manage on the pound. The new sum was wealth, superfluity. They would expect more of her in future. Surely it would be possible to give more; with so much money; to find the spirit to come punctually at nine; always to have everything in complete readiness in all three surgeries; to keep all the books up to date.... But they would not have given her the rise at the end of five months, if they had not felt she was worth it.... It would make all the difference to the summer. Hopefully she took a loose sheet of paper and made two lists of the four pages of the week's entries—dissecting them under the heads of workshop and surgery. About fifteen pounds had been spent. Again and again with heating head she added her pages of small sums, getting each time slightly different results, until at last they balanced with the dissected lists—twice in succession. The hall clock struck one and Mr Leyton came downstairs rattling, and rattled into her room. "How d'you like this get-up?" The general effect of the blue-grey uniform and brown leather belt and bandolier[1] was pleasing. "Oh, *jolly*," she said abstractedly to his waiting figure. He clattered downstairs to

---

1 A pocketed belt worn at a slant across the chest, usually for holding ammunition and often forming part of soldiers' uniforms.

lunch. *Everybody* had outside interests. Mr Hancock would be on the Broads[1] by now. Her afternoon beckoned, easy with the superfluity of money. Anxiously she counted over the balance in the cash box. It was two and ninepence short. Damnation. Damnation. "Put it down to stamps—or miscellanea; not accounted for." She looked back through her entries. Stamps, one pound, at the beginning of the week. Stamps, ten shillings yesterday. It could not be that. It was some carelessness—something not entered—or a miscalculation. Something she had paid out to the workshop in the middle of a rush, and forgotten to put down. She went back through her entries one by one with flaring cheeks; recovering the history of the week and recalling incidents. Nothing came that would account for the discrepancy. It was simply a mistake. Something had been put down wrong. The money had been spent. But was it a workshop or a surgery expense that had gone wrong? "Postage, etc.: two and nine," would make it all right—but the account would not be right. Either the workshop or the surgery account must suffer. It would be another of those little inaccurate spots that came every few weeks; that she would always have to remember ... her mind toiled, goaded and hot.... Mr Orly had borrowed five pounds to buy tools at Buck & Hickman's,[2] and come back with the money spent and some of the tools to be handed to the practice. Perhaps it was in balancing that up that the mistake had occurred ... or the electric lamp account; some for the house, some for the practice, and some for the workshop. Thoroughly miserable, she made a provisional entry of the sum against surgery, in pencil, and left the account unbalanced. Perhaps on Monday it would come right. When the ledgers were all in place and the safe and drawers locked, she stretched her limbs and forced away her misery. The roses reproached her, but only for a moment. They understood, in detail, as clearly as she did, all the difficulties. They took her part. Standing there waiting, they too felt that there was nothing now but lunch and Irving.

With the basket of roses over her arm she walked as rapidly as possible down to Oxford Circus, taking the first turning out of Wimpole Street to hurry the more secretly and conveniently. A

---

1   The Norfolk Broads, in Eastern England, were a popular holiday destination in the late nineteenth century, particularly for boaters. The area is crossed by several rivers and lakes.

2   A London hardware store, founded in 1830 and still running today.

bus took her to Charing Cross,[1] where she jumped off as soon as it began pulling up and ran down the Strand. As soon as she felt herself flying towards her bourne, the fears that last week's magic would have disappeared left her altogether. Last week had been wonderful, an adventure, her first deliberate piece of daring in London. Inside the theatre the scruples and the daring had been forgotten. To-day, again, everything would be forgotten, everything; to-day's happiness was more secure; it would not mean going almost foodless over the week-end and without an egg for supper all next week; there was no anticipation of disapproving eyes in the theatre this week; the sense of the impropriety of going alone had gone; it would never return; the feeling of selfishness in spending money on a theatre alone was still there, but a voice within answered that—saying that there was no one at hand to go, and no one she knew who would find at the Lyceum performance just what she found, no one to whom it would mean much more than a theatre; like any other theatre and a play, amongst other plays, with a celebrated actor taking the chief part ... except Mag. Mag had been with her as she gazed. Mag was with her now. Mag, fulfilling one or other of her exciting Saturday afternoon engagements, would sit at her side.

Easy and happy, she fled along ... her heart greeting each passenger in the scattered throng she threaded, her eyes upon the traffic in the roadway. A horseless brougham[2] went by, moving smoothly and silently amongst the noisy traffic—the driver looked as though he were fastened to the front of the vehicle, a little tin driver on a clockwork toy; there was nothing between him and the road but the platform of the little tank on which his feet were set. He looked as if he were falling off. If anything ran into him there was nothing to protect him. It left an uncomfortable memory ... it would only be for carriages; the well-loved horse omnibuses would go on ... it must be somewhere near here ... "Lyceum Pit," there it was, just ahead, easily discernible. Last week when she had had to ask, she had not noticed the words printed on the side of the passage that showed as you came down the Strand. The pavement was clear for a moment, and she rounded the near angle and ran home down the passage without

---

1 Just south of Trafalgar Square, Charing Cross is considered the centre of London, and has been used as a major navigation point since the eighteenth century.

2 A brougham is a horse-drawn carriage; this one is a very early motor car.

slackening her pace, her half-crown ready in her hand, a Lyceum pittite.[1]

The dark pit seemed very full as she entered the door at the left-hand corner; dim forms standing at the back told her there were no seats left; but she made her way across to the right and down the incline, hoping for a neglected place somewhere on the extreme right. Her vain search brought her down to the barrier, and the end of her inspection of the serried ranks of seated forms to her left swept her eyes forward. She was just under the over-hanging balcony of the dress circle;[2] the well of the theatre opened clear before her as she stood against the barrier, the stalls[3] half full and filling with dim forms gliding in right and left, the upward sweep of the theatre walls covered with boxes[4] from which white faces shone in the gloom, a soft pervading saffron light, bright light heavily screened. There was space all round her, the empty gangway behind, the gangway behind the stalls just in front of the barrier, the view clear away to the stage over the heads of the people sitting in the stalls.... Why not stay here? If people stood at the back of the pit they might stand in front. She retreated into the angle made by the out-curving wall of the pit and the pit barrier. Putting down the basket of roses on the floor at her side she leaned against the barrier with her elbows on its rim.

He was there before he appeared ... in the orchestra, in the audience, all over the house. Presently, in a few moments, he was going to appear, moving and speaking on the stage. Someone might come forward and announce that he was ill or dead. He would die; perhaps only years hence; but long before one was old ... death of Henry Irving. No more thoughts of that; he is there— perhaps for twenty years; coming and going, having seasons at the Lyceum. He knew he must die; he did not think about it. He would turn with a smile and go straight up, in a rosy chariot ...

---

1 One who sits in the "pit" section of the theatre. The Lyceum has a large orchestral pit, in which audiences could sit during plays. The pit tickets were among the cheapest and were typically unreserved. Henry Irving, who was managing the theatre in the late nineteenth century, appreci-ated the pit audience and made a project of improving the seating con-ditions.

2 The lowest tier of seats; the most expensive seats.

3 Seats.

4 Partially enclosed seating areas on either side of the theatre.

well done, thou good and faithful and happy servant. He would go, closing his eyes upon the vision that was always in them, upon something they saw, something they gave out every moment. Whom the gods love die young ... not always young in years, but young always; trailing clouds of glory. It is always the unexpected that happens. Things you dread never happen. That is Weber—or Meyerbeer.[1] Who chooses the music? Perhaps he does.

The orchestration brought back last week's performance. It was all there, behind the curtain. Shylock,[2] swinging across the stage with his halting dragging stride; halting, standing with bent head; shut-in, lonely sweetness. She looked boldly now, untrammelled in her dark corner, at the pictures which had formed part of her distant view all last week in the far-away life at Wimpole Street; the great scenes ... beautifully staged; "Irving always *stages* everything perfectly"—and battled no longer against her sympathy for Shylock. It no longer shocked her to find herself sharing something of his longing for the blood of the Christians.[3] It was wrong; but were not they, too, wrong? They must be; there must be some reason for this certainty of sympathy with Shylock and aversion from Antonio. It might be a wrong reason, but it was there in her. Mag said "that's his genius; he makes you sympathize even with Shylock...." He shows you that you *do* sympathize with Shylock; Mag thinks that is something to admit shamefacedly. Because those other people were to her just "people." Antonio—was it not just as wrong to get into debt and raise money from the Jews as to let money out on usury? But it was his friend. He was innocent. Never mind. They were all, all, smug and complacent in their sunshine. Polished lustful man, with his coarse lustful men friends. Portia and Nerissa were companions in affliction. Beautiful first of all; as lovely and wandering and full of visions as Shylock, until their lovers came. Hearn was right.[4]

---

1 Carl Maria von Weber (1786-1826) and Giacomo Meyerbeer (1791-1864), German composers.

2 The eponymous protagonist of William Shakespeare's play, *The Merchant of Venice*.

3 In what follows Miriam recounts some elements of the play, interspersed with her reactions to them.

4 That is, Lafcadio Hearn (1850-1904) see p. 98, note 1. Thomson notes that "According to Hearn, the reason English lovers would shock was because, for the Japanese, any public display of emotion was unacceptable, and as for passion, it was an emotion rigorously excluded even in private from the well-conducted home." George H.   (*continued*)

English lovers would shock any Japanese. Not that the Japanese were prudish. According to him they were anything but ... they would not talk as Englishmen did, among themselves, and, in mixed society, in a sort of code; thinking themselves so clever; any one could talk a code who chose to descend to a mechanical trick.

How much more real was the relation between Portia and Nerissa than between either of the sadly jesting women and their complacently jesting lovers. Did a man *ever* speak in a natural voice—neither blustering, nor displaying his cleverness, nor being simply a lustful slave? Women always despise men under the influence of passion or fatigue. What horrible old men those two would be—still speaking in put-on voices to hide their shame, pompous and philosophizing.... "Man's love is of man's life a thing apart ..."[1] so much the worse for man; there must be something very wrong with his life. But it would go on, until men saw and admitted this.... Portia was right when she preached her sermon—it made every one feel sorry for all harshness—then one ought not to be harsh to the blindness of men ... somebody had said men would lose all their charm if they lost their vanity and childish cocksureness about their superiority—to force and browbeat them into seeing themselves would not help—but that is what I want to do. I am like a man in that, overbearing, bullying, blustering. I am something between a man and a woman; looking both ways. But to pretend one did not see through a man's voice, would be treachery. Nearly all men will hate me—because I can't play up for long. Harshness must go; perhaps that was what Christ meant. But Portia only wanted to save Antonio's life; and did it by a trick. It was not a Daniel come to judgment;[2] it showed the folly of law; pettifogging;[3] the abuse of the letter of the law. She was harsh to Shylock. Which is most cruel, to take life or to torture the living? The Christians were so self-satisfied; going off to their love-making; that spoiled the play. Their future was much more dark and miserable than the struggle between the sensual Englishman and the wily Jew. The play ought to have

Thomson, *Notes on "Pilgrimage": Dorothy Richardson Annotated* (Greenboro, SC: ELT P, 1999), 96.

1 From George Gordon, Lord Byron's (1788-1824) *Don Juan* (1819-24): "Man's love is of man's life a thing apart / 'Tis woman's whole existence" (stanza 194).

2 See p. 102, note 3.

3 "To plead (a case) with legal chicanery or petty quibbling" (*OED*), which occurs in *The Merchant of Venice*.

ended there, with the woman in the cap and gown pleading, showing something that could not be denied—ye are all together in one condemnation. In that moment Portia was great, her red robe shone and lit the world. She ought to have left them all, and gone through all the law courts of the world; showing up the law. Wit. Woman's wit. Men at least bowed down to that; though they did not know what it was. "Wit" used to mean knowledge— "inwit," conscience. The knowledge of woman is larger, bigger, deeper, less wordy and clever than that of men. Certainly. But why do not men acknowledge this? They talk about mother-love and mother-wit and instinct, as if they were mysterious tricks. They have no real knowledge, but of things; a sort of superiority they get by being free to be out in the world amongst things; they do not understand people. If a woman is good it is all right; if she is bad it is all wrong. Cherchez la femme.[1] Then everything in life depends upon women? "A civilization can never rise above the level of its women."[2] Perhaps if women became lawyers, they would change things.[3] Women do not respect law. No wonder, since it is folly, an endless play on words. Portia? She had been quite complacent about being unkind to the Jew. She had been invented by a man. There was no reality in any of Shakespeare's women. They please men because they show women as men see them. All the other things are invisible; nothing but their thoughts and feelings about men and bothers. Shakespeare did not know the meaning of the words and actions of Nerissa and Portia when they were alone together, the beauty they knew and felt and saw, holy beauty everywhere. Shakespeare's plays are "universal" because they are about the things that everybody knows and hands about, and they do not trouble anybody. They make every one feel wise. It isn't what he says, it's the way he says all these things that don't matter and leave everything out. It's all a sublime fuss.[4]

---

1 French: Look for the woman. A popular phrase suggesting that when something is amiss, there must be a woman behind it.

2 George H. Thomson, in Notes on "Pilgrimage," suggests that Miriam may echo Ralph Waldo Emerson's essay "Civilization," in which he claims that women's "essential charm" has had a positive influence on the progress of civilization (97).

3 The Sex Disqualification (Removal) Act, passed by British Parliament in 1919, stated that people could not be disqualified by sex or marriage from working in the civil service, or in the professions, including law.

4 This could be an allusion to the title of Shakespeare's comedy Much Ado About Nothing.

Italians! Of course. Well—Europeans. It is the difference between the Europeans and the Japanese that Hearn had meant.

Then there *is* tragedy! Things are not simple right and wrong. There are a million sides to every question; as many sides as there are people to see and feel them, and in all big national struggles two clear sides, both right and both wrong. The man who wrote *The Struggle against Absolute Monarchy*[1] was a Roundhead;[2] and he made me a Roundhead; Green's *History*[3] is Roundhead. I never saw Charles's[4] point of view or thought about it; but only of the unjust levies and the dissolution of Parliament and the dissoluteness of the Court. If I had seen Irving[5] then, it would have made a difference. He could never have been Cromwell.[6] He is Charles. Things happen. People tell him things and he cannot understand. He believes in divine right[7] ... sweet and gentle, with perfect manners for all ... perfect in private life ... the first gentleman in the land, the only person free to have perfect manners; the representative of God on earth. "Decaying feudalism." But they ought not to have killed him. He cannot *understand*. He is the scapegoat. Freedom looks so fine in your mind. Parliaments and Trial by Jury and the abolition of the Star Chamber and the triumph of Cromwell's visionaries.[8] But it means this gentle velvet-coated figure with its delicate ruffled hands, its sweetness

---

1 An 1899 book by Bertha Meriton Gardiner, about resistance movements against the British monarchy during the English Civil War (1642-51).

2 A derogatory term for the Puritans who sought to contain the power of Charles I and to put an end to absolute monarchy.

3 John Richard Green's (1837-83) *A History of the English People* (1880).

4 King Charles I sat on the English throne from 1625 until his execution, for treason, in 1649.

5 Henry Irving played the title role in *Charles I*, a play by William Gorham Wills (Thomson 98).

6 Oliver Cromwell (1599-1658) was a political and military figure instrumental in the defeat of the Royalists during the English Civil War. He was appointed Lord Protector of the Commonwealth of England, Scotland, and Ireland, during a brief period in which the nation completely overthrew the monarchy and became a republic. After Cromwell's death, the monarchy was restored.

7 The belief that a king, and his line of succession, is appointed by God.

8 The Star Chamber was a powerful English law court that had become notoriously corrupt by the time Charles I came to the throne. The court under Charles was used to protect the royals from opposition and was abolished by Parliament in 1640.

and courtesy, going with bandaged eyes—to death. Was there no way out? Must one either be a Royalist[1] or a Roundhead. Must monarchies decay? Then why did the Restoration[2] come? What do English people want? "A limited monarchy"; a king controlled by Parliament.[3] As well not have a king at all. Who would not rather live with Charles than with Cromwell? Charles would have entertained a beggar royally. Cromwell was too busy with "affairs of state" to entertain beggars. Charles dying for his faith was more beautiful than Cromwell fighting for his reason. Yet the people must be free; there must be justice. Kings ought to be taught differently. He did not understand. No one believing in divine right can understand. Was the idea of divine right a mistake? Can no one be trusted? Cromwell's son was a weak fool.[4] How can a country be ruled? People will never agree. What ought one to be if one can neither be quite a Roundhead nor quite a Cavalier?[5] They worshipped two gods. Are there two Gods? ... Irving ... walking gently about inside Charles, feeling, as Charles felt the beauty of the sunlit garden, the delicate clothes, the refinement of fine living, the charm of perfect association, the rich beauty of each day as it passed.... Charles died with all that in his eyes, *knowing* it *good*. Cromwell was a farmer. Christ was a carpenter. Christ did not bother about kings. "Render unto Caesar."[6]

---

1 A supporter of the monarchy.
2 The historical period during which the English monarchy was restored, beginning in 1660.
3 I.e., a constitutional monarchy.
4 After Oliver Cromwell's death, his son Richard succeeded as Lord Protector, but was only able to maintain rule for just under a year, at which point the Protectorate ended and the Restoration began.
5 A popular term for supporters of King Charles I during the English Civil War.
6 "Render unto Caesar that which is Caesar's," a phrase attributed to Jesus in the Gospel of Matthew (22:21) suggesting that secular duty should be kept separate from religious duty.

CHAPTER XVI

They had walked swiftly and silently along through the bright evening daylight of the Finchley Road.[1] Miriam held her knowledge suspended, looking forward to the enclosure at the end of the few minutes' walk. But the conservatoire[2] was not enclosed. The clear bright light flooding the rows and rows of seated summer-clad Hampstead people, and lighting up every corner of the level square hall was like the outside evening daylight. The air seemed as pure as the outside air. She followed Mr Hancock to their seats at the gangway end of the fourth row, passing between the sounds echoing thinly from the platform and the wave of attention sweeping towards the platform from the massed rows of intelligent faces. As they sat down, the chairman's voice ceased and the lights were lowered; but so slightly that the hall was still perfectly exposed and clear. The people still looked as though they were out of doors or in their large houses. This was modern improvement—hard clear light. Their minds and their thoughts and their lives and their clothes were always in it. She stared at the screen. A large slide was showing, lit from behind. It made a sort of stage scenery for the rest of the scene, all in one light. She fixed her attention. An enormous vessel with its side stove in, yes, "stove in";[3] in a dock. They got *information* at any rate, and then, perhaps, got free and thought their own thoughts. No. They would follow and think and talk intelligently about the information. Rattling their cultured voices. Mad with pretences.... In *dry* dock,[4] going to be repaired. Gazing sternly at the short man with the long pointer talking in an anxious high thin voice, his head with its upstanding crest of hair half-turned towards the audience, she suppressed a giggle. Folding her hands she gazed, shaking in every limb, not daring to follow what he said, for fear of laughing aloud. Shreds of his first long sentence caught in her thoughts and gave her his meaning, shaking her into giggles. Her features quivered under her skin as she held them, in forcing her eyes towards the distances of sky beyond the ship. Her customary expletives shot through her mind in rapid succession. With each one, the scarves and silk

---

1 A major thoroughfare in North London.
2 French: a music school.
3 That is, smashed in. Normally used in reference to a ship that has struck a rock and been smashed in.
4 When ships are taken out of the water for repairs they are in dry dock.

and velvet of the audience grew brighter about the edge of her circle of vision.

She was an upstart and an alien and here she was. It was more extraordinary in this Hampstead clarity than at a theatre or concert in town. It was a part of his world ... and theirs; one might get the manner and still keep alive.... Was he out of humour because he had realized what he had done or because she had been late for dinner? Was he thinking what his behaviour amounted to, in the eyes of his aunt and cousins; even supposing they did not know that the invitation to dinner and the lecture had been given only this afternoon? He must have known it was necessary to go home and tidy up. When he said the conservatoire was so near that there would be plenty of time, was not that as good as saying she might be a little late? Why had he not said they were staying with him? Next week was full of appointments for their teeth. So he knew they were coming ... and then to go marching into the midst of them, three-quarters of an hour late, and to be so dumbfounded as to be unable to apologize ... my dear, I shall *never* forget the faces of those women. I could not imagine, at first, what was wrong. He was looking so strange. The women barely noticed me—barely noticed me. "I'm afraid dinner will be spoiled," he said, in his way. They had all been sitting round the fire three mortal quarters of an hour waiting for *me*! How they would talk. Their thoughts and feelings about employees could be seen at a glance. It was bad enough for them to have a secretary appearing at dinner, the first evening of their great visit. And now they were sitting alone round the fire and she was at the lecture alone, unchaperoned, with him, "she had the effrontery to come to dinner three-quarters of an hour late ..." feathery hair and periwinkle eyes and white noses; gentle die-away voices. Perhaps the thought of his favourite cousins coming next week buoyed him up. No wonder he wanted to get away to the lecture. He had come, reasonably; not seeing why he should not; just as he would have gone if they had not been there. Now he saw it as they saw it. There he sat. She gazed at the shifting scenes ... ports and strange islands in distant seas, sunlit coloured mountains tops peaking up from forests. The lecturing voice was far away, irrelevant and unintelligible. Peace flooded her.

CHAPTER XVII

The patient sat up with a groan of relief. His dark strong positive liverish profile turned away towards the spittoon. There was a clean broad gap of neck between the strong in-turned ending of his hair and the narrow strip of firm, heavily glazed blue-white collar[1] fitting perfectly into the collar of the well-cut grey coat clothing the firm bulk of his body. "To my mind, there's no reason why they shouldn't do thoroughly well," he said into the spittoon. "All the hospitals would employ 'em in the end. They're more natty and conscientious than men, and there's nothing in the work they can't manage."

"No, I think that's so."

Miriam cleared her throat emphatically. They had no right to talk in that calm disposing way, in the presence of a woman. Mr Hancock felt that too. That kind of man was always nice to women. Strong and cheerful and helping them; but with his mind full of quotations and generalizations. He would bring them out, anywhere. It would never occur to him that the statement of them could be offensive. His newspaper office would be full of little girls. "It's those little ph'girls." But the Amalgam Company probably had quite uneducated girls. Nobody ought to be asked to spend their lives calculating decimal quantities. The men who lived on these things had their drudgery done for them. They did it themselves first. Yes, but then it meant their *future*. A woman clerk never becomes a partner. There was no hope for women in business. That man's wife would be wealthy and screened and looked after all her days; he working. He would live as long as she—a little old slender nut-brown man.

"What was the employment Mr Dolland was speaking of?"

"Dispensing.[2] I think he's quite right. And it's not at all badly paid."

"It ought not to be. Think of the responsibility and anxiety."

"It's a jolly stiff exam, too."

"I like the calm way he talks, as if it were his business to decide what is suitable."

Mr Hancock laughed. "He's a very influential man, you know," he said going to the tube. "Yes?—Oh, show them up."

Miriam detected the note that meant a trial ahead, and went

---

1 Collars were at this time detachable from coats and shirts so they could be cleaned and starched more easily.

2 Distribution of materials or medications.

about her clearing with quiet swift busy sympathy. But Mr Dolland had been a good introduction to the trying hour. Her thoughts followed his unconsciousness down to his cab. She saw the spatted[1] boot on the footplate,[2] the neat strong swing of the body, the dip of the hansom, the darkling face sitting inside under the shiny hat ... the room had become dreadful; empty and silent; pressed full with a dreadful atmosphere; those women from Rochester[3]—but they always sat still. These people were making little faint fussings of movement, like the creakings of clothes in church, and the same silent hostile feeling; people being obliged to be with people. There were two or three besides the figure in the chair. Mr Hancock had got to work with silent assiduity. His face when he turned to the cabinet was disordered, separate from the room and from his work; a most curious expression. He turned again, busily. It was something in the mouth, resentful, and a bad-tempered look in the eyes; a look of discomposed youth. Of course. The aunt and cousins. Had she cut them, standing with her back to the room, or they her? She moved sideways with her bundle of cleaned instruments to the cabinet, putting them all on the flap and beginning to open drawers, standing at his elbow as he stood turned away from the chair mixing a paste.

"You might leave those there for the present," he murmured. She turned and went down the room between the unoccupied seated figures, keeping herself alert to respond to a greeting. They sat vacant and still. Ladies in church. Acrimonious. Querulously dressed in pretty materials and colours that would keep fresh only in the country. She went to the door lingeringly. It was so familiar. There had been all that at Babington.[4] It was that that was in these figures straggling home from school, in pretty successful clothes, walking along the middle of the sunlit road ... *May-bell* deah ... not balancing along the row of drain-pipes nor

---

1 Mr. Dolland is wearing spats, or short covers worn over the instep of the shoe and reaching just above the ankle.

2 The running board on the side of a carriage, for stepping on as one climbs aboard.

3 A town in Kent, just east of London, noted in the nineteenth century for its manufacturing industries.

4 Miriam's childhood home, which she recalls in *Backwater*, the second volume of *Pilgrimage*, and at other points in the series. Richardson based it on her own childhood home in Abingdon, then in the county of Berkshire, west of London (it is presently in Oxfordshire, the boundaries having been redrawn). (Thanks to Scott McCracken for his help here.)

pulling streaks of Berkshire goody[1] through their lips. This was their next stage. When she reached the stairs, she felt herself wrapped in their scorn. It was true; there was something impregnable about them. They sat inside a little fortress, letting in only certain people. But they did not know she could see everything inside the fortress, hear all their thoughts much more clearly than the things they said. To them, she was a closed book. They did not want to open it. But if they had wanted to they could not have read.

The *insolence* of it. Her social position had been identical with theirs and his. Her early circumstances a good deal more ambitious and generous.... "A moment of my consciousness is wider than any of theirs will be in the whole of their lives." ... If she could have stayed in all that, she would have been as far as possible just the same, sometimes ... for certain purposes. A little close group, loyal and quarrelsome for ends that any woman could see through. Fawning and flattering and affectionate to each other and getting half-maddened by the one necessity. The girls would repeat the history of their mother, and get her sour-faced, pretty, delicate refinement. They were so exquisite, now, to look at—the flower-like edges of their faces, unchanging from morning to night; warmth and care and cleanliness and rich clean food; no fatigue or worry or embarrassment, once they had learned how to sit and move and eat. To many men, they would appear angels. They would not meet many in the Berkshire valley. But their mother would manœuvre engagements for them and their men would see them as angels fresh from their mother's hands; miracles of beauty and purity....

Refined shrews, turning in circles, like moths on pins; brainless, mindless, heartless, the prey of the professions; priests, doctors, and lawyers. These two groups kept each other going. There was something hidden in the fact that these women's men always entered professions.

Large portions of the mornings and afternoons of that week were free from visits to the upstairs surgery. From Tuesday morning, she kept it well filled with supplies; guessing that she was to be saved further contact with the aunt and cousins; and drew from the stimulus of their comings and goings, the sound of their voices in the hall and on the stairs, a fund of energy that

---

1 A confection, probably taffy.

filled her unexpected stretches of leisure with unceasing methodical labour. Uninterrupted work on the ledgers awakened her interest in them, the sense that the books were nearly all up to date, the possibility of catching up altogether before the end of the week, brought a relief and a sense of mastery that made the June sunshine gay morning after morning as she tramped through it along the Euston Road. Every hour was full of a strange excitement. Wide vistas shone ahead. On the first of September shone a blinding radiance. She would get up that morning in her dusty garret in the heat and dust of London, with nothing to do for a month; and ride away, somewhere, ride away through the streets, free, out to the suburbs, like a Sunday morning ride, and then into the country. She had weathered the winter and the strange beginnings and would go away to come back; the rest of the summer till then would go dancing, like a dream. There was all that coming; making her heart leap when she thought of it, unknown Wiltshire[1]—with Leader[2] landscapes for a week, and then something else. And meanwhile Wimpole Street. She went about her work, borne along unwearied upon a tide that flowed out in glistening sunlit waves over the sunlit shore of the world. The doors and windows of her cool shaded room opened upon a life that spread out before her fanwise towards endless brilliant distances. Moments of fatigue, little obstinate knots and tangles of urgent practical affairs, did their utmost to convince her that life was a perpetual conflict, nothing certain and secure but the thwarting and discrediting of the dream-vision; every contact seemed to end in an assurance of her unarmed resourceless state. Pausing now and again to balance her account, to try to find a sanction for her joy, she watched and felt the little stabs of the actual facts as they would be summarized by some disinterested observer, and again and again saw them foiled. Things danced, comically powerless against some unheard piping; motes, funny and beloved, in the sunbeam of her life.... Next week, and the coming of the favourite cousins, made a bright barrier across the future and a little fence round her labours. Everything must be ordered and straight before then. She must be free and reproachless for the wonders and terrors of

---

1   A county in southwest England, known for its plains and valleys, most notably Salisbury Plains. Wiltshire is also the home of Stonehenge, the country's most famous ancient stone monument.
2   Benjamin William Leader (1831-1923), a famous English landscape painter.

their visit.... Perhaps there might be only the one meeting; the evening already arranged might be all the week's visit would bring. The week would pass unseen by her and everything would be as before. As before; was not that enough, and more than enough?

Her rare visits to the surgery were festivals. Free from the usual daily fatigue of constant standing for reiterated clearances and cleansings of small sets of instruments, she swept full of cheerful strength, her mind free for method, her hands steady and deft, upon the accumulations left by long sittings, rapping out her commentary upon his prolonged endurance by emphatic bumpings of basins and utensils; making it unnecessary for him to voice the controlled exasperation that spoke for her from every movement and tone. Once or twice she felt it wavering towards speech, and whisked about and bumped things down with extra violence. Once or twice he smiled into her angry face, and she feared he was going to speak of them.

CHAPTER XVIII

It was a sort of formality. They all three seemed to be waiting for something to begin. They were not at ease. Perhaps they had come to the end of everything they had to say to each other, and had only the memory of their common youth to bind them to each other. Members of the same family never seemed to be quite at ease sitting together doing nothing. These three met so seldom that they were obliged when they met to appear to be giving their whole attention to each other, sitting confronted and trying to keep talk going all the time. That made every one speak and smile and look self-consciously. Perhaps they reminded each other, by their mutual presence, that the dreams of their youth had not been fulfilled. And the cousins were formal. Like the other cousins, they belonged to the prosperous provincial middle class that always tries to get its sons into professions. Without the volume of Sophocles,[1] one would have known he was part of a school and she could have been nothing but the wife or daughter or sister of an English professional man. It was always the same world; once the only world that was worthy of one's envious admiration and respect; changed now ... "hardworked little textbook people and here and there an enlightened thwarted man." ... Was Mr Canfield thwarted? There was a curious look of lonely enlightenment about his head. At the university, and now and again with a head master or a fellow assistant-master, he had had moments of exchange and been happy for a moment and seen the world alight. But his happiest times had been in loneliness, with thoughts coming to him out of books. They had been his solace and his refuge since he was fifteen; and in spite of the hair greying his temples he was still fifteen; within him were all the dreams and all the dreadful crudities of boyhood ... he had never grown to man's estate.... He had understood at once. "It always seems unnecessary to explain things to people; you feel while you are explaining that they will meet the same thing themselves, perhaps in some different form; but certainly, because things are all the same." "Oh, yes; that's certainly so." He had looked pleased and lightened. Darkness and cold had come in an instant, with Mrs Canfield's unexpected reverent voice. "I don't quite understand what that means; tell me." She had put down her fancy work and lifted her flowerlike face, not suspiciously as the other cousins

---

1 Sophocles (496-406 BCE), the Greek playwright, was most famous for his tragedies *Oedipus Rex* and *Antigone*.

would have done, but with their type of gentle formal refinement and something of their look. She could be sour and acid if she chose. She could curl her lips and snub people. What was the secret of the everlasting same awfulness of even the nicest of refined sheltered middle-class Englishwoman? He had stumbled and wandered through a vague statement. He knew that all the long loneliness of his mind lay revealed before one—and yet she had been the dream and wonder and magic of his youth and was still his dear companion. The "lady" was the wife for the professional Englishman—simple, sheltered, domesticated, trained in principles she did not think about, and living by them; revering professional and professionally successful men; never seeing the fifth-form[1] schoolboys they all were. No woman who saw them as they were, with their mental pride and vanity and fixity, would stay with them; no woman who saw their veiled appetites.... But where could all these wives go?

Throughout the evening, she was kept quiet and dull and felt presently very weary. Her helpless stock-taking made it difficult to face the strangers, lest painful illumination and pity and annoyance should stream from her too visibly.... Perhaps they, too, took stock and pitied; but they were interested, a little eager in response and, though too well bred for questions, obviously full of unanswered surmises, which perhaps presently they would communicate to each other. There were people who would say she was too egoistic to be interested in them, a selfish, unsocial, unpleasant person, and they were kind charming people, interested in everybody. That might be true.... But it was also true that they were eager and interested because their lives were empty of everything but principles and a certain fixed way of looking at things; and one could be fond of their niceness and respectful to their goodness but never interested, because one knew everything about them, even their hidden thoughts and the side of them that was not nice or good, without having any communication with them.... He had another side; but there was no place in his life which would allow it expression. It could only live in the lives of people met in books; in sympathies here and there for a moment; in people who passed "like ships in the night";[2] in moments at

---

1 Fifteen or sixteen years old; in the last three years of secondary school.
2 Though these words have appeared elsewhere, this may be a reference to the best-selling novel *Ships that Pass in the Night* (1893) by Beatrice Harraden (1864-1936).

the beginning and end of holidays when things would seem real, and as if henceforth they were going to be real every day. If it found expression in his life, it would break up that life. Any one who tried to make it find personal expression would be cruel; unless it were to turn him into a reformer or the follower of a reformer. That could happen to him. He was secretly interested in adventurers and adventuresses.

CHAPTER XIX

It had evidently been a great festival. One of the events of Mr Hancock's summer; designed by him for the happiness and enjoyment of his friends, and enjoyed by him in labouring to those ends. It was *beautiful* to look back upon; in every part; the easy journey, the approach to the cottage along the mile of green-feathered river, the well-ordered feast in the large clean cottage; the well-thought-out comfort of the cottage bedrooms, the sight of the orchard lit by Chinese lanterns, the lantern-lit boats, the drifting down the river in the soft moonlit air; the candle-lit supper table, morning through the cottage windows, upstairs and down, far away from the world, people meeting at breakfast like travellers in a far-off country, pleased to see well-known faces ... the morning on the green river ... the gentleness and kindliness and quiet dignity of everybody, the kindly difficult gently jesting discussion of small personal incidents; the gentle amiable strains; the mild restrained self-effacing watchfulness of the women; the uncompeting mutual admiration of the men; the general gratitude of the group when one or other of the men filled up a space of time with a piece of modestly narrated personal reminiscence....

Never, never could she belong to that world. It was a perfect little world; enclosed; something one would need to be born and trained into; the experience of it as an outsider was pure pain and misery; admiration, irritation, and resentment running abreast in a fever. Welcome and kindliness could do nothing; one's own straining towards it, nothing; a night of sleepless battering at its closed doors, nothing. There was a secret in it, in spite of its simple-seeming exterior; an undesired secret. Something to which one could not give oneself up. Its terms were terms on which one could not live. That girl could live on them, in spite of her strenuous different life in the East End[1] settlement ... in spite of her plain dull dress and red hands. She knew the code; her cheap straw hat waved graciously, her hair ruffled about her head in soft clouds. Why had he never spoken of her uncle's cottage so

---

1   This is a Christian settlement in the East End, a chronically poor part of London. Such settlements were devoted to helping the poor and cultivating religious feeling. See Martha Vicinus, *Independent Women* (Chicago: U of Chicago P, 1992) for the kinds of opportunities such work gave to middle-class women. The East End is best described as East London north of the river Thames. See also p. 66, note 2.

near his own? She must be always there. When she appeared in the surgery she seemed to come straight out of the East End ... his respect for workers amongst the poor ... his general mild revulsion from philanthropists; but down here she was not a philanthropist ... outwardly, a girl with blowy hair and a wavy hat, smiling in boats, understanding botany and fishing ... inwardly a designing female, her mind lit by her cold intellectual "ethical"—hooooo—the very *sound* of the word—"ethical Pantheism"; cool and secret and hateful. "Rather a nice little thing"; "pretty green dress"; *nice!*

CHAPTER XX

Miriam turned swiftly in her chair and looked up. But Mr Hancock was already at the door. There was only a glimpse of his unknown figure, arrested for a moment with its back to her as he pulled the door wide enough to pass through. The door closed crisply behind him and his crisp unhastening footsteps went away out of hearing along the thickly carpeted hall.

"*Dear* me!" she breathed through firmly held lips, standing up. Her blood was aflame. The thudding of her heart shook the words upon her breath. She was fighting against something more than amazement. She knew that only part of her refused to believe. In a part of her brain illumination, leaving the shock already far away in the past, was at work undisturbed, flowing rapidly down into thoughts set neatly in the language of the world. She held them back, occupying herself irrelevantly about the room, catching back desperately at the familiar trains of reverie suggested by its objects; cancelling the incident and summoning it again and again without prejudice or afterthought. Each time the shock recurred unchanged, firmly registered, its quality indubitable. She sat down at last to examine it and find her thoughts. Taking a pencil in a trembling hand, she began carefully adding a long column of figures. A system of adding that had been recommended to her by the family mathematician now suggested itself for the first time in connection with her own efforts....

How *dare* he?

It was deliberate. A brusque casual tone, deliberately put on; a tone he sometimes used to the boys downstairs, or to cabmen. How did he dare to use it to her? It must cease instantly. It was not to be suffered for a moment. Not for a moment could she hold a position which would entitle any one, particularly any man, to speak to her in that—outrageous—*official* tone. Why not? It was the way of business people and officials all the world over.... Then he should have begun as he meant to go on.... I won't endure it now. No one has ever spoken to me in that way— and no one shall, with impunity. I have been fortunate. They have spoiled me.... I should never have come, if I had found they had that sort of tone. It was his difference that made me come.

Those two had talked to him and made him think. The aunt and cousins had prepared the way. But their hostility had been harmless. These two had approved. That was clear at the week-end. They must have chaffed him, and given him their blessing.

Then, for the first time, he had thought, sitting alone and pondering reasonably. It was he himself who had drawn back. He was quite right. He belonged to that side of society and must keep with them and go their way. Very wise and right ... but damn his insolent complacency....

"Everything a professional man does must stabilize his position." Perhaps that is true. But then his business relationships must be business relationships from the first ... that was expected. The wonder of the Wimpole Street life was that it had not been so. Instead of an employer there had been a sensitive isolated man; prosperous and strong outwardly, and as suffering and perplexed in mind as any one could be. He had not hesitated to seek sympathy.

Any fair-minded onlooker would condemn him. Any one who could have seen the way he broke through resistance to social intercourse outside the practice. He may have thought he was being kind to a resourceless girl. It was *not* to resourcelessness that he had appealed. It was not that. That was not the truth.

He would have cynical thoughts. The truth was that something came in and happened of itself before one knew. A woman always knows first. It was not clear until Babington. But there was a sharp glimpse then. He must have known how amazed they would be at his cycling over after he had neglected them for years, on that one Sunday. They had concealed their amazement from him. But it was they who had revealed things. There was nothing imaginary, after that, in taking one wild glance and leaving things to go their way. Nothing. No one was to blame. And now he knew and had considered, and had made an absurd reasonable decision and taken ridiculous prompt action.

A business relationship ... by *all* means. But he shall acknowledge and apologize. He shall explain his insulting admission of fear. He shall admit in plain speech what has accounted for his change of manner.

Then that little horror is also condemned. *She* is not a wealthy efficient woman of the world.

Men are simply paltry and silly—all of them.

In pain and fear, she wandered about her room, listening for her bell. It had gone; the meaning of their days had gone; trust and confidence could never come back. A door was closed. His life was closed on her for ever....

The bell rang softly in its usual way. The incident had been an accident; an illusion. Even so; she had been prepared for it, without knowing she was prepared, otherwise she would not have understood so fully and instantly. If she had only imagined it, it had changed everything, her interpretation of it was prophetic; just as before he had not known where they were, so now the rupture was imminent whether he knew it or no. She found herself going upstairs breathing air thick with pain. This was dreadful.... She could not bear much of this.... The patient had gone. He would be alone. They would be alone. To be in his presence would be a relief ... this was appalling. This pain could not be endured. The sight of the room holding the six months would be intolerable. She drew her face together, but her heart was beating noisily. The knob of the door handle rattled in her trembling hand ... large flat brass knob with a row of grooves to help the grasp ... she had never observed that before. The door opened before her. She flung it wider than usual and pushed her way, leaving it open ... he was standing impermanently with a sham air of engrossment at his writing table, and would turn on his heel and go the moment she was fairly across the room. Buoyant with pain, she flitted through the empty air towards the distant bracket-table. Each object upon it stood marvellously clear. She reached it and got her hands upon the familiar instruments ... no sound; he had not moved. The flame of the little spirit-lamp burned unwavering in the complete stillness ... now was the moment to drop thoughts and anger. Up here was something that had been made up here, real and changeless and independent. The least vestige of tumult would destroy it. It was something that no one could touch; neither his friends nor he nor she. They had not made it and they could not touch it. Nothing had happened to it; and he had stood quietly there long enough for it to re-assert itself. Steadily, with her hands full of instruments, she turned towards the sterilizing tray. The room was empty. Pain ran glowing up her arms from her burden of nauseating relics of the needs of some complacent patient ... the room was stripped, a West End surgery, among scores of other West End surgeries, a prison claiming her by the bonds of the loathsome duties she had learned.

CHAPTER XXI

To-day the familiar handwriting brought no relief. This letter must be the final explanation. She opened it, standing by the hall table. "Dear Miss Henderson—you are very persistent." She folded the letter up and walked rapidly out into the sunshine. The way down to the Euston Road was very long and sunlit. It was radiant with all the months and weeks and days. She thought of going on with the unread letter and carrying it into the surgery, tearing it up into the waste-paper basket and saying "I have not read this. It is all right. We will not talk any more." One thing would have gone. But there would be a tremendous cheerfulness and independence, and the memory of the things in the other letters. The letter once read, two things would have gone, everything. She paused at the corner of the gardens, looking down at the pavement. There was, in some way that would not come quite clear, so much more at stake than personal feelings about the insulting moment. It was something that stuck into everything, made everything intolerable until it was admitted and cancelled. As long as he went on hedging and pretending it was not there, there could be no truth anywhere. It was something that must go out of the world, no matter what it cost. It would be smiling and cattish and behaving to drop it. Explained, it would be wiped away, and everything else with it. To accept his assertions would be to admit lack of insight. That would be treachery. The continued spontaneity of manner which it would ensure would be the false spontaneity that sat everywhere ... all over that woman getting into the bus; brisk cheerful falsity. She glanced through to the end of the letter ... "foolish gossip which might end by making your position untenable." *Idiot.* Charming chivalrous gentleman.

I want to have it both ways. To keep the consideration and flout the necessity for it. No one shall dare to protect me from gossip. To prove myself independent and truth-demanding I would break up anything. That's damned folly. Never mind. Why didn't he admit it at once? He hated being questioned and challenged. He may have thought that manner was "the kindest way." It is not for him to choose ways of treating me. This cancels the past. But it admits it. Not to admit the past would be to go on for ever in a false position. He still hides. But he knows that I know he is hiding. Where we have been we have been. It may have been through a false estimate of me, to begin with. That does not matter. Where we have been we have been. That is not imagination. One day he will know it is not imagination. There is something that is making me very glad. A painful relief. Something forcing me back upon something. There is something that I have smashed, for some reason I do not know. It's something in my temper, that flares out about things. Life allows no chance of getting at the bottom of things....

I have nothing now but my pained self again, having violently rushed at things and torn them to bits. It's all my fault from the very beginning. But I stand for something. I would dash my head against a wall rather than deny it. I make people hate me by *knowing* them and dashing my head against the wall of their behaviour. I should never make a good chess-player. Is God a chess-player? I shan't leave until I have proved that no one can put me in a false position. There is something that is untouched by positions....

I did not know what I had.... Friendship is fine fine porcelain. I have sent a crack right through it....

Mrs Bailey ... numbers of people I never think of would like to have me always there....

The sky, fitting down on the irregular brown vista, bore an untouched life.... There were always mornings; at work. I am free to work zealously and generously with and for him.

At *least* I have broken up his confounded complacency.

He will be embarrassed. *I* shan't.

CHAPTER XXII

"... And at fifty, when a woman is beginning to sit down intelligently to life—behold, it is beginning to be time to take leave...."

That woman was an elderly woman of the world; but a dear. She understood. She had spent her life in amongst people, having a life of her own going on all the time; looking out at something through the bars, whenever she was alone and sometimes in the midst of conversations; but no one would see it, but people who *knew*. And now she was free to step out and there was hardly any time left. But there was a little time. Women who *know* are quite brisk at fifty. "A man must never be silent with a woman unless he wishes for the quiet development of a relationship from which there is no withdrawing ... if ordinary social intercourse cannot be kept up he must fly ... in silence a man is an open book and unarmed. In speech with a man a woman is at a disadvantage— because they speak different languages. She may understand his. Hers he will never speak nor understand. In pity, or from other motives, she must therefore, stammeringly, speak his. He listens and is flattered and thinks he has her mental measure when he has not touched even the fringe of her consciousness.... Outside the life relationship men and women can have only conversational, and again conversational, interchange." ...That's the truth about life. Men and women never meet. Inside the life relationship you can see them being strangers and hostile; one or the other or both, completely alone. That was the world. Social life. In social life no one was alive but the lonely women keeping up half-admiring half-pitying endless conversations with men, with one little ironic part of themselves ... until they were fifty and had done their share of social life. But outside the world—one could be alive always. Fifty. Thirty more years....

When I woke in the night I felt nothing but tiredness and regret for having promised to go. Now, I never felt so strong and happy. This is how Mag is feeling. Their kettle is bumping on their spirit lamp, too. She loves the sound just in this way, the Sunday morning sound of the kettle, with the air full of coming bells and the doors opening—I'm half-dressed, without any effort—and shutting up and down the streets is *perfect*, again, and again; at seven o'clock in the silence, with the air coming in from the squares smelling like the country, is bliss. "You know, little child, you have an extraordinary capacity for happiness." I suppose I have. Well; I can't help it.... I *am* frantically, frantically happy. I'm up here alone, frantically happy. Even Mag has to *talk* to Jan about the happy things. Then they go, a little. The only thing to do is either to be silent or make cheerful noises. Bellow. If you do that too much, people don't like it. You can only keep on making cheerful noises if you are quite alone. Perhaps that is why people in life are always grumbling at "annoyances" and things; to hide how happy they are ... "there is a dead level of happiness all over the world"—hidden. People go on about things, because they are always trying to remember how happy they are. The worse things are, the more despairing they get, because they are so happy. You know what I mean. It's there—there's nothing else there.... But some people *know* more about it than others. Intelligent people. I suppose I am intelligent. I can't *help* it. I don't want to be different. Yes, I do—oh Lord, yes, I *do*. Mag knows. But she goes in amongst people and the complaints and the fuss, and takes sides. But they both come out again; to be by themselves and talk about it all ... they sit down intelligently to life.... They do things that have nothing to do with their circumstances. They were always doing things like this all the year round. Spring and summer and autumn and winter things. They had done, for years. The kind of things that made independent elderly women, widows and spinsters who were free to go about, have that look of intense appreciation ... "a heart at leisure from itself to soothe and sympathize"; no, that type was always inclined to revel in other people's troubles. It was something more than that. Never mind. Come on. Hurry up. Oh—for a man, oh for a man, *oh* for a man—*sion* in the skies....[1] Wot a big voice I've got, mother.

"Cooooooo—ooo—er, Bill." The sudden familiar sound came just above her head. Where was she? *What* a pity. The boys had wakened her. Then she had been asleep! It was perfect. The footsteps belonging to the voice had passed along just above her head; nice boys, they could not help chi-iking[2] when they saw the sleeping figures, but they did not mean to disturb. They had wakened her from her first daytime sleep. Asleep! She had slept in broad sunlight, at the foot of the little cliff. Waking in the daytime is *perfect* happiness. To wake suddenly and fully,

---

1   These are lines from popular nineteenth-century hymns.
2   Slang for shouting "a hurrah, a good word, or hearty praise." John
     Camden Hotten, *A Dictionary of Modern Slang, Cant, and Vulgar Words*
     (London: Piccadilly, 1860).

nowhere; in paradise; and then to see sharply with large clear strong eyes the things you were looking at when you fell asleep. She lay perfectly still. Perhaps the girls were asleep. Presently they would all be sitting up again, and she would have to begin once more the tiring effort to be as clever as they were. But it would be a little different now that they had all lain stretched out at the foot of the cliffs, asleep. She was changed. Something had happened since she had fallen asleep disappointed in the east-coast sea and the little low cliff, wondering why she could not see and feel them like the seas and cliffs of her childhood. She could see and feel them now, as long as no one spoke and the first part of the morning remained far away. She closed her eyes and drifted drowsily back to the moment of being awakened by the sudden cry. In the instant before her mind had slid back, and she had listened to the muffled footsteps thudding along the turf of the low cliff above her head, waiting angrily and anxiously for further disturbance, she had been perfectly alive, seeing; perfect things all round her, no beginning or ending ... there had been moments like that, years ago, in gardens, by seas and cliffs. Her mind wandered back amongst these; calling up each one with perfect freshness. They were all the same. In each one she had felt exactly the same; outside life, untouched by anything, free. She had thought they belonged to the past, to childhood and youth. In childhood she had thought each time that the world had just begun and would always be like that; later on, she now remembered, she had always thought when such a moment came that it would be the last, and had clung to it with wide des-perate staring eyes until tears came and she had turned away from some great open scene, with a strong conscious body flooded suddenly by a strong warm tide, to the sad dark world to live for the rest of her time upon a memory. But the moment she had just lived was the same, it was exactly the *same* as the first one she could remember, the moment of standing, alone, in bright sunlight on a narrow gravel path in the garden at Babing-ton between two banks of flowers, the flowers level with her face, and large bees swinging slowly to and fro before her face from bank to bank, many sweet smells coming from the flowers and, amongst them, a strange pleasant smell like burnt paper.... It was the same moment. She saw it now in just the same way; not remembering going into the garden or any end to being in the bright sun between the blazing flowers, the two banks linked by the slowly swinging bees, nothing else in the world, no house behind the little path, no garden beyond it. Yet she must somehow have got out of the house and through the shrubbery and along the plain path between the lawns.

All the six years at Babington were that blazing alley of flowers without beginning or end, no winters, no times of day or changes to be seen. There were other memories, quarrelling with Harriett in the nursery, making paper pills, listening to the bells on Sunday afternoon, a bell and a pomegranate, a bell or a pomegranate round about the hem of Aaron's robe,[1] the squirting of water into one's aching ear, the taste of an egg after scarlet fever,[2] the witch in the chimney,[3] cowslip balls,[4] a lobster walking upstairs on its tail,[5] dancing in a ring with grown-ups, the smell of steam and soap, the warm smell of the bath towel, Martha's fingers warming one's feet, her lips kissing one's back, something going to happen to-morrow, crackling green paper clear like glass and a gold paper fringe in your hand before the cracker[6] went off; an eye blazing out of the wall at night, "Thou God seest me,"[7] apple pasties[8] in the garden; coming up from the mud pies round the summer-house to bed, being hit on the nose by a swing and going indoors screaming at the large blots of blood on the white pinafore,[9] climbing up the cucumber frame and falling through the glass at the top,[10] blowing bubbles in the hay-loft and singing *Rosalie the Prairie Flower*,[11] and whole pieces of life indoors and out, coming up bit by bit as one thought, but all mixed with sadness and pain and bothers with people. They did not come first, or without

---

1 From Exodus 28:34-35, where the robes of the high priest are described and prescribed to be worn by Aaron, Moses' brother.

2 A streptococcal infection that can lead to strep throat.

3 This may refer to the folk belief that a bend in the chimney will keep witches from flying down it, or to a charm placed in the flue or hearth to prevent witches entering the house.

4 A ball made of the petals of the cowslip (*Primula veris*) flower, often by children, as with daisy chains and similar crafts.

5 Obscure.

6 Christmas cracker, a tube with little novelties inside, and packed with a cap that bangs when both ends of the cracker are pulled apart.

7 Genesis 16:13 (King James Version).

8 An English baked pastry, made with various fillings.

9 A collarless, sleeveless dress, like an apron, often worn by children over their clothes to keep them from getting dirty (*OED*).

10 That is, a cold frame or structure of glass and wood used to cultivate vegetables outdoors in winter.

11 An 1855 ballad by popular American hymn and songwriting duo George Frederick Root (1820-95) and Fanny Crosby (1820-1915).

thought. The blazing alley came first without thought or effort of memory. The flowers all shining separate and distinct and all together, indistinct in a blaze. She gazed at them ... sweet-williams of many hues, everlasting flowers, gold and yellow and brown and brownish purple, pinks and petunias and garden daisies white and deep crimson ... then *memory* was happiness, one happiness linked to the next.... It was the same already with Germany ... the sunny happy beautiful things came first ... in a single glance, the whole of the time in Germany was beautiful, golden happy light, and people happy in the golden light, garlands of music, and the happy ringing certainty of voices, no matter what they said, the way the whole of life throbbed with beauty when the hush of prayer was on the roomful of girls ... the wonderful house, great dark high wooden doors in the distance thrown silently open, great silent space of sunlight between them, high windows, alight against the shadows of rooms; the happy confidence of the open scene.... Germany was a party, a visit, a gift. It *had* been, in spite of every-thing in the difficult life, what she had dreamed it when she went off; all woods and forests and music ... Hermann and Dorothea[1] happiness in the summer twilight of German villages. It had become that now. The heart of a German town was that, making one a little homesick for it.... The impulse to go and the going had been right. It was part of something ... with a meaning; perhaps there is happiness only in the things one does deliberately, without a visible reason; drifting off to Germany, because it called; coming here to-day ... in freedom. If you are free, you are alive ... nothing that happens in the part of your life that is not free, the part you do and are paid for, is alive. To-day, because I am free I am the same person as I was when I was there, but much stronger and happier because I know it. As long as I can sometimes feel like this nothing has mattered. Life is a chain of happy moments that cannot die.

"Damn those boys—they woke me up."

"Did they, Mag? so they did me; did you dream?" Perhaps Mag would say something ... but people never seemed to think anything of "dropping off to sleep."

"I drempt that I dwelt in Marble Halls;[2] you awake von Bohlen?"

---

1 "Hermann and Dorothea" (1796-97), an epic poem by Goethe.

2 An aria, also called "The Gipsy Girl's Dream," from the opera *The Bohemian Girl* (1843) by Irish composer Michael William Balfe (1808-70), with lyrics by English theatre manager Alfred Bunn (1796-1860).

"I don't quite know."

"But speaking tentatively ..."

"A long lean mizzerable *tent*ative——"

"I perceive that you are still asleep. Shall I sing it?—'I *durr-r*-empt, I da-*we*-elt, in ma-ha-har-ble halls.'"

"Cooooo—oooo—er, Bill." The response sounded faintly from far away on the cliffs.

"Cooooo—ooo—er, Micky," warbled Miriam. "I like that noise. When they are further off I shall try doing it very loud, to get the proper crack."

"I think we'd better leave her here, don't you von Bohlen?"

Was it nearly tea-time? Would either of them soon mention tea? The beauty of the rocks had faded. Yet, if they ceased being clever and spoke of the beauty, it would not come back. The weariness of keeping things up went on. When the gingernuts and lemonade were at last set out upon the sand, they shamed Miriam with the sense of her long preoccupation with them. The girls had not thought of them. They never seemed to flag in their way of talking. Perhaps it was partly their regular meals. It was dreadful always to be the first one to want food....

But she was happier down here with them than she would have been alone.

Going alone for a moment in the twilight across the little scrub, as soon as she had laughed enough over leaving the room in the shelter of a gorse bush, she recovered the afternoon's happiness. There was a little fence, bricks were lying scattered about, and half-finished houses stood along the edge of the scrub. But a soft land-breeze was coming across the common carrying the scent of gorse; the silence of the sea reminded her of its presence beyond the cliffs; her own gorse-scented breeze, and silent sea and sunlit cliffs.

CHAPTER XXIII

Cool with sound short sleep, she rose early, the memory of yesterday giving a Sunday leisure to the usual anxious hurry of breakfast. She was strong with her own possessions. Wimpole Street held nothing but her contract of duties to fulfil. These she could see in a clear vexatious tangle, against the exciting oncoming of everybody's summer; an excitement that was enough in itself. Patients were pouring out of town—in a fortnight the Orlys would be gone; all Mr Orly's accounts must be out by then. In a month, Mr Hancock would go. For a month before her own holiday there would be almost nothing to do. If every one's accounts were examined before then, she could get them off at leisure during that month ... then for this month there was nothing to do but the lessening daily duties and to get every one to examine accounts; then the house to herself, with only Mr Leyton there; the cool ease of summer in her room, and her own month ahead.

The little lavatory with its long high window sending in the light from across the two sets of back-to-back tree-shaded Bloomsbury gardens, its little shabby open sink cupboard facing her with its dim unpolished taps and the battered enamel cans on its cracked and blistered wooden top, became this morning one of her own rooms, a happy little corner in the growing life that separated her from Wimpole Street. There were no corners such as this in the beautiful clever Hampstead house; no remote shabby happy corners at all; nothing brown and old and at peace. Between him and his house were his housekeeper and servants; between him and his life was his profession ... and the complex group of people with whom he must perpetually deal, with whom he dealt in alternations of intimacy and formality. He was still at his best in his practice. That was still his life. There was nothing more real, as yet, in his life than certain times and moments in his room at Wimpole Street.... Life had answered no other questions for him.... His thought-life and his personal life were troubled and dark and cold ... in spite of his attachment to some of his family group ... he could buy beautiful things, and travel freely in his leisure ... perhaps that, those two glorious things, were sufficient compensation. But there was something wrong about them; they gave a false sense of power ... the way all those people smiled at each other when they went about and bought things, picked up a fine thing at a bargain, or gave a price whose size they were proud of ... thinking other people's thoughts ... apart from this worldly side of his life, he was entirely at Wimpole Street; the whole of him; an open book; there was nothing else in his life, yet ... his holiday with those two men—even the soft-voiced sensuous one who would quote poetry and talk romantically and cynically about women in the evenings—would bring nothing else. Yet he was counting upon it so much that he could not help unbending about his boat and his boots and his filters ... perhaps all that was the best of the holiday—men were never tired of talking about the way they did this and that ... clever difficult things that made all the difference; but they missed all the rest. Even when they sat about smoking, their minds were fussing. The women in their parties dressed, and smiled and appreciated. There would be no real happiness in such a party ... except when the women were alone, doing the things with no show about them. Supposing I were able to go anywhere on this page ... Ippington[1]... 295 m.; pop. 760 ... trains to Tudworth[2] and thence two or three times daily ... Spray Bay Hotel ... A sparrow cheeped on the window sill and fluttered away. The breath of happiness poured in at the high window; all the places in the railway guide told over their charms; mountains and lakes and rivers, innumerable strips of coast, village streets to walk along for the first time, leading out ... going, somewhere, in a train. Standing on tiptoe, she gazed her thoughts across the two garden spaces towards the grimed backs of the large brown houses. Why was one allowed to be so utterly happy? There it was ... happily here and happily going away ... away.

---

1 Unidentified. Ippington Church is in Cambridgeshire, but there is no record of an Ippington village. There are places such as Rippington and Chippington, so it is possible that Richardson simply means to invoke any such small hill town.
2 An ancient town in Yorkshire, listed in the *Domesday Book* of 1066.

CHAPTER XXIV

"There; how d'ye like that, eh? A liberal education in twelve volumes, with an index,[1] Read them when ye want to. See?" ...

They looked less, set up like that in a row, than when they had lain about on the floor of the den ... taking up Dante[2] and Beethoven at tea time.

"Books posted? I wonder I'm not more rushed. I say—v'you greased all Hancock's and the pater's instruments?"

He knows I'm slacking ... he'll tell the others when they come back....

Mr Leyton's door shut with a bang. He would be sitting reading the newspaper until the next patient came. The eternal sounds of laughter and dancing came up from the kitchen. The rest of the house was perfectly still. Her miserable hand reopened the last page of the index. There were five or six more entries under "Woman."[3]

If one could only burn all the volumes; stop the publication of them. But it was all books, all the literature in the world, right back to Juvenal[4] ... whatever happened, if it could all be avenged by somebody in some way, there was all that ... the classics, the finest literature—"unsurpassed." Education would always mean coming in contact with all that. Schoolboys got their first ideas.... *How* could Newnham and Girton women[5] endure it? How could they go on living and laughing and talking?

---

1 Joanne Winning has argued convincingly that this refers to the ninth edition of the *Encyclopædia Britannica*, 1875-89 and updated with an additional ten volumes in the tenth edition of 1902 (53-54). The disparities between the two, including the number of volumes and the differences in the index, leave room for doubt, however. Joanne Winning, *The Pilgrimage of Dorothy Richardson* (Madison: U of Wisconsin P, 2000).

2 Dante Alighieri (1265-1321), an Italian poet most notable for his *Divine Comedy*.

3 The entry on "Women" in the ninth edition of the *Encyclopaedia Britannica* is signed by the Honourable Lady Jeune: Susan Jeune, Baroness St. Helier, London City Council Alderman 1910-27, and Dame Commander of the Order of the British Empire from 1925 to her death.

4 Ancient Roman satirist (60-140 CE).

5 Two women's colleges at the University of Cambridge. Prior *(continued)*

And the modern men were the worst ... "We can now, with all the facts in our hands, sit down and examine her at our leisure." There was no getting away from the scientific facts ... *inferior*; mentally, morally, intellectually, and physically ... her development arrested in the interest of her special functions ... reverting later towards the male type ... old women with deep voices and hair on their faces ... leaving off where boys of eighteen began. If that is true everything is as clear as daylight. "Woman is not undeveloped man but diverse" falls to pieces. Woman is undeveloped man ...[1] if one could die of the loathsome visions ... I *must* die. I can't go on living in it ... the whole world full of *creatures*; half-human. And I am one of the half-human ones, or shall be, if I don't stop now.

Boys and girls were much the same ... women stopped being people and went off into hideous processes. What for? What was it all for? Development. The wonders of science. The wonders of science for women are nothing but gynaecology—all those frightful operations in the *British Medical Journal* and those jokes—the hundred golden rules.... Sacred functions[2]... highest possibilities ... sacred for what? The hand that rocks the cradle rules the world?[3] The Future of the Race?[4] What world? What race? Men.... Nothing but men; for ever.

---

to the foundation of Newnham (in 1871) and Girton (in 1869), women were not allowed to attend lectures at Cambridge.

1   These quotations are likely drawn from the *Encyclopaedia Britannica*; see p. 255, note 1.

2   Miriam is thinking of the conventional ideology of womanhood that obtained in the nineteenth century, and saw women as proverbial "angels in the house," as Coventry Patmore styled them in his well-known volume *The Angel in the House* (1854).

3   From William Ross Wallace's (1819-81) poem "What Rules the World" (1865).

4   Concern over perceived degeneration of the European, Caucasian, or white race was widespread at the end of the nineteenth century, finding articulation in Max Nordau's (1849-1923) *Degeneration* (1895). In 1871 Edward Bulwer Lytton (1803-73) published *The Coming Race*, about a subterranean superior race. Although "the future of the race" appears in Bernard Shaw's *Man and Superman* (1902-03), this is too late for Miriam to know it at this point in the narrative (c. 1896). Richardson may be thinking of H.G. Wells's dystopian vision of the future of humanity in *The Time Machine* (1895), which Miriam could have known.

If, by one thought, all the men in the world could be stopped, shaken, and slapped. There *must*, somewhere, be some power that could avenge it all ... but if these men were right, there was not. Nothing but Nature and her decrees. Why was nature there? Who started it? If nature "took good care" this and that ... there must be somebody. If there was a trick, there must be a trickster. If there is a god who arranged how things should be between men and women, and just let it go and go on I have no respect for him. I should like to give him a piece of my mind....

It will all go on as long as women are stupid enough to go on bringing men into the world ... even if civilized women stop the colonials and primitive races would go on. It is a nightmare.

They invent a legend to put the blame for the existence of humanity on woman[1] and, if she wants to stop it, they talk about the wonders of civilization and the sacred responsibilities of motherhood. They can't have it both ways. They also say women are not logical.

They despise women and they want to go on living—to repro- duce—themselves. None of their achievements, no "civilization," no art, no science can redeem that. There is no pardon possible for man. The only answer to them is suicide; all women ought to agree to commit suicide.

The torment grew as the August weeks passed. There were strange interesting things unexpectedly everywhere. Streets of great shuttered houses, their window boxes flowerless, all grey, cool and quiet and untroubled, on a day of cool rain; the restau- rants were no longer crowded; torturing thought ranged there unsupported, goaded to madness, just a mad feverish swirling in the head, ranging out, driven back by the vacant eyes of little groups of people from the country. Unfamiliar people appeared in the parks and streets, talking and staring eagerly about, women in felt boat-shaped hats trimmed with plaid ribbons—Americans. They looked clever—and ignorant of worrying thoughts. Men carried their parcels. But it was just the same. It was impossible

---

1 Miriam refers here to the Catholic doctrine of original sin, which derives from the biblical story that sin and suffering only came into the world because Eve eats the forbidden fruit of the Tree of Knowledge of Good and Evil and induces Adam to do so as well (Gen. 3:1-24).

to imagine these dried, yellow-faced women with babies. But if they liked all the fuss and noise and talk as much as they seemed to do.... If they did *not*, what were they doing? What was everybody *doing*? So busily.

Sleeplessness, and every day a worse feeling of illness. Every day the new torture. Every night the dreaming and tossing in the fierce, stifling, dusty heat, the awful waking, to know that presently the unbearable human sounds would begin again; the torment of walking through the streets, the solitary torment of leisure to read again in the stillness of the office; the moments of hope of finding a fresh meaning; hope of having misread.

There was nothing to turn to. Books were poisoned. Art. All the achievements of men were poisoned at the root. The beauty of nature was tricky femininity. The animal world was cruelty. Humanity was based on cruelty. Jests and amusements were tragic distractions from tragedy. Religion was the only hope. But even there there was no hope for women. No future life could heal the degradation of having been a woman. Religion in the world had nothing but insults for women. Christ was a man. If it was true that he was God taking on humanity—he took on *male* humanity ... and the people who explained him, St Paul[1] and the priests, the Anglicans[2] and the Nonconformists,[3] it was the same story everywhere. Even if religion could answer science and prove it wrong there was no hope, for women. And no intelligent person can prove science wrong. Life is poisoned, for women, at the very source. Science is true and will find out more and more, and things will grow more and more horrible. Space is full of dead worlds. The world is cooling and dying.[4] Then why not stop *now*?

---

1   St. Paul, or Paul the Apostle (5-67 CE), was one of the earliest Christian missionaries.
2   See p. 67, note 3.
3   Either non-Christian or, more commonly, non-Anglican Christians.
4   The idea that the universe, as a closed system, must tend towards heat-death, or entropy, originated in 1851 with William Thomson, 1st Baron Kelvin (see p. 143, note 4), and quickly gained popular credence through the second half of the nineteenth century.

"Nature's great Salic Law will never be repealed."[1] "Women can never reach the highest places in civilization." Thomas Henry Huxley. With side-whiskers. A bouncing complacent walk. Thomas Henry Huxley. (*Thomas Babington Macaulay.*)[2] The same sort of walk. Eminent men. Revelling in their cleverness. "The Lord has delivered him into my hand."[3] He did not believe in any future for anybody. But he built his life up complacently on home and family life while saying all those things about women, lived on them and their pain, ate their food, enjoyed the comforts they made ... and wrote conceited letters to his friends about his achievements and his stomach and his feelings.

What is it in me that stands back? Why can't it explain? My head will burst if it can't explain. If I die now in wild anger it only makes the thing more laughable on the whole.... That old man lives quite alone in a little gas-lit lodging. When he comes out, he is quite alone. There is nothing touching him anywhere. He will go quietly on like that till he dies. But he is me. I saw myself in his eyes that day. But he must have money. He can live like that with nothing to do but read and think and roam about, because he has money. It isn't fair. Some woman cleans his room and does

---

1   The correct quotation from Thomas Henry Huxley's (1825-95) 1865 essay "Emancipation Black and White" is: "Nature's old salique law will not be repealed, and no change of dynasty will be effected" (73). Huxley argues that women should be allowed better education if they would like, but that their social positions will not and should not change as a result. Men will remain stronger, and better women will only result in yet better sons. (T.H. Huxley, *Science and Education: Essays* [London: MacMillan & Co. 1895]). Salic Law is an ancient legal code that formed the basis for modern law through much of Europe. It stated that women were not qualified for inheritance. According to Joanne Winning, in the ninth edition of the *Encyclopædia Britannica*, "Salic Law is defined in connection with property and inheritance, and legislation which precludes women's access to either" (54).

2   Thomas Babington Macaulay (1800-59), English historian and politician, is most famous for his "Minute" on Indian education, urging an education based on English literature to remake Indians as nearly as possible in the image of the English.

3   In an 1860 debate with Archbishop Samuel Wilberforce (1805-73), Huxley is reputed to have said this line just before launching into a convincing defence of Darwin's theory of evolution, in response to Wilberforce mocking it.

his laundry. His thoughts about women are awful. It's the best way ... but I've made all sorts of plans for the holidays. After that, I will save and never see anybody and never stir out of Bloomsbury. The woman in black works. It's only in the evenings she can roam about seeing nothing. But the people she works for know nothing about her. She knows. She is sweeter than he. She is sweet. I like her. But he is more me.

CHAPTER XXV

The room still had the same radiant air. Nothing looked worn. There was not a spot anywhere. Bowls of flowers stood about. The Coalport tea-service[1] was set out on the little black table. The drawn-thread work table cover.... She had arranged the flowers. That was probably all she did; going in and out of the garden, in the sun, picking flowers. *The Artist's Model* and *The Geisha*[2] and the *Strand Musicals*[3] still lay about; the curious new smell still came from the inside of the piano. But there was this dreadful tiredness. It was dreadful that the tiredness should come nearer than the thought of Harriett. A pallid worried disordered face looked back from the strip of glass in the overmantel. No need to have looked. Always now, away from London, there was this dreadful realization of fatigue, dreadful empty sense of worry and hurry ... feeling so *strong* riding down through London, everything dropping away, nothing to think of; off and free, the holiday ahead, nothing but lovely, lonely freedom all round one.

Perhaps Harriett would be nervous and irritable. She had much more reason to be. But even if she were, it would be no good. It would be impossible to conceal this frightful fatigue and nervousness. Harriett *must* understand at once how battered and abject one was. And it was a misrepresentation. Harriett knew nothing of all one had come from; all one was going to in the distance. Maddening.... Lovely; how rich and good they looked, more honest than those in the London shops. Harriett or Mrs Thimm or Emma had ordered them from some confectioner in Chiswick.[4] Fancy being able to buy anything like that without

---

1 "Tea-service" is the name for the actual tea set made by Coalport, an English fine China company established in 1750.

2 Edwardian musical comedies *An Artist's Model*, opened in 1895 and *The Geisha* in 1896 in London. Both are productions of the writing team of Owen Hall (1853-1907), Harry Greenbank (1865-99), and Sidney Jones (1861-1946). Drawing on a successful formula, both musicals turn on romantic entanglements involving mistaken identities and/or mistaken attractions. They were among the most popular stage productions of the Edwardian period.

3 Copies of *The Strand Musical Magazine*, sister publication to *The Strand Magazine* (1891-1950).

4 A suburb of London that experienced significant growth during the nineteenth century.

thinking. How well they went with the black piano and the Coalport tea-service and the garden light coming in. Gerald did not think that women were inferior or that Harriett was a dependent.... But Gerald did not think at all. He knew nothing was too good for Harriett. Oo, *I* dunno, she would say with a laugh. She thought all men were duffers.[1] Perhaps that was the best way. Selfish babies. But Gerald was not selfish. He would never let Harriett wash up, if he were there. He would never pretend to be ignorant of "mysteries" to get out of doing things. I get out of doing things—in houses. But women won't let me do things. They all know I want to be mooning about. How do they know it? What is it? But they like me to be there. And now in houses there's always this fearful worry and tiredness. What is the meaning of it?

Heavy footsteps came slowly downstairs.

"I put tea indoors. I thought Miss Miriam'd be warm after her ride."

A large undulating voice with a shrewd consoling glance in it. She must have come to the kitchen door to meet Harriett in the hall.

"Yes, I'ke spect she will." It was the same voice Harriett had had in the nursery, resonant with practice in speaking to new people. Miriam felt tears coming.

"Hallo, you porking? Isn't it porking?"[2]

"Simply porked to death, my dear. Porked to *Death*," bawled Miriam softly, refreshed and delighted. Harriett was still far off, but she felt as if she had touched her. Even the end of the awful nine months was not changing her. Her freshly shampooed hair had a leisurely glint. There was colour in her cheeks. She surreptitiously rubbed her own hot face. Her appearance would improve now, with every hour. By the evening she would be her old self. After tea she would play *The Artist's Model* and *The Geisha*.

"Let's have tea. I was asleep. I didn't hear you come."

She sank into one of the large chairs, her thin accordion-pleated black silk tea-gown billowing out round her squared little body. Even her shoulders looked broader and squarer. From the little pleated white chiffon chemisette,[3] her radiant firm little

---

1 "A fool, or worthless person" (Hotten 134).

2 Apparently, Miriam and Harriet are using the slang term "porking" to mean either hot or tired.

3 A light article of women's clothing worn to fill in the neckline of a garment.

head rose up, her hair glinting under the light of the window behind her. She looked so fine—such a "fine spectacle"—and seemed so strong. How did she feel? Mrs Thimm brought the teapot. The moment she had gone, Harriett handed the rich cakes. Mrs Thimm *beaming*, shedding strong beams of happiness and approval....

"Come on," said Harriett. "Let's tuck in. There's some thin bread and butter somewhere, but I can't eat anything but these things."

"Can't you?"

"The last time I went up to town, Mrs Bollingdon and I had six between us at Slater's and when we got back we had another tea."

"Fancy *you*!"

"I know. I can't *'elp* it."

"I can't 'elp it, Micky. *Love*lay b-hird."

The fourth cup of creamy tea; Harriett's firm ringed hand; the gleaming serene world; the sunlit flower-filled garden, shaded at the far end by the large tree the other side of the fence, coming in, one with the room; the sun going to set and bring the evening freshness and rise to-morrow. Twenty-eight leisurely teas, twenty-eight long days; a feeling of strength and drowsiness. Nothing to do but clean the bicycle and pump up the tyres on the lawn, to-morrow. Nothing—after carrying the bicycle from the coal cellar up the area steps and through the house into the Tansley Street back yard. Nothing more but setting out after two nights of sleep in a cool room.

"That your machine in the yard, Mirry?"

"Yes; I've hired it, thirty bob[1] for the whole month."

"Well, if you're going a sixty-mile ride on it, I advise you to tighten up the nuts a bit."

"I will if you'll show me where they are. I've got a lovely spanner.[2] Did you look in the wallet?"[3]

"I'll have a look at it all over, if you like."

"Oh, Gerald, you saint...."

"Now he's happy," said Harriett, as Gerald's white-flannelled figure flashed into the sunlight and disappeared through the yard gate.

---

1 Slang for a shilling.

2 British term for "wrench."

3 A tool pouch attached to the bicycle for emergency repairs.

"Ph—how hot it is; it's this summer-house."

"Let's go outside if you like," said Miriam lazily, "it seems to me simply perfect in here."

"It's all right—ph—it's hot everywhere," said Harriett languidly. She mopped her face. Her face emerged from her handkerchief fever-flushed, the eyes large and dark and brilliant; her lips full and drawn in and down at the corners with a look of hopeless anxiety.

Anger flushed through Miriam. Harriett at nineteen, in the brilliant beauty of the summer afternoon, facing hopeless fear.

"That's an awfully pretty dress," she faltered nervously.

Harriett set her lips and stretched both arms along the elbows of her basket chair.

"You could have it made into an evening gown."

"I loathe the very sight of it. I shall burn it the minute I've done with it."

It was awful that anything that looked so charming could seem like that.

"D'you feel bad? Is it so awful?"

"I'm all right, but I feel as if I were bursting. I wish it would just hurry up and be over."

"I think you're simply splendid."

"I simply don't think about it. You don't think about it, except now and again when you realize you've got to go through it, and then you go hot all over."

"The head's[1] a bit wobbly," said Gerald riding round the lawn.

"Does that matter?"

"Well, it doesn't make it any easier to ride, especially with this great bundle on the handle-bars. You want a luggage-carrier."

"I dare say. I say, Gerald, show me the nuts to-morrow, not now."

The machine was lying upside down on the lawn, with its back wheel revolving slowly in the air.

"The front wheel's out of the true."[2]

"What do you think of the saddle?"

"The saddle's all right enough."

---

1 That is, the headset, the set of bearings that hold the handlebar stem to the fork and provide the steering capacity.

2 That is, it has a bend or wobble to it.

"It's a Brooks's, B 40;[1] about the best you can have. It's my own, and so's the Lucas's Baby bell."[2]

"By Jove, she's got an adjustable spanner."

"That's not mine, nor the repair outfit; Mr Leyton lent me those."

"And vaseline on the bearings."

"Of course."

"I don't think much of your gear-case, my dear."

"Gerald, do you think it's all right on the whole?"

"Well, it's sound enough as far as I can see; bit squiffy and wobbly. I don't advise you to ride it in traffic, or with this bundle."

"I *must* have the bundle. I came down through Tottenham Court Road and Oxford Street and Bond Street and Piccadilly all right."

"Well, there's no accounting for tastes. Got any oil?"

"There's a little oil can in the wallet, wrapped up in the rag. It's lovely; perfectly new."

1   J.B. Brooks & Co. patented a variety of bicycle seats. The B40 model came in either a ladies' or gents' version. The 1890 Brooks catalogue boasts that the Ladies' B40 has a "special dress protector, which, while neat and unobtrusive, is thoroughly effective, and renders it impossible for the dress to catch."
    <http://www.brooksengland.com/press/2009_01/1890_Catalogue.pdf>.
2   Lucas Industries (founded 1860) built automotive and bicycle parts, in particular bicycle lamps and bells.

CHAPTER XXVI

There was a strong soft grey light standing at the side of the blind ... smiling and touching her as it had promised. She leaped to the floor and stood looking at it, swaying with sleep. Ships sailing along with masts growing on them, poplars streaming up from the ships, all in a stream of gold.... Last night's soapy water poured away, and the fresh poured out ready standing there all night, everything ready.... I must not forget the extra piece of string.... Je-ru-sa-*lem* the Gol-den, with-milk-and-hun-ny— blest.... Sh, not so much noise ... beneath thy con, tem, *pla*, tion, sink, heart, and, voice, o, ppressed.

I *know* not, oh, I, *know*, not.[1]

Sh—Sh ... hark hark my soul angelic songs are swelling O'er earth's green fields, and ocean's wave-beat shore[2] ... damn—blast where are my bally knickers?[3] Sing us sweet fragments of the songs above.

The green world everywhere, inside and out ... all along the dim staircase, waiting in the dim cold kitchen.

No blind, brighter. Cool grey light, a misty windless morning. Shut the door.

They STAND—those HALLS *of* ZI-ON
ALL JUBILANT *with* SONG.[4]

As she neared Colnbrook[5] the road grew heavier and a closer mist lay over the fields. It was too soon for fatigue, but her knees

---

1 Opening lines of the ancient hymn, "Jerusalem, the Golden." Originally a Latin poem by the twelfth-century monk Bernard of Cluny, it was translated into English in 1851 by John M. Neale (1818-66).
2 Opening lines of the 1854 hymn "Hark! Hark! My Soul," by Frederick William Faber (1814-63).
3 "Blast" and "bally" are slang curse words, "blast" meaning something like "damn" and "bally" meaning "bloody." "Knickers" is slang for undergarments.
4 Further lines from "Jerusalem, the Golden."
5 A small village, then in Buckinghamshire, but later incorporated into Berkshire county, west of London. Colnbrook was noted for centuries for its many inns.

already seemed heavy with effort. Getting off at the level crossing she found that her skirt was sodden and her zouave[1] spangled all over with beads of moisture. She walked shivering across the rails and remounted rapidly, hoisting into the saddle a draggled person that was not her own, and riding doggedly on beating back all thoughts but the thought of sunrise.

"Is this Reading?"[2]

The cyclist smiled as he shouted back. He knew she knew. But he liked shouting too. If she had yelled Have you got a *soul*, it would have been just the same. If every one were on bicycles all the time you could talk to everybody, all the time, about anything[3] ... sailing so steadily along with two free legs ... how much easier it must be with your knees going so slowly up and down ... how *funny* I must look with my knees racing up and down in lumps of skirt. But I'm here, at the midday rest. It must be nearly twelve.

Drawing into the kerb near a confectioner's, she thought of buying two bars of plain chocolate. There *was* some sort of truth in *The Swiss Family Robinson*.[4] If you went on, it was all right. There was only death. People frightened you about things that were not there. I will never listen to anybody again; or be frightened. That cyclist knew, as long as he was on his bicycle. Perhaps he has people who make him not himself. He can always get away again. Men can always get away. I am going to lead a man's life, always getting away....

Wheeling her machine back to the open road, she sat down on a bank and ate the cold sausage and bread and half of the chocolate and lay down to rest on a level stretch of grass in front of a gate. Light throbbed round the edges of the little high white fleecy clouds. She swung triumphantly up. The earth throbbed beneath her with the throbbing of her heart ... the sky steadied and stood further off, clear, peaceful, blue, with light neat soft bunches of cloud drifting slowly across it. She closed her eyes

---

1 See p. 203, note 1.

2 A Berkshire county town that became a major manufacturing centre in the nineteenth century.

3 Reminiscent of a perhaps apocryphal comment attributed to H.G. Wells: "When I see an adult on a bicycle, I do not despair for the future of the human race."

4 A popular 1812 novel by Swiss pastor Johann David Wyss (1743-1818) about a shipwrecked family that builds a new home on a remote island. There were a number of English translations published throughout the nineteenth century.

upon the dazzling growing distances of blue and white, and felt the horizon folding down in a firm clear sweep round her green cradle. Within her eyelids fields swung past green, cornfields gold and black, fields with coned clumps of harvested corn, dusty gold, and black, on either side of the bone-white grass-trimmed road. The road ran on and on, lined by low hedges and the strange everlasting back-flowing fields. Thrilling hedges and out-stretched fields of distant light, coming on mile after mile, winding off, left behind ... "It's the Bath Road[1] I shall be riding on; I'm going down to Chiswick to see which way the wind is on the Bath Road...." Trees appeared, golden and green and shadowy, with warm cool strong shaded trunks coming nearer and larger. They swept by, their shadowy heads sweeping the lower sky. Poplars shot up, drawing her eyes to run up their feath-ered slimness and sweep to the top of the pointed plumes pierc-ing the sky. Trees clumped in masses round houses leading to vil-lages that shut her into little corridors of hard hot light ... the little bright sienna form of the hen she had nearly run over; the land stretching serenely out again, rolling along, rolling along in the hot sunshine with the morning and evening freshness at either end ... sweeping it slowly in and out of the deeps of the country night ... eyelids were transparent. It was *light* coming through one's eyelids that made that clear soft buff; soft buff light filtering through one's body ... little sounds, insects creeping and humming in the hedge, sounds from the grass. Sudden single quiet sounds going up from distant fields and farms, lost in the sky.

I've got my sea-legs[2] ... this is *riding*—not just straining along trying to forget the wobbly bicycle, but feeling it wobble and being able to control it ... being able to look about easily ... there will be a harvest moon this month, rolling up huge and hot, sud-denly over the edge of a field; the last moon. I shall see that

---

1　The Old Bath Road is the old main road that runs between London and the ancient Roman town of Bath, in the southwestern county of Somer-set. The quoted words here appear to be from a ballad or popular song about the ancient road. Though the suggestion is tempting, they are not from John Poole's (1786-1872) *Intrigue, or The Bath Road, A Comical Interlude, In One Act* (1865).

2　Slang for finding one's balance while on something other than solid ground.

anyhow, whatever the holiday is like. It will be cold again in the winter. Perhaps I shan't feel so cold this winter.

She recognized the figure the instant she saw it. It was as if she had been riding the whole day to meet it. Completely forgotten, it had been all the time at the edge of the zest of her ride. It had been everywhere all the time and there it was at last, dim and distant and unmistakable ... coming horribly along, a murk in the long empty road. She slowed up looking furtively about. The road had been empty for so long. It stretched invisibly away behind, empty. There was no sound of anything coming along; nothing but the squeak squeak of her gear-case; bitter empty fields on either side, greying away to the twilight, the hedges sharp and dark, enemies; nothing ahead but the bare road, carrying the murky figure; there all the time; and bound to come. She rode on at her usual pace, struggling for an absorption so complete as to make her invisible, but was held back by her hatred of herself for having wondered whether he had seen her. The figure was growing more distinct. Murky. Murk from head to foot. Wearing openly like a coat the expression that could be seen hidden inside everybody. She had made an enemy of him. It was too late. The voice in her declaring sympathy, claiming kinship, faded faint and far away within her ... hullo old boy, isn't it a bloody world ... he would know it had come too late. He came walking along, slowly walking like someone in a procession or a quickly moving funeral; like someone in a procession, who must go on. He was sur- rounded by people, pressed in and down by them, wanting to kill every one with a look and run, madly, to root up trees and tear down the landscape and get outside ... he is myself.... He stood still. Her staring eyes made him so clear that she saw his arrested face just before he threw out an arm and came on, stumbling. Measuring the width of the roadway she rode on slowly along the middle of it, pressing steadily and thoughtlessly forward, her eyes fixed on the far-off spaces of the world she used to know, towards a barrier of swirling twilight. He was quite near, slouching and thinking and silently talking, on and on. He was all right, poor thing. She put forth all her strength and shot past him in a sharp curve, her eye just seeing that he turned and stood, swaying.

What a blessing he was drunk, what a blessing he was drunk, she chattered busily, trying to ignore her trembling limbs. Again and again as she steadied and rode sturdily and blissfully on, came the picture of herself saying with confidential eagerness as she dismounted: "I *say*—make haste—there's a madman coming down the road—get behind the hedge till he's gone—I'm going for the police." A man would not have been afraid. Then men *are* more independent than women. Women can never go very far from the protection of men—because they are physically inferior. But men are afraid of mad bulls.... They have to resort to tricks. What was that I was just thinking? Something I ought to remember. Women have to be protected. But men explain it the wrong way. It was the same thing.... The polite protective man was the same; if he relied on his strength. The world is the most sickening hash.... I'm so sorry for you. *I* hate humanity too. *Isn't* it a lovely day? *Isn't* it? Just look.

The dim road led on into the darkness of what appeared to be a private estate. The light from the lamp fell upon wide gates fastened back. The road glimmered on ahead with dense darkness on either side. There had been no turning. The road evidently passed through the estate. She rode on and on between the two darknesses, her light casting a wobbling radiance along her path. Rustling sounded close at hand, and quick thuddings startled her, making her heart leap. The hooting of an owl echoed through the hollows amongst the trees. Stronger than fear, was the comfort of the dense darkness. Her own darkness by right of riding through the day. Leaning upon the velvety blackness she pushed on, her eyes upon the little circle of light, steady on the centre of the pathway, wobbling upon the feet of the trees emerging in slow procession on either side of the way.

The road began to slope gently downwards. Wearily back-pedalling, she crept down the incline, her hand on the brake, her eyes straining forward. Hard points of gold light—of course. She had put them there herself. Marlborough[1] ... the prim polite lights of Marlborough; little gliding moving lights, welcoming, coming safely up as she descended. They disappeared. There must have been a gap in the trees. Presently she would be down among them.

"*Good* Lord—it's a woman."
She passed through the open gate into the glimmer of a

---

1 A town in Wiltshire county, on the Old Bath Road, about 80 miles (120 km) west of London.

descending road. Yes. Why not? Why that amazed stupefaction? Trying to rob her of the darkness and the wonderful coming out into the light. The man's voice went on with her down the dull safe road. A young lady, taking a bicycle ride in a daylit suburb. That was what she was. That was all he would allow. It's something in men.

"You don't think of riding up over the downs[1] at this time of night?" It was like an at-home.[2] Everybody in the shop was in it, but she was not in it. Marlborough thoughts rattling in all the heads; with Sunday coming. They had sick and dying relations. But it was all in Marlborough. Marlborough was all round them all the time, the daily look of it, the morning coming each day excitingly, all the people seeing each other again and the day going on. They did not know that that was it; or what it was they liked. Talking and thinking, with the secret hidden all the time even from themselves. But it was that that made them talk and make such a to-do about everything. They had to hide it because, if they knew, they would *feel* fat and complacent and wicked. They were fat and complacent because they did not know it.

"Oh yes I do," said Miriam in feeble husky tones.

She stood squarely in front of the grating. The people became angrily gliding forms; cheated; angry in an eternal resentful silence; pretending. The man began thoughtfully ticking off the words.

"How far have you come?" he asked, suddenly pausing and looking up through the grating.

"From London."

"Then you've just come down through the Forest."

"Is that a forest?"

"You must have come through Savernake."[3]

"I didn't know it was a forest."

"Well, I don't advise you to go on up over the downs at this time of night."

If only she had not come in, she could have gone on without knowing it was "the downs."

"My front tyre is punctured," she said conversationally, leaning a little against the counter.

---

1 A range of chalk hills that extends along the southern coast of England.

2 That is, times when the house was open to guests or visitors. See p. 203, note 3.

3 Savernake Forest sits on a chalk plateau and stretches about 7 miles between Marlborough and Great Bedwyn, to the east.

The man's face tightened. "There's Mr Drake next door would mend that for you, in the morning."

"Next door. Oh, thank you." Pushing her sixpence under the rail, she went down the shop to the door seeing nothing but the brown dusty floor leading out to the helpless night.

Why did he keep making such impossible suggestions? The tyre was absolutely flat. How much would a hotel cost? How did you stay in hotels ... hotels ... her hands went busily to her wallet. She drew out the repair outfit and Mr Leyton's voice sounded, emphatic and argumentative, "You know where you are and they don't rook you." There was certain to be one in a big town like this. She swished back into the shop and interrupted the man with her eager singing question.

"Yes," came the answer, "there's a quiet place of that sort up the road, right up against the Forest."

"Has my telegram gone? Can I alter it?"

"No, it's not gone, you're just in time."

It was the loveliest thing that could have happened. The day was complete, from morning to night.

Someone brought in the meal and clattered it quietly down, going away and shutting the door without a word. A door opened and the sound of departing footsteps ceased. She was shut in with the meal and the lamp in the little crowded world. The musty silence was so complete that the window hidden behind the buff-and-white blinds and curtains must be shut. The silence throbbed. The throbbing of her heart shook the room. Something was telling the room that she was the happiest thing in existence. She stood up, the beloved little room moving as she moved, and gathered her hands gently against her breast, to ... get through, through into the soul of the musty little room.... "Oh! ..." She felt herself beating from head to foot with a radiance, but her body within it was weak and heavy with fever. The little scene rocked, crowding furniture, antimacassars,[1] ornaments, wool mats. She looked from thing to thing with a beaming, feverish, frozen smile. Her eyes blinked wearily at the hot crimson flush of the mat under the lamp. She sank back again, her heavy light limbs glowing with fever. "By Jove, I'm tired.... I've had nothing since

---

1   A small cloth placed over the back or arm of a chair or couch to protect its fabric.

breakfast m—but a m-bath *bun*[1] and an acidulatudd *drop."*[2] ...
She laughed and sat whistling softly ... Jehoshaphat[3]—Manchester[4]—Mesopotamia[5]—beloved—you sweet, sweet thing—
Veilchen, unter Gras versteckt[6]—out of it all—here I am. I shall
always stay in hotels.... Glancing towards the food spread out on
a white cloth near the globed lamp, she saw behind the table a
little stack of books. Ham and tea and bread and butter....
Leaning unsteadily across the table ... battered and ribbed green
binding and then a short moral story or natural history—blue,
large and fat, a "story-book" of some kind ... she drew out one of
the undermost volumes.... *Robert Elsmere!*[7] Here, after all these
years in this little outlandish place. She poured out some tea and
hurriedly slid a slice of ham between two pieces of bread and
butter and sat back with the food drawn near, the lamplight
glaring into her eyes, the printed page in exciting shadow. Everything in the room was distinct and sharp—morning strength
descended upon her.

How he must have liked and admired. It must have amazed
him; a woman setting forth and putting straight the muddles of
his own mind. "Powerful," he probably said. It was a half-jealous
keeping to himself of a fine, good thing. If he could have known
that it would have been, just at that very moment, the answer to
my worry about Christ, he would have been jealous and angry
quite as much as surprised and pleased and sympathetic ... he

---

1 A Bath Bun is a sweet roll with sugar sprinkled on top.

2 An acidulated drop is a candy, similar to a lemon drop.

3 A Biblical king of Judah, a kingdom in the Middle East, in the ninth
century BCE.

4 A city in Northern England, which was a major industrial centre in the
nineteenth century.

5 An ancient region of the Middle East, between the Tigris and Euphrates
rivers, now Iraq.

6 Title of a German poem by Hoffmann Von Fallersleben, translated into
English by Alfred Baskerville in 1882 as "Violet on Grassy Slope."
Alfred Baskerville, *The Poetry of Germany* (Philadelphia: Shaefer &
Koradl, 1882), p. 247. A more accurate translation would be "violet
hidden under the grass."

7 A best-selling 1888 novel by Mary Augusta Ward (1851-1920), published under the name Mrs. Humphry Ward, that tells the story of a
clergyman who loses his faith.

was afraid *himself* of the idea that any one can give up the idea of the divinity of Christ and still remain religious and good. He ought to have let me read it.... If he could have stated it himself as well, that day by the gate he would have done so ... "a very reasonable dilemma, my dear." He knew I was thinking about things. But he had not read *Robert Elsmere* then. He was jealous of a thunderbolt flung by a woman....

And now I've got beyond *Robert Elsmere*.... That's Mrs Humphry Ward and Robert Elsmere; that's gone. There's no answering science. One must choose. Either science or religion. They can't both be true. This is the same as *Literature and Dogma*[1].... Only in *Literature and Dogma* there is that thing that is perfectly true—that thing—what is it? What was that idea in *Literature and Dogma*?

I wonder if I've strained my heart. This funny feeling of sinking through the bed. Never mind. I've done the ride. I'm alive and alone in a strange place. Everything's alive all round me in a new way. Nearer. As the flame of the candle had swelled and gone out under her blowing, she had noticed the bareness of everything in the room—a room for chance travellers, nothing that any one could carry away. She could still see it as it was when she moved and blew out the candle, a whole room swaying sideways into darkness. The more she relinquished the idea of harm and danger, the nearer and more intimate the room became.... No one can prevent my being alone in a strange place, near to things and loving them. It's more than worth half killing yourself. It makes you ready to die. I'm not going to die, even if I have strained my heart. "Damaged myself for life." I am going to sleep. The dawn will come, no one knowing where I am. Because I have no money, I must go on and stay with these people. But I have been alive here. There's hardly any time. I *must* go to sleep.

---

1 See p. 151, note 1.

CHAPTER XXVII

Being really happy or really miserable makes people like you and like being with you. They need not know the cause. Someone will speak now, in a moment.... Miriam tried to return to the falling rain, the soft light in it, the soft light on the greenery, the intense green glow everywhere ... misty green glow. But her eyes fell and her thoughts went on. They would have seen. Her face must be speaking of their niceness in coming out on the dull day, so that she might drive about once more in Lord Lansdowne's estate. Someone will speak. Perhaps they had not found forgetfulness in the green through the rain under the grey. Moments came suddenly in the lanes between the hedges, like that moment that always came where the lane ran up and turned, and the fields spread out in the distance. But usually you could not forget the chaise and the donkey and the people. In here amongst the green, something always came at once and stayed. Perhaps they did not find it so, or did not know they found it, because of their thoughts about the "fine estate." They seemed quite easy driving in the lanes, as easy as they ever seemed when one could not forget them. What were they doing when one forgot them? They knew one liked some things better than others; or suddenly liked everything very much indeed ... she said you were apathetic ... what does that mean? ... what did she mean? ... with her, one could see nothing and sat waiting ... I said I don't think so, I don't think she is apathetic at all. Then they understood when one sat in a heap.... They had been pleased this morning because of one's misery at going away. They did not know of the wild happiness in the garden before breakfast, nor that the garden had been so lovely because the strain of the visit was over, and London was coming. They did not know that the happiness of being in amongst the greenery to-day, pouring out one's heart in farewell to the great trees, had grown so intense because the feeling of London and freedom was there. They could not see the long rich winter, the lectures and books, out of which something was coming....

"It's a pity the rain came."

Ah no, that is not rain. It is not raining. What is "raining"? What do people *think* when they say these things?

"We are like daisies, *drenched* in dew." She pursed up her face towards the sky.

They laughed and silence came again. Heavy and happy.

"I'm glad you came up. I want to ask you what is to be done about Hendie."

Miriam looked about the boudoir.[1] Mrs Green had hardly looked at her. She was smiling at her fancy work. But if one did not say something soon, she would speak again, going on into things from her point of view. Doctor and medicine. Eve liked it all. She *liked* Mrs Green's clever difficult fancy work, and the boudoir smell of Tonquin beans,[2] and the house and garden and the bazaars and village entertainments, and the children's endless expensive clothes and the excitements and troubles about that fat man. Down here she was in a curious flush of excitement all the time herself....

"I think she wants a rest."

"I told her so. But resting seems to make her worse. We all thought she was worse after the holidays."

Miriam's eyes fell before the sudden glance of Mrs Green's blue-green eye. She must have seen her private vision of life in the great rich house ... misery, death with no escape. But they had Eve. Eve did not know what was killing her. She liked being tied to people.

"She is very nervous."

"Yes. I know it's only nerves. I've told her that."

"But you don't know what nerves are. They're not just nothing...."

"*You*'re not nervous."

"Don't you think so?"

"Not in the way Hendie is. You're a solid little person."

Miriam laughed, and thought of Germany and Newlands and Banbury Park. But this house would be a thousand times worse. There was no one in it who knew anything about anything. That was why, when she was not too bad, Eve thought it was good for her to be there.

"I think she's very happy here."

"I'm glad you think that. But something must be done. She can't go on with these perpetual headaches and sleeplessness and attacks of weepiness."

"I think she wants a long rest."

"What does she do with her holidays? Doesn't she rest then?"

---

1   French: a woman's private dressing room.

2   More commonly called tonka beans, these are the seeds from a South American tree. They smell like vanilla, and were used in perfumes and other products.

"Yes, but there are always *worries*," said Miriam desperately.

"You have had a good deal of worry—how is your father?"

How much do you know about that.... How does it strike you....

"He is all right, I think."

"He lives with your eldest sister."

"Yes."

"That's very nice for him. I expect the little grandson will be a great interest."

"Yes."

"And your youngest sister has a little girl?"

"Yes."

"Do you like children?"

"Yes."

"I expect you spend a good deal of your time with your sisters."

"Well—it's a fearful distance." Why didn't you ask me all these things when I was staying with you. There's no time now....

"Do you like living alone in London?"

"Well—I'm fearfully *busy*."

"I expect you are. I think it's wonderful. But you must be awfully lonely sometimes."

Miriam fidgeted and wondered how to go.

"Well—come down and see us again. I'm glad I had this chance of talking to you about Hendie."

"Perhaps she'll be better in the winter. I think she's really better in the cold weather."

"Well—we'll hope so," said Mrs Green getting up. "I can't think what's the matter with her. There's nothing to worry her, down here."

"No," said Miriam emphatically in a worldly tone of departure. "Thank you so much for having me," she said feebly as they passed through the flower-scented hall, the scent of the flowers hanging delicately within the stronger odour of the large wood-fire.

"I'm glad you came. We thought it would be nice for both of you."

"Yes it was very kind of you. I'm sure she wants a complete rest." Away from us, away from you, in some new place....

In the open light of the garden, Mrs Green's eyes were almost invisible points. She ought to do her hair smaller. The fashionable bundle of little sausages did not suit a large head. The eyes looked more sunken and dead than Eve's with her many headaches. But she was strong—a strong hard thunder-cloud at breakfast. Perhaps very unhappy. But wealthy. Strong, cruel wealth, eating up lives it did not understand. How did Eve manage to read *Music and Morals*[1] and Olive Schreiner[2] here?

---

1 A popular 1871 book by cleric Hugh Reginald Haweis (1838-1901) that examines his philosophy on music and provides biographies of a number of important composers.
2 British South African feminist, activist, and writer Olive Schreiner (1855-1920), best known for the significant role she played in the women's suffrage movement in Britain and for her novel *The Story of an African Farm* (1883).

CHAPTER XXVIII

"Miss Dear to see you, Miss."

"Is there any one else in the waiting-room?"

"No, miss—nobody."

Miriam went in briskly.... "Well?· How is the decayed gentle-woman?" she said briskly from the doorway. She hardly looked. She had taken in the close-fitting bonnet and chin-bow, and the height-giving look of the long blue uniform cloak together with the general aspect of the heavily shaded afternoon room....

"Oh, she's very well."

Miss Dear had stood quite still in her place half-way down the room between the sofa and the littered waiting-room table. She made a small controlled movement with her right hand as Miriam approached. Miriam paused with her hand on a *Navy League*,[1] absorbed in the low sweet even tone. She found herself standing reverently, pulled up a few inches from the dark figure. Suddenly she was alight with the radiance of an uncontrollable smile. Her downcast eyes were fixed upon a tall slender figure in a skimpy black dress, tendrils of fine gold hair dancing in the rough wind under a cornflower-blue toque,[2] a clear living rose-flush.... Something making one delicate figure more than the open width of the afternoon, the blue afternoon sea and sky. She looked up. The shy sweet flower-pink face glowed more intensely under the cap of gold hair clasped flatly down by the blue velvet rim of the bonnet. The eyes, now like Weymouth Bay,[3] now like Julia Doyle's,[4] now a clear expressionless blue, were fixed on hers; the hesitating face was breaking again into watchful speech. But there was no speech in the well-remembered outlines moulding the ominous cloak. Miriam flung out to stem the voice, rushing into phrases to open the way to the hall and the front door. Miss Dear stood smiling, and laughing her little smothered obsequious laugh, just as she had done at Bognor,[5] making one feel like a man.

"Well—I'm most frightfully busy," wound up Miriam cheer-fully, turning to the door. "That's London—isn't it? One never has a minute."

---

1 *The Navy League Journal* (1895-1908).

2 See p. 182, note 2.

3 A bay on the south coast of England, in Dorset.

4 A character from *Backwater* (vol. 2 of *Pilgrimage*), she is a fellow teacher at Wordsworth House, where Miriam works.

5 A resort town on the south coast of England.

Miss Dear did not move. "I came to thank you for the concert tickets," she said in the even thoughtful voice that dispersed one's thoughts.

"Oh yes. Was it any good?"

"I enjoyed it immensely," said Miss Dear gravely. "So did Sister North," she added, shaking out the words in delicate laughter.

... *I* don't know "Sister *North*." ... "Oh, good," said Miriam opening the door.

"It was most kind of you to send them. I'm going to a case[1] to-morrow, but I shall hope to see you when I come back."

"Sister North sported a swell new blouse," said Miss Dear in clear intimate tones as she paused in the hall to take up her umbrella.

"I hope it won't rain," said Miriam formally, opening the front door.

"She was no *end* of a swell," pursued Miss Dear, hitching her cloak and skirt from her heels with a neat cuffed gloved hand, quirked compactly against her person just under her waist, and turned so that her elbow and forearm made a small compact angle against her person. She spoke over her shoulder, her form slenderly poised forward to descend the steps: "I told her she would knock them." She was aglow with the afternoon sunlight streaming down the street.

Miriam spoke as she stepped down with delicate plunges. She did not hear and paused, turning, on the last step.

"It was too *bad* of you," shouted Miriam smiling, "to leave my sister alone at the Decayed Gentlewomen's."[2]

"I couldn't help myself," gleamed Miss Dear. "My time was up."

"Did you *hate* being there?"

Miss Dear hung, poised and swaying to some inner breeze. Miriam gazed, waiting for her words, watching the in-turned eyes control the sweet lips flowering for speech.

"It was rather comical"—the eyes came round, clear pure blue—"until your sister came." The tall slender figure faced the length of the street; the long thin blue cloak, flickering all over,

---

1 Miss Dear is a nurse who pays calls on those who are ill to treat them.
2 First founded by Irish novelist Anna Maria Hall (1800-81), Decayed Gentlewomen's homes were charitable institutions established to care for unmarried women whose fortunes had declined as a result of being unwed and without material support.

gave Miriam a foresight of the coming swift hesitating conversational progress of the figure along the pavement, the poise of the delicate surmounting head, slightly bent, the pure brow foremost, shading the lowered thoughtful eyes, the clear little rounded dip of the indrawn chin.

"I'm glad she gave me your address," finished Miss Dear, a little furrow running along her brow in control of the dimpling flushed oval below it. "I'll say au revoir[1] and not good-bye, for the present."

"Good-bye," flung Miriam stiffly at the departing face. Shutting the neglected door, she hurried back through the hall and resumed her consciousness of Wimpole Street with angry eager swiftness.... Eve, getting mixed up with people ... it is right ... *she* would not have been angry if I had asked her to be nice to somebody.... I did not mean to do anything ... I was proud of having the tickets to send ... if I had not sent them, I should have had the thought of all those nurses, longing for something to do between cases. They are just the people for the Students' Concerts ... if she comes again ... "I can't have social life, unfortunately," how furious I shall feel saying that, "you see I'm so fearfully full up— lectures every night and I'm away every week-end ... and I'm not supposed to see people here——"

---

1   French: Good-bye; literally, until we meet again.

CHAPTER XXIX

Miriam had no choice but to settle herself on the cane-seated chair. When Miss Dear had drawn the four drab-coloured curtains into place, the small cubicle was in semi-darkness.

"I hope the next time you come to tea with me it will be under rather more comfortable circumstances."

"This is all right," said Miriam, in abstracted impatient continuation of her abounding manner. Miss Dear was arranging herself on the bed as if for a long sitting. The small matter of business would come now. Having had tea, it would be impossible to depart the moment the discussion was over. How much did the tea cost here? That basement tea-room, those excited young women and middle-aged women, watchful and stealthy and ugly with poverty and shifts, those teapots and shabby trays and thick bread and butter were like the Y.W.C.A.[1] public restaurant at the other end of the street—fourpence at the outside; but Miss Dear would have to pay it. She felt trapped ... "a few moments of your time to advise me," and now half the summer twilight had gone and she was pinned in this prison face to face with anything Miss Dear might choose to present; forced by the presences audible in the other cubicles to a continuation of her triumphant tea-room manner.

"You must excuse my dolly."[2] She arranged her skirt neatly about the ankle of the slippered bandaged foot.

Any one else would say, "What is the matter with your foot?" ... It stuck out, a dreadfully padded mass, dark in the darkness of the dreadful little enclosure in the dreadful dark hive of women, collected together only by poverty.

"Have you *left* your association?"

"Oh *no*, dear; not *permanently* of course," said Miss Dear, pausing in her tweakings and adjustments of draperies to glance watchfully through the gloom.

"I'm still a member there."

"Oh yes."

"But I've got to look *after* myself. They don't give you a chance."

"No——"

---

1 The Young Women's Christian Association, an organization established in the late nineteenth century, first in England, then spreading worldwide. Its mandate was to support women, both socially and spiritually.
2 That is, her bandage.

"It's rush in and rush out and rush in and rush out."

"What are you going to do?" ... what do you want with me? ...

"What do you mean, de-er?"

"Well, I mean, are you going on nursing?"

"Of *course*, de-er. I was going to tell you."

Miriam's restive anger would not allow her to attend fully to the long story. She wandered off with the dreadful idea of nursing a "semi-mental" sitting in a deck-chair in a country garden, the hopeless patient, the nurse half intent on a healthy life and fees for herself, and recalled the sprinkling of uniformed figures amongst the women crowded at the table, all in this dilemma, all eagerly intent; all overworked by associations claiming part of their fees or taking the risks of private nursing,[1] all getting older; all, anyhow as long as they went on nursing, bound to live on illness; to live with illness knowing that they were living on it. Yet Mr Leyton had said that no hospital run by a religious sisterhood was any good ... these women were run by doctors....

"You see, de-er, it's the best thing any sensible nurse can do as soon as she knows a sufficient number of influenchoo peopoo—physicians and others."

"Yes, I see." ... But what has all this to do with me....

"I shall keep in correspondence with my doctors and friends and look *after* myself a bit."

"Yes, I see," said Miriam eagerly. "It's a *splendid* plan. What did you want to consult me about?"

"Well, you see it's like this. I must tell you my little difficulty. The folks at thirty-three don't know I'm here, and I don't want to go back there, just at present. I was wondering if, when I leave here, you'd mind my having my box sent to your lodgings. I shan't want my reserve things down there."

"Well—there isn't much *room* in my room."

"It's a flat box. I got it to go to the colonies with a patient."

"*Oh*, did you go?" ... Nurses did see life; though they were never free to see it in their own way. Perhaps some of them ... but then they would not be good nurses.

"Well, I didn't *go*. It was a chance of a lifetime. Such a de-er old gentleman—one of the Fitz-Duff family. It would have been nurse-companion. He didn't want me in uniform. My word. He gave me a complete outfit, *took* me round, coats and skirts at

---

1 Nurses either belonged to associations that organized them and found them cases but took a portion of their fees or worked independently at greater risk of not having work, or of poor working conditions.

Peters, gloves at Penberthy's, a *lovely* gold-mounted umbrella, everything the heart could desire. He treated me just like a daughter." During the whole of this speech she redeemed her words by little delicate bridling movements and adjustments, her averted eyes resting in indulgent approval on the old gentleman.

"Why didn't you go?"

"He *died*, dear."

"Oh, I see."

"It could go under your bed, out of the way."

"I've got hat-boxes and things. My room is full of things, I'm afraid."

"P'raps your landlady would let it stand somewhere."

"I might ask her—won't they let you leave things here?"

"They *would*, I dare say," frowned Miss Dear, "but I have special reasons. I don't wish to be beholden to the people here." She patted the tendrils of her hair, looking about the cubicle with cold disapproval.

"I dare say Mrs Bailey wouldn't mind. But I hardly like to ask her, you know. There seems to be luggage piled up everywhere."

"Of course I should be prepared to pay a fee."

... What a wonderful way of living ... dropping a trunk full of things and going off with a portmanteau;[1] starting life afresh in a new strange place. Miriam regarded the limber capable form outstretched on the narrow bed. This dark little enclosure, the forced companionship of the crowd of competing adventuresses, the sounds of them in the near cubicles, the perpetual sound, filling the house like a sea, of their busy calculations ... all this was only a single passing incident ... beyond it were the wide well-placed lives of wealthy patients.

"Miss Younger is a sweet woman."

Miriam's eyes awoke to affronted surprise.

"You know, de-er; the wan yow was sitting by at tea-time. I told you just now."

"Oh," said Miriam guiltily.

Miss Dear dropped her voice: "She's told me her whole story. She's a dear sweet Christian woman. She's working in a settlement.[2] She's privately engaged, to the bishop. It's not to be published yet. She's a sweet woman."

---

1 A small case for carrying clothing; from the (literal) French: coat-carrier.

2 See p. 240, note 1. Either "Legal residence or establishment in a particular parish, entitling a person to relief from the poor rates; the right to

Miriam rose. "I've got to get back, I'm afraid."

"Don't hurry away, dear. I hoped you would stay and have some supper."

"I really can't," said Miriam wearily.

"Well, perhaps we shall meet again before Thursday. You'll ask Mrs Bailey about my box," said Miss Dear getting to her feet.

"Fancy you remembering her name," said Miriam with loud cheerfulness, fumbling with the curtains.

Miss Dear stood beaming indulgently.

All the way down the unlit stone staircase they rallied each other about the country garden with the deck chairs.

"Well," said Miriam from the street, "I'll let you know about Mrs Bailey."

"All right, dear, I shall expect to hear from you; au revoir!" cried Miss Dear from the door. In the joy of her escape into the twilight Miriam waved her hand towards the indulgently smiling form and flung away, singing.

relief acquired by such residence" (*OED* Def. 3) or "An establishment in the poorer quarters of a large city where educated men or women live in daily personal contact with the working class for co-operation in social reform" (*OED* Def. 16). The *OED* lists most occurrences of the word from 1884 to 1904.

CHAPTER XXX

"Regular field-day, eh, Miss Hens'n? Look here——" Mr Orly turned towards the light coming in above the front door to exhibit his torn waistcoat and broken watch-chain. "Came for me like a fury. They've got double strength y' know, when they're under. Ever seen anything like it?"

Miriam glanced incredulously at the portly frontage.

"Fancy breaking the *chain*," she said, sickened by the vision of small white desperately fighting hands. He gathered up the hanging strings of bright links, his powerful padded musicianly hands finding the edges of the broken links and holding them adjusted with the discoloured ravaged fingers of a mechanic. "A good tug would do it," he said kindly. "A chain's no stronger than the weakest link," he added with a note of dreamy sadness, drawing a sharp sigh.

"Did you get the tooth out?" clutched Miriam, automatically making a mental note of the remark that flashed through the world with a sad light, a lamp brought into a hopeless sickroom ... keeping up her attitude of response to show that she was accepting the apology for his extremities of rage over the getting of the anaesthetist. Mrs Orly appearing in the hall at the moment, still flushed from the storm, joined the group and outdid Miriam's admiring amazement, brilliant smiles of relief garlanding her gentle outcry. "Hancock busy?" said Mr Orly, in farewell, as he turned and swung away to the den followed by Mrs Orly, her unseen face busy with an interrupted errand. He would not hear that her voice was divided.... No one seemed to be aware of the divided voices ... no men. Life went on and on, a great oblivious awfulness, sliding over everything. Every moment things went that could never be recovered ... on and on, and it was always too late, there was always some new thing obliterating everything, something that looked new, but always turned out to be the same as everything else, grinning with its sameness in an awful blank where one tried to remember the killed things.... If only every one would stop for a moment and let the thing that was always hovering be there, let it settle and intensify. But the whole of life was a conspiracy to prevent it. Was there something wrong in it? It could not be a coincidence the way life *always* did that ... she had reached the little conservatory[1] on the half

---

1 Sunroom.

landing, darkened with a small forest of aspidistra.[1] The dull dust-laden leaves identified themselves with her life. What had become of her autumn of hard work that was to lift her out of her personal affairs and lead somewhere? Already the holiday freshness and vigour had left her; and nothing had been done. Nothing was so strong as the desire that everything would stop for a moment, and allow her to remember.... Wearily she mounted the remaining stairs to Mr Hancock's room. "I think," said a clear high confident voice from the chair and stopped. Miriam waited with painful eagerness while the patient rinsed her mouth; "that that gentleman thinks himself a good deal cleverer than he is," she resumed, sitting back in the chair.

"I am afraid I'm not as familiar with his work as I ought to be, but I can't say I've been very greatly impressed as far as I have gone."

"Don't go any further. There's nothing there to go for."

Who are you speaking of? How do you know? What have *you* got that makes you think he has nothing?—Miriam almost cried aloud. Could she not see, could not both of them see that the quiet sheen of the green-painted window-frame cast off their complacent speech? Did they not hear it tinkle emptily back from the twined leaves and tendrils, the flowers and butterflies painted on the window in front of them? The patient had turned briskly to the spittoon again, after her little speech. She would have a remark ready when the brisk rinsing was over. There could be no peace in her presence. Even when she was gagged, there would be the sense of her sending out little teasing thoughts and comments. They could never leave anything alone ... oh, it was *that* woman ... the little gold knot at the back of the cheerful little gold head; hair that curled tightly about her head when she was a baby and that had grown long and been pinned up, as the clever daughter of that man; getting to know all he had said about women. If she believed it she must loathe her married state and her children ... how *could* she let life continue through her? Perhaps it was the sense of her treachery that *gave* her that bright brisk amused manner. It was a way of carrying things off, that maddening way of speaking of everything as if life were a jest at everybody's expense.... All "clever" women seemed to have that,

---

1 A common flowering houseplant. In his novel *Keep the Aspidistra Flying* (1936), George Orwell (1903-50) elevated it into an icon of philistine bourgeois commercialism.

never speaking what they thought or felt, but always things that sounded like quotations from men; so that they always seemed to flatter or criticize the men they were with, according as they were as clever as some man they knew, or less clever. *What* was she like when she was alone and dropped that bright *manner*.... "Have you made any New Year resolutions? I don't make any. My friends think me godless, *I* think *them* lacking in common sense" ... exactly like a man; taking up a fixed attitude ... having a sort of prepared way of taking everything ... like the Wilsons ... anything else was "unintelligent" or "absurd" ... their impatience meant something. Somehow all the other people were a reproach. If, some day, every one lived in the clear light of science, "waiting for the pronouncements of science in all the affairs of life," waiting for the pronouncements of those sensual dyspeptic men with families, who thought of women as existing only to produce more men ... admirably fitted by nature's inexorable laws for her biological role ... perhaps she agreed or pretended to think it all a great lark ... the last vilest flattery ... she had only two children ... si la femme avait plus de sensibilité, elle ne retomberait pas si facilement dans la grossesse.... La femme, c'est peu galant de le dire, est la femelle de l'homme.[1] The Frenchman at any rate *wanted* to say something else. But why want to be gallant ... and why not say: man, it is not very graceful to say it, is the male of woman? If women had been the recorders of things from the beginning it would all have been the other way round ... Mary. Mary, the Jewess, write something about Mary the Jewess; the Frenchman's Queen of Heaven.[2]

Englishmen; the English were "the leading race." "England and America together—the Anglo-Saxon peoples—could govern the destinies of the world."[3] *What* world? ... millions and millions of child-births ... colonial women would keep it all going ... and religious people ... and if religion went on there would always be all the people who took the Bible literally ... and if religion were

---

1 French: if woman were more sensible, she would not become pregnant so easily.... Woman, it is not very gallant to say, is the female of man. We have been unable to identify the source of this quotation.
2 Refers to the Virgin Mary, the mother of Jesus Christ, who was Jewish. In France, historically a Catholic nation, Mary is highly revered and frequently prayed to; this is often called "the cult of Mary."
3 Common sentiments from the jingoistic last decade of the nineteenth century, the very height of the British Empire.

not true, then there was only science. Either way was equally abominable ... for women.

The far end of the ward was bright sunlight ... there she was, enthroned, commanding the whole length of the ward, sitting upright, her head and shoulders already conversational, her hands busy with objects on the bed towards which her welcoming head was momentarily bent; like a hostess moving chairs in a small drawing-room ... chrysanthemums all down the ward—massed on little tables ... a *parrot* sidling and bobbing along its perch, great big funny solemn French grey,[1] fresh clean living French grey, pure in the sunlight, a pure canary-coloured beak ... clean grey and yellow ... in the sun ... a curious silent noise in the stillness of the ward.

"I couldn't hear; I wasn't near enough."

"Better late than never, I *said*."

"D'you *know*, I thought you'd only been here a few days, and to-day when I looked at your letter I was simply *astounded*. You're sitting up."

"I should hope I am. They kept me on my back, half starving, for three weeks."

"You look very pink and well now."

"That's what Dr Ashley-Densley said. You ought to have seen me when I came in. You see I'm on chicken now."

"And you feel better."

"Well—you can't really tell how you are till you're up."

"When are you going to get up?"

"To-morrow, I hope, dear. So you see you're just in time."

"Do you mean you are going away?"

"They turn you out as soon as you're strong enough to stand."

"But—*how* can you get about?"

"Dr Ashley-Densley has arranged all that. I'm going to a convalescent home."

"*Oh*, that's very nice."

"Poor Dr Ashley-Densley, he was dreadfully upset."

"You've had some letters to cheer you up." Miriam spoke impatiently, her eyes rooted on the pale leisurely hands, mechanically adjusting some neatly arranged papers.

"*No*, de-er. My friends have all left me to look after my*self* this

---

1   A breed of parrot.

time, but since I've been sitting up, I've been trying to get my affairs in order."

"I thought of bringing you some flowers, but there was not a single shop between here and Wimpole Street."

"There's generally women selling them outside. But I'm glad you didn't; I've too much sympathy with the poor nurses."

Miriam glanced fearfully about. There were so many beds with forms seated and lying upon them ... but there seemed no illness or pain. Quiet eyes met hers; everything seemed serene; there was no sound but the strange silent noise of the sunlight and the flowers. Half-way down the ward stood a large threefold screen covered with dark American cloth.

"She's unconscious to-day," said Miss Dear; "she won't last through the night."

"Do you mean to say there is someone *dying* there?"

"*Yes, de-*er."

"Do you mean to say they don't put them into a separate room to *die*?"

"They can't, dear. They haven't got the *space*," flashed Miss Dear.

Death, shut in with one lonely person. Brisk nurses putting up the screen. Dying eyes cut off from all but those three dark surrounding walls, with death waiting inside them. Miriam's eyes filled with tears. There, just across the room, was the end. It had to come, somewhere; just that; on any summer's afternoon ... people did things; hands placed a screen, people cleared you away.... It was a relief to realize that there were hospitals to die in; worry and torture of mind could end here. Perhaps it might be easier with people all round you than in a little room. There were hospitals to be ill in and somewhere to die neatly, however poor you were. It was a relief ... "she's always the last to get up; still snoring when everybody's fussing and washing." That would be me ... it lit up the hostel. Miss Dear liked that time of fussing and washing, in company with all the other cubicles fussing and washing. To be very poor meant getting more and more social life, with no appearances to keep up, getting up each day with a holiday feeling of one more day and the surprise of seeing everybody again; and the certainty that if you died somebody would do something. Certainly it was this knowledge that gave Miss Dear her peculiar strength. She was a nurse and knew how everything was done. She knew that people, all kinds of people, were *people* and would do things. When one was quite alone one could not believe this. Besides no one *would* do anything, for me. I don't want any one to. I should hate the face of a nurse who put a screen round my bed. I shall not die like that. I shall die in some other way, out in the sun, with—yes—oh, yes—Tah-dee, t'*dee*, t'dee—t'dee.

"It must be funny, for a nurse, to be in a hospital."

"It's a little too funny sometimes, dear—you know too much about what you're in for."

"Ilikeyourredjacket."

"Good *heavens!*"

"That's nothing, dear. He does that all the afternoon."

"How can you stand it?"

"It's Hobson's choice,[1] madam."

The parrot uttered three successive squawks, fuller and harsher and even more shrill than the first.

"He's just tuning up; he always does in the afternoon, just as everybody is trying to get a little sleep."

"But I never *heard* of such a thing! It's monstrous, in a hospital. Why don't you all complain?"

"'Sh, dear; he belongs to matron."

"Why doesn't she have him in her room? Shut *up*, Polly."

"He'd be rather a roomful in a little room."

"Well—what is he *here?* It's the wickedest thing of its kind I've ever heard of; some great fat healthy woman ... why don't the *doctors* stop it?"

"Perhaps they hardly notice it, dear. There's such a bustle going on in the morning when they all come round."

"But hang it all, she's here to look after you, not to leave her luggage all over the ward."

The ripe afternoon light ... even outside a hospital ... the strange indistinguishable friend, mighty welcome, unutterable happiness. O death, where is thy sting? O grave, where is thy victory?[2] The light has no end. I know it and it knows me, no misunderstanding, no barrier. I love you—people say things. But

---

1 When no alternative option is available, so the only choice one can make is to either accept the situation at hand, or remove oneself from the situation entirely. From English stable owner Thomas Hobson (c. 1544-1631), who would offer customers the choice of just one of his horses or none at all.

2 1 Corinthians 15:55 (King James Version).

nothing that anybody says has any meaning. Nothing that anybody says has any meaning. There is something more than anything that anybody says, that comes first, before they speak ... vehicles travelling along through heaven; everybody in heaven without knowing it; the sound the vehicles made all together, sounding out through the universe ... life touches your heart like dew; that is *true* ... the edge of his greasy knowing selfish hair touches the light; he brushes it; there is something in him that remembers. It is in everybody; but they won't stop. Maddening. But they know. When people die, they must stop. Then they remember. Remorse may be complete; until it is complete you cannot live. When it is complete something is burned away ... ou-agh, flows out of you, burning, inky, acid, flows right out ... purged ... though thy sins are as *scarlet*, they shall be white as snow.[1] *Then* the light is there, nothing but the light, and new memory, sweet and bright; but only when you have been killed by remorse.

This is what is meant by a purple twilight. Lamps alight, small round lights, each in place, shedding no radiance, white day lingering on the stone pillars of the great crescent,[2] the park railings distinct, the trees shrouded but looming very large and permanent, the air wide and high and purple, darkness alight and warm. Far, far away beyond the length of two endless months, is Christmas. This kind of day lived for ever. It stood still. The whole year, funny little distant fussy thing, stood still in this sort of day. You could take it in your hand and look at it. Nobody could touch this. People and books and all those things that men had done, in the British Museum, were a crackling noise, outside.... Les yeux gris, vont au paradis.[3] That was the two poplars, standing one each side of the little break in the railings, shooting up; the space between them shaped by their shapes, leading somewhere. I *must* have been through there; it's the park. I don't remember. It isn't. It's waiting. One day I will go through. Les yeux gris, vont au paradis. Going along, along, the twilight hides your shabby clothes. They are not shabby. They are clothes you go along in, funny; jolly. Everything's here, any bit of anything, clear in your brain; you can look at it. What a terrific thing a person is; bigger than anything. How *funny* it is to be a

---

1 Isaiah 1:18 (King James version).
2 Also known as the Royal Crescent, in Holland Park, London.
3 French: Grey eyes go to paradise; French nursery rhyme.

person. You can never not have been a person. Bouleversement.[1] It's a fait bouleversant.[2] *Christ*-how-rummy. It's enough.[3] Du, Heilige, rufe dein Kind zurück, ich habe genossen das irdische Glück; ich habe geliebt und gelebet[4].... Oh let the solid ground not fail beneath my feet, until I am quite quite sure[5].... Hallo, old Euston Road,[6] beloved of my soul,[7] my own country,[8] my native heath.[9] There'll still be a glimmer on the table when I light the lamp ... how shall I write it down, the *sound* the little boy made as he carefully carried the milk jug? ... going along, trusted, *trusted*, you could see it, you could see his mother. His legs came along, little loose feet, looking after themselves, pottering, behind him. All his body was in the hand carrying the milk jug. When he had done carrying the milk jug he would run; running along the pavement amongst people, with cool round eyes, not looking at anything. Where the crowd prevented his running, he would jog up and down as he walked, until he could run again, bumping solemnly up and down amongst the people; boy.

The turning of the key in the latch was lively with the vision of the jumping boy. The flare of the match in the unlit hall lit up eternity. The front door was open, eternity poured in and on up the stairs. At one of those great staircase windows, where the last of the twilight stood, a sudden light of morning would not be surprising. Of course a letter; curly curious statements on the hallstand.

---

1 French: upset, upheaval.

2 French: upsetting fact.

3 Possibly a reference to Matthew 10:25: "It is enough for the disciple that he be as his master."

4 German: You, the Holy, call your child back, I have enjoyed earthly happiness; I have loved and lived. From *Des Mädchens Klage*, music by Franz Schubert (1797-1828), libretto by Friedrich von Schiller (1759-1805).

5 From Tennyson's poem "Maud."

6 See p. 59, note 1.

7 "Beloved of my soul," Jeremiah 12:7 (King James Version).

8 "My own country" may be a misremembered line from Sir Walter Scott's (1771-1832) poem "My Native Land," which appeared in his novel *The Lay of the Last Minstrel* (1805).

9 "My native heath," a line from Sir Walter Scott's novel *Rob Roy* (1817).

That is mother-of-pearl, nacre; twilight nacre; crépuscule nacre;[1] I must wait until it is gone. It is a visitor; pearly freshness pouring in; but, if I wait, I may feel different. With the blind up, the lamp will be a lamp in it; twilight outside, the lamp on the edge of it, making the room gold, edged with twilight.

I *can't* go to-night. It's all *here*; I *must* stay here. Botheration. It's Eve's fault. Eve would rather go out and see Nurse Dear than stay here. Eve *likes* getting tied up with people. I *won't* get tied up; it drives everything away. Now I've read the letter, I must go. There'll be afterwards when I get back. No one has any power over me. I shall be coming back. I shall always be coming back.

Perhaps it had been Madame Tussaud's[2] that had made this row of houses generally invisible; perhaps their own awfulness. When she found herself opposite them, Miriam recognized them at once. By day, they were one high long lifeless smoke-grimed facade fronted by gardens colourless with grime, showing at its thickest on the leaves of an occasional laurel. It had never occurred to her that the houses could be occupied. She had seen them now and again as reflectors of the grime of the Metropolitan Railway.[3] Its smoke poured up over their faces as the smoke from a kitchen fire pours over the back of a range. The sight of them brought nothing to her mind but the inside of the Metropolitan Railway; the feeling of one's skin prickling with grime, the sense of one's smoke-grimed clothes. There was nothing in that strip between Madame Tussaud's and the turning into Baker Street but the sense of exposure to grime ... a little low grimed wall surmounted by paintless sooty iron railings.[4] On the other side of the road, a high brown wall, protecting whatever was behind, took the grime in one thick covering, here it spread over

---

1 Mother-of-pearl, also known as nacre, is the shiny outer layer of a pearl. Twilight nacre is a black pearl; "crepuscule": French for "twilight."

2 Waxworks museum exhibiting figures of famous historical figures; named after its founder (in London in 1835) Marie Tussaud (1761-1850), who began by taking death masks in wax of men who died in the French Revolution. The museum moved to Marylebone Road in 1884.

3 The first underground railway, which began running in 1863 and linked central London to a number of important outlying terminus stations.

4 By the late nineteenth century, pollution by coal-burning factories in and around London had blanketed much of the city with sooty residue; where it was not frequently cleaned away, it accumulated.

the exposed gardens and façades turning her eyes away. To-night they looked almost as untenanted as she had been accustomed to think them. Here and there on the black expanse, a window showed a blurred light. The house she sought appeared to be in total darkness. The iron gate crumbled harshly against her gloves as she set her weight against the rusty hinges. Gritty dust sounded under her feet along the pathway and up the shallow steps leading to the unlit doorway.

Her flight up through the sickly, sweet-smelling murk of the long staircase ended in a little top back room brilliant with un-globed gaslight. Miss Dear got her quickly into the room and stood smiling and waiting for a moment for her to speak. Miriam stood nonplussed, catching at the feelings that rushed through her and the thoughts that spoke in her mind. Distracted by the picture of the calm tall gold-topped figure in the long grey skirt and the pale pink flannel dressing-jacket. Miss Dear was smiling the smile of one who has a great secret to impart. There was a saucepan or frying-pan or something—with a handle—sticking out.... "I'm glad you've brought a book," said Miss Dear. The room was closing up and up ... the door was shut. Miriam's exasperation flew out. She felt it fly out. What would Miss Dear do or say? "I 'oped you'd come," she said, in her softest, most thoughtful tones. "I've been rushing about and rushing about." She turned with her swift limber silent-footed movement to the thing on the gas-ring. "Sit down dear," she said, as one giving permission, and began rustling a paper packet. A haddock came forth and the slender thoughtful fingers plucked and picked at it and lifted it gingerly into the shallow steaming pan. Miriam's thoughts whirled to her room, to the dark sky-domed streets, to the coming morrow. They flew about all over her life. The cane-seated[1] chair thrilled her with a fresh sense of anger.

"I've been shopping and rushing about," said Miss Dear, disengaging a small crusty loaf from its paper bag. Miriam stared gloomily about and waited.

"Do you like haddock, dear?"

"Oh—well—I don't know—yes, I think I do."

The fish smelled very savoury. It was wonderful and astonishing to know how to cook a real meal, in a tiny room; cheap ... the lovely little loaf and the wholesome solid fish would cost less than

---

1 The seat is woven of wicker.

a small egg and roll and butter at an A.B.C. How did people find out how to do these things?

"You know how to cook?"

"Haddock doesn't hardly need any cooking," said Miss Dear, shifting the fish about by its tail.

"What is your book, dear?"

"Oh—*Villette*."[1]

"Is it a pretty book?"

She didn't want to know. She was saying something else.... How to mention it? Why say anything about it? But no one had ever asked. No one had known. This woman was the first. She, of all people, was causing the first time of speaking of it.

"I bought it when I was fifteen," said Miriam vaguely, "and a Byron[2]—with some money I had; seven and six."[3]

"Oh yes."

"I didn't care for the Byron; but it was a jolly edition; padded leather with rounded corners and gilt-edged leaves."

"*Oh!*"

"I've been reading this thing ever since I came back from my holidays."

"It doesn't look very big."

Miriam's voice trembled. "I don't mean that. When I've finished it, I begin again."

"I wish you would read it to me."

Miriam recoiled. Anything would have done; *Donovan*[4] or anything.... But something had sprung into the room. She gazed at the calm profile, the long slender figure, the clear grey and pink, the pink frill of the jacket falling back from the soft fair hair turned cleanly up, the clean fluffy curve of the skull, the serene line of the brow bent in abstracted contemplation of the steaming pan. "I believe you'd like it," she said brightly.

"I should love you to read to me when we've 'ad our supper."

"Oh—I've had my supper."

---

1 An 1853 novel by Charlotte Brontë (1816-55) about a woman teaching in an all-girls' school.

2 George Gordon, Lord Byron (1788-1824), leading English Romantic poet known for his libertine lifestyle and at-times risqué verse.

3 The book cost seven shillings and sixpence; the books were not inexpensive.

4 A popular 1882 novel by Edna Lyall (1857-1903), written under the name Ada Ellen Bayly.

"A bit of haddock won't hurt you, dear.... I'm afraid we shall have to be very knockabout; I've got a knife and a fork but no plates at present. It comes of living in a *box*," said Miss Dear pouring off the steaming water into the slop-pail.

"I've had my supper—really. I'll read while you have yours."

"Well, don't sit out in the middle of the room, dear."

"I'm all right," said Miriam impatiently, finding the beginning of the first chapter. Her hands clung to the book. She had not made herself at home as Eve would have done, and talked. Now, these words would sound aloud, in a room. Someone would hear and see. Miss Dear would not know what it was. But she would hear and see something.

"It's by a woman called Charlotte Brontë," she said, and began, headlong, with the gaslight in her eyes.

The familiar words sounded chilly and poor. Everything in the room grew very distinct. Before she had finished the chapter, Miriam knew the position of each piece of furniture. Miss Dear sat very still. Was she listening patiently like a mother, or wife, thinking of the reader as well as of what was read, and with her own thoughts running along independently, interested now and again in some single thing in the narrative, something that reminded her of some experience of her own, or some person she knew? No, there was something different. However little she saw and heard, something was happening. They were looking and hearing together ... did she feel anything of the grey ... grey ... grey made up of all the colours there are; all the colours, seething into an even grey ... she wondered as she read on almost by heart, at the rare freedom of her thoughts, ranging about. The book was cold and unreal compared with what it was when she read it alone. But something was happening. Something was passing to and fro between them, behind the text; a conversation between them that the text, the calm quiet grey that was the outer layer of the tumult, brought into being. If they should read on, the conversation would deepen. A glow ran through her at the thought. She felt that in some way she was like a man reading to a woman, but the reading did not separate them like a man's reading did. She paused for a moment on the thought. A man's reading was not reading; not a looking and a listening so that things came into the room. It was always an assertion of himself. Men read in loud harsh unnatural voices, in sentences, or with voices that were a commentary on the text, as if they were telling you what to think ... they preferred reading to being read to; they read as if they were the authors of the text. Nothing could get through them but what they saw. They were like showmen....

"Go on, dear."

"My voice is getting tired. It must be all hours. I ought to have gone; ages ago," said Miriam settling herself in the little chair with the book standing opened on the floor at her side.

"The time does pass quickly, when it is pleasantly occupied."

A cigarette, now, would not be staying on. It would be like putting on one's hat. Then the visit would be over; without having taken place. The incident would have made no break in freedom. They had been both absent from the room nearly all the time. Perhaps that was why husbands so often took to reading to their wives, when they stayed at home at all; to avoid being in the room listening to their condemning silences or to their speech, speech with all the saucepan and comfort thoughts simmering behind it.

"I haven't had much time to attend to study. When you've got to get your living, there's too much else to do."

Miriam glanced sharply. Had she wanted other things in the years of her strange occupation? She had gone in for nursing sentimentally, and now she knew the other side; doing everything to time, careful carrying out of the changing experiments of doctors. Her reputation and living depended on that; their reputation and living depended on her. And she had to go on, because it was her living.... Miss Dear was dispensing little gestures with bent head held high and in-turned eyes. She was holding up the worth and dignity of her career. It had meant sacrifices that left her mind enslaved. But, all the same, she thought excuses were necessary. She resented being illiterate. She had a brain somewhere, groping and starved. What could she do? It was too late. What a *shame* ... serene golden comeliness, slender feet and hands, strange ability and knowledge of the world, and she knew, *knew* there was something that ought to be hers. Miriam thrilled with pity. The in-turned eyes sent out a challenging blue flash that expanded to a smile. Miriam recoiled, battling in the grip of the smile.

"I wish you'd come round earlier to-morrow, dear, and have supper here."

"How long are you going to stay here?" ... to come again and read further and find that strange concentration that made one see into things. Did she really like it?

"Well, dear, you see, I don't know. I must settle up my affairs a little. I don't know where I am with one thing and another. I must leave it in the hands of an 'igher power." She folded her hands and sat motionless with in-turned eyes, making the little movements with her lips that would lead to further speech, a flashing forth of something....

"Well, I'll see," said Miriam getting up.

"I shall be looking for you."

CHAPTER XXXI

It was ... jolly; to have something one was obliged to do every evening—but it could not go on. Next week-end, the Brooms, that would be an excuse for making a break. She must have other friends she could turn to ... she must *know* one could not go on. But bustling off every evening regularly to the same place with things to get for somebody was evidently good in some way ... health-giving and strength-giving....

She found Miss Dear in bed; sitting up, more pink and gold than ever. There was a deep lace frill on the pink jacket. She smiled deeply, a curious deep smile that looked like "a smile of perfect love and confidence" ... it *was* partly that. She was grateful, and admiring. That was all right. But it could not go on; and now illness. Miriam was aghast. Miss Dear seemed more herself than ever, sitting up in bed, just as she had been at the hospital.

"Are you ill?"

"Not really ill, de-er. I've had a touch of my epileptiform neuralgia."[1] Miriam sat staring angrily at the floor.

"It's enough to *make* any one ill."

"*What* is?"

"To be sitoowated as I am."

"You haven't been able to hear of a case?"

"How can I take a case, dear, when I haven't got my uniforms?"

"Did you sell them?"

"*No*, de-er. They're with all the rest of my things at the hostel. Just because there's a small balance owing, they refuse to give up my box. I've told them I'll settle it as soon as my pecooniary affairs are in order."

"I see. That was why you didn't send your box on to me? You know I could pay that off if you like, if it isn't too much."

"No, dear, I couldn't hear of such a thing."

"But you *must* get work, or something. Do your friends know how things are?"

"There is no one I should care to turn to at the moment."

"But the people at the Nursing Association?"

Miss Dear flushed and frowned. "Don't think of *them*, dear. I've told you my opinion of the superintendent, and the nurses

---

1 Recurring, severe pain in the facial nerves.

are in pretty much the same box as I am. More than one of them owes me money."

"But surely if they knew——"

"I tell you I don't *wish* to apply to Baker Street at the present time."

"But you *must* apply to *someone. Something* must be done. You see I can't, I shan't be able to go on indefinitely."

Miss Dear's face broke into weeping. Miriam sat smarting under her own brutality ... poverty is brutalizing, she reflected miserably, excusing herself. It makes you helpless and makes sick people fearful and hateful. It ought not to be like that. One can't even give way to one's natural feelings. What ought she to have done? To have spoken gently ... you see, dear ... she could hear women's voices saying it ... my resources are not unlimited, we must try and think what is the best thing to be done ... humbug ... they would be feeling just as frightened, just as self-protecting, inside. There were people in books who shouldered things and got into debt, just for any casual, helpless person. But it would have to come on somebody, in the end. What then? Bustling people with plans ... "it's no good sitting still waiting for Providence,"[1] ... but that was just what one wanted to avoid ... it had been wonderful, sometimes in the little room. It was *that* that had been outraged. It was as if she had struck a blow.

"I *have* done something, dear."

"What?"

"I've sent for Dr Ashley-Densley."

"There is our gentleman," said Miss Dear tranquilly, just before midnight. Miriam moved away and stood by the window as the door split wide and a tall grey-clad figure plunged lightly into the room. Miriam missed his first questions in her observation of his well-controlled fatigue and annoyance, his astonishing height and slenderness and the curious wise softness of his voice. Suddenly she realized that he was going. He was not going to take anything in hand or do anything. He had got up from the chair by the bedside and was scribbling something on an envelope ... no sleep for two nights he said, evenly, in the soft musical girlish tones. A prescription ... then he'd be off.

"Do you know Thomas's?" he said colourlessly.

---

1 Good fortune that issues from God's mercy.

"Do you know Thomas's—the chemist[1]—in Baker Street?" he said, casting a half-glance in her direction as he wrote on.

"I do," said Miriam coldly.

"Would you be afraid to go round there now?"

"What is it you want?" said Miriam acidly.

"Well, if you're not afraid, go to Thomas's, get this made up, give Miss Dear a dose and, if it does not take effect, another in two hours' time."

"You may leave it with me."

"All right. I'll be off. I'll try to look in some time to-morrow," he said turning to Miss Dear. "Bye-bye," and he was gone.

When the grey of morning began to show behind the blind, Miriam's thoughts came back to the figure on the bed. Miss Dear was peacefully asleep, lying on her back with her head thrown back upon the pillow. Her face looked stonily pure and stern; and colourless in the grey light. There was a sheen on her forehead, like the sheen on the foreheads of old people. She had probably been asleep ever since the beginning of the stillness. Everybody was getting up. "London was getting up." That man in the *Referee*[2] knew what it was, that feeling when you live right *in* London, of being a Londoner, the thing that made it *enough* to be a Londoner, getting up, in London; the thing that made real Londoners different from every one else, going about with a sense that made them *alive*. The very idea of living anywhere but in London, when one thought about it, produced a blank sensation in the heart. What was it I said the other day? "London's got me. It's taking my health, and eating up my youth. It may as well have what remains...." Something stirred powerfully, unable to get to her through her torpid body. Her weary brain spent its last strength on the words, she had only half meant them when they were spoken. *Now*, once she was free again, to be just a Londoner, who would ask nothing more of life? It would be the answer to all questions; the perfect unfailing thing, guiding all one's decisions. And an ill-paid clerkship was its best possible protection; keeping one at a quiet centre, alone in a little room, untouched by human relationships, undisturbed by the necessity of being anything. Nurses and teachers and doctors, and all the people who were doing special things surrounded by people and

1 A pharmacist.
2 See p. 67, note 1.

talk, were not Londoners. Clerks were, unless they lived in suburbs. The people who lived in St Pancras and Bloomsbury and in Seven Dials[1] and all round Soho and in all the slums and back streets everywhere were. She would be again, soon ... not a woman ... a Londoner.

She rose from her chair feeling hardly able to stand. The long endurance in the cold room had led to nothing but the beginning of a day without strength—no one knowing what she had gone through. Three days and nights of nursing Eve had produced only a feverish gaiety. It *was* London that killed you.

"I will come in at lunch-time," she scribbled on the back of an envelope, and left it near one of the hands outstretched on the coverlet.

Outdoors it was quite light, a soft grey morning, about eight o'clock. People were moving about the streets. The day would be got through somehow. To-morrow she would be herself again.

"Has she applied to the Association to which she belongs?"

"I think she wishes for some reason to keep away from them just now. She suggested that I should come to you, when I asked her if there was any one to whom she could turn. She told me you had helped her to have a holiday in a convalescent home." These were the right people. The quiet grey house, the high-church[2] room, the delicate outlines of the woman, clear and fine in spite of all the comfort.... The All Souls Nursing Sisters[3].... They *were* different ... emotional and unhygienic ... cushions and hot-water bottles ... good food ... early service—Lent[4]—stuffy churches—fasting. But they would not pass by on the other side.... She sat waiting ... the atmosphere of the room made much of her weeks of charity and her long night of watching, the quiet presence in it knew of these things without being told. The weariness of her voice had poured out its burden, meeting find flowing into the patient weariness of the other woman and changing. There was

---

1 An intersection in the West End of London, where seven streets meet; in the nineteenth century, a well-known slum.

2 That is, high Anglican, Protestant in doctrine but very nearly identical with Catholicism in its emphasis on ritual and ceremony.

3 Many of the nursing associations were run by religious orders; nurses were often also nuns.

4 A Christian event: the 40 days leading up to Easter, during which worshippers fast and pray extensively in spiritual preparation for Easter celebrations.

no longer any anger or impatience. Together, consulting as accomplices, they would see what was the best thing to do— whatever it was would be something done on a long long road going on for ever; nobody outside, nobody left behind. When they had decided, they would leave it, happy and serene, and glance at the invisible sun and make little confident jests together. She was like Mrs Bailey—and someone farther back—mother. This was the secret life of women. They smiled at God. But they all flattered men. All these women....

"They ought to be informed. Will you call on them—to-day? Or would you prefer that I should do so?"

"I will go—at lunch-time," said Miriam promptly.

"Meanwhile I shall inform the clergy. It is a case for the parish.[1] You must not bear the responsibility a moment longer."

Miriam relaxed in her capacious chair, a dimness before her eyes. The voice was going on, unnoticing, the figure had turned towards a bureau. There were little straggles about the fine hair— Miss Jenny Perne—the Pernes. She was a lonely old maid.... One must listen ... but London had sprung back ... in full open midday roar; brilliant and fresh; dim, intimate, vast, from the darkness. This woman preferred some provincial town ... Wolverhampton[2] ... Wolverhampton ... in the little room in Marylebone Road Miss Dear was unconsciously sleeping—a pauper.

There was a large bunch of black grapes on the little table by the bedside, and a book.

"Hullo, you literary female," said Miriam, seizing it ... *Red Pottage*[3] ... a curious novelish name, difficult to understand. Miss Dear sat up, straight and brisk, blooming smiles. What an easy life. The light changing in the room and people bringing novels and grapes, smart new novels that people were reading.

"What did you do at lunch time, dear?"

"Oh I had to go and see a female unexpectedly."

---

1 The church in the neighbourhood had responsibility for the spiritual and often physical welfare of its congregants.
2 A city in England's West Midlands. In the nineteenth century, it was a wealthy city.
3 A popular 1899 novel by British writer Mary Cholmondeley (1859-1925). It was a "New Woman" novel, one of many early feminist novels of the period that challenged marriage, domesticity, and Victorian ideals of femininity.

"I found your note and thought perhaps you had called in at Baker Street."

"At your Association, d'you mean? Oh, my dear lady!" Miriam shook her thoughts about, pushing back "She owes money to almost every nurse in this house and seems to have given in in every way," and bringing forward "one of our very best nurses for five years."

"Oh, I went to see the woman in Queen Square[1] this morning."

"I know you did, dear." Miss Dear bridled in her secret way, averted, and preparing to speak. It was over. She did not seem to mind. "I liked her," said Miriam hastily, leaping across the gap, longing to know what had been done, beating out anywhere to rid her face of the lines of shame. She was sitting before a judge ... being looked through and through.... Noo, Tonalt, suggest a tow-pic....

"She's a sweet woman," said Miss Dear patronizingly.

"She's brought you some nice things" ... poverty was worse if you were not poor enough....

"Oh, *no*, dear. The curate brought these. He called twice this morning. You did me a good turn. He's a real friend."

"Oh—oh, I'm so glad."

"Yes—he's a nice little man. He was most dreadfully upset."

"What can he do?"

"How do you mean, dear?"

"Well, in general?"

"He's going to do everything, dear. I'm not to worry."

"How splendid!"

"He came in first thing and saw how things stood, and came in again at the end of the morning with these things. He's sending me some wine, from his own cellar."

Miriam gazed, her thoughts tumbling incoherently.

"He was most dreadfully upset. He could not write his sermon. He kept thinking it might be one of his own *sisters* in the same sitawation. He couldn't rest till he came back."

Standing back ... all the time ... delicately preparing to speak ... presiding over them all ... over herself too ...

"He's a real friend."

"Have you looked at the book?" There was nothing more to do.

"No, dear. He said it had interested him very much. He reads

---

1 A square in the Bloomsbury neighbourhood of London.

them for his sermons, you see" ... she put out her hand and touched the volume ... John's books ... Henry is so interested in photography ... unknowing patronizing respectful gestures.... "Poor little man. He was dreadfully upset."

"We'd better read it."

"What time are you coming, dear?"

"Oh—well."

"I'm to have my meals regular. Mr Taunton has seen the landlady. I wish I could ask you to join me. But he's been so generous. I mustn't run expenses up, you see, dear."

"Of course not. I'll come in after supper. I'm not quite sure about to-night."

"Well—I hope I shall see you on Saturday. I can give you tea."

"I'm going away for the week-end. I've put it off and off. I must go this week."

Miss Dear frowned. "Well dear, come in and see me on your way."

Miss Dear sat down with an indrawn breath.

Miriam drew her Gladstone bag[1] a little closer. "I have only a second."

"All *right*, dear. You've only just *come*."

It was as if nothing had happened the whole week. She was not going to say anything. She was ill again, just in time for the week-end. She looked fearfully ill. Was she ill? The room was horrible—desolate and angry....

Miriam sat listening to the indrawn breathings.

"What is the matter?"

"It's my epileptiform neuralgia again. I thought Dr Ashley-Densley would have been in. I suppose he's off for the week-end."

She lay back pale and lifeless-looking with her eyes closed.

"All right, I won't go, that's about it," said Miriam angrily.

"Have another cup, dear. He said the picture was like me and like my name. He thinks it's the right name for me—'You'll always be able to inspire affection,' he said."

"Yes, that's true."

---

1   A small, deep, leather suitcase, popular in the nineteenth century and named after English Prime Minister, William Gladstone (1809-98).

"He wants me to change my first name. He thought Eleanor would be pretty."

"I *say*; look here."

"Of course I can't make any decision until I know certain things."

"D'you mean to say ... *good*ness!"

Miss Dear chuckled indulgently, making little brisk movements about the tea-tray.

"So I'm to be called Eleanor Dear. He's a dear little man. I'm very fond of him. But there is an earlier friend."

"Oh——"

"I thought you'd help me out."

"*I?*"

"Well, dear, I thought you wouldn't mind calling and finding out for me how the land lies."

Miriam's eyes fixed the inexorable shapely outlines of the tall figure. That dignity would never go; but there was something that would never come ... there would be nothing but fuss and mystification for the man. She would have a house and a dignified life. He, at home, would have death. But these were the women. But she had liked the book. There was something in it she had felt. But a man reading, seeing only bits and points of view, would never find that far-away something. She would hold the man by being everlastingly mysteriously up to something or other behind a smile. He would grow sick to death of mysterious nothings; of things always centring in her, leaving everything else outside her dignity. Appalling. What *was* she doing all the time, bringing one's eyes back and back each time after one had angrily given in, to question the ruffles of her hair and the way she stood and walked and prepared to speak?

"*Oh* ...! of *course* I will—you wicked woman."

"It's very puzzling. You see, he's the earlier friend."

"You think if he knew he had a rival—— Of course. Quite right."

"Well, dear, I think he ought to *know*."

"So I'm to be your mamma. What a *lark*."

Miss Dear shed a fond look. "I want you to meet my little man. He's longing to meet you."

"Have you mentioned me to him?"

"Well, dear, who should I mention if not you?"

"So I thought the best thing to do would be to come and ask you what would be the best thing to do for her."

"There's nothing to be done for her." He turned away and moved things about on the mantelpiece. Miriam's heart beat rebelliously in the silence of the consulting-room. She sat waiting stifled with apprehension, her thoughts on Miss Dear's familiar mysterious figure. In an unendurable impatience she waited for more, her eye smiting the tall averted figure on the hearthrug, following his movements ... small framed coloured pictures—very brilliant—photographs?—of dark and fair women, all the same, their shoulders draped like "The Soul's Awakening,"[1] their chests bare, all of them with horrible masses of combed out waving hair like the woman in the Harlene shop, only waving naturally. The most awful minxes ... his ideals. What a man. What a ghastly world. "If she were to go to the south of France, at once, she might live for years" ... this is hearing about death, in a consulting-room ... no escape ... everything in the room holding you in. The Death Sentence.... People would not die if they did not go to consulting-rooms ... doctors make you die ... they watch and threaten.

"What is the matter with her?" Out with it, don't be so important and mysterious.

"Don't you know, my dear girl?" Dr Densley wheeled round with searching observant eyes.

"Hasn't she told you?" he added quietly, with his eyes on his nails. "She's phthisical.[2] She's in the first stages of pulmonary tuberculosis."[3]

The things in the dark room darkled with a curious dull flash along all their edges and settled in a stifling dusky gloom. Everything in the room dingy and dirty and decaying, but the long lean upright figure. In time, too, he would die of something. Phthisis ... that curious terrible damp mouldering smell, damp warm faint human fungus ... in Aunt Henderson's bedroom.... But she had got better.... But the curate ought to know. But perhaps he, too, perhaps she had *imagined* that....

---

1   A popular (much-reproduced) painting, a portrait of a young girl, by English artist James Sant (1820-1916), official portraitist to Queen Victoria.

2   Suffering from "a wasting disease, esp. one involving the lungs" (*OED* "phthisis").

3   A disease in which bacteria attack the lungs, leading to a chronic cough, pulmonary bleeding, fever, and if not treated, eventually death. Tuberculosis is now far less common and can be treated with antibiotics; however, it was one of the most common causes of death in nineteenth-century England.

"It seems strange she has not told such an old friend."

"I'm not an old friend. I've only known her about two months. I'm hardly a friend at all."

Dr Densley was roaming about the room. "You've been a friend in need to that poor girl," he murmured contemplating the window curtains. "I recognized that when I saw you in her room last week." How superficial....

"Where did you meet her?" he said, a curious gentle high tone on the where and a low one on the meet, as if he were questioning a very delicate patient.

"My sister picked her up at a convalescent home."

He turned very sharply and came and sat down in a low chair opposite Miriam's low chair.

"Tell me all about it, my dear girl," he said sitting forward so that his clasped hands almost touched Miriam's knees.

"And she told you I was her oldest friend," he said, getting up and going back to the mantelpiece.

"I first met Miss Dear," he resumed after a pause, speaking like a witness, "last Christmas. I called in at Baker Street and found the superintendent had four of her disengaged nurses down with influenza.[1] At her request, I ran up to see them. Miss Dear was one of the number. Since that date she has summoned me at all hours on any and every pretext. What I can, I have done for her. She knows perfectly well her condition. She has her back against the wall. She's making a splendid fight. But the one thing that would give her a chance, she obstinately refuses to do. Last summer I found for her employment in a nursing home in the south of France. She refused to go, though I told her plainly what would be the result of another winter in England."

"Ought she to marry?" said Miriam suddenly, closely watching him.

"Is she thinking of marrying, my dear girl?" he answered, looking at his nails.

"Well of course she *might*——"

"Is there a sweetheart on the horizon?"

"Well, she inspires a great deal of affection. I think she is inspiring affection *now*."

---

1   The flu was much more dangerous at the turn of the twentieth century than it is today; after World War I, the Spanish Influenza killed 20-50 million people globally.

Dr Densley threw back his head with a laugh that caught his breath and gasped in and out on a high tone, leaving his silent mouth wide open, when he again faced Miriam with the laughter still in his eyes.

"Tell me, my dear girl," he said, smiting her knee with gentle affection, "is there someone who would like to marry her?"

"What I want to *know*," said Miriam very briskly "is whether such a person ought to know about the state of her health." She found herself cold and trembling as she asked. Miss Dear's eyes seemed fixed upon her.

"The chance of a tuberculous woman in marriage," recited Dr Densley, "is a holding up of the disease with the first child; after the second, she usually fails."

Why children? A doctor could see nothing in marriage but children. This man saw women with a sort of admiring pity. He probably estimated all those women on the mantelpiece according to their child-bearing capacity.

"Personally, I do not believe in forbidding the marriage of consumptives; provided both parties know what they are doing; and if they are quite sure they cannot do without each other. We know so little about heredity and disease,[1] we do not know always what life is about. Personally, I would not divide two people who are thoroughly devoted to each other."

"No?" said Miriam coldly.

"Is the young man in a position to take her abroad?"

"I can't tell you more than I know," said Miriam impatiently getting up.

Dr Densley laughed again and rose.

"I'm very glad you came, my dear girl. Come again soon and report progress. You're so near you can run in any time when you're free."

---

1 Following from Charles Darwin's theory of natural selection, or the "survival of the fittest," in the 1860s Sir Frances Galton (1822-1911) began to develop theories about human heredity that gained popular currency. His ideas were developed into the science of eugenics, which aims to control genetics in order to improve the human species. In the late nineteenth and early twentieth centuries, theories of eugenics were quite popular; however criticisms against it began to arise in the 1920s, and then escalated after World War II. The doctor here alludes to the related concern about whether disease is hereditary, and thus a potential detriment to future generations, although he shows some skepticism towards the idea, recognizing it is simply theory, rather than proven fact.

"Thank you," said Miriam politely, scrutinizing him calmly as he waved and patted her out into the hall.

Impelled by an uncontrollable urgency, she made her way along the Marylebone Road. Miss Dear was not expecting her till late. But the responsibility, the urgency. She must go abroad. About Dr Densley. That was easy enough. There was a phrase ready about that somewhere. Three things. But she could not go abroad to-night. Why not go to the Lyons[1] at Portland Road station,[2] and have a meal and get calm and think out a plan? But there was no time to lose. There was not a moment to lose. She arrived at the dark gate breathless and incoherent. A man was opening the gate from the inside. He stood short and compact in the gloom, holding it open for her.

"Is it Miss Henderson?" he said nervously as she passed.

"Yes," said Miriam stopping dead, flooded with sadness.

"I have been hoping to see you for the last ten days," he said hurriedly and as if afraid of being overheard. In the impenetrable gloom, darker than the darkness, his voice was a thread of comfort.

"Oh, yes."

"Could you come and see me?"

"Oh, yes, of course."

"If you will give me your number in Wimpole Street, I will send you a note."

"My *dear*!"

The tall figure, radiant, lit from head to foot, "as the light on a falling wave" ... "as the light on a falling wave." ...

Everything stood still as they gazed at each other. Her own self gazed at her out of Miss Dear's eyes.

"Well, I'm *bothered*," said Miriam at last, sinking into a chair.

"No need to be bothered any more, dear," laughed Miss Dear.

"It's extraordinary." She tried to recover the glory of the first moment in speechless contemplation of the radiant figure now

---

1 A popular chain of tea shops, the first of which opened in Piccadilly in 1894.

2 A London tube station near Regent's Park, it was part of the Metropolitan Railway.

moving chairs near to the lamp. The disappearance of the gas, the shaded lamp, the rector's wife's manner, the rector's wife's quiet stylish costume; it was like a prepared scene. How funny it would be to know a rector's wife.

"He's longing to meet you. I shall have a second room to-morrow. We will have a tea-party."

"It was to-day, of course."

"Just before you came," said Miss Dear, her glowing face bent, her hands brushing at the new costume. "You'll be our greatest friend."

"But how grand you are."

"He made my future his care some days ago, dear. 'As long as I live, you shall want for nothing,' he said."

"And to-day it all came out."

"Of course he'll have to get a *living*, dear. But we've decided to ignore the world."

What did she mean by that? ...

"You won't have to."

"Well, dear, I mean let the world go by."

"I see. He's a jewel. I think you've made a very good choice. You can make your mind easy about that. I saw the great medicine-man to-day."

"It was all settled without that, dear. I never even thought about him."

"You needn't. No woman need. He's a man who doesn't know his own mind and never will. I doubt very much whether he has a mind to know. If he ever marries he will marry a *wife*, not any particular woman; a smart worldly woman for his profession, or a thoroughly healthy female who'll keep a home in the country for him and have children and pour out his tea and grow things in the garden, while he flirts with patients in town. He's most *awfully* susceptible."

"I expect we shan't live in London."

"Well, that'll be better for you, won't it?"

"How do you mean, de-er?"

"Well, I ought to tell you Dr Densley told me you ought to go abroad."

"There's no need for me to go abroad, dear, I shall be all right if I can look *after* myself and get into the air."

"I expect you will. Everything's happened just right, hasn't it?"

"It's all been in the hands of an 'igher power, dear."

Miriam found herself chafing again. It had all rushed on, in a few minutes. It was out of her hands completely now. She did not want to know Mr and Mrs Taunton. There was nothing to hold her any longer. She had seen Miss Dear in the new part. To watch the working out of it, to hear about the parish, sudden details about people she did not know—intolerable.

CHAPTER XXXII

The short figure looked taller in the cassock, funny and hounded, like all curates; pounding about and arranging a place for her and trying to collect his thoughts while he repeated how good it was of her to have come. He sat down at last to the poached eggs and tea, laid on one end of the small, book-crowded table.

"I have a service at four-thirty," he said, busily eating and glaring in front of him with unseeing eyes, a little like Mr Grove[1] only less desperate because his dark head was round and his eyes were blue—"so you must excuse my meal. I have a volume of Plato[2] here."

"Oh, yes," said Miriam doubtfully.

"Are you familiar with Plato?"

She pondered intensely and rushed in just in time to prevent his speaking again.

"I *should* like him, I know—I've come across extracts in other books."

"He is a great man; my favourite companion. I spend most of my leisure up here, with Plato."

"What a delightful life," said Miriam enviously, looking about the small crowded room.

"As much time as I can spare from my work at the Institute and the Mission chapel; they fill my *active* hours."

Where would a woman, a wife-woman, be, in a life like this? He poured himself out a cup of tea; the eyes turned towards the tea-pot were worried and hurried; his whole compact rounded form was a little worried and anxious. There was something—bunnyish about him. Reading Plato, the expression of his person would still have something of the worried rabbit about it. His face would be calm and intent. Then he would look up from the page, taking in a thought, and something in his room would bring him back again to worry. But he was too stout to belong to a religious order.

"You must have a very busy life," said Miriam, her attention wandering rapidly off hither and thither.

"Of course," he said turning away from the table to the fire beside which she sat, "I think the clergy should keep in touch to

---

1   See p. 74, note 3.
2   Plato (c. 427-347 BCE), famous Greek philosopher and student of philosopher Socrates. His most noted work, the *Republic*, deals with ethics and the roles and responsibilities of the state.

some extent with modern thought—in so far as it helps them with their own particular work."

Miriam wondered why she felt no desire to open the subject of religion and science; or any other subject. It was so extraordinary to find herself sitting tête-à-tête[1] with a clergyman, and still more strange to find him communicatively trying to show her his life from the inside. He went on talking, not looking at her, but gazing into the fire. She tried in vain to tether her attention. It was straining away to work upon something, upon some curious evidence it had collected since she came into the room; and even with her eyes fixed upon his person and her mind noting the strange contradiction between the thin, rippling many-buttoned cassock and the stout square-toed boots protruding beneath it, she could not completely convince herself that he was there.

"... novels; I ask my friends to recommend any that might be helpful."

He had looked up towards her with this phrase.

"Oh yes, *Red Pottage*," she said grasping hurriedly and looking attentive.

"Have you read that novel?"

"No. I imagined that *you* had, because you lent it to Miss Dear."

"Miss Dear has spoken to you of me?"

"Oh yes."

"Of you, she has spoken a great deal. You know her very well. It is because of your long friendship with her that I have taken courage to ask you to come here and discuss with me about her affairs."

"I have known Miss Dear only a very short time," said Miriam, sternly, gazing into the fire. Nothing should persuade her to become the caretaker of the future Mrs Taunton.

"That surprises me very much indeed," he said propping his head upon his hand by one finger held against a tooth. He sat brooding.

"She is very much in need of friends just now," he said suddenly and evenly towards the fire, without removing his finger from his tooth.

"Yes," said Miriam gravely.

"You are, nevertheless, the only intimate woman friend to whom just now she has access."

---

1   French: literally, head to head: to meet alone, without the mediation of a third party.

"I've done little things for her. I couldn't do much."

"You were sorry for her." Mr Taunton was studying her face and waiting.

"Well—I don't know; she"—she consulted the fire intensely, looking for the truth—"she seems to me too strong for that." Light! Women have no pity on women ... they *know* how *strong* women are; a sick man *is* more helpless and pitiful than a sick woman; almost as helpless as a child. People in order of strength ... women, men, children. This man without his worldly props, his money and his job and his health, had not a hundredth part of the strength of a woman ... nor had Dr Densley....

"I think she *fascinated* me."

Mr Taunton gathered himself together in his chair and sat very upright.

"She has an exceptional power of inspiring affection—affection and the desire to give her the help she so sorely needs."

"Perhaps that is it," said Miriam judicially. But you are very much mistaken in calling on me for help ... "domestic work and the care of the aged and the sick"[1]—very convenient—all the stuffy nerve-racking never-ending things to be dumped on to women—who are to be openly praised and secretly despised for their unselfishness—I've got twice the brain-power you have. You are something of a scholar; but there is a way in which my time is more valuable than yours. There is a way in which it is more right for you to be tied to this woman than for me. Your reading is a habit, like most men's reading, not a quest. You don't want it disturbed. But you are kinder than I am. You are splendid. It will be awful—you don't know how awful yet—poor little man.

"I think it has been so, in my case, if you will allow me to tell you."

"Oh, yes, *do*," said Miriam a little archly—"of course—I know—I mean to say Miss Dear has told me."

"Yes," he said eagerly.

"How things are," she finished, looking shyly into the fire.

"Nevertheless, if you will allow me, I should like to tell you exactly what has occurred and to ask your advice as to the future. My mother and sisters are in the midlands."

"Yes," said Miriam in a carefully sombre non-committal tone; waiting for the revelation of some of the things men expect from

---

1   This unidentified quotation alludes to accepted roles for women at the time.

mothers and sisters and wondering whether he was beginning to see her unsuitability for the role of convenient sister.

"When my rector sent me to look up Miss Dear," he began heavily, "I thought it was an ordinary parish case, and I was shocked beyond measure to find a delicately nurtured, ladylike girl in such a situation. I came back here to my rooms and found myself unable to enter into my usual employments. I was haunted by the thought of what that lonely girl, who might have been one of my own sisters, must be suffering and enduring and I returned to give what relief I could, without waiting to report the case to my rector for ordinary parish relief. I am not dependent on my stipend and I felt that I could not withhold the help she ought to have. I saw her landlady and made arrangements as to her feeding, and called each day myself to take little things to cheer her—as a rule when my day's work was done. I have never come in contact with a more pathetic case. It did not occur to me for ... a moment, that she viewed my visits and the help I was so glad to be able to give ... in ... in any other light ... that she viewed me as other than her parish priest."

"Of *course* not," said Miriam violently.

"She is a singularly attractive and lovable nature. That, to my mind, makes her helplessness and resourcelessness all the more painfully pathetic. Her very name——" He paused, gazing into the fire. "I told her lately in one of her moments of deep depression that she would never want for friends, that she would always inspire affection wherever she went, and that as long as I lived she should never know want. Last week—the day I met you at the gate—finding her up and apparently very much better, I suggested that it would be well to discontinue my visits for the present, pointing out the social reasons and so forth ... I had with me a letter from a very pleasant Home in Bournemouth.[1] She had hinted, much earlier, that a long rest in some place such as Bournemouth was what she wanted, to set her up in health. I am bound to tell you what followed. She broke down completely, told me that, socially speaking, it was too late to discontinue my visits; that people in the house were already talking."

---

1 A medical facility (sanatorium) in the southern coastal town of Bournemouth, in Dorset. Consumptives were frequently sent to sanatoriums on the coast, as medical professionals believed the best treatment to be rest and fresh air. Mountain air was thought to be ideal for consumptives' health, but coastal towns were considered healthier than the city in countries such as England where large mountain ranges were less accessible.

"People in *that* house!"—you little simpleton—"Who? It is the most monstrous thing I ever heard."

"Well—there you have the whole story. The poor girl's distress and dependence were most moving. I have a very great respect for her character and esteem for her personality—and of course I am pledged."

"I see," said Miriam narrowly regarding him. Do you want to be saved?—ought I to save you?—why should I save you?—it is a solution of the whole thing, and a use for your money—you won't marry her when you know how ill she is.

"It is of course the immediate future that causes me anxiety and disquietude. It is there I need your advice and help."

"I see. Is Miss Dear going to Bournemouth?"

"Well; that is just it. Now that the opportunity is there, she seems disinclined to avail herself of it. I hope that you will support me in trying to persuade her."

"Of course. She *must* go."

"I am glad you think so. It is obvious that definite plans must be postponed until she is well and strong."

"You would be able to go down and see her."

"Occasionally, as my duties permit, oh, yes. It is a very pleasant place, and I have friends in Bournemouth who would visit her."

"She ought to be longing to go," said Miriam on her strange sudden smile. It had come from somewhere; the atmosphere was easier; suddenly in the room with her was the sense of bluebells, a wood blue with bluebells, and dim roofs, roofs in a town ... sur les toits[1]... and books; people reading books under them.

Mr Taunton smiled too.

"Unfortunately that is not so," he said leaning back in his chair and crossing his legs comfortably.

"You know," he said turning his blue gaze from the fire to Miriam's face, "I have never been so worried in my life as I have during the last ten days. It's upsetting my winter's work. It is altogether too difficult and impossible. I cannot see any possible

---

1 French: on the roofs. This is also the title of an 1897 short film by famous French director Georges Méliès. Though the film is not thematically connected to this scene in the novel, Richardson may have had the film in mind while Miriam thinks of "dim roofs, roofs in a town." Richardson had a keen interest in film; see p. 149, note 1.

adjustment. You see, I cannot possibly be continually interrupted and in such—strange ways. She came here yesterday afternoon with a list of complaints about her landlady. I *really* cannot attend to these things. She sends me *telegrams*. Only this morning there was a telegram. 'Come at once. Difficulty with chemist.' Of course it was impossible for me to leave my work at a moment's notice. This afternoon, I called. It seems that she was under the impression that there had been some insolence ... it absorbs so much *time* to enter into long explanations with regard to all these people. I cannot do it. That is what it comes to. I cannot do it."

Ah! You've lost your temper; like any one else. You want to shelve it. Any one would. But, being a man, you want to shelve it on to a woman. You don't care who hears the long tales as long as you don't....

"Have you seen her doctor?"

"No. I think, just now, he is out of town."

"*Really?* Are you sure?"

"You think I should see him."

"Certainly."

"I will do so on the first opportunity. That is the next step. Meantime I will write, provisionally, to Bournemouth."

"Oh, she must go to Bournemouth anyhow; that's settled."

"Perhaps her medical man may help there."

"He won't make her do anything she doesn't mean to do."

"I see you are a reader of character."

"I don't think I am. I always begin by idealizing people."

"Do you indeed?"

"Yes, always; and then they grow smaller and smaller."

"Is that your invariable experience of humanity?"

"I don't think I'm an altruist."[1]

"I think one must have one's heroes."

"In life or in books?"

"In both perhaps—one has them certainly in books—in records. Do you know this book?"

Miriam sceptically accepted the bulky volume he took down from the book-crowded mantelshelf.

"Oh, how interesting," she said insincerely when she had read *Great Thoughts from Great Lives*[2] on the cover.... I ought to have

---

1   Someone who does good for others without any expectation of or intent for personal gain.

2   Unidentified, but typical of popular books that culled life lessons from the biographies of great men.

said I don't like extracts. "Lives of great men all remind us We can make our lives sublime," she read aloud under her breath from the first page.... I ought to go. I can't enter into this.... I hate "great men," I think....

"That book has been a treasure-house to me—for many years. I know it now almost by heart. If it interests you, you will allow me, I hope, to present it to you."

"Oh, you must not let me deprive you of it—oh *no*. It is very kind of you; but you really mustn't." She looked up and returned quickly to the fascinating pages. Sentences shone out striking at her heart and brain ... names in italics; Marcus Aurelius[1] ... Lao-Tse.[2] Confucius[3] ... Clement of Alexandria[4]... Jacob Boehme.[5] "It's full of the most fascinating things. Oh no; I couldn't think of taking it. You must keep it. Who is Jacob Boehme? That name always *fascinates* me. I must have read something, somewhere, a long time ago. I can't remember. But it is such a *wonderful* name."

"Jacob Boehme was a German visionary. You will find, of course, all shades of opinion there."

"All contradicting each other; that's the worst of it. Still, I suppose all roads lead to Rome."[6]

"I see you have thought a great deal."

"Well," said Miriam feverishly, "there's always *science*, always all that awful business of science, and no getting rid of it."

"I think—in that matter—one must not allow one's mind to be led away."

"But one must keep an *open* mind."

"Are you familiar with Professor Tyndall?"[7]

---

1 Marcus Aurelius (121-180 CE) was a Roman Emperor. He was greatly admired as a philosopher and ruler.

2 An ancient Chinese philosopher (b. 604 BCE), and founder of Taoism, a philosophy that emphasizes the unity of all things.

3 Confucius (551-479 BCE) was an ancient Chinese philosopher. His teachings centred on morality and ethics.

4 Clement of Alexandria (c. 150-215 CE) was a Christian theologian.

5 German philosopher (1575-1624) whose works made claims for an unconventional vision of mysticism and the divine. He was a major influence on the Quakers, a religious society that Richardson joined in her mid- to late-thirties.

6 An ancient proverb suggesting that all routes, literal or metaphorical, converge on a powerful centre. The phrase is based on the fact that all major roads in the Roman Empire converged on the imperial city.

7 John Tyndall (1820-93), Professor of Natural History at the Royal Institution (which ran public scientific lectures) best known for his research on light waves and radiant heat.

"Only by meeting him in books about Huxley."

"Ah—he was very different; very different."

"Huxley," said Miriam with intense bitterness, "was an egoistic *adolescent*—all his life. I *never* came across *anything* like his conceited complacency in my life. The very look of his side-whiskers—well, there you have the whole man." Her heart burned and ached, beating out the words. She rose to go, holding the volume in hands that shook to the beating of her heart. Far away in the bitter mist of the darkening room was the strange little figure.

"Let me just write your name in the book."

"Oh, well, really, it is too bad—thank you very much."

He carried the book to the window-sill and stood writing, his bent head very dark and round in the feeble grey light. Happy monk, alone up under the roof with his Plato. It was a *shame*.

CHAPTER XXXIII

"What a *huge* room!"

"Isn't it a big room? Come in, young lady."

Miriam crossed to the fireplace through a warm, faintly sweet atmosphere. A small fire was smoking and the gas was partly turned down, but the room was warm with a friendly brown warmth. Something had made her linger in the hall until Mrs Bailey had come to the dining-room door and stood there, with the door wide open and something to communicate waiting behind her friendly greetings. As a rule, there was nothing behind her friendly greetings but friendly approval and assurance. Miriam had never seen the dining-room door open before, and sought distraction from the communicativeness by drifting towards it and peering in. Once in, and sitting in the chair between the fireplace and Mrs Bailey's tumbled work-basket standing on the edge of the long table, bound to stay taking in the room until Mrs Bailey returned, she regretted looking in. The hall and the stairs and her own room would be changed now she knew what this room was like. In her fatigue she looked about, half taking in, half recoiling from the contents of the room. "He stopped and got off his bicycle, and I said you don't seem very pleased to *see* me." Already he knew that they were tiresome strangers to each other. "I can't go dancing off to Bournemouth at a moment's notice, dear." "Well, I strongly advise you to go as soon as you can." "Of *course* I'm going, but I can't just dance off." "Don't let him get into the habit of associating you with the idea of worry." If she didn't *worry* him, and was always a little ill, and pretty.... "He says he can't do without her. I've told him, without reserve, what the chances are, and given them my blessing." Did he really feel that, suddenly sitting there in the consulting-room? If only she wouldn't be so mysterious and important about nothing....

There was a hugeness in the room, radiating from the three-armed dim-globed chandelier, going up and up; to the high heavily-moulded smoke-grimed ceiling, spreading out right and left along the length of the room, a large enclosed quietness, flowing up to the two great windows, hovering up and down the dingy rep[1] and dingy lace curtains and the drab-coloured Venetian blinds, through whose chinks the street came in. Tansley Street was there, pressing its secret peace against the closed

---

1 See p. 105, note 2.

windows. Between the windows a long strip of mirror, framed in tarnished gilt, reflected the peace of the room. Miriam glanced about, peering for its secret; her eye running over the length of the faded, patterned, deep-fringed table cover, the large cracked pink bowl in the centre, holding an aspidistra[1] ... brown cracked leaves sticking out; the faded upholstery of the arm-chair opposite her, the rows of dining-room chairs across the way, in line with the horsehair[2] sofa; the piano in the space between the sofa and the window; the huge mirror in the battered tarnished gilt frame sweeping half-way up the wall above the mantelpiece, reflecting the pictures and engravings hung rather high on the opposite wall, bought and liked long ago, the faded hearthrug under her feet, the more faded carpet disappearing under the long table, the dark stare of the fireplace, the heavy marble mantelpiece, the marble-cased clock, the opaque pink glass fat-bodied jugs scrolled with a dingy pattern, dusty lustres, curious objects in dull metal....

"It'll give my chicks a better chance. It isn't fair on them—living in the kitchen and seeing nobody."

"And you mean to risk sending the lodgers away?"

"I've been thinking about it some time. When the dining-room left, I thought I wouldn't fill up again. Miss Campbell's going too."

"Miss Campbell?"

"The drawn-room and drawn-room bedroom ... my word ... had her rooms turned out every week, carpets up and all."

"Every *week*!"

"Always talking about microbes. My *word*."

"How awful. And all the other people?"

"I've written them," smiled Mrs Bailey at her busily interlacing fingers.

"Oh!"

"For the 14th prox.;[3] they're all weekly."

"Then, if they don't stay as boarders, they'll have to trot out at once."

"Well, I thought if I was going to begin I'd better take the bull

---

1 See p. 287, note 1.
2 The sofa is stuffed with horse hair, as was common prior to synthetic stuffing.
3 Next; that is, the 14th of the next month.

by the horns. I've heard of two. Norwegian young gentlemen. They're coming next week, and they both want large bedrooms."

"I think it's awfully plucky, if you've had no experience."

"Well, young lady, I see it like this. What *others* have done, I can. I feel I must do something for the children. Mrs Reynolds has married three of her daughters to boarders. She's giving up. Elsie is going into the typing."[1]

"You haven't written to *me*."

"You stay where you are, young lady."

"Well—I think it's awfully sweet of you, Mrs Bailey."

"Don't you think about that. It needn't make any difference to you."

"Well—of course—if you heard of a boarder——"

Mrs Bailey made a little dab at Miriam's knee. "You stay where you *are*, my dear."

"I do hope it will be a success. The house will be completely changed."

"I know it's a risk. But if you get on it pays better. There's less work in it and you've got a house to live in. Nothing venture, nothing *have*. It's no good to be backward in coming forward, nowadays. We've got to march with the times."

Miriam tried to see Mrs Bailey presiding, the huge table lined with guests. She doubted. Those boarding-houses in Woburn Place, the open windows in the summer, the strange smart people, in evening dress, the shaded lamps; Mrs Bailey would be lost. She could never hold her own. The quiet house would be utterly changed. There would be people going about, in possession, all over the front steps and at the dining-room windows and along the drawing-room balcony.

---

1 Elsie will train to become a typist, as Miriam earlier considered she must do to earn more as a secretary.

Appendix A: Reviews

[The reviews gathered in this appendix provide an unvarnished perspective on how Richardson's contemporaries, many of them experimental writers themselves, received her work. These assessments do not have the benefit of historical hindsight, but appeared nearly contemporaneously with the novels themselves, and thus articulate first impressions of a body of work that would ultimately be vast and span decades. Of particular interest here is the aspect of tone. When Woolf,[1] or Rodker,[2] or Mansfield[3] indicates that Richardson's technique is interesting but ultimately boring, we must attend closely to whether that is an honest professional appraisal or possibly such an appraisal tainted with envy.[4] After all, Woolf and Mansfield certainly were also experimenting with narrative innovations such as stream of consciousness, and with representing women's lives through the apparently mundane happenings of the everyday. Richardson did it before them, though, and arguably with greater commitment to the principles she sought to exemplify. Nonetheless, readers who have experienced some frustration with Richardson's coy, at times obscure, prose will no doubt be relieved to find that they have illustrious company. They will also discover the charms and admiration expressed in these reviews, and recognize—as her contemporaries did—Richardson's central place in literary modernism.]

1. Virginia Woolf, "*The Tunnel*," *Times Literary Supplement* (13 February 1919), p. 81

Although *The Tunnel* is the fourth book that Miss Richardson has written, she must still expect to find her reviewers paying a great deal of attention to her method. It is a method that demands attention, as a door whose handle we wrench ineffectively calls our attention to the fact that it is locked. There is no slipping smoothly down the accustomed channels; the first chapters provide an amusing spectacle of hasty critics seeking them in vain. If this were the result of perversity,

---

1 Virginia Woolf (1882-1941): major English modernist writer.
2 John Rodker (1894-1955): English writer and publisher.
3 Katherine Mansfield (1888-1923): New Zealand writer best known for her short stories.
4 Woolf, in particular, expresses ungenerous feelings towards Richardson, as recorded in her diary entries for 22 March 1919 and 21 February 1921. See p. 41 in the Introduction, above.

we should think Miss Richardson more courageous than wise; but being, as we believe, not wilful but natural, it represents a genuine conviction of the discrepancy between what she has to say and the form provided by tradition for her to say it in. She is one of the rare novelists who believe that the novel is so much alive that it actually grows. As she makes her advanced critic, Mr. Wilson,[1] remark: "There will be books with all that cut out—him and her—all that sort of thing. The book of the future will be clear of all that." And Miriam Henderson herself reflects: "but if books were written like that, sitting down and doing it cleverly and knowing just what you were doing and just how somebody else had done it, there was something wrong, some mannish cleverness that was only half right. To write books knowing all about style would be to become like a man." So "him and her" are cut out, and with them goes the old deliberate business: the chapters that lead up and the chapters that lead down; the characters who are always characteristic; the scenes that are passionate and the scenes that are humorous; the elaborate construction of reality; the conception that shapes and surrounds the whole. All these things are cast away, and there is left, denuded, unsheltered, unbegun and unfinished, the consciousness of Miriam Henderson, the small sensitive lump of matter half transparent and half opaque, which endlessly reflects and distorts the variegated procession, and is, we are bidden to believe, the source beneath the surface, the very oyster within the shell.

The critic is thus absolved from the necessity of picking out the themes of the story. The reader is not provided with a story; he is invited to embed himself in Miriam Henderson's consciousness, to register one after another, and one on top of another, words, cries, shouts, notes of a violin, fragments of lectures, to follow these impressions as they flicker through Miriam's mind, waking incongruously other thoughts, and plaiting incessantly the many coloured and innumerable threads of life. But a quotation is better than description.

She was surprised now at her familiarity with the details of the room ... that idea of visiting places in dreams. It was something more than the ... all the real work of your life has a real dream in it; some of the real dream part of you coming true. You know in advance when you are really following your life. These things are familiar because reality is here. Coming events cast light. It is like dropping everything and walking backward to something you know is there. However far you go out you come back.... I am back now where I was before I began trying to do things like other

---

1   That is, Hypo Wilson, the character introduced in *The Tunnel* and based on H.G. Wells (1866-1946), the English writer and social critic with whom Richardson had a long intellectual, and a brief romantic, relationship.

people. I left home to get here. None of those things can touch me here. They are mine.

Here we are thinking, word by word, as Miriam thinks. The method, if triumphant, should make us feel ourselves seated at the centre of another mind, and, according to the artistic gift of the writer, we should perceive in the helter-skelter of flying fragments some unity, significance, or design. That Miss Richardson gets so far as to achieve a sense of reality far greater than that produced by the ordinary means is undoubted. But, then, which reality is it, the superficial or the profound? We have to consider the quality of Miriam Henderson's consciousness, and the extent to which Miss Richardson is able to reveal it. We have to decide whether the flying helter-skelter resolves itself by degrees into a perceptible whole. When we are in a position to make up our minds we cannot deny a slight sense of disappointment. Having sacrificed not merely "hims and hers," but so many seductive graces of wit and style for the prospect of some new revelation or greater intensity, we still find ourselves distressingly near the surface. Things look much the same as ever. It is certainly a very vivid surface. The consciousness of Miriam takes the reflection of a dentist's room to perfection. Her senses of touch, sight and hearing are all so excessively acute. But sensations, impressions, ideas and emotions glance off her, unrelated and unquestioned, without shedding quite as much light as we had hoped into the hidden depths. We find ourselves in the dentist's room, in the street, in the lodging-house bedroom frequently and convincingly; but never, or only for a tantalizing second, in the reality which underlies these appearances. In particular, the figures of other people on whom Miriam casts her capricious light are vivid enough, but their sayings and doings never reach that degree of significance which we, perhaps unreasonably, expect. The old method seems sometimes the more profound and economical of the two. But it must be admitted that we are exacting. We want to be rid of realism, to penetrate without its help into the regions beneath it, and further require that Miss Richardson shall fashion this new material which has the shapeliness of the old accepted forms. We are asking too much; but the extent of our asking proves that "The Tunnel" is better in its failure than most books in their success.

2. John Rodker,[1] "*The Tunnel*," *The Little Review* 6.5 (September 1919): 40-41

Dorothy Richardson appears in this new instalment of her cycle to have made a tiresome practise of what was originally a rather engag-

---

1 For Rodker, see p. 325, note 2.

ing manner. One feels—and perhaps that is what one is expected to feel—that nothing now will ever be able to interpose between herself and this Juggernath of her WORK. With extraordinary and arachnoid patience she persists in still rebuilding her web under some strange persecution-delusion that the observing scientist has destroyed it. This is absurd; the original statement stands the additional respinning only results in what was a bright and not unoriginal conception becoming thickened to the diameter of a hawser.

In this welter of material the reader feels like a Kafir[1] carefully searching for the diamond swallowed the day before. Much is irrelevant, sundry sparkles attract but they are not the indubitable article. Still he cannot conceive of the stone being elsewhere and the search is protracted indefinitely.

Read for a brief half hour Miss Richardson is interesting, her perception is just, her comments show a lively mind; but while the writer with a fresh mind on several consecutive mornings, shall we say, worked out in a thousand words or more the passage of Miriam through a front door, the reader can hardly be expected to consider it relevant, or in any case to remember it. The method of whipping up enormous masses of material to coagulate a skeleton may be new; it may be even exciting in an age where all our curiosity is a kind of sunday-morning-paper society gossip; but there can be no doubt that if anything in life may be said to be a waste of time this kind of gossip is it. Carefully avoiding all hills Miss Richardson keeps brilliantly to exotic valleys so full of life that one is suffocated.

For myself I would rather have an impression created in one phrase than in ten. Miss Richardson will probably say "yes! if you can get the same impression," but when one gets no impression one has a legitimate grievance. The best literature allows a very small latitude but certainly there, i.e. from indications given, one is allowed a real if circumscribed manoeuvring ground, but Miss Richardson is a too familiar familiar, her jogging elbow is always in your ribs—disaster waits you on either side. But no brain could want all this detail. Yet Miss Sinclair's article[2] remains true: there is quality in this work, sympathy even, but as a scientific study,—else why so ponderous,—it is fairly valueless since with every appearance of allowing herself a free rein Miss Richardson has a particularly firm hand on the reins. Her

---

1 Racist term for a black South African.
2 May Sinclair (1863-1946): English writer. Her 1918 review of Richardson's novels in *The Little Review* furnishes the first use of "stream of consciousness" to describe a literary technique. See Sinclair's review in the Broadview Press edition of *Pointed Roofs* (2014), pp. 236-42.

method has been compared to that of Joyce.[1] This is mere footling since anyone with a sufficiently sympathetic and cultured brain can follow Joyce and be moved by him; but Miss Richardson's associations are as free as a choppy sea and with the same effect. Miss Richardson is too intellectually subtle. It's a very clever game; a very dreary analysis. Reverberation of thought carried to a certain point has no further value—"he knew she knew he knew she knew—."

3. Katherine Mansfield,[2] "Three Women Novelists (Review of *The Tunnel*)," *Athenaeum* 4640 (4 April 1919): 140-41

Why was it written? The question does not present itself—it is the last question one would ask after reading *The Tunnel*. Miss Richardson has a passion for registering every single thing that happens in the clear, shadowless country of her mind. One cannot imagine her appealing to the reader or planning out her novel; her concern is primarily, and perhaps ultimately, with herself. "What cannot I do with this mind of mine!" one can fancy her saying. "What can I not see and remember and express!" There are times when she seems deliberately to set it a task, just for the joy of realizing again how brilliant a machine it is, and we, too, share her admiration for its power of absorbing. Anything that goes into her mind she can summon forth again, and there it is, complete in every detail, with nothing taken away from it—and nothing added. This is a rare and interesting gift, but we should hesitate before saying it was a great one.

The Tunnel is the fourth volume of Miss Richardson's adventures with her soul-sister Miriam Henderson. Like them, it is composed of bits, fragments, flashing glimpses, half scenes and whole scenes, all of them quite distinct and separate, and all of them of equal importance. There is no plot, no beginning, no middle or end. Things just "happen" one after another with incredible rapidity and at break-neck speed. There is Miss Richardson, holding out her mind, as it were, and there is Life hurling objects into it as fast as she can throw. And at the appointed time Miss Richardson dives into its recesses and reproduces a certain number of these treasures—a pair of button boots, a night in Spring, some cycling knickers, some large, round biscuits—as many as she can pack into a book, in fact. But the pace kills.

There is one who could not live in so tempestuous an environment as her mind—and he is Memory. She has no memory. It is true that Life is sometimes very swift and breathless, but not always. If we are to be truly alive there are large pauses in which we creep away into our

---

1 James Joyce (1882-1941): Irish writer.
2 For Mansfield, see p. 325, note 3.

caves of contemplation. And then it is, in the silence, that Memory mounts his throne and judges all that is in our minds—appointing each his separate place, high or low, rejecting this, selecting that—putting this one to shine in the light and throwing that one into the darkness.

We do not mean to say that those large, round biscuits might not be in the light, or the night in Spring be in the darkness. Only we feel that until these things are judged and given each its appointed place in the whole scheme, they have no meaning in the world of art.

4. Katherine Mansfield,[1] "Dragonflies," in *Novels and Novelists*. Ed. J. Middleton Murry. NY: Knopf, 1930, p. 310

Who can tell, watching the dragonfly, at what point in its swift angular flight it will suddenly pause and hover, quivering over this or that? The strange little jerk—the quivering moment of suspension—we might almost fancy they were the signs of a minute inward shock of recognition felt by the dragonfly. "There is something here; something here for me. What is it?" it seems to say. And then, at the same instant, it is gone. Away it darts, glancing over the deep pool until another floating flower or golden bud or tangle of shadowy weeds attracts it, and again it is still, curious, hovering over....

But this behaviour, enchanting thought [sic] it may be in the dragonfly, is scarcely adequate when adopted by the writer of fiction. Nevertheless, there are certain modern authors who do not appear to recognize its limitations. For them the whole art of writing consists in the power with which they are able to register that faint inward shock of recognition. Glancing through life they make the discovery that there are certain experiences which are, as it were, peculiarly theirs. There is a quality in the familiarity of these experiences or in their strangeness which evokes an immediate mysterious response—a desire for expression. But now, instead of going any further, instead of attempting to relate their "experiences" to life or to see them against any kind of background, these writers are, as we see them, content to remain in the air, hovering over, as if the thrilling moment were enough and more than enough. Indeed, far from desiring to explore it, it is as though they would guard the secret for themselves as well as for us, so that when they do dart away all is as untouched, as unbroken as before.

But what is the effect of this kind of writing upon the reader? How is he to judge the importance of one thing rather than another if each is to be seen in isolation? And is it not rather cold comfort to be

---

1 For Mansfield, see p. 325, note 3.

offered a share in a secret on the express understanding that you do not ask what the secret is—more especially if you cherish the uncomfortable suspicion that the author is no wiser than you, that the author is in love with the secret and would not discover it if he could? ...

Interim,[1] which is the latest slice from the life of Miriam Henderson, might almost be described as a nest of short stories. There is Miriam Henderson, the box which holds them all, and really it seems there is no end to the number of smaller boxes that Miss Richardson can make her contain. But *Interim* is a very little one indeed. In it Miriam is enclosed in a Bloomsbury[2] boarding-house, and though she receives, as usual, shock after shock of inward recognition, they are produced by such things as well-browned mutton, gas jets, varnished wallpapers. Darting through life, quivering, hovering, exulting in the familiarity and the strangeness of all that comes within her tiny circle, she leaves us feeling, as before, that everything being of equal importance to her, it is impossible that everything should not be of equal unimportance.

---

1   *Interim*, the fifth chapter-volume in *Pilgrimage*, was serialized alongside James Joyce's *Ulysses* in *The Little Review* in 1919, and published as a book in 1920.
2   Bloomsbury is an artistic and intellectual neighbourhood of London, where Virginia Woolf and her circle lived and met. For Woolf, see p. 325, note 1.

Appendix B: Letters

[As did many writers of the early twentieth century, Richardson wrote letters prolifically and kept most of her correspondence. It is fortunate for us that she did, since her letters have become the chief source of information about how she felt about her work and, more importantly still, about her life. Richardson notoriously withheld information about her personal life, preferring to let her work speak for itself. As such, some biographers have had to rely upon information contained in the novels to discern even the basic contours of Richardson's life and personality. The letters afford some of the few glimpses we have into her way of thinking and the details of her life, as well as chronicling her engagements with other writers, publishers, and scholars.[1]]

1. **To Samuel Solomonovich Koteliansky,[2] 11 December 1933. In Gloria G. Fromm, ed., *Windows on Modernism*, Athens, GA: U of Georgia P, 1995. 253-55**

Constantine Bay. Padstow N. Cornwall.
Dec 11th, 1933.

Dear Kot:
    [...] And here, for you, is Pilgrimage, which has, so to speak, never been published. Ten chapter-volumes have found their way into print, into an execrable lay-out & disfigured by hosts of undiscovered printer's errors & punctuation that is the result of corrections, intermittent, by an orthodox 'reader' & corrections of these corrections, also intermittent, by the author. (Whose system, if such it can be called—Beresford[3] discovered & pointed it out to me—cannot be bad, or a dissertation I wrote after Beresford's discovery had made me punctuation-conscious, would not have been incorporated by Columbia University in their volume for the use of students of journalism.) The order in which these "chapters" appeared is apparently undiscov-

---

1   This angle of approach to Richardson's life and work is gaining an invaluable resource in the Richardson Editions Project's publication of a three-volume *Collected Letters of Dorothy Richardson*, as of 2015.

2   Samuel Solomonovich Koteliansky (1880-1955): Russian-born translator and man of letters.

3   J.D. Beresford (1873-1947): English writer and first editor of *Pointed Roofs*. For his Introduction to *Pointed Roofs*, see pp. 255-57 in the Broadview Press edition (2014).

erable either by booksellers or librarians. They offer, as the first, or the latest, any odd volume they happen to have. The intervals between their appearance has [*sic*] been disastrously long. Yet, at snail's pace, they all go on selling. In every one of Duckworth's biennial statements each one of the volumes appears; & the last year or two has shown a slight increase.[1] Letters, & reviews, indicated that young persons liked the last volume, who had read none of its predecessors. I believe, all told, that a decent corrected edition—in the form of two, or three, of the short volumes bound together—would pay its way. Duckworth agrees, but is prevented from venturing, by having (mysteriously) set the books up in varying types. I hold his promise to release me. But the publisher taking over would have to acquire his stock, not large, and settle my overdraft on Duckworth, once £300, reduced, by attrition, to something like £60. In regard to the first volume, I would accept a small royalty agreement. If it did fairly well, my share in the next to be larger. [...]

   Yours sincerely,
   Dorothy M.R.

2. To Bryher,[2] May 1936. In Gloria G. Fromm, ed., *Windows on Modernism*, Athens, GA: U of Georgia P, 1995. 311-12

Trevone Cottage.
Trevone Padstow.
May '36.

Dear Bryher,

  I must thank you, too, for George Orwell's book, so beloved of Compton Mackenzie, whose own work it resembles, technically only, as Orwell's mind lacks a metaphysical background, is horizontal &, supposedly "realist," whereas Mackenzies [*sic*] is vertical, having roots in the earth & a summit in the sky.[3] He shares many of the illusions of the Wells[4] school & begs, all the while, exactly the same questions; being based on exactly the same unhistorical, unscientific, uneverything nightmare vision of reality, & may be compared to a medical diagnosis, useful & interesting as an enumeration of symptoms, but mistaking these symptoms for causes rather than recognising them as results. [...]

---

1 Gerald Duckworth & Co.: English publishing house founded in 1898.
2 Annie Winnifred Ellerman (1894-1983): English writer, editor, and patron who went by the pen-name Bryher.
3 George Orwell: pseudonym of the English writer and propagandist Eric Arthur Blair (1903-50). Compton MacKenzie (1883-1972): Scottish writer.
4 That is, H.G. Wells. See p. 326, note 1.

After a years [*sic*] suspense, since last May, when I discovered Dent's[1] believed P[ilgrimage]. finished, I can alight & breathe. They have come round to my plan, of issueing [*sic*] sets of vols. rather than the whole at once, but, under pretext of "awakening public interest," are postponing the first of these till 1938.[2] They hope, by the time all are out, the book will be complete; though they undertake to go on publishing if it is not. All I can do, is to indicate that this delay will not assist the production of the final volumes. But it comforts me to have the matter settled & to know that there will be, one day, a decent corrected edition, possibly complete. This assurance has helped to release my paralysed faculties & get me back to my centre, for so long inaccessible.

We look forward to the new L. & L.[3]

With love

Dorothy.

3. To Vincent Brome,[4] 16 January 1950. In Gloria G. Fromm, ed., *Windows on Modernism*, Athens, GA: U of Georgia P, 1995. 631-32

Hillside. Trevone. Padstow. Cornwall.

Jan.16th.'50

Dear Mr[.] Brome:

In vain I have been hunting, amidst the accumulations of months, for your last letter, hoping that perhaps you will have discovered in Pilg[rimage]. The answers to your questions, for nothing short of an essay could convey more or less what I feel you want.

H.G.[5] was of course a mass of contradictions. Poor little Artie Kipps[6] found his way to the door of the church founded on Huxley's

---

1 J.M. Dent: publishers, founded 1888.

2 1938 saw the first Collected Edition of *Pilgrimage*, though Richardson continued to produce new installments. A second Collected Edition was published by Dent in 1967, with the latest Collected Edition appearing under the Virago Press imprint in 1970.

3 *Life and Letters*: English journal published 1928-1935.

4 Vincent Brome (1910-2004): English writer and journalist best-known for his biographies of public and literary figures such as Clement Atlee (1947), H.G. Wells (1951), Frank Harris (1959), Sigmund Freud and his followers (1967), Carl Jung (1978), Havelock Ellis (1981), and J.B. Priestly (1988).

5 H.G. Wells. See p. 326, note 1.

6 Arthur ("Artie") Kipps is the protagonist of H.G. Wells's 1905 novel *Kipps*, a tale of class difference and social inequality in turn-of-the-century England.

reading of Darwin[1] (in the hey-day of SCIENCE before her limitations as an explorer of reality became evident) and spent his life there taking notes and writing epistles in all kinds of forms (as a novelist, his characters were devised to illustrate his theories). As a transcendent journalist of science, no one can touch him for imaginative power. Largely he transformed the average consciousness of his earlier days and undoubtedly hoped to lead the abstraction labelled "humanity," eager and unanimous, to a new world. Up to a point, he was a prophet, but only in regard to things. (Of people he knew [insert: relatively] nothing). This planet he kept saying, is a misfit. We will find our way out, amongst the stars—"beyond our wildest dreams." Enlargement of the premises and improvement of the furniture leaving individuals unchanged. His final realisation of the failure of his gospel, coupled with a complete inability to understand why his dictatorship was refused, was the tragedy of his last days. For his pathetically amusing pontificality was excha[n]ged blind anger and dismay, and we had "humanity at the end of its tether."[2] Perhaps, for towards the very end he became gentler and more considerate to those surrounding him, when all was lost and he could fight no more, illumination may have dawned.

He tried, in his way, all doors save that of philosophy. First and Last Things seemed to suggest a turning-point.[3] But soon, quicker in the uptake than anyone I have ever known, he was chasing after the latest discovery and advertising it in categorical generalisations.

Jane[4] is difficult to state. Growing up in undiluted Philistia,[5] she escaped, towards the end of her schooldays into Science. Had, as he notes in his tribute after her death, reservations in regard to much of his ideology, but never stated them, always, because she realised their importance to him, supporting and applauding. Yes, indeed (answering one of your questions) she gave him carte blanche until one of his affairs and the relative failure of that year's book, necessitated a change of residence—the move to Hampstead—and modified her

---

1 Thomas Henry Huxley (1825-95): English biologist and vociferous proponent of English naturalist Charles Darwin (1809-82), whose theories of evolution transformed our understanding of human history and species relationships.

2 *Mind at the end of its Tether* (1945): H.G. Wells's last book.

3 *H[.]G[.] W[ells]'s First and Last Things: A Confession of Faith and Rule of Life (1908)* was revised several times, finally appearing as *The Conquest of Time (1942)*.

4 Jane: nickname of Amy Catherine Robins (1872-1927), Wells's second spouse, with whom he supposedly had an open marriage.

5 That is, a land of tasteless anti-intellectualism, named for the land of the Philistines in the Bible.

plans for the boys, she put her foot down and exacted a promise that for a time was kept.

[rest of letter by hand]

"Free-love" formed part of the gospel of the younger Fabians.[1] The family was to be liquidated (H.G.'s "Socialism & the Family")[2] I recall a solemn discussion, at a meeting of young women, on the desirability of selecting a suitable male, producing an infant & going on the rates. Most of us were what Lawson Dodd labeled "poor law girls," independent, existing, (quite happily) just above the poverty-line on very small salaries.

Please don't hesitate, if I've not answered all your questions, to let me know[.]

Yours sincerely,

Dorothy M. Richardson.

[type resumed]

PS. Your letter has turned up.

---

1   Fabian Society: British socialist society (founded 1884) that espoused gradual reform of society along socialist lines, through the example of clean living and promotion of European renaissance ideals. It was named for the Roman General Fabius Maximus (c. 280-203 BCE), who defeated the Carthaginian army with a strategy of harassment and attrition rather than direct military engagement.

2   Published in 1906, *Socialism and the Family* contained two articles, "Socialism and the Middle Classes" and "Modern Socialism and the Family." [Fromm's note]. In these essays, Wells outlines the Fabian/Socialist attitude towards the family, opposing the patriarch's ownership of the members of the family as it opposes all other forms of private property, and advocating for free and open relationships that eschew the forms of ownership entailed under institutions such as marriage.

Appendix C: Essays

[In addition to the novels in *Pilgrimage*, Richardson wrote numerous essays and contributed articles to a variety of publications, beginning with *The Dental Record*. Her topics ranged from writerly method through hygiene, gender politics, feminism, and the future of the novel. In them, she shows herself to be extremely well read and grounded in the history of Western art and letters, as well as remarkably up-to-date on scientific and hygienic matters. Much of this comes, of course, from her experience working as Miriam does in a dentist's office, but it also bespeaks a generous curiosity. If her novels have been characterized in terms of finding nothing too trivial to include, these essays show that Richardson herself possessed just the sort of mind that likewise found everything about it worthy of attention.]

1. "About Punctuation," *Adelphi* 1 (April 1924): 990-96

[In this essay, Richardson tackles the question of punctuation and the role it plays in experimental narrative techniques such as those she pioneered in *Pilgrimage*. She had been criticized for some of the unconventional punctuation she used in the first three chapter-volumes of *Pilgrimage*, and sought to meet that criticism head-on and honestly. Taking the problem of whether and how to experiment with punctuation seriously, Richardson considers both what is gained by irregular punctuation and what can be lost—and urges those who would try it to be sure of an uncommonly good copy editor. In sum, she suggests, writers ought to be free to punctuate as they see most fit for their aims, since punctuation is key to presentation, though the practicalities of the publishing process make experimenting with punctuation fraught.]

Only to patient reading will come forth the charm concealed in ancient manuscripts. Deep interest there must be, or sheer necessity, to keep eye and brain at their task of scanning a text that moves along unbroken, save by an occasional full-stop. But the reader who persists finds presently that his task is growing easier. He is winning familiarity with the writer's style, and is able to punctuate unconsciously as he goes ... It is at this point that he begins to be aware of the charm that has been sacrificed by the systematic separation of phrases. He finds himself *listening*. Reading through the ear as well as through the eye. And while in any way of reading the ear plays its part, unless it is most cunningly attacked it co-operates, in our modern way, scarcely at all. It is left behind. For as light is swifter than sound so is the eye swifter than the ear. But in the slow, attentive reading demanded by unpunctuated texts, the faculty of hearing has its chance, is enhanced until the text *speaks* itself. And it is of this enhancement that the strange lost charm is born. Quite modest matter, read thus, can arouse and fuse the faculties of mind and heart.

Only the rarest of modern prose can thus arouse and affect. Only now and again, to-day, is there any strict and vital relationship between the reader and what he reads. Most of our reading is a superficial swift gathering, as we loll on the borderland between inertia and attention, of the matter of a text. An easy-going collaboration, with the reader's share reduced to the minimum. So much the better, it may be said. Few books, ancient or modern, are worth a whole self. Very few can call us forth to yield all we are and suffer change. Yet it is not to be denied that the machinery of punctuation and type, while lifting burdens from reader and writer alike and perfectly serving the purposes of current exchange, have also, on the whole, devitalized the act of reading; have tended to make it less organic, more mechanical.

There is no discourtesy, since punctuation has come to be regarded as invariable, in calling it part of the machinery of book production. An invisible part. For so long as it conforms to rule punctuation is invisible. After the school years it is invisible; its use, for most people, as unconscious as the act of breathing. Most of us were taught punctuation exactly as we were taught rule of three. Even if we were given some sense of the time-value of the stop and its subdivisions, the thing that came first and last, the fun of the game, was the invariability of the rules. And so charming is convention, so exhilarating a deliberate conformity to tradition, that it is easy to forget that the sole aim of law is liberty; in this case, liberty to express.

It is not very long since an English gentleman's punctuation was as romantic as his spelling. The formal law was strictly observed only by scholars. Not until lately have infringements, by the ordinary, been regarded as signs of ill-breeding. And in high places there have always been those who have honoured the rules in the breach, without rebuke. Sterne, for example, joyously broke them all, and it has been accounted unto him for righteousness.[1] Beside him stands Rabelais, wielding form as Pantaloon wields his bladder.[2] Were they perhaps

---

1 Laurence Sterne (1713-68): English writer most famous for his 1759 comic novel *The Life and Opinions of Tristram Shandy*.

2 François Rabelais (1494-1553): French comic writer. "Pantaloon" seems to be an error on Richardson's part, substituting the popular comic figure of avarice in the tradition of the English Harlequinade, for the character Panta-

castigated for their liberties by the forgotten orthodox of the period? Or is it that the stickler for stereotyped punctuation makes his first appearance in our own time? Why, in either case, have Mr. Wells's experiments, never going further than a reinforcement of the full-stop and a free use of the dash, been dragged into the market-place and lynched, while the wholesale depredations of Sterne and Rabelais are merely affectionately hugged? Is it because their rows and rows of dots, their stars, and their paragraphs built of a single word are so very often a libidinous digging of the reader's ribs? Because their stars wink? It is noteworthy that so long as his dots were laughter Mr. Wells was not called over the coals for mannerism. There was no trouble until those signs were used to italicize an idea or drive home a point; until they became pauses for reflection, by the reader. From that time onwards there have been, amongst his opponents, those who take refuge in attack on his method. Scorn of the dot and the dash has come forward to play its part in the business of answering Mr. Wells. Sterne and Rabelais and the earlier Wells, genially aware of the reader and with nothing to fear from him, offer open hospitality on their pages, space, while their wit detonates, for the responsive beat of the reader's own consciousness. The later Wells, usually the prey of dismay, anger or despair, handles the resources of the printed page almost exclusively as missiles, aimed full at the intelligence alone.

Of the value of punctuation and, particularly, of its value as pace-maker for the reader's creative consciousness, no one has had a keener sense than Mr. Henry James.[1] No one has more sternly, or more cunningly, secured the collaboration of the reader. Along his prose not even the most casual can succeed in going at top-speed. Short of the casting off of burdens, the deep breath, the headlong plunge, the sustained steady swimming, James gives nothing at all. To complete

---

gruel in Rabelais' *La vie de Gargantua et de Pantagruel* (*The Life of Gargantua and Pantagruel*), a series of five novels (1532-64). Compounding the error, though shedding some light on what Richardson means here, is the fact that though Pantagruel inflates a pig's bladder and puts stones in it to make a musical instrument, Triboulet takes it and strikes Pantagruel with it before wandering off, taking "huge Delight in the melody of the rickling, crackling Noise of the Pease" (François Rabelais, *Gargantua and Pantagruel*, trans. by Sir Thomas Urquhart and Peter Le Motteux (1653-94), ed. W.E. Henley [London: David Nutt, 1900], III, 228).

1 Henry James (1843-1916): American writer. James towers over turn-of-the-century fiction, writing a huge number of popular and influential novels between *Roderick Hudson* (1875) and *The Golden Bowl* (1904). Known colloquially as "the master," James became something of a touchstone for early twentieth-century writers intent upon honing their technique.

renunciation he offers the recreative repose that is the result of open-eyed concentration. As aesthetic exercise, with its peculiar joys and edifications, the prose of James keeps its power, even for those in utmost revolt against his vision, indefinitely. It is a spiritual Swedish Drill.[1] Gently, painlessly, without shock or weariness, as he carries us unhasting, unresting, over his vast tracts of statement, we learn to stretch attention to the utmost. And to the utmost James tested, suspending from the one his wide loops, and from the other his deep-hung garlands of expression, the strength of the comma and the semi-colon. He never broke a rule. With him, punctuation, neither made, nor created, nor begotten, but proceeding directly from its original source in life, stands exactly where it was at its first discovery. His text, for one familiar with it, might be reduced, without increase of the attention it demands, to the state of the unpunctuated scripts of old time. So rich and splendid is the fabric of sound he weaves upon the appointed loom, that his prose, chanted to his punctuation, in an unknown tongue, would serve as well as a mass—in D minor.

Yet even James, finding within bonds all the freedom he desired, did not quite escape the police. Down upon almost his last written words came the iron hand of Mr. Crosland, sternly, albeit most respectfully, recommending a strait-jacket in the shape of full-stops to be borrowed—from Mr. Bart Kennedy.[2,3] Whose stops are shouts. A pleasant jest. Relieving no doubt a long felt desire for the presence in Mr. James of a little ginger. But Crosland is austere. Sternly, with no intervals for laughter, he drags us headlong, breathless, belaboured, from jest to jest with never a smile or pause. It is his essential compactness that makes him a so masterly sonneteer. His sonnets gleam, now like metalled ships, now like jewels. Prose, in his sense, might be written like a sonnet. First the form, a well-balanced distribution of stops for each paragraph, and then the text. An interesting experiment.

---

1   A form of light physical exercise akin to calisthenics or yoga, emphasizing grace, balance, and attention, popular in the first quarter of the twentieth century.

2   Thomas William Hodgson Crosland (c. 1865-1924): English writer and editor, and a close friend of Lord Alfred Douglas (1870-1945), Oscar Wilde's (1854-1900) lover. After Wilde was jailed for homosexuality and Douglas converted to Catholicism, Crosland joined Douglas in persecuting another homosexual, Wilde's friend and literary executor, Robbie Ross (1869-1918).

3   Bart Kennedy (1861-1930): English writer. As a young man, Kennedy left England to work his way across the Atlantic Ocean and the North American continent, drawing upon those experiences for his series of "tramp" novels *A Man Adrift* (1899), *A Sailor Tramp* (1902), and *A Tramp in Spain* (1904). When he returned to England he married and pursued a successful writing career.

As interesting as that now on trial in a prose that is a conscious protest against everything that has been done to date by the hand of talent at work upon inspiration. But the dadaists, in so far as they are paying to the law the loud tribute of anarchy, are the counterparts of the strictly orthodox.

Meanwhile, for those who stand between purists and rebels, the rules of punctuation are neither sacred, nor execrable, nor quite absolute. No waving of the tablets of the law has been able to arrest organic adaptation. The test of irregularities is their effectiveness. Verbless phrases flanked by full-stops, the use of and at the beginning of a sentence, and kindred effective irregularities, are safe servants, for good, in the cause of the written word. And always there has been a certain variability in the use of the comma. As the shortest breath of punctuation it is allowed, without controversy, to wander a little.

Yet the importance of the comma cannot be exaggerated. It is the angel, or the devil, amongst the stops. In prose, everything turns upon its use. Misplaced, it destroys sense more readily than either of its fellows. For while their wanderings are heavy-footed, either at once obvious, or easily traceable, the comma plays its pranks unobtrusively. Used discreetly, it clears meaning and sets both tone and pace. And it possesses a charm denied to other stops. Innocence, punctuating at the bidding of a prompting from within, has the comma for its darling. Spontaneous commas are as delightful in their way as spontaneous spelling; as delightful as the sharp breath drawn by a singing child in the middle of a word.

Experiment with the comma, as distinct from recourse to its recognised variability, is to be found, since the stereotyping of the rules, only here and there and takes one form: its exclusion from sequences of adjectives. This exclusion suggests an awareness of the power of the comma as a holder-up, a desire to allow adjectives to converge, in the mind of the reader, as swiftly as possible upon their object. But one would expect to find, together with such awareness, discrimination. And, so far as I know, the exclusion of the comma when it is practised at all, is unvarying; the possibilities are missed as surely here, as they are in conformity to the letter of the law.

The use of the comma, whether between phrases or in sequences of adjectives, is best regulated by the consideration of its time-value. If, for example, we read:—

"Tom went singing at the top of his voice up the stairs at a run that ended suddenly on the landing in a collision with the sweep,"

we are brought sensibly nearer to sharing the incident than if we read:—

"Tom went, singing at the top of his voice, up the stairs, at a run that ended, suddenly, on the landing, in a collision with the sweep."

Conversely, if we read:—

"Tom stupid with fatigue fearing the worst staggered without word or sign of greeting into the room,"

we are further off than in reading:—

"Tom, stupid with fatigue, fearing the worst, staggered, without word or sign of greeting, into the room."

Even more obvious is the time-value of the comma in sequences of adjectives:—

"Suave low-toned question-begging excuses"

bears the same meaning as:—

"Suave, low-toned, question-begging excuses."

But the second is preferable.

"Huge soft bright pink roses"

may be written:—

"Huge, soft, bright, pink roses."

But the first wins.

It is a good plan, in the handling of phrases, to beware of pauses when appealing mainly to the eye, and to cherish them when appealing to reflection. With sequences of single words, and particularly of adjectives, when the values are concrete, reinforcing each other, accumulating without modification or contradiction upon a single object of sight, the comma is an obstruction. When the values are abstract, qualifying each other and appealing to reflection, or to vision, or to both vision and reflection at once, the comma is essential. If there is a margin of uncertainty, any possibility of ambiguity or misapprehension, it is best, no matter what is sacrificed of elasticity or of swiftness, to load up with commas. Or the reader may pay tax. And it is dangerous in these days of hurried readings to ask for the re-scanning even of a single phrase.

But there is woe in store, unless he be a prince of proof-readers, for the writer who varies his punctuation. The kindly hands that regulate his spelling will regulate also his use of stops; and, since hands are human, they will regulate irregularly. The result, when the author has altered the alterations, also irregularly, sometimes reading punctuation on to the page when it is not there—is chaos.

2. "The Disabilities of Women," *The Freewoman* 2.39 (15 August 1912): 254-55

[In this and the next three essays, Richardson works out some aspects of her feminism. As discussed in the Introduction to this volume (pp. 9-45), feminism and "the woman question" were extremely hot topics in the first half of the twentieth century, and Richardson was keenly interested in them. In addition to developing Miriam into a New

Woman through the novels, Richardson tackled the larger questions of social hygiene, women's health, and women's roles as cultural producers. This last in particular haunts all her engagements with feminism and sexism. Richardson advances from the beginning a perspective made much more famous by Virginia Woolf's 1929 essay *A Room of One's Own*: that given the same freedom from domestic worries, financial hardship, and dependency upon others that men enjoy, they would have produced as much if not more great art as men have. Richardson finds fault with the increasingly difficult circumstances under which women have had to work if they wished to write, and suggests that rather than wonder that women haven't produced more art, we should stand in awe of what they *have* done. Arguing, for example, that genius is common enough, but that talent and hard work are in short supply, Richardson claims that women have an abundance of the latter and would happily put it to use if they were not charged with ensuring the wellness and happiness of their families and indeed society as a whole. As these essays show, Richardson's is an eloquent voice in the cause of gender equality, and provides a strong endorsement of women's fundamental abilities as artists.]

The Feminist movement has been accompanied at every stage of its progress by an undertow of commentary from the medical profession. From eminent members of the fraternity hypnotic cries go up. For anti-feminists, of course, the statements of medical science have afforded the best possible arguments. They reproduce both the data and the ensuing deductions of the gynaecologists in a chorus of triumphant finality. The Feminists have also, almost with one accord, accepted the data of gynaecology; but they have at the same time disputed the conclusions—an attitude which is, in consideration of the necessary limitations of science (a point to which I shall return a little later), a much more reasonable one.

They have refused the conclusions, but have accepted the damning data; and with regard to these damning data they have taken up, in the main, two positions. They have agreed that what the doctors say is true enough as far as it goes, but that it applies only to pathological women, the class of women with which the medical profession is constantly dealing, and which inevitably colours their whole picture of life. Either they have agreed thus far, and then, as it were, taken out a brief for the rest of womankind, or they have admitted for all women whatsoever comparative physical disabilities, coupled with fundamental characteristics to be interpreted in terms of social value according to individual opinion, to personal assumptions and standards. They have claimed freedom in the name of these differences, and they have refused to accept masculine readings of life, masculine schemes of value. Generally they have accompanied this relatively constructive attitude with the assertion that the special functions of women need be no more disturbing to mental balance and judgment than are any functions of the body.

There is, however, a third possibility, one which has been, within the ranks of the protagonists, strangely neglected. This third way is open to anyone who will consider for a moment the necessary limitations of scientific work. The scientist for his business of observation and experiment is obliged to isolate one set of facts, to tear them from the context of reality. His perpetual occupation with this one set, his constant fixed gaze from one angle of vision, produces in him an increasing tendency to see all life through the peep-hole of his special science. Invaluable as are his results from the merely intellectual point of view, from the point of view of the accumulation and the classification of data in the interest of our progressive understanding and control of natural forces, the result of allowing him to step outside his special business of observation and report is, in the very large majority of cases, disaster. There is, it is true, here and there a man who can retain, even amidst the utmost complex of spectacular minutiae, his independence of mind, who escapes becoming the tool of his own point of view, who is capable of questioning and criticising the hypotheses, the original assumptions on which his science is based. But these types are rare. The vast majority of scientifically trained men are, as far as their science is concerned, followers. When the exceptional type occurs, it is likely that orthodox conclusions from data outspread are about to be swept away by some simplifying generalisation.

Simplifying generalisations have, of late years, been made by men and women here and there regarding the true nature, that is to say the actual position in the context of reality of such chronic infections as cancer and tuberculosis.

In the teeth of the increasing armies of orthodoxy, of the increasing acreage of hospitals and appliances, of the enormous sums of money devoted to research, they have maintained the falsity, for anything beyond diagnostic purposes, of looking at cancer and tuberculosis as things in themselves. They have, metaphorically, swept away the imposing paraphernalia of the bacteriologists, they have used and not been used by the science of bacteriology, and, undaunted by its mass of curious detail, have declared simply that these diseases are by-products of alimentary digestive errors, and must be treated via the nutritional function. I have chosen these instances because they are, now, comparatively flagrant and familiar. But this same "scrapping" of the deductions of orthodox medical science, both theoretically and practically, is taking place under our eyes to-day with regard to "feminine ailments."

Rational practice in this matter has been spreading sporadically over our civilisation for a couple of generations, and the simple underlying generalisation is reaching out feelers now into the very precincts of orthodoxy, and rescuing here and there a medical practitioner who has preserved his mental flexibility in spite of the schools. While orthodoxy is adding an extra week to the time a mother must remain in bed after the birth of her child, and become wiser and wiser as to the phenomenon known as "change of life,"[1] and its mental and moral accompaniments, independent common sense is maintaining the absolute controllability of the whole series of feminine ailments and disturbances.

The finest results in this direction have so far been attained by the fruitarians—i.e., those who base their dietary on raw fruit and salads. The food reform press of Europe produces, as I have pointed out elsewhere, every month increasing documentary evidence as to the immunity of fruitarian mothers from the disturbances and most of the unsightliness of pregnancy, the pain of childbirth, and the succeeding exhaustion, testimony as to the fineness of the children born, the easy persistence of ample natural nourishment for them, their freedom from tooth troubles, from those infectious disorders which are generally considered part of the programme of childhood, the disappearance of difficulties in relation to the arrival of maturity in girls, and to the cessation in women of the special functions.

Very significant in this connection is a book recently published on the Diseases of Women by an orthodox gynaecologist, who is not, however, a dietetic faddist. It is significant in three ways: First, as confessing in its preface that a leading idea of a most grave and fundamental character revolutionising his scientific outlook, came to him from outside: "The experience," he says, "has not been unmixed indeed with a certain amount of regret that such a suggestion in a medical matter of prime importance should have come from one who is not himself a qualified medical man. Truth, however, must be humbly received and assented to, from whatever quarter it may come; and for my part I welcome it gladly." Secondly, that many of the commonplaces of the "vegetarians" (many of the immunities above cited) are achieved by Dr. Rabagliati's patients by the application of their common-sense rules as to the how and the when of feeding, the distinction between hunger and its perversion—nervous appetite, the folly of "tempting" children to eat, the wisdom of accepting the hint of a day's voluntary fasting on the part of a child, the incompatibility of the digestive processes with perfect sleep, etc., etc. Thirdly, it is significant in that Dr. Rabagliati pays tribute to the

---

1 Menopause.

fruitarians for the reduction of childbirth to a comparatively painless and swift affair.

I may, perhaps, in this connection, profitably refer to a letter appearing earlier in the year in a German health paper, from a mother who, after four comparatively easy "vegetarian" confinements, achieved on a raw fruit and salad dietary, with occasional days of fasting, a pregnancy which passed unnoticed until the eleventh hour, and ended in the painless birth of her best child, brought into the world by her without assistance from man or woman, and without subsequent exhaustion.

The fact that infectious diseases and chronic infections such as tuberculosis and cancer, that influenzas, catarrhs, viscosities, all the migraines and "nerves" pains and penalties of the physical life of women are due to the imprisonment of the eager spirit of life in bodies clogged and weakened by malnutrition, the fact that they give way before rational diet is, in the opinion of the writer, worth a very great deal to the Feminist movement, and should effectually arm even those who are at present pathological against orthodoxy's list of "inherent disabilities."

3. "The Reality of Feminism," *The Ploughshare* 2 (September 1917): 241-46[1]

We commend our contributor's important essay to the attention of our readers; it passes in review several recent books, namely: "Towards a Sane Feminism," by Wilma Meikle (Grant Richards); "Woman and the Church," by the Rev. B.H. Streeter (T. Fisher Unwin); "Women in the Apostolic Church," by T.B. Allworthy (W. Heffer & Sons, Ltd.); "Woman's Effort," by A.E. Metcalfe (B.H. Blackwell).[2]

During the first few decades of its existence, English feminism was the conscious acceptance by women of the diagnosis of the cynics and an attempt to deal with this diagnosis by placing upon environment the major part of the responsibility for feminine "failings." It declared that the faults of women were the faults of the slave, and were due to repressions, educational and social. Remove these repressions, and the failings would disappear. Feminists of both sexes devoted them-

---

1 See the headnote to Appendix C2, p. 344.

2 Wilma Meikle (1887-1964): feminist thinker and activist. Meikle was a lover of both Rebecca West (1892-1983) and Mary Butts (1890-1937), as well as an acquaintance of Richardson's and H.G. Wells's. Rev. B.H. Streeter: Reverend Burnett Hillman Streeter (1876-1937) was a gospel scholar; "Woman and the Church" was co-authored with Edith Picton Turbervill (1872-1960), a social reformer and writer. T.B. Allworthy (1879-1964): an English vicar.

selves to securing for women educational and social opportunities equal to those of men. The "higher" education of women was their watchword, the throwing open of the liberal professions their goal, and the demonstration of the actual equality of women and men the event towards which they confidently moved. It followed that only a very small number of women was affected. Only one class of women, the class well-dowered by circumstance, could be counted upon to supply recruits for the demonstration of the intellectual "quality" of women. This feminism was, therefore, in practice, a class feminism—feminism for ladies. In principle much had been gained. The exclusively sexual estimate of women had received its death-blow. But it soon became apparent that academic education and the successful pursuit of a profession implied a renunciation of domesticity. The opening heaven of "emancipation" narrowed to the sad and sterile vista—feminism for spinsters. From that moment public opinion see-sawed between the alternatives of discrediting domesticity and of dividing women into two types—"ordinary" women, who married, and "superior" women, who did not. But for at least one whole generation the belief in academic distinction as the way of emancipation for women was unclouded by any breath of doubt. The reaction which was later on to produce the formula of "university standards in home training" had barely set in when the whole fabric of feminist theory was challenged by the appearance of Charlotte Stetson's "Women and Economics."[1] Opening her attack with a diagnosis of the female sex, which outdoes all the achievements of the cynics, she joined the earlier feminists in laying the responsibility for the plight of womanhood at the door of circumstance; but in a much more thorough-going fashion and with a backward and forward sweep which not only lifted the question out of the dimensions of an empirical problem and related it to the development of life as a whole, but purged it of the note of antagonism that characterises the bulk of feminist literature.

Agnes Edith Metcalfe (1870-1923): feminist activist and author of one other work in the same vein as *Woman's Effort*, *Woman: A Citizen* (1918), featuring a preface by "Mrs. Sidney Webb," that is, Beatrice Webb, Baroness Passfield (née Potter) (1858-1943). We are grateful to J. Matthew Huculak, Christine Walde, and Elizabeth Crawford for their help in identifying some of these individuals.

1   Charlotte Perkins Stetson (née Gilman) (1860-1935): American writer most famous for her short story "The Yellow Wallpaper" (1890), although some consider *Women and Economics* (1898) to be her single greatest work; its subtitle is "A Study of the Economic Relation between Men and Women as a Factor in Social Evolution."

Woman as a purely sexual product, said this American feminist, is a quite recent development in the western world; and it is commerce that has produced her. Woman was a differentiated social human being earlier than man. The "savage" woman who first succeeded in retaining her grown son at her side, invented social life. Up to the era of machinery, i.e., during the agricultural and civic centuries, the home was the centre of productive service. The scientific development of industry, while it did much to humanise the male—even though his commerce was as aggressive as his flint implements and his fleets of coracles—worked upon the female as a purely desocialising influence. By driving the larger industries from the homestead, it forced her either to follow them into the factory and workshop, to the destruction of home life, or to remain in a home that was no longer a centre of vital industries, but an isolated centre of consumption and destruction on a scale regulated entirely by the market value of its male owner. She became either an industrial pawn or a social parasite. Success on the part of the man completed her parasitic relationship to life by turning her into an increasingly elaborate consumer. Henceforth her sole asset was her sex, her sole means of expression her personal relationship to some specific male—father, brother, husband or son. She lived on her power to "charm." Sentiment flourished like a monstrous orchid. Home-life, over-focussed and over-heated, was cut off finally from the life of the world. Men kept their balance by living in two spheres, but the two spheres, "the world" and "the home" were so completely at variance that he could realise himself fully in neither, and was condemned to pose in each, to the annulling of his manhood. The average female, living by and through sex, missed womanhood, but achieved a sort of harmony by a thorough-going exploitation of sex. The home, all over-emphasised femininity, and the world, all over-specialised maleness, cancelled and nullified each other.

The way through this *impasse*, said Mrs. Stetson, was for women to follow the commercialised home industries into the world and to socialise them. Armies of women have been driven perforce into the industrial machine, heavily handicapped underlings, working under conditions they have been powerless to alter. They must now advance in a body, boldly and consciously, taking their old rank as producers, administrators, doing the world's housekeeping in the world. In order that they may do this, "homelife" as we know it, must be reorganised. The millions of replicas of tiny kitchens and nurseries, served by isolated women, must disappear. The world must become a home. In it women will pursue socially valuable careers, responsible to the community for their work, assured by the community of an economic status clear of sex and independent of their relationship to any specific male. They will spend their days at the work they can do best, whether nursery work, education, or mechanical engineering, finding their places in the social fabric as freely as do their brothers. Houses, communally cleansed and victualled,[1] will remain as meeting-places for rest and recreation.

It was impossible to ignore Mrs. Stetson's facts. Her challenge left English feminists in two distinct groups, the one standing for the sexual and economic independence of all women, irrespective of class, and working towards the complete socialisation of industry, the other ignoring or deprecating the industrial activities of women and standing for the preservation of the traditional insulated home; seeking to improve the status of women by giving them votes, solving woman's economic problem by training her in youth to earn her living, "if need be."

These two mutually exclusive groups were caught up into the suffrage campaign;[2] the one with the motive of transforming the conditions of female labour, the other because the capture of political power was part of the process of securing the recognition of the essential equality of women and men. The war has played into the hands of both parties by demonstrating the social efficiency of women and by giving an unprecedented urgency to the problem of woman in industry. The "equality" suffragists have secured a partial victory on the score of the proven ability of women to act as substitutes for men. The industrial suffragists rejoice in the spectacle of the disintegrated home, the inauguration of the municipal kitchen, and the fact that the promoters of infant welfare are more and more insistently emphasising the necessity for the municipal crèche.

Mrs. Stetson's forecast appears to be on the way to fulfilment, and those who are looking to the co-operation of women as the decisive factor in the achievement of the industrial revolution joyously welcome the independent and powerful restatement of Mrs. Stetson's main proposition that has recently come from the pen of Miss Wilma Meikle.[3] Miss Meikle is a very thorough-going feminist, and the vigour and beauty of her work—by far the best attempt at constructive feminism which has yet appeared in England—is obviously the product of a profound faith. She evidently sympathises with the militant phases of the suffrage movement in its spirit of pure revolt and self-assertion rather than with the aspects represented by "women delicately unaware of the kitchen side of politics, genteelly unacquainted with the stupendous significance of commerce, women who had been bred in drawing-rooms where the ruling class posed as men whose power was

---

1 Stocked with food.
2 The campaign to allow women to vote; it was not fully successful until 1928.
3 See headnote to this essay and p. 348, note 2.

based upon culture and oratory," women for whom "life was bowdlerised into a Mary Ward novel";[1] and she sympathises with the men who reach Parliament through sheer individual worth in public life rather than "obscure men like Thomas Babington Macaulay and Benjamin Disraeli,[2] who had been rushed into social eminence by their flowing rhetoric at Westminster."[3] But she is only incidentally a suffragist. The main argument of her book is a recantation of the whole of the suffrage movement. She is entirely sceptical as to the value of a parliamentary franchise[4] which leaves the industrial masses at the mercy of political legislation, and believes that the way to political power is through industrial power, through the trades union and the power of the worker to transform his environment and make his own terms. Women must build up their power upon the basis of industrial organisation. "They must serve and work, and they must join the workers' surging revolt against the denial of things that make existence life, their hunger for knowledge and their desire for leisure, and their determination to have both." It follows that "the lady," "delicately sympathetic, alluringly reticent, consistently courteous and skilfully environed," must go. She is, even at her best, comparable to the Circassian,[5] bred charmingly from her infancy to be the light of some good man's harem. Her caprices were an incentive to industrial enterprise, she helped the troubadours to invent "manners," she provided a market for the wares of the artist. But science and commerce and art are now no longer dependent on her greed. She is an anachronism. Home life must be re-organised to set her free to work.

"The great Domestic Cant of Good Wifehood and Good Motherhood has tied the average woman into such a tangle of hypocrisies

---

1   Mary Augusta Ward (1851-1920): Australian-born English writer who published under the name Mrs. Humphry Ward.
2   Thomas Babington Macaulay (1800-59): English historian and politician; his "Minute on Indian Education" (1835) introduced British-style education as a means of governing India. Benjamin Disraeli (1804-81): British politician and twice Prime Minister. The only British Prime Minister of Jewish descent, Disraeli was central in establishing the Conservative party in Britain. He closely aligned British Conservatism with the British Empire, and proved himself a formidable statesman. Alongside his political career, Disraeli was a prolific novelist, perhaps best known for his 1845 novel *Sybil, or The Two Nations*, which concerns the plight of the working class.
3   The English parliament is in Westminster, London.
4   Vote.
5   Circassia was an independent mountainous country in the Caucasus; Richardson refers here to the belief that Circassian women were often raised to be courtesans.

that she cannot unravel herself sufficiently to be a distinct personality.... Before long she is exhausted by hypocrisy. Her self-distrust lashes her to a duster, her determining to appear what she is not is a magnet that keeps her inextricably fastened to her servants or her cooking stove ... her nerves are racked by the effort to live up to the Good Mother ideal. There is no fun left in her."

With the Great Domestic Cant weighing our women down under "the absurdly complicated organisation of the family there remains no cause for wonder that in spite of higher education, in spite of feminism, original thought amongst women is almost non-existent." Her financial independence must be secured. She must learn to think her own thoughts and form her own judgments in contact with actuality. All the freedoms there are can be claimed by her without the vote once she demonstrates her industrial indispensability and organises her ranks against those who would exploit her. Parliamentary life will follow rather than precede feminine emancipation. Finally, women in the mass, set free from their dependence upon a single masculine pocket for everything they desire in addition to food and clothing, will find it possible to live a full life,

> "and the old restlessness which has almost universally lowered the value of their work will at last be stilled ... and with the full and final accomplishment of women's lives will come the end of feminism by its ultimate absorption into the common cause of humanity."

To many minds this vision of homeless womanhood caught equally with man in the industrial machine, interested equally with man in "earning a living," differentiated from man only by her occasional evanescent relationship to an infant, will bring nothing but dismay. They will see life shorn of roses and turned into a workshop. They will see the qualities that are "far above rubies"[1] and can never be paid for, going by the board. In other words, they attach more importance to environment than to humanity. They have no faith in the qualities they wish to "preserve." They have no faith in womanhood. The apparent overpreoccupation of the feminists with environment is a very different thing. It is based on faith in womanhood, although both its reasoning and its demands make it appear that they regard women as

---

1   Proverbs 31:10: "Who can find a virtuous woman? for her price is far above
    rubies" (King James Version). Richardson uses the line critically to suggest
    that it is part of a general misogyny that oppresses women in the name of pro-
    tecting their higher or more spiritual qualities from the rough-and-tumble of
    the working world.

potential men, obstructed by the over-elaborated machinery of the home.

But the fact of woman remains, the fact that she is relatively to man, *synthetic*. Relatively to man she sees life whole and harmonious. Men tend to fix life, to fix aspects. They create metaphysical systems, religions, arts, and sciences. Woman is metaphysical, religious, an artist and scientist in life. Let anyone who questions the synthetic quality of women ask himself why it is that she can move, as it were in all directions at once, why, with a man-astonishing ease, she can "take up" everything by turns, while she "originates" nothing? Why she can grasp a formula, the "trick" of male intellect, and the formula once grasped, so often beat a man at his own game? Why, herself "nothing," she is such an excellent critic of "things"? Why she can solve and reconcile, revealing the points of unity between a number of conflicting males—a number of embodied theories furiously raging together. Why the "free lance," the woman who is independent of any specific male, does this so excellently, and why the one who owes subsistence to a single male is usually loyally and violently partisan in public, and the wholesome opposite in private? And let him further ask himself why the great male synthetics, the artists and mystics, are three-parts woman? That women are needed "in the world" in their own right and because of their difference to men is clearly recognised in Canon Streeter's book on "Woman in the Church."[1] But for him difference constitutes inferiority. He confesses that the present bankruptcy of the church is largely owing to the exclusion of women, and he calls for a cautious and partial admission of women into the ministry. It is not, he thinks, advisable that they should be admitted to the priesthood as long as the priest stands in a position of authority. In a democratised church system women as priests might, in time, be thinkable. For the present, the completion of the male church might be brought about by a large co-operation of women in the work and the deliberations of the church. Incidentally, it occurs to him that such a recognition of the feminine element in religion would act as a curb to the heresy of Mariolatry.[2] In other words, women are to be admitted into a carefully regulated share in the working of a divine institution because during the centuries of their exclusion it has become progressively impotent, but they are to be excluded from its full powers and privileges because there is no divine principle in womanhood. Canon Streeter has never asked himself why Mariolatry has established itself tyrannously at the very heart of the liveliest system of man-made theology. He has made

---

1 See headnote to this essay and p. 348, note 2.
2 Excessive adoration or worship of the Virgin Mary, the mother of Jesus Christ; it is a charge often levelled at Catholics by Protestants.

nothing of the fact that a male priesthood, having usurped authority and driven women from the early position of workers side by side with men, ordained priests equally with men by the laying on of hands, immediately reinstated her, enthroned above them as the Queen of Heaven.[1] The Hebrew Jehovah, imagined as male, could not satisfy them. The deifying of Mary was an unconscious expression of their need to acknowledge the feminine element in Godhead.[2] Canon Streeter is the male Protestant, caught in the Protestant cul-de-sac "he for God only, she for God in him." The acknowledgment reached unconsciously in Mariolatry has been reached consciously by the "heresy" of Quakerism.[3] The early Quakers, wrapped as they were as "men" in secular fear and distrust of "woman," did not dare to deny her her human heritage of divine light and bravely took in the dark the leap of admitting her to full ministry. Only the Protestants have left her out altogether. Canon Streeter may reply that Quakerism is a democratised faith, and is heretical in its exclusion of priest and sacrament, thus underlining his dilemma. There is no alternative. Woman springs to the centre of an aristocratic church system—because men will have her there. She walks into a democratic church system, man's equal, in her own right. If Anglicanism,[4] to save its life, democratises itself and admits women to full fellowship, it will leave Catholicism in possession of the field as the typical classical church with Mariolatry a part of its system, the memorial for all time of the emptiness of the dream of male supremacy. A similar begging of the whole question of women in the ministry distinguishes Mr. T.B. Allworthy's[5] recent valuable contribution to the history of women in the Apostolic church.[6] He accounts for the activities of women in the early church by the fact that this church was social and not separated. Let the church once more become an integral part of social life and women will achieve their proper share in church life. How, one would like to ask, is the church to achieve the becoming an integral part of social life save by the free admission of women in their own right? The last book on our

---

1 Queen of Heaven is one of the epithets used to refer to the Virgin Mary in Catholicism.

2 Godhead: the substantial nature or essence of God.

3 Protestant movement, also known as the Religious Society of Friends, founded in the late seventeenth century and based upon belief in a direct personal relationship with God, without mediation by ordained priests or ministers.

4 A Protestant off-shoot of Catholicism, founded by English King Henry VIII in 1534, after the Pope opposed his request for a divorce from his wife.

5 See headnote to this essay and pp. 348-49, note 2.

6 A Pentecostal Christian denomination (i.e., Protestant).

list is a resume of all that women have done and suffered in their contest with the idea that a woman cannot be a legislator. Its author is of opinion that political enfranchisement is an essential part of feminine education, and Mr. Houseman, who contributes a preface, agrees in the sense that the great need of women is the need of a corporate consciousness, that such a consciousness was unattainable by her during the years of artificial segregation, and that it has been achieved by means of the agitation which has arisen for the ending of this segregation.

Taken together, these four books are a fairly inclusive statement of feminist thought to date. They are, in spite of their common tendency to contrast a "dark" past with a "bright" future, to separate environment from life and to regard environment as the more potent factor, a very remarkable convergence of recognition, coming from minds differing as to the why and wherefore, the ways and means of "feminism" upon the divine-human fact of womanhood. This is the essential thing. A fearless constructive feminism will re-read the past in the light of its present recognition of the synthetic consciousness of woman; will recognise that this consciousness has always made its own world, irrespective of circumstances. It can be neither enslaved nor subjected. Man, the maker of formulae, has tried in vain, from outside, to "solve the problem" of woman. He has gone off on lonely quests. He has constructed theologies, arts, sciences, philosophies. Each one in turn has stiffened into lifelessness or become the battleground of conflicting theories. He has sought his God in the loneliness of his thought-ridden mind, in the beauty of the reflex of life in art, in the wonder of his analysis of matter, in the curious maps of life turned out by the philosophising intellect. Woman has remained curiously untroubled and complete. He has hated and loved and feared her as mother nature, feared and adored her as the unattainable, the Queen of Heaven; and now, at last, nearing the solution of the problem, he turns to her as companion and fellow pilgrim, suspecting in her relatively undivided harmonious nature an intuitive solution of the quest that has agonised him from the dawn of things. At the same moment his long career as fighter and destroyer comes to an end; an end that is the beginning of a new glory of strife. In the pause of deadly combat he sees the long past in a flash. He had ceased in principle to be a fighter before the war. With the deliberate conscious ending of his role of fighter, with his deliberate renunciation of the fear of his neighbour will come the final metamorphosis of his fear of "woman." Face to face with the life of the world as one life he will find it his business to solve not the problem of "woman" who has gained at last the whole world for her home, but of man the specialist; the problem of the male in a world where his elaborate outfit of characteristics as fighter, in warfare, in trade, and in politics, is left useless on his hands.

4. "Talent and Genius: Is Not Genius Far More Common than Talent?," *Vanity Fair* 21 (October 1923): 118, 120[1]

When Plato[2] was planning his ideal commonwealth, he found the poets would not fit the pattern and proposed running them out of the town. Today, the poets, once discovered, run of their own accord. But genius, though its prestige has grown enormously since Plato's day, is still a thorn in the side of authority. It is also the central problem of modern psychology; and in their efforts to draw a circle round the phenomenon the psychologists have given the genius worshipping capacity of modern society some severe shocks. There was a bad quarter of an hour at the end of the century when they discovered its streak of madness, and the pundits of Decadence followed with much slaughtering of heroes.[3]

A little later we began to hear of the subconscious.[4] Uncanny but comforting, a capacious hold-all for mysteries. And common humanity, discovered in possession of this amazing *arrière-boutique*,[5] was more interesting than ever. Hidden away within the workaday being of every one of us, unchanging, illimitable, and ever new, was the source of art, love and religion; the smiling kingdom of Heaven. We had heard this before. But here was the science for it. Science and faith had kissed each other. We could rejoice in peace.

We rejoiced. Until we were startled by the announcement that someone had found the way into the subconscious, investigated the premises and discovered all our activities at their single simple source. His report was humiliating, until we realized that we were hearing, not bad news about humanity, but good news about sex.[6] If not only our "genius," art, philosophy and religion, but every one of our activities, is a sublimation of—or a failure to sublimate—the sex impulse, we are not less wonderful, but sex much more wonderful than we had sup-

---

1   See the headnote to Appendix C2, p. 344.
2   Greek philosopher (427-347 BCE) whose *Republic* (c. 380 BCE) outlined an ideal society governed by philosopher-kings and from which poets were banished as professional liars.
3   Decadence was a movement of the 1890s (or *fin-de-siècle*) in which people relished artifice over the natural.
4   Allusion to the psychoanalytic work of Sigmund Freud (1856-1939), Austrian psychologist and founder of psychoanalysis.
5   French: back room.
6   Freud posited that libido (sexual energy as sublimated by the ego) drives much, if not all, human behaviour.

posed. And psychology, in shifting the smile of the sphinx, is as far as ever from solving her riddle.[1]

There was once an irritable man of genius who brushed the problem away. Tush, said he, genius is a plain and simple thing. Genius is an infinite capacity for taking pains. His formula has deservedly held its own. It fulfils the one demand of a good definition. It defines. But it does not define genius. It defines talent, which is something far rarer.

THE SECRET OF DARWIN

It defines the ants, amongst the humbler orders of consciousness the most talented. It defines the great Darwin.[2] We are accustomed to speak of the mighty genius of Darwin. Because his theory shattered our world, and rebuilt it, very far away from our hearts' desire. It forced us to live, until the genius of Samuel Butler[3] set Darwin's facts in their right order in the context of reality, in a gloomy and uncertain twilight. Looking back to the sunshine of earlier days, we were tempted to wish that Darwin had never been born to enlighten our minds and sadden our hearts. Between whiles we were inordinately proud of him; hard-headed Darwinians with no nonsense about us. What a Titan England had produced! A Colossus, bestriding the world![4]

Then the human documents began to appear. His life and letters, the lives and letters of those who had known him. And the Colossus

---

1   The Egyptian statue of the sphinx, a mythical half-woman/half-lion figure, stood at a crossroads near the ancient Greek city of Thebes. Its enigmatic smile gave rise to the legend that it once lived and posed a riddle to all travellers: what has four legs in the morning, two legs at mid-day, and three in the evening? The answer is humans, who crawl on four legs in infancy (morning), walk on two legs in the middle of life (mid-day), and use a cane as a third "leg" in old age (evening). When Oedipus solved the riddle, the sphinx was so angry that she threw herself from a cliff to her death.

2   For Darwin, see p. 60, note 3.

3   Samuel Butler (1835-1902): controversial English writer whose writings, whether on evolution (*Evolution, Old & New* [1879]), Christianity (*God the Known and God the Unknown* [1879]), Homeric myth (*Authoress of the Odyssey* [1897]) or technology (*The Book of the Machines* [1863]), managed to upset all sides of any debate he entered. He is best remembered for the satirical utopian novel *Erewhon, or Over the Range* (1872) and *The Way of all Flesh* (1903).

4   Titans: in Greek myth, a race of giant gods eventually overthrown by the Olympian gods, led by Zeus. Colossus: legendary enormous statue with one foot planted on either side of the harbour entrance on the isle of Rhodes.

was nowhere to be found. In the whole record there is not a trace of any one of the characteristics of genius. From first to last not a single eccentricity. Nothing in the least gey ill to live with. And so distressed was this sweet and simple soul over the moral earthquake he had produced, so far from desiring to change the placid little world of his day, that he flouted his own theory to the extent of saying that it need not interfere with religious belief.

Our Darwin was no genius. He was a supremely talented naturalist. A naturalist with an infinite capacity for taking pains. With the enormous, unflagging industry of the semi-invalid, he collected and observed in his own small field; and presently there stood before his eyes his theory, ready-made.

THE MIDWIFE OF GENIUS

But in regarding genius as ordinary, Carlyle was right.[1] If anything can be called ordinary, genius can. To say that genius is universal, that we all have it more or less, is to give utterance to a truism that has never had a night out. But more specifically, we may assert that genius is very ordinary and talent rare; that genius exists potentially in every woman and is sometimes found in men; that many men and a few women have talent.

But though separable, talent, that which does, and genius, that which sees, ought never to be separated. Talent, though the more independent of the two and able, given sufficient specialist knowledge, without possessing a scrap of wisdom, to make a tremendous noise in the world and draw down much limelight, does its best with genius behind it. Genius is helpless without talent. If anything is to be born of it there must be conscious laborious work on the original inspiration. Talent is the midwife of genius. Unschooled genius is apt to reel to its doom, dealing out destruction as it goes. The gift of genius in the individual is nothing for human boasting. Its only righteousness is in the development of the talents that belong to it.

What then of Jane Austen, producing a masterpiece, a perfect balance of genius and talent, in girlhood? What of Shakespeare?[2]

Well, in the first place, we are all, even though we may not lisp in numbers, born within the medium of literary art, and begin our struggle with it even before we can speak. And the phenomenon of Jane

1   Thomas Carlyle (1795-1881): Scottish philosopher, writer, and historian.
2   Jane Austen (1775-1817): English writer. It is not clear to what Richardson refers here. Austen's earliest significant work is *Sense and Sensibility* (1811), published when Austen was 36 years old and nearly twenty years in the making. William Shakespeare (1564-1616): English playwright.

Austen's masterpiece produced casually in a few weeks has recently been changed to the normal spectacle of long patient labor upon the original conception. Shakespeare is admittedly inexplicable. A child essayist described him the other day as "a man who wrote plays with a marvelous command of highflown language."

The "highflown" language could be picked up in the fifteenth century almost anywhere. A poet of simple birth, by frequenting the best circles, would find himself swimming in it. But the command, the intensive culture, the perfect gentlemanly sophistication—these things together in a casual barn-strutter, a man humbly reared, and excluded from the best circles by what, in his day, was held to be a low trade, have so shocked our sense of probability that many minds have clutched willingly at any theory, no matter how grotesque, that offered escape from the outrage on common sense. And now there is Mr. Looney, whose careful, unflustered observation of the surrounding facts, has at last unearthed and given to the world the simple, obvious, astounding explanation.[1]

THE ABUSE OF TALENT

There is, of course, the other side of the picture. Genius either in the community or in the individual, may be stifled by talent. See the havoc played with the synthetic stupor of woman when first she emerged, in numbers, into the analytic partisan fighting world of men.

The feminine intelligentsia, the product of fifty years "higher education," are usually brilliant creatures. There is a great show of achievement in the arts and sciences to their credit. Almost none of it bears the authentic feminine stamp. Almost the whole could be credited to men. But this blind docility, so disastrous to women, and still more disastrous to the men who mould them, is a phase already passing. Feminine genius is finding its way to its own materials.

Of the lack of balance between talent and genius in the individual, there is a painfully perfect example in a man whose work is a permanent battle-ground of *doctrinaires*, Gustave Flaubert.[2] Lack of balance is always comic, to the spectator. But comedy is tragedy standing on its head. And the comedy of Gustave Flaubert is like all other comedies, exasperating the spectacle of needless tumult.

Flaubert's genius was a passion for pure form. It gave birth to the

---

1 John Thomas Looney (1870-1944): English teacher and originator of the Oxfordian theory, which holds that the plays ascribed to William Shakespeare were in fact written by Edward de Vere, 17th Earl of Oxford (1550-1604).

2 Gustave Flaubert (1821-80): French writer best known for his 1857 novel *Madame Bovary*.

now famous stylistic dogma of statement without commentary. But his magnificent talents, his infinite capacity for taking literary pains, were too much for him. His lifelong struggle leaves us *Salammbô* a pure exotic and one of the sacred books of the aesthetes; *Saint Antoine*, his masterpiece *manqué*, a grand conception reduced to nullity by too much scholarliness; *Madame Bovary*, a study from a living model chosen for him by brother artists to keep his literary genius within bounds, and chosen later by the reading public to represent him.[1] Here his genius and his talent run neck to neck, and his friends stand justified in their choice. But an examination *de haut en bas* of a "small soul" is not great literature.

Then there is the neglected document of the *Education Sentimentale*, the unfinished cynical extravaganza, *Bouvard et Pécuchet* and three short stories, two of which, *St. Julien* and *Un Coeur Simple*, are miniature masterpieces, perhaps the most perfect miniatures in literature.[2] They stand also the decisive test of great literature; the wayfaring man, though a fool, shall not err therein.

One man, two small masterpieces. What more, it may be asked, is needed? But one cannot get away from the pity of the limitation of Flaubert's production, from the waste of his life, the vanity of his sufferings. With the whole document before us in his most self-revealing letters, his letters to George Sand,[3] the trouble is insipidly lucid. His loathing of humanity, his continuous depression, his lauding of his martyrdom to the skies, all cry aloud his mishandling of his genius.

George, she who was all genius and precious little talent, might have freed him if she had been younger and had had him for a while under her thumb. She would have cured his spinsterish inability to leave his work alone, to refrain from niggling over it until it went stale on his hands. As it was, she sat amongst her family and friends at Nohant,[4] pouring out her novels on the backs of envelopes and tradesman's bills, and begged him to refrain from bitterness, to come out

---

1 *Salammbô* (1862); *La tentation de Saint Antoine* (1874); *Madame Bovary* (1857). By comparison with some of his contemporaries (e.g., Honoré de Balzac [1799-1850] or Émile Zola [1840-1902]), Flaubert's literary output is scant, in large part because he insisted on finding *le mot juste* (the correct word), avoiding cliché and honing his style obsessively.

2 *L'Éducation sentimentale* (1869); *Bouvard et Pécuchet* (1881); "St. Julien" and "Un Coeur Simple" are collected in *Trois Contes* (1877).

3 George Sand (1804-76), pen-name of French writer Amantine Lucile Aurore Dupin, was a prolific novelist, critic, and political commentator. Her correspondence with Flaubert (a close friend) holds some of the key insights into Flaubert's thinking about his literary efforts, and his commitment to style.

4 A small town in central France. Sand was raised in Nohant, eventually dying there in 1876; she is buried on the grounds of her family's home there.

into life and enlarge himself. It was his method, not his life, that needed enlarging. "Try," he writes to George, "to have a great deal of talent, and even genius if you can." *Try* to have genius. These words epitomize his life.

GENIUS AND LIFE

In life, as in art, our achievements are born of the marriage of genius and talent. The driving force behind success is genius. The name of the firm is Vision & Practical Ability, Inc.

The personal records of great public men almost invariably reveal feminine genius in the background. Yet, so far in our history, it is obvious that the balance has been weighted on the side of talent. That specialist knowledge, the ability to do, has been divorced from wisdom, the ability to see. It is not for nothing that men have been defined as those who look without seeing and women as those who see without looking. Again and again civilization, that proud achievement of the talents of men, getting ahead of vision, has led with monotonous reiteration, down to disaster. Each picture has been proudly hung, but the surrounding household has been wrecked in the process. And though nothing is more foolish than to cry up one sex at the expense of the other, and to imagine that the single genius of woman will "save the world," it is perhaps not quite unreasonable to suppose that the vicious circle will be broken by the inclusion, in public affairs, of the dynamic power that has been, so far, almost universally short-circuiting in the home.

5. **"Women and the Future: A Trembling of the Veil before the Eternal Mystery of 'La Giaconda,'"** *Vanity Fair 22* **(April 1924): 39-40**[1]

Most of the prophecies born of the renewed moral visibility of woman, though superficially at war with each other, are united at their base. They meet and sink, in the sands of the assumption that we are, today, confronted with a new species of woman.

Nearly all of the prophets, nearly all of those who are at work constructing hells, or heavens, upon this loose foundation, are men. And their crying up, or down, of the woman of today, as contrasted to the woman of the past, is easily understood when we consider how difficult it is, even for the least prejudiced, to *think* the feminine past, to

---

1 See the headnote to Appendix C2, p. 344. *La Gioconda* is the Italian original name of the painting better known in English as the *Mona Lisa*.

escape the images that throng the mind from the centuries of masculine expressiveness on the eternal theme: expressiveness that has so rarely reached beyond the portrayal of woman, whether Madonna, Diana, or Helen, in her moments of relationship [*sic*] to the world as it is known to men.[1]

Even the pioneers of feminism, Mill, Buckle,[2] and their followers, looked only to woman as she was to be in the future, making, for her past, polite, question-begging excuses. The poets, with one exception, accepted the old readings. There is little to choose between the visions of Catholic Rossetti and Swinburne the Pagan. Tennyson, it is true, crowns woman, elaborately, and withal a little irritably, and with much logic-chopping. But he never escapes patronage, and leaves her leaning heavily, albeit most elegantly, upon the arm of man. Browning stands apart, and Stopford Brooke will not be alone in asking what women themselves think of Browning's vision of woman as both queen and lord, outstripping man not only in the wisdom of the heart, but in that of the brain also.[3]

And there is Meredith—with his shining reputation for understanding; a legend that by far outruns his achievement. Glimpses of woman as a full cup unto herself, he certainly had. And he reveals much knowledge of men as they appear in the eyes of such women. This it is that has been accounted unto him for righteousness. He never sees that he is demanding the emancipation of that which he has shown to be independent of bonds. Hardy, his brother pagan and counterpart, is Perseus hastening to Andromeda, seeking the freedom of the bound.[4]

Since the heyday of Meredith and Hardy, batallions [*sic*] of women have become literate and, in the incandescence of their revelations, masculine illusions are dying like flies. But, even today, most men are

---

1 Madonna: the Virgin Mary; Diana: Greek goddess of the hunt; Helen: in Homer's *Iliad* (c. 1190 BCE), the woman over whom the Trojan War was fought.

2 John Stuart Mill (1806-73): English philosopher and political economist; Henry Thomas Buckle (1821-62): English historian.

3 Dante Gabriel Rossetti (1828-82): English poet, illustrator, and painter; Algernon Charles Swinburne (1837-1909): English poet and novelist; Alfred, Lord Tennyson (1809-92): English poet; Robert Browning (1812-89): English poet and playwright; Stopford Brooke (1832-1916): Irish churchman and writer.

4 George Meredith (1828-1909): English writer; Thomas Hardy (1840-1928): English writer; Perseus: hero of Greek myth who rescues Andromeda, who has been chained to a rock as a sacrifice to a sea monster to appease Poseidon after Andromeda's mother Cassiopeia has bragged that she is even more beautiful than Poseidon's daughters, the Nereids.

scarely [*sic*] aware of the searchlight flung by these revelations across the past. These modern women, they say, are a new type.

It does not greatly matter to women that men cling to this idea. The truth about the past can be trusted to look after itself. There is, however, no illusion more wasteful than the illusion of beginning all over again; nothing more misleading than the idea of being divorced from the past. It is, nevertheless, quite probable that feminine insistence on exhuming hatchets is not altogether a single-hearted desire to avoid waste and error.

Many men, moreover, are thoroughly disconcerted by the "Modern Woman."[1] They sigh for ancient mystery and inscrutability. For La Giaconda ... And the most amazing thing in the history of Leonardo's[2] masterpiece is their general failure to recognize that Lisa[3] stands alone in feminine portraiture because she is centered, unlike her nearest peers, those dreamful, passionately blossoming imaginations of Rossetti, neither upon humanity nor upon the consolations of religion.

THE ESSENTIAL EGOIST

It is because she is so completely there that she draws men like a magnet. Never was better artistic bargain driven than between Leonardo and this lady who sat to him for years; who sat so long that she grew at home in her place, and the deepest layer of her being, her woman's enchanted domestication within the sheer marvel of existing, came forth and shone through the mobile mask of her face. Leonardo of the innocent eye, his genius concentrated upon his business of making a good picture, caught her, unawares, on a gleeful cosmic holiday. And in seeking the highest, in going on till he got what he wanted, he reaped also the lesser things. For there is in Lisa more than the portrayal of essential womanhood. The secondary life of the lady is clearly visible. Her traffic with familiar webs, with her household and the external shapings of life. When Pater[4] said that her eyelids were a little weary, he showed himself observant. But he misinterpreted the weariness.

On the part of contemporary artists, there are, here and there,

---

1 "The Woman Question," or the problem presented by the "New Woman" who eschewed domestic life for a career, education, and independence, was a prominent social issue in the first quarter of the twentieth century. See Introduction, pp. 9-45.

2 Leonardo da Vinci (1452-1519): Italian artist, musician, inventor, mathematician, cartographer, botanist, and writer. He painted the *Gioconda* (*Mona Lisa*).

3 That is, Mona Lisa.

4 Walter Pater (1839-94): English writer and critic.

attempts to resuscitate man's ancient mystery woman, the beloved-hated abyss. The intensest and the most affrighted of these essayists are D.H. Lawrence and Augustus John.[1] Perhaps they are nearer salvation than they know.

For the essential characteristic of women is egoism. Let it at once be admitted that this is a masculine discovery. It has been offered as the worst that can be said of the sex as a whole. It is both the worst and the best. Egoism is at once the root of shameless selfishness and the ultimate dwelling place of charity. Many men, of whom Mr. Wells[2] is the chief spokesman, read the history of woman's past influence in public affairs as one long story of feminine egoism. They regard her advance with mixed feelings, and face her with a neat dilemma. Either, they say, you must go on being Helens and Cinderellas,[3] or you must drop all that and play the game, in so far as your disabilities allow, as we play it. They look forward to the emergence of an army of civilized, docile women, following modestly behind the vanguard of males at work upon the business of reducing chaos to order.

Another group of thinkers sees the world in process of feminisation, the savage wilderness, where men compete and fight, turned into a home. Over against them are those who view the opening prospect with despair. To them, feminism is the invariable accompaniment of degeneration.[4] They draw back in horror before the oncoming flood of mediocrity. They see ahead a democratized world, overrun by hordes of inferior beings, organized by majorities for material ends; with primitive, uncivilizable woman rampant in the midst.

Serenely apart from these small camps is a large class of delightful beings, the representatives of average masculinity at its best, drawing

---

1 David Herbert Lawrence (1885-1930): English writer; Augustus John (1878-1961): Welsh artist. In novels such as *Sons and Lovers* (1913), *The Rainbow* (1915), and *Lady Chatterley's Lover* (1928), Lawrence queries the nature of authentic, free sexual relationships between men and women, even as he affirms standard or conventional understandings of masculinity and femininity. John was associated with post-impressionist painting techniques akin to those of Paul Gauguin (1848-1903) and Henri Matisse (1869-1954), and made his name as a portraitist. In keeping with the "beloved-hated" ambivalence Richardson attributes to their depictions of true womanly women, Richardson reads Lawrence's and John's public comments as signs of both intensity and fear (hence "affrighted").

2 For H.G. Wells, see p. 326, note 1.

3 Helen: see p. 363, note 1; Cinderella: heroine of a folk tale first published in 1697 as part of Charles Perrault's (1628-1703) *Histoires ou contes du temps passés*.

4 This view is epitomized by Max Nordau's (1849-1923) 1892 book *Entartung (Degeneration)*.

much comfort from the spectacle of contradictory, mysterious woman at last bidding fair to become something recognizably like itself. Women, they say, are beginning to take life like men; are finding in life the things men have found. They make room for her. They are charming. Their selfishness is social, gregarious. Woman is to be the jolly companion; to co-operate with man in the great business of organizing the world for jollity. But have any of these so variously grouped males any idea of the depth and scope of feminine egoism? Do they not confound it with masculine selfishness? Do they realize anything of the vast difference between these two things?

It is upon the perception of this difference that any verdict as to the result of woman's arrival "in the world" ultimately rests. Though, *it is true* certain of these masculine forecasts *are* being abundantly realized. There is abroad in life a growing army of man-trained women, brisk, positive rational creatures with no nonsense about them, living from the bustling surfaces of the mind; sharing the competitive partisanships of men; subject, like men, to fear; subject to national panic; to international, and even to cosmic panic. There is also an army let loose of the daughters of the horse-leech; part of the organization of the world for pleasure. These types have always existed. The world of the moment particularly favours them. But their egoism is as nothing to the egoism of the womanly woman,[1] the beloved-hated abyss, at once the refuge and the despair of man.

For the womanly woman lives, all her life, in the deep current of eternity, an individual, self-centered. Because she is one with life, past, present, and future are together in her, unbroken. Because she thinks flowingly, with her feelings, she is relatively indifferent to the fashions of men, to the momentary arts, religions, philosophies, and sciences, valuing them only in so far as she is aware of their importance in the evolution of the beloved. It is man's incomplete individuality that leaves him at the mercy of that subtle form of despair which is called ambition, and accounts for his apparent selfishness. Only completely self-centered consciousness can attain to unselfishness the celebrated unselfishness of the womanly woman. Only a complete self, carrying all its goods in its own hands, can go out, perfectly, to others, move freely in any direction. Only a complete-self can afford to man the amusing spectacle of the chameleon woman.

---

1 Richardson advances here her notion of the woman who is at once in tune with her femininity and yet not oppressed by men, neither emulating them nor submitting to them. The notion is central to her commitment to discovering a feminine form of prose that would articulate women's consciousness and experience on its own terms, in contrast to both staying silent and imitating men's writing.

Apart from the saints, the womanly woman is the only human being free to try to be as good as she wants to be. And it is to this inexorable creature, whom even Nietzsche[1] was constrained to place ahead of man, that man returns from his wanderings with those others in the deserts of agnosticism.[2] She is rare. But wherever she is found, there also are found the dependent hosts.

But is not the material of this intuitive creature strictly limited? Is she not fettered by sex? Seeking man, while man, freed by nature for his divine purpose, seeks God, through blood and tears, through trial and error, in every form of civilization? He for God only, she for God in him? She is. She does. When man announces that the tree at the door of the cave is God, she excels him in the dark joy of the discovery. When he reaches the point of saying that God is a Spirit and they that worship him must worship him in spirit and in truth, she is there waiting for him, ready to parrot any formula that shows him aware of the amazing fact of life.

And it is this creature who is now on the way to be driven out among the practical affairs of our world, together with the "intelligent" woman; i.e., with the woman who is intelligible to men. For the first time. Unwillingly. The results cannot be exactly predicted. But her gift of imaginative sympathy, her capacity for vicarious living, *for* being simultaneously in all the warring camps, will tend to make her within the council *of nations* what the Quaker is within the council of religions.[3]

---

1   Friedrich Nietzsche (1844-1900): German philosopher who celebrated an affirmative brand of nihilism, averring that there is no absolute truth, but also that this absence of truth affords unlimited opportunity for fulfilling human potential. He celebrated the power of the will over any constraint. Though he is popularly thought to be misogynistic and anti-Semitic, his work is nuanced and sophisticated in ways that make such charges difficult to sustain.

2   A stance of indecision about the existence of God or an afterlife, based upon the assertion that it is not possible for humans to know to a certainty one way or the other.

3   For Quakers, see p. 355, note 3 above. With "council of religions," Richardson may be referring to the World's Parliament of Religions, first convened in Chicago in 1893 in an attempt to create a global dialogue of faiths. As pacifists and non-proselytizing, the Quakers are notable for going their own quiet way, prioritizing a personal relationship with God over doctrinal issues and/or expansion of the faith.

6. "Women in the Arts: Some Notes on the Eternally Conflicting Demands of Humanity and Art," *Vanity Fair* 24 (May 1925): 47, 100[1]

It is only lately that the failure of women in the fine arts has achieved pre-eminence in the *cause célèbre*, Man versus Woman, as a witness for the prosecution. In the old days, not only was art not demanded of women, but the smallest sign of genuine ability in a female would put a man in the state of mind of the lady who said when she saw the giraffe: "I don't believe it."

Thus Albrecht Dürer, travelling through the Netherlands in 1521 and happening upon the paintings of Susanne Horebout, makes appreciative notes in his diary, but is constrained to add: "Amazing that a she-creature should accomplish so much." And some three hundred years later, Gustave Flaubert, standing at the easel of Madame Commanville, smiles in*dulgently* and murmurs: "Yes, she has talent; *it is odd*."[2]

But today, under pressure of the idea that women in asserting equality, have also asserted identity with men, the demand for art as a supporting credential has become the parrot-*cry* of the masculinists of both sexes. A cry that grows both strident and hoarse. For this pre-eminent witness for the prosecution is, poor fellow, shockingly over-worked. And not only *over-worked* but also a little uneasy. Feeling *no* doubt, since most of his fellows have been hustled away in disgrace and those that remain are apt to wilt in the hands of defending counsel, that his own turn may be at hand.

But though towering a little insecurely still he towers, at once the last refuge of all who are frightened by anything that disturbs their vision of man as the dominant sex, and the despair of those feminists who believe fine art to be the highest human achievement.

There are of course many, an increasing band, who flatly deny that art is the highest human achievement and place ahead of it all that is called science, which they are inclined to regard as the work of human-ity's post-adolescence. But it is a curious and notable fact, a fact quite as curious and notable as the absence of first-class feminine art, that all these people, whenever they want to enlighten the layman on the subject of the scientific imagination, are at pains to explain that the sci-entific imagination, at its best, is the imagination of the artist. It is not

---

1 See the headnote to Appendix C2, p. 344.

2 Albrecht Dürer (1471-1528): German artist and mathematician; Susanne Horebout, actually Susanna(h) Hornebolt (or Horenbout) (1503-45): first known female artist in England; for Flaubert, see p. 360, note 2; Caroline Commanville (née Hamard) (1846-1931): Flaubert's niece.

less odd that the man of science if he is masculinist, will, when hard-pressed, seize, to belabour his opponent, not the test-tube, but the mahlstick.[1] (It is of course to be remembered that while the mahlstick is solid and persists unchanging, the test-tube is hollow and its contents variable.) And the rush for the mahlstick goes on in spite of the fact that the witness for science does not, on the whole, have a bad time. He has perhaps lost a little of his complacency. But he can still, when counsel for the defense reminds the jury how recently women have had access to scientific material and education, point to the meager, uninstructed beginnings of some of the world's foremost men of science.

Side by side with the devotees of science we find those who count religion as the highest human achievement. They are a house divided. In so far as they set in the van the mystic—the religious genius who uses not marble or pigment or the written word, but his own life as the medium of his art—they supply a witness for the defense who points to Catherine and Teresa walking abreast with Francis and Boehme.[2] But their witness is always asked what he makes of the fact that Jesus, Mahomed, and Buddha are all of the sex male.[3] His prompt answer: that he looks not backward but ahead, leaves things, even after he has pointed to Mrs. Eddy and Mrs. Besant, a little in the air.[4] For Catholic feminists there is always the Mother of God. But they are rare, and as it were under an editorial ban. Privately they must draw much comfort from the fact that the Church which, since the days of its formal organization has excluded woman from its ultimate sanctities, is yet constrained to set her above it, crowned Queen of Heaven.[5]

---

1   A metre-long pole with a ball at one end, used as a lever/platform to keep one's arm off the wet part of a painting while finishing detail work.

2   St. Catherine of Alexandria (c. 282-c. 305), St. Teresa of Avila (1515-82), St. Francis of Assisi (1182-1226), and Jakob Böhme (1575-1624) are all canonical figures in Christian history; three are saints and Böhme, a Protestant, is a mystic and theologian.

3   Jesus Christ (c. 7 BCE-33 CE): the messiah and son of God in Christian religions; Mahomed (or Mohammed) (570-632): the chosen prophet of Allah in Islamic religions; Buddha: the sacred name of Siddhartha Gautama (563-483 BCE), the spiritual leader of Buddhist religions.

4   Mary Baker Eddy (1821-1910): founder of the Christian Science religious movement; Annie Besant (1847-1933): famous secularist and activist. Politically active from an early age, Besant soon gravitated toward Theosophy, her work with which took her to India. In India, she became involved with politics, joined the Indian National Congress, and fought for Home Rule for India (i.e., relative independence from the British Empire). She was elected president of the Indian National Congress in 1917, and worked for both Theosophy and Indian independence until her death in 1933.

5   I.e., the Virgin Mary, mother of Christ.

Last, but from the feminist point of view by no means least of those who challenge the security of the one solidly remaining hope of the prosecution, are the many who believe, some of them having arrived at feminism via their belief, that the finest flowers of the human spirit are the social arts including the art of dress. In vain is their witness reminded of the man modiste,[1] the pub and the club. He slays opposition with lyrics, with idylls of the Primitive Mother forming, with her children, society, while father slew beasts and ate and slept.[2] And side by side with the pub at its best he places the salon at its best, and over against Watt and his dreamy contemplation of the way the light steam plays with the heavy lid of the kettle—a phenomenon, thunders the prosecution, that for centuries countless women have witnessed daily in animal stupidity—he sets Watt's mother, seeing the lifting lid as tea for several weary ones.[3]

But in all this there is no comfort for the large company of feminists who sincerely see the fine arts as humanity's most godlike achievement. For them the case, though still it winds its interminable way, is settled. There is no escape from the verdict of woman's essential inferiority. The arraignment is the more flawless because just here, in the field of art, there has been from time immemorial, a fair field and no favour. Always women have had access to the pen, the chisel and the instrument of music. Yet not only have they produced no Shakespeare, no Michelangelo and no Beethoven, but in the civilization of today, where women artists abound, there is still scarcely any distinctive feminine art. The art of women is still on the whole either mediocre or derivative.

There is, of course, at the moment, Käthe Kollwitz,[4] Mother and Hausfrau to begin with, and, in the estimation of many worthy critics, not only the first painter in Europe today but a feminine painter—one that is to say whose work could not have been produced by a man. She

---

1 French: milliner.
2 Richardson alludes here to the argument that it was mothers in settlements who established society while the men were hunting and resting.
3 James Watt (1736-1819): Scottish inventor and engineer who most famously invented the steam engine after watching the heavy iron lid of a kettle lifted off the pot by built-up steam pressure. Richardson refers here to the notion that it took Watt but one observation to invent one of the most important devices in the industrial world, while women have observed the same phenomenon for centuries without ever making the connection, because they saw not a mechanical phenomenon but nourishment for their families instead. Richardson is gesturing toward the backhanded anti-feminism that argues that women are essential to society, perhaps even its very originators, but ultimately unsuited for science, industry, politics, and public life.
4 Käthe Kollwitz (1867-1945): German artist. Hausfrau: German: housewife.

it may be is the Answer to Everything. For though it is true that one swallow does not make a summer, the production by the female sex of even one supreme painter brings the whole fine arts argument to the ground and we must henceforth seek the cause of woman's general lack of achievement in art elsewhere than in the idea that first-class artistic expression is incarnate in man alone.

Let us, however suppose that there is no Käthe Kollwitz, assume art to be the highest human achievement, accept the great arraignment and in the interest of the many who are driven to cynicism by the apparent impossibility of roping women into the scheme of salvation, set up the problem in its simplest terms. Cancel out all the variable factors; the pull of the home on the daughter, celibacy, the economic factor and the factor of motherhood, each of which taken alone may be said by weighting the balance to settle the matter out of court and taken all together make us rub our eyes at the achievements of women to date—cancel out all these and imagine for a moment a man and a woman artist side by side with equal chances and account if we can for the man's overwhelming superiority.

There is before we can examine our case one more factor to rule out—isolated here because it grows, in the light of modern psychological investigation, increasingly difficult to state, and also because as a rule it is either omitted from the balance, or set down as a good mark to the credit of one party. This elusive and enormously potent factor is called ambition. And its definition, like most others, can never be more or less than a statement of the definer's philosophy of life. But it may at least be agreed that ambition is rich or poor. Childishly self-ended or selflessly mature. And a personal ambition is perhaps not ill-defined as the subtlest form of despair—though a man may pass in a lifetime from the desire for personal excellence, the longing to be sure that either now or in the future he shall be recognized as excellent, to the reckless love of excellence for its own sake, leaving the credit to the devil—and so on to becoming, as it were behind his own back, one with his desire. And though the ambition of the artist need not of necessity be personal, he is peculiarly apt to suffer in the absence of recognition—and here at once we fall upon the strongest argument against fine art as the highest human achievement. These are altitudes. But we are discussing high matters. And though the quality of a man's ambition takes naught from the intrinsic value of his work, an ambition to the extent that it remains a thirst to be recognized as personally great, is a form of despair. And it is a form of despair to which men are notoriously more liable than are women. A fact that ceases to surprise when one reflects that, short of sainthood, a man must do rather than be, that he is potent not so much in person as in relation to the things he makes.

And so with ambition ruled out and our case thus brought down to the bare bones of undebatable actuality, back to our artists of whom immediately we must enquire what it is that they most urgently need for the development of their talents, the channels through which their special genius is to *operate*. The question has been answered by genius—on its bad days and always to the same effect. Da Vinci, called simultaneously by almost everything that can attract the mind of man, has answered it. Goethe, the court official, answered it.[1] And by way of casting a broad net we will quote here the testimonies of an eleventh century Chinese painter and a modern writer, a South African.

"Unless I dwell in a quiet house, seat myself in a retired room with the window open, the table dusted, incense burning and the thousand trivial thoughts crushed out and sunk, I cannot have good feeling for painting or beautiful taste, and cannot create the you" (the mysterious and wonderful—Fennelosa's [*sic*] translation) Kakki.[2]

"It's a very wise curious instinct that makes all people who have imaginative work (whether it's scientific or philosophic thinking, or poetry, or story-making, of course it doesn't matter so it's original work, and has to be spun out of the *texture of the mind itself*) try to creep away into some sort of solitude."…. "It's worry, tension, painful emotion, anxiety that kills imagination out as surely as a bird is killed by a gun." Olive Schreiner.[3]

Quiet, and solitude in the sense of freedom from preoccupations, are the absolute conditions of artistic achievement. Exactly, it may be answered, and your male artist will pay for these things any price that may be asked. Will pay health, respectability, honour, family claims and what not. And keep fine. And there are in the world of art women who make the same payments and yet do not achieve supremacy and, indefinably, do not remain fine. What is the difference? Where is it that the woman breaks down? She should with a fair field and her fascinating burdensome gift of sight, her gift for expansive vicarious living, be at least his equal? She should. But there are, when we come down to the terms of daily experience, just two things that queer the pitch. One abroad and one at home. For the woman, and particularly the woman painter, going into the world of art is immediately surrounded

---

1   For da Vinci, see p. 364, note 2; Johann Wolfgang von Goethe (1749-1832): German Romantic writer and politician. Trained as a lawyer, Goethe became a member of Carl August, Duke of Saxe-Weimar-Eisenach's privy council in 1775 and served the Duke in a number of roles for the rest of his life.

2   Ernest Fenollosa (1846-1908): American art historian of Japanese art. Kakki (or Hsia Kuei) (c. eleventh century): Chinese landscape painter.

3   Olive Schreiner (1855-1920): South African writer best known for *The Story of an African Farm* (1883).

by masculine traditions. Traditions based on assumptions that are largely unconscious and whose power of suggestion is unlimited. Imagine the case reversed. Imagine the traditions that held during a great period of Egyptian art, when women painters were the rule—the nude male serving as model, as the "artist's model" that in our own day is synonym for nude femininity.

But even the lifting away from our present gropings after civility in the world at large of the diminishing shadow of that which, for want of a more elegant term, is being called men-state mentality, would do nothing towards the removal of the obstruction in the path of the woman artist at home. She would still be left in an environment such as has surrounded no male artist since the world began. For the male artist, though with bad luck he may be tormented by his womankind, or burdened by wife and family, with good luck may be cherished by a devoted wife or mistress, or neglectful char,[1] by someone, that is to say, who will either reverently or contemptuously let him be. And with the worst of luck, living in the midst of debt and worry and pressure, still somehow he will be tended and will live serenely innocent of the swarming detail that is the basis of daily life.

It is not only that there exists for the woman no equivalent for the devoted wife or mistress. There is also no equivalent for the most neglectful char known to man. For the service given by women to women is as different from that given by women to men as is chalk from cheese. If hostile, it will specialize in manufacturing difficulties. If friendly, it will demand unfaltering response. For it knows that living sympathy is there. And in either case service is given on the assumption that the woman at work is in the plot for providing life's daily necessities. And even vicarious expansion towards a multitude of details, though it may bring wisdom, is fatal to sustained creative effort.

Art demands what, to women, current civilization won't give. There is for a Dostoyevsky[2] writing against time on the corner of a crowded kitchen table a greater possibility of detachment than for a woman artist no matter how placed. Neither motherhood nor the more continuously exacting and indefinitely expansive responsibilities of even the simplest housekeeping can so effectively hamper her as the human demand, besieging her wherever she is, for an inclusive awareness, from which men, for good or ill, are exempt.

---

1 Cleaning woman.

2 Fyodor Dostoyevsky (1821-81): Russian writer. Richardson imagines him "writing against time" possibly because, due to increasingly failing health, constant financial difficulties, and imprisonment, Dostoyevsky frequently wrote with a sense of urgency and impending catastrophe.

7. Foreword, *Pilgrimage*, Collected Edition. London: J.M. Dent, 1938. 9-12

[This Foreword, written on the occasion of the first Collected Edition of *Pilgrimage* in 1938 (another incorporating new material was produced in 1967), is the first retrospective Richardson takes on her work. It offers an explanation for the motive behind writing *Pilgrimage*, for making some of the stylistic choices that characterize it, and for continuing the enterprise even as reviewers and the reading public seemed to lose interest in the later chapter-volumes. It is an honest look back that also seeks to place Richardson's work in the longer tradition of the realist novel and, though she does not call it by name, of modernist experimentation. Without claiming too much, Richardson notes that she is one of the very first innovators of stream of consciousness (though she continued to hate that particular expression throughout her life) and similar techniques, and makes a modest case for her own achievement.]

Although the translation of the impulse behind his youthful plan for a tremendous essay on *Les Forces humaines* makes for the population of his great cluster of novels with types rather than with individuals, the power of a sympathetic imagination, uniting him with each character in turn, gives to every portrait the quality of a faithful self-portrait, and his treatment of backgrounds, contemplated with an equally passionate interest and themselves, indeed, individual and unique, would alone qualify Balzac to be called the father of realism.[1]

Less deeply concerned with the interplay of human forces, his first English follower portrays with complete fidelity the lives and adventures of inconspicuous people, and for a while, when in the English literary world it began its career as a useful label, realism was synonymous with Arnold Bennett.[2]

---

1 Honoré de Balzac (1799-1850): French writer. As a precocious student he had planned an essay on "Les Forces humaines" ("Human Strength"), but instead wrote his magnum opus, *La Comédie humaine* (*The Human Comedy*), a massive series of short stories and novels published over the course of his adult life.

2 Arnold Bennett (1867-1931): English writer and journalist best known for his popular realist novels. He was held by many young experimental writers to be an icon of the old guard, writing conventional, often bad, novels. This view is most clearly articulated in Virginia Woolf's (1912-1941) essay *Mr. Bennett and Mrs. Brown* (London: Hogarth P, 1924).

But whereas both Balzac and Bennett, while representing, the one in regard to a relatively concrete and coherent social system, the other in regard to a society already showing signs of disintegration, the turning of the human spirit upon itself, may be called realists by nature and unawares, their immediate successors possess an articulate creed. They believe themselves to be substituting, for the telescopes of the writers of romance whose lenses they condemn as both rose-coloured and distorting, mirrors of plain glass.

By 1911, thought not yet quite a direct supply of documentary material for the dossiers of the *cause célèbre*, Man versus conditions impeached as the authors of his discontent, realist novels are largely explicit satire and protest, and every form of conventionalized human association is being arraigned by biographical and autobiographical novelists.

Since all these novelists happened to be men, the present writer, proposing at this moment to write a novel and looking round for a contemporary pattern, was faced with the choice between following one of her regiments and attempting to produce a feminine equivalent of the current masculine realism. Choosing the latter alternative, she presently set aside, at the bidding of a dissatisfaction that revealed its nature without supplying any suggestion as to the removal of its cause, a considerable mass of manuscript. Aware, as she wrote, of the gradual falling away of the preoccupations that for a while had dictated the briskly moving script, and of the substitution, for these inspiring pre-occupations, of a stranger in the form of contemplated reality having for the first time in her experience its own say, and apparently justify-ing those who acclaim writing as the surest means of discovering the truth about one's own thoughts and beliefs, she had been at the same time increasingly tormented, not only by the failure, of this now so independently assertive reality, adequately to appear within the text, but by its revelation, whencesoever focused, of a hundred faces, any one of which, the moment it was entrapped within the close mesh of direct statement, summoned its fellows to disqualify it.

In 1913, the opening pages of the attempted chronicle became the first chapter of "Pilgrimage," written to the accompaniment of a sense of being upon a fresh pathway, an adventure so searching and, some-times, so joyous as to produce a longing for participation; not quite the same as a longing for publication, whose possibility, indeed, as the book grew, receded to vanishing point.

To a publisher, nevertheless, at the bidding of Mr J.D. Beresford,[1] the book was ultimately sent. By the time it returned, the second

1 See p. 237, note 1; in Beresford's Introduction, pp. 255-57, in the Broadview Press edition of *Pointed Roofs* (2014).

chapter was partly written and the condemned volume, put away and forgotten, would have remained in seclusion but for the persistence of the same kind friend, who acquired and sent it to Edward Garnett, then reading for Messrs Duckworth.[1] In 1915, the covering title being at the moment in use elsewhere, it was published as "Pointed Roofs."

The lonely track, meanwhile, had turned out to be a populous highway. Amongst those who had simultaneously entered it, two figures stood out. One a woman mounted upon a magnificently caparisoned charger, the other a man walking, with eyes devoutly closed, weaving as he went a rich garment of new words wherewith to clothe the antique dark material of his engrossment.

News came from France of one Marcel Proust,[2] said to be producing an unprecedentedly profound and opulent reconstruction of experience focused from within the mind of a single individual, and, since Proust's first volume had been published and several others written by 1913, the France of Balzac now appeared to have produced the earliest adventurer.

Finally, however, the role of pathfinder was declared to have been played by a venerable gentleman, a charmed and charming high priest of nearly all the orthodoxies, inhabiting a softly lit enclosure he mistook, until 1914, for the universe, and celebrated by evolving, for the accommodation of his vast tracts of urbane commentary, a prose style demanding, upon the first reading, a perfection of sustained concentration akin to that which brought it forth, and bestowing, again upon the first reading, the recreative delights peculiar to this form of spiritual exercise.

And while, indeed, it is possible to claim for Henry James,[3] keeping the reader incessantly watching the conflict of human forces through the eye of a single observer, rather than taking him, before the drama begins, upon a tour amongst the properties, or breaking in with descriptive introductions of the players as one by one they enter his enclosed resounding chamber where no plant grows and no mystery pours in from the unheeded stars, a far from inconsiderable technical influence, it was nevertheless not without a sense of relief that the present writer recently discovered, in "Wilhelm Meister," the following manifesto:

---

1 Edward Garnett (1868-1937): English writer and editor who played a major role in publishing much early modernist work. "Messrs. Duckworth": Gerald Duckworth & Co., English publishing house founded in 1898.
2 Marcel Proust (1871-1922): French novelist and critic. *Du Côté de Chez Swann* (*Swann's Way*) is the first volume of *A la recherche du temps perdu* (*In Search of Lost Time*), his magnum opus, a multi-volume series of novels (1913-27).
3 See p. 341, note 1.

In the novel, reflections and incidents should be featured; in drama, character and action. The novel must proceed slowly, and the thought-processes of the principal figure must, by one device or another, hold up the development of the whole.... The hero of the novel must be acted upon, or, at any rate, not himself the principal operator.... Grandison, Clarissa, Pamela, the Vicar of Wakefield, and Tom Jones himself, even where they are not acted upon, are still retarding personalities and all the incidents are, in a certain measure, modelled according to their thoughts.[1]

Phrases began to appear, formulae devised to meet the exigencies of literary criticism. "The Stream of Consciousness" lyrically led the way, to be gladly welcomed by all who could persuade themselves of the possibility of comparing consciousness to a stream. Its transatlantic successors, "Interior Monologue" and "Slow-Motion Photography," may each be granted a certain technical applicability leaving them, to this extent, unhampered by the defects of their qualities.

Lives in plenty have been devoted to the critic's exacting art and a lifetime might be spent in engrossed contemplation of the movements of its continuous ballet. When the dancers tread living boards, the boards will sometimes be heard to groan. The present writer groans, gently and resignedly, beneath the reiterated tap-tap accusing her of feminism, of failure to perceive the value of the distinctively masculine intelligence, of pre-War sentimentality, of post-War Freudianity. But when her work is danced upon for being unpunctuated and therefore unreadable, she is moved to cry aloud. For here is truth.

Feminine prose, as Charles Dickens and James Joyce[2] have delightfully shown themselves to be aware, should properly be unpunctuated, moving from point to point without formal obstructions. And the author of "Pilgrimage" must confess to an early habit of ignoring, while writing, the lesser of the stereotyped system of signs, and, further, when finally sprinkling in what appeared to be necessary, to a small unconscious departure from current usage. While meeting

---

1 *Wilhelm Meister's Apprenticeship* (*Wilhelm Meisters Lehrjahre*, 1795-96) by Goethe (see p. 166, note 1). Grandison, Clarissa, Pamela: characters in the novels *The History of Sir Charles Grandison* (1753), *Clarissa; or, the History of a Young Lady* (1748), and *Pamela; or, Virtue Rewarded* (1740): all novels by Samuel Richardson (1689-1761), an English writer. *The Vicar of Wakefield* (1766): novel by Oliver Goldsmith (1730-74), an English writer. Tom Jones: *The History of Tom Jones, a Foundling* (1749), a novel by Henry Fielding (1707-54), another English writer. All are sentimental realist novels, often epistolary in form (i.e., presented as a series of letters).

2 Charles Dickens (1812-70): English writer; for Joyce, see p. 329, note 1.

approval, first from the friend who discovered and pointed it out to her, then from an editor who welcomed the article she wrote to elucidate and justify it, and, recently, by the inclusion of this article in a text-book for students of journalism and its translation into French, the small innovation, in further complicating the already otherwise sufficiently complicated task of the official reader, helped to produce the chaos for which she is justly reproached.

For the opportunity, afforded by the present publishers, of eliminating this source of a reputation for creating avoidable difficulties, and of assembling the scattered chapters of "Pilgrimage" in their proper relationship, the author desires here to express her gratitude and, further, to offer to all those readers who have persisted in spite of every obstacle, a heart-felt apology.

D.M.R.
Trevone, 1938.

Select Bibliography

Blake, Caesar R. *Dorothy M. Richardson*. Ann Arbor: U of Michigan P, 1960.

Bluemel, Kristin. "'Civilization Is Based Upon the Stability of Molars': Dorothy Richardson and Imperialist Dentistry." Ed. Lisa Rado. *Modernism, Gender, and Culture: A Cultural Studies Approach.* New York, NY: Garland, 1997. 301-18.

——. *Experimenting on the Borders of Modernism: Dorothy Richardson's "Pilgrimage."* Athens: U of Georgia P, 1997.

——. "The Feminine Laughter of No Return: James Joyce and Dorothy Richardson." Ed. Gail Finney. *Look Who's Laughing: Gender and Comedy.* Langhorne, PA: Gordon and Breach, 1994. 161-71.

——. "Missing Sex in Dorothy Richardson's *Pilgrimage*." *English Literature in Transition (1880-1920)* 39.1 (1996): 20-38.

Bronfen, Elisabeth, and Victoria Appelbe. *Dorothy Richardson's Art of Memory: Space, Identity, Text.* Manchester, UK: Manchester UP, 1999.

Buchanan, Averill. "Dorothy Miller Richardson: A Bibliography 1900 to 1999." *Journal of Modern Literature* 24.1 (2000): 135-60.

Cucullu, Lois. "Over-Eating: *Pilgrimage*'s Food Mania and the Flânerie of Public Foraging." *Modernist Cultures* 2.1 (2006): 42-57.

Drewery, Claire. *Modernist Short Fiction by Women: The Liminal in Katherine Mansfield, Dorothy Richardson, May Sinclair and Virginia Woolf.* Surrey, UK: Ashgate, 2011.

Eagleson, Harvey. *Pedestal for Statue: The Novels of Dorothy M. Richardson.* Sewanee, TN: UP at the University of the South, 1934.

Egger, Rebecca. "Deaf Ears and Dark Continents: Dorothy Richardson's Cinematic Epistemology." *Camera Obscura: A Journal of Feminism, Culture, and Media Studies* 30 (1992): 5-33.

Fahy, Thomas. "The Cultivation of Incompatibility: Music as a Leitmotif in Dorothy Richardson's *Pilgrimage*." *Women's Studies: An Interdisciplinary Journal* 29.2 (2000): 131-47.

Felber, Lynette. "A Manifesto for Feminine Modernism: Dorothy Richardson's *Pilgrimage*." Ed. Lisa Rado. *Rereading Modernism: New Directions in Feminist Criticism.* New York: Garland, 1994. 23-39.

Finn, Howard. "At the Margins of Modernism." *Women: A Cultural Review* 11.1-2 (2000): 175-78.

——. "'In the Quicksands of Disintegrating Faiths': Dorothy Richardson and the Quakers." *Literature & Theology: An International Journal of Religion, Theory, and Culture* 19.1 (2005): 34-46.

——. "Objects of Modernist Description: Dorothy Richardson and the Nouveau Roman." *Paragraph: A Journal of Modern Critical Theory* 25.1 (2002): 107-24.

Fouli, Janet (ed.). *The Letters of John Cowper Powys and Dorothy Richardson.* London: Cecil Wolf, 2008.

——. *Structure and Identity: The Creative Imagination in Dorothy Richardson's "Pilgrimage."* Tunis: Faculté des Lettres de la Manouba, 1995.

Frattarola, Angela. "Developing an Ear for the Modernist Novel: Virginia Woolf, Dorothy Richardson and James Joyce." *Journal of Modern Literature* 33.1 (2009): 132-53.

Frigerio, Francesca. "Musical Aesthetics and Narrative Forms in Dorothy Richardson's Prose." *Textus: English Studies in Italy* 16.2 (2003): 311-28.

Fromm, Gloria G. *Dorothy Richardson: A Biography.* Urbana: U of Illinois P, 1977.

——. "Epistolary Counterpoint: The Letters of Dorothy Richardson and John Cowper Powys." *The Powys Review* 8.1 [25] (1990): 29-38.

——. "Objects of Modernist Description: Dorothy Richardson and the Nouveau Roman." *Paragraph: A Journal of Modern Critical Theory* 25.1 (2002): 107-24.

——. "What Are Men to Dorothy Richardson?" *Women & Literature* 2 (1982): 168-88.

—— (ed.). *'Windows on Modernism': Selected Letters of Dorothy Richardson.* Athens, GA: U of Georgia P, 1995.

Garrity, Jane. *Step-Daughters of England: British Women Modernists and the National Imaginary.* Manchester, UK: Manchester UP, 2003.

Gillespie, Diane Filby. "Political Aesthetics: Virginia Woolf and Dorothy Richardson." Ed. Jane Marcus. *Virginia Woolf: A Feminist Slant.* Lincoln: U of Nebraska P, 1983. 132-51.

Glaubitz, Nicola. "Cinema as Mode(l) of Perception: Dorothy Richardson's Novels and Essays." Ed. Klaus Kreimeier and Annemone Ligensa. *Film 1900: Technology, Perception, Culture.* New Barnet, UK: Libbey, 2009. 237-47.

Glikin, Gloria. "Checklist of Writings by Dorothy M. Richardson." *English Literature in Transition (1880-1920)* 8 (1965): 1-11.

Gregory, Horace. *Dorothy Richardson: An Adventure in Self-Discovery.* New York: Holt, Rinehart & Winston, 1967.

Hanscombe, Gillian E. *The Art of Life: Dorothy Richardson and the*

Development of Feminist Consciousness. London: Owen, 1982; Athens: Ohio UP, 1983.

———. "Dorothy Richardson versus the Novel." Ed. and intro. Ellen G. Friedman and Miriam Fuchs. *Breaking the Sequence: Women's Experimental Fiction.* Princeton: Princeton UP, 1989. 85-98.

Harvey, Melinda. "Dwelling, Poaching, Dreaming: Housebreaking and Homemaking in Dorothy Richardson's *Pilgrimage.*" Ed. Teresa Gómez Reus and Aránzazu Usandizaga. *Inside Out: Women Negotiating, Subverting, Appropriating Public and Private Space.* Amsterdam, Netherlands: Rodopi, 2008. 167-88.

Henke, Suzette A. "Male and Female Consciousness in Dorothy Richardson's *Pilgrimage.*" *Journal of Women's Studies in Literature* 1 (1979): 51-60.

Kaplan, Sydney Janet. "'Featureless Freedom' or Ironic Submission: Dorothy Richardson and May Sinclair." *College English* 32.8 (1971): 914-17.

———. *Feminine Consciousness in the Modern British Novel.* Urbana and London: U of Illinois P, 1975.

Kemp, Sandra. "'But How Describe a World Seen Without a Self?': Feminism, Fiction and Modernism." *Critical Quarterly* 32.1 (1990): 99-118.

Kumar, Shiv K. "Dorothy Richardson and the Dilemma of 'Being Versus Becoming.'" *Modern Language Notes* 74.6 (1959): 494-501.

Levy, Anita. "Gendered Labor, the Woman Writer and Dorothy Richardson." *Novel: A Forum on Fiction* 25.1 (1991): 50-70.

Linett, Maren. "'The Wrong Material': Gender and Jewishness in Dorothy Richardson's *Pilgrimage.*" *Journal of Modern Literature* 23.2 (1999): 191-208.

Llantada Díaz, Maria Francisca. "An Analysis of Poetic and Cinematic Features in Dorothy M. Richardson's *Pilgrimage.*" *English Studies: A Journal of English Language and Literature* 90.1 (2009): 57-77.

———. "Proust's Traces on Dorothy Richardson. Involuntary Memory and Metaphors." *Études britanniques contemporaines: Revue de la Société d'études anglaises contemporaines* 36 (2009): 125.

Maddison, Isobel. "'Trespassers Will Be Prosecuted': Dorothy Richardson among the Fabians." *Literature and History* 19.2 (2010): 52-68.

McCracken, Scott. "Embodying the New Woman: Dorothy Richardson, Work and the London Café." Ed. Avril Horner and Angela Keane. *Body Matters: Feminism, Textuality, Corporeality.* Manchester, UK: Manchester UP, 2000. 58-71.

——. "From Performance to Public Sphere: The Production of Modernist Masculinities." *Textual Practice* 15.1 (2001): 47-65.

Omichi, Chiho. "Pilgrimage in London: Dorothy Richardson and the Search for Feminine Space in Science and Socialism." *Poetica: An International Journal of Linguistic-Literary Studies* 63 (2005): 63-81.

Parsons, Deborah L. "The 'Passante' as 'Flâneuse' in Dorothy Richardson's *Pilgrimage*." Ed. Valeria Tinkler-Villani. *Babylon or New Jerusalem? Perceptions of the City in Literature.* Amsterdam, Netherlands: Rodopi, 2005. 155-67.

——. *Theorists of the Modernist Novel: James Joyce, Dorothy Richardson, Virginia Woolf.* Abingdon: Routledge, 2007.

——. "'There's More Space within than Without': Agoraphobia and the Bildungsroman in Dorothy Richardson's *Pilgrimage*." Ed. Gail Cunningham and Stephen Barber. *London Eyes: Reflections in Text and Image.* New York, NY: Berghahn, 2007. 79-90.

Podnieks, Elizabeth. "The Ultimate Astonisher: Dorothy Richardson's *Pilgrimage*." *Frontiers: A Journal of Women Studies* 14.3 (1994): 67-94.

Poresky, Louise A. "The Egotist and the Peacock: Virginia Woolf and Dorothy Richardson Revisited." *Virginia Woolf Miscellany* 37 (1991): 5-6.

Powys, John Cowper. *Dorothy M. Richardson.* London: Joiner & Steele, 1931.

Radford, Jean. *Dorothy Richardson.* New York and London: Harvester Wheatsheaf, 1991; Bloomington: Indiana UP, 1991.

——. "Impersonality and the Damned Egotistical Self: Dorothy Richardson's *Pilgrimage*." Ed. Christine Reynier and Jean-Michel Ganteau. *Impersonality and Emotion in Twentieth-Century British Literature.* Montpellier, France: Université Montpellier III, 2005. 87-95.

Randall, Bryony. *Modernism, Daily Time and Everyday Life.* Cambridge, UK: Cambridge UP, 2007.

Richardson, Dorothy Miller. *Backwater.* London: Duckworth, 1916.

——. *Clear Horizon.* London: J.M. Dent and Cresset P, 1935.

——. *Dawn's Left Hand.* London: Duckworth, 1931.

——. *Deadlock.* London: Duckworth, 1921.

——. *Gleanings from the Works of George Fox.* London: Headley Brothers, 1914.

——. *Honeycomb.* London: Duckworth, 1917.

——. *Interim.* London: Duckworth, 1920.

——. *John Austen and the Inseparables.* London: William Jackson, 1930.

———. *Journey to Paradise: Short Stories and Autobiographical Sketches.* London: Virago, 1989.

———. *Oberland.* London: Duckworth, 1927.

———. *Pilgrimage* (4 vols.). London: Dent and Cresset, 1938.

———. *Pilgrimage* (4 vols.). London: J.M. Dent, 1967.

———. *Pilgrimage* (4 vols.). London: Virago, 1979.

———. *Pointed Roofs.* London: Duckworth, 1915.

———. *The Quakers Past and Present.* London: Constable, 1914.

———. *Revolving Lights.* London: Duckworth, 1923.

———. *The Trap.* London: Duckworth, 1925.

———. *The Tunnel.* London: Duckworth, 1919.

Rose, Shirley. "Dorothy Richardson: The First Hundred Years, a Retrospective View." *Dalhousie Review* 53 (1973): 92-96.

———. "Dorothy Richardson's Theory of Literature: The Writer as Pilgrim." *Criticism: A Quarterly for Literature and the Arts* 12 (1970): 20-37.

Rosenberg, John D. *Dorothy Richardson: The Genius They Forgot. A Critical Biography.* London: Duckworth; New York: Knopf, 1973.

Staley, Thomas F. *Dorothy Richardson.* Boston: Twayne, 1976.

Stamm, David. *A Pathway to Reality: Visual and Aural Concepts in Dorothy Richardson's "Pilgrimage."* Tübingen, Germany: Francke, 2000.

Thomson, George H. *Dorothy Richardson: A Calendar of Letters.* Greensboro, NC: ELT P, 2007.

———. "Dorothy Richardson: Letters to a Sister in America." *English Literature in Transition (1880-1920)* 43.4 (2000): 410-88.

———. *Notes on "Pilgrimage": Dorothy Richardson Annotated.* Greensboro, NC: ELT P, 1999.

———, and Kristin Bluemel. *A Reader's Guide to Dorothy Richardson's "Pilgrimage."* Greensboro, NC: ELT P, 1996.

———, with Dorothy F. Thomson. *The Editions of Dorothy Richardson's "Pilgrimage": A Comparison of Texts.* Greensboro, NC: ELT P, 2001.

Thorn, Arline R. "'Feminine' Time in Dorothy Richardson's *Pilgrimage.*" *International Journal of Women's Studies* 1 (1978): 211-19.

Tucker, Eva. *"Pilgrimage": The Enchanted Guest of Spring and Summer: Dorothy Richardson 1873-1954: A Reassessment of Her Life and Work.* Penzance: Hypatia P, 2003.

Vanacker, Sabine. "Stein, Richardson and H.D.: Women Modernists and Autobiography." *Bête Noire* 6 (1988): 111-23.

Wang, Han-sheng. "Observing the City: Dorothy Richardson and Her Film Criticism." *NTU Studies in Language and Literature* 22 (2009): 77-106.

Watts, Carol. *Dorothy Richardson*. Plymouth, UK: Northcote House, with the British Council, 1995.

Winning, Joanne. *The Pilgrimage of Dorothy Richardson*. Madison: U of Wisconsin P, 2000.

Wittman, Livia Käthe. "Desire in Feminist Narrative: Reading Margit Kaffka and Dorothy Richardson." *Canadian Review of Comparative Literature/Revue canadienne de littérature comparée* 21.3 (1994): 399-415.

Wollaeger, Mark. "Richardson, Woolf, Lawrence: The Modernist Novel's Experiments with Narrative (I)." Ed. Robert L. Caserio and Clement Hawes. *The Cambridge History of the English Novel*. Cambridge, UK: Cambridge UP, 2012. 596-611.